Praise for Nadine Matheson

'Another absolute cracker. Gruesome and gritty'
Liz Nugent, *Sunday Times* bestselling author of *Strange Sally Diamond*

'With a deft hand and fresh, original voice, Matheson weaves a story that's dark, tense, action-packed, and so, so clever. Once I started *The Kill List*, I couldn't stop until the very last page. Outstanding'
Andrea Mara, number one *Sunday Times* bestselling author of *No One Saw a Thing*

'Nadine Matheson pulls it out of the bag again . . . you'll only close *The Kill List* when you've finished it. Another masterpiece'
Graham Bartlett, author of *Bad for Good*

'This engrossing and visceral read has all the series' signature grit . . . impossible to put down'
Crime Monthly

'The most invigoratingly grisly new crime writer on the block . . . Matheson writes with a light, witty touch very welcome in the often-humourless gorefest genre'
The Telegraph

'Gritty, compelling storytelling'
Daily Mail

'Expertly paced and plotted . . . You will need to leave the lights on'
Platinum

'If you like your crime on the gruesome side, this will certainly satisfy'
Heat

'Delightfully creepy and unsettling . . . this is a stay-up-all-night read from a masterful storyteller. Clever and intelligently complex. (Not advised if you're alone in the house.)'
Orlando Murrin, author of *Knife Skills for Beginners*

'A chilling and gripping serial killer thriller from a woman who knows her crime. Accomplished and disturbing. I raced through it'
Anna Mazzola, author of *The Clockwork Girl*

Nadine Matheson was born and raised in Deptford and now practises as a criminal defence lawyer. She won the City University Crime Writing competition, and she has an MA in Creative Writing. *The Jigsaw Man* was her first crime novel and was loved by readers around the world. It was shortlisted for the Dead Good Reader and the Adult Diverse Book Awards in 2022, and it has been translated into fifteen languages. *The Kill List* was longlisted for the Theakston Crime Novel of the Year in 2025.

Nadine is currently the chair for the Crime Writers' Association, and she is also the host of the podcast, *The Conversation with Nadine Matheson*. For more information about Nadine and her writing, visit her website at www.nadinematheson.com, sign up for her mailing list, or follow her on X @nadinematheson, and on Instagram @queennads.

Also by Nadine Matheson

The Jigsaw Man
The Binding Room
The Kill List

THE SHADOW CARVER

NADINE MATHESON

ONE PLACE. MANY STORIES

HQ
An imprint of HarperCollins*Publishers* Ltd
1 London Bridge Street
London SE1 9GF

www.harpercollins.co.uk

HarperCollins*Publishers*
Macken House, 39/40 Mayor Street Upper
Dublin 1, D01 C9W8, Ireland
This edition 2026

1
First published in Great Britain by HQ,
an imprint of HarperCollins*Publishers* Ltd 2026

Emoji(s) © Shutterstock.com

Copyright © Nadine Matheson 2026

Nadine Matheson asserts the moral right to be identified as the author of this work.

A catalogue record for this book is available from the British Library.

ISBN: HB: 978-0-00-854848-3
TPB: 978-0-00-854849-0

Set in Sabon LT Pro by HarperCollins*Publishers* India

This novel is entirely a work of fiction. The names, characters and incidents portrayed in it are the work of the author's imagination. Any resemblance to actual persons, living or dead, events or localities is entirely coincidental.

All rights reserved. No part of this publication may be reproduced, stored in a retrieval system, or transmitted, in any form or by any means, electronic, mechanical, photocopying, recording or otherwise, without the prior permission of the publishers.

Without limiting the exclusive rights of any author, contributor or the publisher of this publication, any unauthorised use of this publication to train generative artificial intelligence (AI) technologies is expressly prohibited. HarperCollins also exercise their rights under Article 4(3) of the Digital Single Market Directive 2019/790 and expressly reserve this publication from the text and data mining exception.

Printed and bound in the UK using 100% Renewable
Electricity at CPI Group (UK) Ltd

To Charlene

PROLOGUE

4 March 2013
Ealing, London

He can breathe today. Every exhale and inhale no longer felt as though barbed wire was being dragged across his lungs, but it's still painful to open his swollen eyes. He tries to focus but all he can see is shadows. He can't see her, but he can smell her. He gazes at the shadow which he knows is his wife, Deborah. Family and friends no longer pop in for a chat and a drink or to sit idly in the garden on the long summer nights but instead visit him as a patient. They talk in hushed, pained and pitiful whispers; unsure how to sit in a room that is no longer used for living but for end-of-life care.

The leather creaks as Deborah rises from the armchair.

'He looks like he's turned a corner,' Deborah whispers and gently places a hand on his leg. 'The doctor came by this morning and was really pleased.'

'We often find patients make a vast improvement when they're being cared for at home. Less stress, familiar smells.'

He feels gloved fingers rest on the dry and flaccid skin on his right arm and he smiles. He knows her touch. His nurse.

'Sian. Knew that you couldn't resist me,' he says.

'How could anyone resist you. You're a superstar,' Sian replies as she places the blood pressure cuff around his arm.

He can sense the smile in her voice. It has occurred to him, more than once, that there aren't many people in the world who make you feel seen. Sian never treats him as another item to tick off her itinerary. He winces as the machine sings and the cuff tightens around his arm.

'There we go,' Sian says brightly as the cuff on his arm quickly depresses. 'All done.'

'And I'm still here,' he replies.

'Of course, you're still here,' Sian says gently. She steps back and records his blood pressure and pulse readings in his chart.

'Are you staying over?' he asks, eagerness managing to break through the hoarseness.

'I told my husband I was spending the night with another man.'

He smiles as he hears his wife, laughing for the first time in weeks.

'Unfortunately, you're not my only bit on the side,' Sian says. 'I've got other patients to see this afternoon, but I'll be back.'

Sian clears a space on the kitchen island and lays out the vials of medication, sealed packets of needles and syringes.

'Are you sure I can do this?' Deborah asks anxiously as she pushes aside the shopping bags she hasn't had a chance to unpack.

'You'll be fine. You've been practising and I have faith in you,' Sian replies, picking up a vial. 'This is the easy one. Morphine, which you will deliver orally in three hours. How many mils?'

'Five,' Deborah answers nervously.

Sian smiles with approval as she picks a second vial. 'Warfarin,' she says. 'You will inject 5mil into his thigh. What do you need to do before you inject?'

Deborah straightens herself and places her hands – her fingernails bitten to the quick – on the island as though she needs the extra support.

'Check for air bubbles in the syringe and if there are any I should—' Deborah pauses as doubt fills her eyes.

Sian nods encouragingly.

'Hold the syringe up, gently tap it and wait for the bubbles to rise to the top. Then I will push the plunger until the air bubbles are gone. Double check the dosage and then inject,' says Deborah.

'I promise you everything will be fine,' Sian reassures her. 'I'll be back at 8.30 p.m. and you can finally get a decent night's sleep.'

'I don't know what we would do without you,' Deborah says as she grabs Sian and hugs her both with relief and gratitude. 'You're an angel.'

The sirens are now silent but the sharp wailing of a woman falling into grief can be heard on the street. A curtain in the upstairs window of the house on the opposite side of the street twitches as the front door of number 25 opens. A paramedic walks out with no sense of urgency. A silver BMW, its engine quiet, drives at speed and brakes sharply outside number 25, blocking the driveway. From her position, next to a large ash tree on the opposite side of the street, Sian can see and hear everything. The car door opens, and a man attempts to exit but he hasn't unclipped his seatbelt and he's forced back. He finally releases it and stumbles out of the car as the door of number 27 opens and a young woman steps out, barefooted, into her front garden.

'What's happened?' she asks.

'It's Dad,' the man replies as he runs through the open door of number 25. Sian places her hand against her chest to slow down the rapid pace of her heart. She knows exactly what happened at number 25. Her patient's body had grown rigid fifteen minutes after he'd ingested the strychnine that had been mixed into the vial of morphine, which she will later replace with the untampered bottle in her pocket. His muscles had spasmed and he'd become hyperaware as the poison invaded his nervous system and his already damaged kidneys began to fail. His eyes had protruded and grown bloodshot as he began to convulse. His pale and fragile skin had turned blue as his blood stopped feeding oxygen to his skin. Death was not quick. Sian checks her watch: 8.23 p.m.. She could have been at his side ten minutes before the poison took hold of his body but that would mean she would have had to perform her duty; to save him. Sian Fox-Carnell was not that sort of angel.

The Chronicle
18 June 2014
Annabeth Lawson

Nurse charged with murder

A district nurse has appeared at Tower Bridge Magistrates' Court charged with the murder of two patients who were under her care.

Sian Fox-Carnell, thirty-five, from Willesden Green has also been charged with two counts of attempted murder. All offences are said to have taken place over the course of six months.

The Homicide and Murder Enquiry Team South began an investigation into Sian Fox-Carnell after the death of television presenter, Leonard Calgary, who was diagnosed with testicular cancer three years ago, and retired charity worker Adesina Onyeka. Fox-Carnell was charged with the attempted murders of primary school headteacher Tabitha Gladstone and nineteen-year-old psychology student Jorge Menjivar following a report of suspected poisoning.

Fox-Carnell, who was dressed in a grey police-station-issued tracksuit, appeared in the dock before District Judge Kalyani and spoke only to confirm her name, date of birth and address. Fox-Carnell was not asked to enter any pleas to the four charges against her. Several members of the victims' families were removed from the public gallery in Court One after they ignored the judge's directions to remain silent and screamed obscenities at Fox-Carnell.

Marcus Valder, prosecuting, told the court that the CPS had authorised a further charge of arson with intent to endanger life.

The judge remanded Ms Fox-Carnell in custody to appear at the Central Criminal Court on 19 June 2014.

Fox-Carnell had been working at Guy's and St Thomas' Hospital since graduating in 2003 and became a district nurse in 2010. Jorge Menjivar who attended court with his parents said he was 'lucky to survive' and described Fox-Carnell as 'more evil than the cancer that was once in my body'.

The Chronicle
13 October 2021
Annabeth Lawson

Court of Appeal overturns Sian Fox-Carnell's murder convictions

A former nurse found guilty of two counts of murder and the attempted murder of two other patients under her care by overdosing them with prescribed medication and the poison strychnine has had her convictions overturned.

Sian Fox-Carnell will now face a retrial after judges ruled new evidence had emerged that was not heard in the first trial and that the original forensic evidence could not be relied upon.

Since the closure of the Forensic Science Services in 2012, forensic work has been contracted to the private sector. LFJ Forensic Services was used by many units within the Metropolitan Police. Toxicology reports in the Fox-Carnell investigation were prepared by Dr Ian Fry who oversaw the criminal division of LFJ Forensic Services from 2007-2019.

Earlier this year Dr Fry, who had previously worked for the FSS, was charged with misconduct in a public office and fraud after an investigation into the falsification of forensic reports. It's also alleged Dr Fry falsified records and accepted bribes in a case that led to the wrongful conviction of the late Andrew Streeter, twenty-five years ago. Dr Ian Fry will stand trial at Southwark Crown Court early next year.

Fox-Carnell, now aged forty-two, was found guilty of two counts of murder and two counts of attempted murder at the Central Criminal Court in April 2015. She was sentenced to four separate life sentences with a twenty-three-year tariff. She had served six years of her sentence.

Fox-Carnell broke down in tears and collapsed at court when Lady Justice Carr delivered the judgement.

The new Director of Public Prosecutions, Dame Stella Gibbons, issued a statement outside of court that the CPS will be seeking a retrial and that Her Majesty's Court Service had assured her that the trial date will be expedited.

Ms Martin, Fox-Carnell's solicitor, said they were delighted that the convictions were quashed and that they were looking forward to the retrial which would successfully absolve Fox-Carnell. 'Ms Fox-Carnell was and remains a woman of good character and she should be able to prepare for her trial without any restrictions on her liberty. We will be applying for bail in due course,' her statement added.

1

There was a cheer from most of the Serial Crimes Unit as Anjelica Henley pressed through the crowd and approached the reserved table in the pub garden. A few days ago, she'd been on a beach in Grenada with her family and avoiding text messages from her boss and her ex, Stephen Pellacia. Now she was back in London, exhausted and trying to understand why the serial killer, Sian Fox-Carnell, was a leading news item.

'You finally decided to grace us with your presence,' said DS Paul Stanford, standing up and giving mock applause. 'I thought you'd emigrated.'

'I'm not here for you,' Henley said as she handed Joanna, the office manager for the SCU, a blue gift bag and a bouquet of flowers.

'I told you she would turn up.' Joanna hugged Henley tightly. 'Thank you, love.'

'If it was anyone else, I would have stayed at home.'

'You really know how to make someone feel wanted, don't you,' said Stanford, shuffling along the bench, making way for Henley.

'Don't start.' Henley stifled a yawn as a wave of jetlag hit her.

'It's good to have you back boss,' said DC Salim Ramouter. He held up his near-empty beer glass in salute.

'Kiss arse,' Joanna sniggered.

'Because it's your birthday, Jo, I'm not going to respond,' said Ramouter.

'Where's Eastwood and Pellacia?' Henley asked, scanning the

crowd for her colleagues, as Joanna and Ramouter continued to banter. The unseasonably warm October weather meant the beer garden was filled to capacity with the post-work crowd, students and locals.

'Getting a round in. I told them you were on your way, so you won't be left out,' Ezra, the unit's forensic computer analyst, replied.

'If I'd known I'd be coming back to this craziness with Sian Fox-Carnell, I wouldn't have got on the bloody plane,' said Henley, catching her boss, Pellacia's eye as he and DS Roxanne Eastwood made their way towards their small group. She felt the unmistakable pang of longing and looked away.

'It's not the best news to come back home to.' Stanford picked up a beer mat and tapped it repeatedly on the table, signalling his annoyance.

'What are we talking about?' asked Eastwood.

'Fox-Carnell,' Stanford answered.

Pellacia groaned, placed the tray on the table and handed out the rest of the drinks. 'Do we have to talk about her?'

'I would gladly not talk about her for the rest of my days but the fact that me and Henley have been summoned to court is going to make that a bit difficult,' said Stanford.

'What for?' Henley asked as Eastwood handed her a glass of wine.

'They've listed Fox-Carnell's case first thing Monday morning and the judge has requested our presence. I was going to wait until you'd at least got two glasses of wine down you, but no time like the present.'

'I tried to get you out of it, but the judge wasn't having it,' Pellacia said. He took a sip of his beer, holding Henley's gaze for a second longer than was necessary.

'I know Fox-Carnell was before my time at the SCU, but I thought she was bang to rights,' said Eastwood.

'She is,' Pellacia responded vehemently. 'Rhimes, Stanford, Henley and I worked that investigation to the ground. Left no stone unturned. We had evidence of Fox-Carnell tampering with medication, witness evidence—'

'None of that matters though. Not when her legal team are saying that there was no direct evidence of Fox-Carnell injecting her patients with lethal doses of medication, and they're not wrong,' said Stanford.

'But that wasn't our case, was it?' countered Henley. 'The evidence showed that she either switched the medication or purposely gave the incorrect dosage directions to the patients' family members who were looking after them. She was the only person responsible for killing two people and nearly killing two more.'

'If the CPS hadn't run scared, we could have charged her with more deaths,' added Pellacia.

'But from what Stanford told me, no one is saying that Rhimes and his team did anything wrong,' said Ramouter as a barman placed two large bowls of nachos on the table.

'Of course we didn't do anything wrong. This is just the inevitable fallout of discovering that Dr Fry was one of the people responsible for putting an innocent man in prison for twenty-five years,' said Henley. She checked her phone as it started ringing and motioned for Stanford to move.

Pellacia frowned 'That man has blood on his hands. How many more people like Andrew Streeter are sitting inside for crimes they didn't commit and how many have got away with literal murder?'

Joanna pulled the nachos towards her. 'Fox-Carnell is chancing her arm, and she won't be the only one. It won't matter if you were charged with shoplifting a car tyre or a mass murder, they're all going to lodge appeals if Dr Ian Fry even breathed near their forensic report.'

'Everything all right?' Pellacia asked, joining Henley outside the pub. He pulled out a box of cigarettes from his pocket and sighed when he saw it was empty.

'Consider that a sign,' Henley said, putting her phone away.

'Yeah, I really should give up.'

They stood in silence that was somehow both comfortable and uncomfortable.

'You didn't answer me,' Pellacia said.

Henley stepped away from the main door to let a couple pass. 'Everything's fine. That was Simon on the phone.'

'How is your brother?'

'Doing what he's best at: being annoying,' Henley said affectionately. 'How are you?'

Pellacia blew out his cheeks and looked disappointingly at the empty cigarette box in his hand. 'Everywhere I turn: stress. Fox-Carnell, and every other twat who's ever crossed our path, protesting their innocence, the SCU being under review and then there's been stuff with—'

Henley stiffened and chastised herself for having such a reaction to the name Pellacia had stopped himself from saying.

'Sorry, you've just come back from holiday and that's actually why I came out here. I wanted to apologise,' Pellacia said.

'You really don't have to.'

'No. I do. I was out of line. You told me where we stood, and I had a hard time accepting it. You asked for space, I should have respected that.'

'It's not all on you,' Henley admitted, a wave of emotion and confusion sweeping over her. 'I know what I've said but that doesn't—'

Henley stopped when a figure in the distance waved and started making their way quickly towards them.

'That doesn't what?' Pellacia asked earnestly, taking hold Henley's arm. 'What were you going to say?'

Henley gently pulled away. 'It's Linh,' she said. 'She's coming this way.'

Pellacia turned around, his shoulders visibly rising and falling with disappointment.

'Sometimes I think I'm imagining things,' he said, facing Henley again. 'That I'm holding onto something that doesn't exist but right now, I know I'm wrong.'

'Good evening,' Linh said brightly, stepping in between Henley and Pellacia; an obvious intervention.

'I'm going back inside. What can I get you, Linh?' asked Pellacia.

'A very large JD and Coke, thanks,' Linh replied as she hugged Henley.

'I didn't know you were going to be here?' Henley said.

Pellacia returned inside.

'Ezra invited me.'

'Of course he did. You know he's got a thing for you?'

Linh laughed. 'Who doesn't have a thing for me? Anyway, what did I just interrupt?'

'You didn't interrupt anything,' Henley replied, lowering her gaze.

'Liar.'

'It was about work.'

Linh smiled and slowly shook her head. 'I can see straight through the pair of you but I'm going to let you off because you look like you're about to cry.'

Henley rubbed underneath her eyes. 'It's jetlag,' she protested.

'That's the trouble with holidays. It's all well and good being in your Caribbean sun-soaked bubble for three weeks but then you have to come home and deal with reality.' Linh placed her arm around Henley. 'And whether you like it or not, Pellacia is very much reality.'

'Can we not do this now, Linh? None of this is easy.'

'Who said life was ever easy.'

2

The blue and white police tape had been wrapped taut between two lampposts across 24 Cullen Lane in Dulwich. Whilst waiting for his coffee order, Ramouter had done his research. All thirty-two houses on Cullen Lane were privately owned, valued no less than £2 million and had become a popular haunt for car thieves. Ramouter adjusted the sleeves of his protective suit and made his way to the crime scene. The signs of a burglary gone wrong were visible in the driveway of number 24: a drying pool of blood a metre from the front door, a broken watch next to the overgrown hydrangea bush, a broken plant pot, visible footprints in the grassless border and a phone – the screen broken – in the grey gravel. And yet a sixty grand Lexus was still parked on the driveway, plugged into the charging point.

Ramouter turned to the uniformed police officer keeping a log of everyone entering and leaving the crime scene, and asked, 'Who was first on the scene?'

'A postwoman, or maybe that should be post person? No one knows anymore,' said PC Keith, flicking the pages of his logbook. 'Postwoman, Frankie Duloise, twenty-six years old. She'd bolted her mail trolley to a lamppost at the junction of Cullen Lane and Druce Road and started her route. She said she had her headphones on and was listening to a podcast. True crime.' He rolled his eyes. 'She pushed the front gate open and tripped over the victim. Then called 999.'

'Any idea how long the victim had been there?'

PC Keith closed his logbook. 'I didn't see the victim. The paramedics had already taken him to King's College Hospital. But I was told he was wearing jeans and a T-shirt when he was found. For all we know he could have been laying here from last night.'

'Thanks,' Ramouter replied. He turned around but found his way into the property blocked by a woman standing in the doorway with her arms crossed defensively.

'You don't look like one of my lot,' she said firmly, unmoving, curls of red hair escaping from the hood of her oversuit.

'DC Ramouter,' he replied.

The woman's face broke into a grin. 'The Serial Crimes Unit. I didn't think they were going to send anyone. I'm DC Copeland. So do you think this is one we can hand over to you?'

'I haven't stepped through the front door yet, so it's impossible to say.'

'Sorry, sorry. I'm always jumping ahead of myself. Overeager but you know, if this case qualifies—'

'It seems as though every CID room is determined to palm off every aggravated burglary case in London to the SCU but, like I said, I haven't been inside yet,' Ramouter replied. He placed his right foot on the doorstep.

'You can't exactly blame us,' Copeland replied, still stuck rigidly in place in the doorway. 'Everyone's caseload is ridiculous. You can tell people to stop committing crimes but you're just pissing in the wind really.'

Ramouter smiled politely as Copeland continued spouting her views on work overload.

'Right,' Copeland said brightly as she finally moved to the side, her back against the open door. 'You better come in, but be careful where you're stepping. We've got broken glass, water, oil and blood all over the floor.'

Ramouter paused in the doorway. The macabre scent of fresh

fig and cassis essential oils mixed with the coppery overtones of spilled blood filled the air. He tracked the blood trail that continued from the doorway, along the hallway floor and into the kitchen. The large ornate mirror to Ramouter's left was lopsided and strands of brown hair stuck in the blood splatter that had settled in the cracks that spider-webbed on the glass. He walked through the hallway observing the jagged wood of the broken spindles on the bannister to his right. 'A lot of violence,' he said.

'Isn't that what you expect from an aggravated burglary?' Copeland mused as a forensic officer, exhibits bags in his hand, made his way down the staircase.

'Not for the cases we're investigating,' said Ramouter. 'The homeowners we've been dealing with haven't been harmed in any way.'

Copeland stopped in her tracks and stared at Ramouter; disbelief contorting her tone. 'I've seen the updates on HOLMES for your home invasion investigation. You call being dragged from your bed, tied up and threats to douse you with petrol as not being harmed?'

'Sorry, that's not what I meant. You've mis—'

'I don't know what they're teaching you over at the SCU, but I would call that the epitome of violence.'

'What I meant to say is that the violence in our cases is psychological. But look around you. This violence is physical.'

Copeland pursed her lips as she stepped back; broken glass crunching under her feet. 'Who knew the SCU only took on cases where they don't have to get their hands dirty,' she muttered.

Ramouter ignored her and walked into a large open plan kitchen and living area.

'From what we can work out, the burglar entered from the rear and forced the back patio door open, here,' Copeland said. She moved swiftly in front of Ramouter and pointed at the bifold door, the windows smeared with grey fingerprint dust.

Ramouter crouched down. 'This has a multi-point locking system.' He ran a gloved finger across the locking mechanism in the door frame. 'They're not usually so easy to break into.'

'No, they're not,' Copeland agreed. 'But the door was open when we came in.'

'The garden gate faces the street,' said Ramouter. 'Makes me think that whoever forced entry must have carried out some kind of reconnaissance. I saw the neighbourhood watch signs when I was walking along the road and most of the houses either have video doorbell monitoring or CCTV cameras. I'd be surprised if there weren't recent reports of suspicious activity.'

'We've just started door-to-door enquiries and, so far, no one has said they saw anything suspicious either last night or this morning.'

'There's still time,' Ramouter replied, walking over to the kitchen counter. Slices of cold and hardening garlic flatbread were on a wooden chopping board next to a bowl of wilting salad. A large wine glass, dregs of red wine staining the sides, was next to a bottle, the cork stuck on the corkscrew beside it.

'Your victim is a man, right?' Ramouter asked, pushing the base of the wine glass with his finger, turning it around.

Copeland nodded. 'We haven't formally confirmed his identity, but we believe him to be the homeowner, Dr Graham Ashcroft.'

Ramouter pointed at the pink lipstick on the edge of the glass.

'Ah, I didn't notice that,' Copeland said.

'And there's another wine glass on the dining table. Is our victim married, girlfriend?'

'We haven't established that yet.'

Ramouter pointed at the knife block on the counter. 'There's a knife missing.'

'Paramedics said the wounds of our victim were consistent with a knife, and the postwoman described cuts and bruises to the victim's face but it's impossible to say if that particular missing knife was used in the attack or—' Copeland shrugged– 'just missing. You know what it's like. I've lost count of the number of forks I've thrown in the bin.'

'I'm assuming your officers have done a search of the area?'

Copeland narrowed her eyes. Ramouter wasn't sure if she was annoyed at the question or was now annoyed with him. The question remained unanswered.

Ramouter left the kitchen area and made his way into the middle of the open-plan room. A seventy-inch TV was on the wall above a brand new PS5 on the wall-mounted TV unit. To Ramouter's left was a solid oak table. In the middle of the table was an open laptop next to two bowls stained with dried pasta sauce. A second wine glass was on its side, in a pool of now-sticky red wine. He walked along the bespoke bookcase filled with recent bestsellers, modern classics and prize winners.

Ramouter pulled out a book from the top shelf and turned the pages, causing Copeland to say, 'This ain't a library. What are you looking for?'

'Your victim is a collector. This is a first edition, first printing copy of Ernest Hemingway's *The Sun Also Rises*,' he said, replacing the book on the shelf. He reached into his oversuit and removed his phone.

Copeland stared blankly at Ramouter. 'Never heard of it.'

'That copy of *The Sun Also Rises* is valued at just under four grand.'

Copeland whistled.

'Don't you find it odd there's no ransacking?'

'Not at all. The burglar didn't get a chance because our victim was home.'

'Mind if I go upstairs?' Ramouter asked.

'Knock yourself out, but be careful. CSI haven't made their way up there yet. I'll be outside if you need me.'

*

There were three bedrooms upstairs. Two large doubles and a single room that had been converted into an office. Ramouter poked his head into the office where a dual monitor screen stood on top of a teak-coloured standing desk. A treadmill and oak rowing machine were on the right facing a smaller version of the television downstairs.

'This isn't a burglary,' Ramouter muttered to himself as he walked into the main bedroom and saw the designer bags on the shelves of the opened wardrobe. The closed drawers in the wardrobe and the jewellery on the dressing table confirmed to Ramouter what his gut had been telling him from the moment he saw the Lexus on the driveway. Whoever had forced their way into the house wasn't interested in stealing anything of value. The only thing that had been on their mind was violence.

'DC Ramouter.'

Copeland's loud voice travelled to the first floor, quickly followed by the sound of her feet landing heavily and rapidly on the stairs.

'What is it?' Ramouter asked. Copeland appeared in front of him, the red flush in her cheeks deepening as she placed a hand on her chest.

'I need you to come with me. Our aggravated burglary might have just turned into an attempted murder.'

'Homeowner's name is Patsy Howe. Sixty-two years old,' said Copeland. She ran her hand through her hair and attempted to smooth down her wayward curls. 'She's a retired teacher but she works as a tarot reader.'

'You've rushed me down here to see a psychic?' Ramouter asked incredulously.

'Don't be ridiculous,' said Copeland as they made towards the front door of number 31 that had been left on the latch.

Copeland pushed the door open and gestured Ramouter inside. 'Mrs Howe,' she called out. 'It's DC Copeland.'

'Give me a sec,' came a disembodied voice.

A few seconds later, a petite woman with striking grey hair cut into a harsh bob, wearing purple-rimmed glasses, entered the hallway.

'Mrs Howe, I'm DC Ramouter.' He removed his warrant card and held it out.

'Oh, it's Patsy,' she replied. She looked at his warrant card and smiled. 'Nice picture.'

'Mrs Howe,' Copeland continued. 'The footage.'

'Of course, but you'll have to excuse the mess,' said Patsy. From the bottom of the stairs, she pushed aside a basket of unfolded clothes, bundles of toilet paper and a shopping bag filled with toiletries.

'Don't worry about it.' Ramouter followed her upstairs.

'Through the door on your left,' said Patsy once they'd reached the landing.

Ramouter was momentarily stunned as he walked into the bedroom that faced the front of the house. A large telescope was pointed at the window, along with a separate camera on a tripod and on the shelves was a multitude of photography equipment and smaller telescopes.

'What did you teach before you retired?' he asked.

'Astronomy,' Patsy answered proudly. 'I'd been teaching for thirty years and one day I decided enough is enough. Academia isn't what it was. It's all business.'

'Patsy, could you show DC Ramouter what you found.' Copeland sounded impatient.

Patsy sat down at her table and woke her computer up from sleep mode.

'I had the telescope, which is attached to the camera, running automatically because I was hoping to catch the Draconids meteor shower. I usually close the door because I've got a crazy cat who likes to jump on anything that resembles a tree, but I must have forgotten because the cat got in and the stupid thing knocked the tripod and detached the camera. So instead of my camera recording the meteor shower it caught this.'

Ramouter's breath caught in his throat as Patsy enlarged and reorientated the video. 'The camera cost me a fortune but it's the absolute best,' Patsy said quietly as the image of a star filled sky quickly fell away and was replaced with Cullen Lane.

'What time was this?' Ramouter asked.

The footage showed a fox on the pavement as a white man, bleeding, barefooted and wearing jeans and a short-sleeved top, ran into shot.

Patsy right clicked and brought up the video's time stamp. '12.16 a.m.. That's why I didn't hear a thing. Our bedroom is at the back of the house.'

'Watch,' Copeland said. 'There's no sound but you don't need it. You can feel everything.'

The man stopped in the middle of the road and the fox ran between the planters. The man leaned forward and placed his hands on his thighs as the bright strobe of car headlights quickly filled the street. He paused for a split second before turning to run as a black car came into view. The car rammed into the man. His body hit the windscreen, propelled off the bonnet and onto the road. The car skidded, the right-side tyres hitting the kerb before braking. The man rolled over onto his back and placed his arm across his chest as his legs moved slowly. The driver's side door opened, and a person dressed all in black, their face concealed by a balaclava, ran out into the road and towards the man. Ramouter leaned closer to the screen as the man in black grabbed the arms of the man on the ground and dragged him back towards the car. He opened the rear passenger door and manoeuvred the man onto the back seat. He quickly ran around the rear of the car and got back behind the wheel. A light switched on in the upstairs window of a house two doors down on the opposite side of the road as the car drove off the kerb and quickly out of view.

'Shit,' Ramouter said. 'And that footage is definitely from this morning?'

'Absolutely,' Patsy replied. 'If I fast forward it, you'll see my husband leaving for work just after six.'

'And are you able to identify the man who—'

'Dr Graham Ashcroft' Patsy said, nodding. 'My husband is a cabbie and he's driven Graham many times. That's definitely him.'

'I was told the victim was found on the driveway this morning,' said Ramouter once Patsy had closed the front door behind them.

'He was,' confirmed Copeland.

'So how did he get there after he was run off the road? Did the driver dump him there or did Graham manage to get out of the car but collapsed before he could get inside and call for help?'

'Hopefully, we'll be able to answer those questions once we've received the street's CCTV footage.'

'Either way, you've definitely got an attempted murder on your hands.'

3

Henley felt trapped. There was nowhere to run. She watched Eloise Rhimes cross the Inner London Crown Court car park and walk directly towards her. Eloise sat as a District Judge at Bromley Magistrates' Court and Henley assumed that a meeting, likely about a youth charged with a serious offence, was the reason behind her presence at the Crown Court. However, paranoia and shame convinced her that Eloise was here for her. She could feel Eloise's unanswered texts and voicemails burning a hole in her pocket. Henley wasn't in the habit of hiding from people but that's exactly what she'd been doing ever since she'd agreed to look into Eloise's husband's death.

'I thought it was you,' Eloise said as she hugged Henley. 'How was your holiday?'

'It was good. Very much needed,' said Henley, feeling embarrassed by Eloise's warmth.

'And how are you and Rob?'

'They definitely weren't joking when they said marriage isn't easy, but we're better,' Henley admitted. Her relationship with her husband had been challenging over the years. No one could ever replace her mum, but Eloise had stepped in, listened, advised and held her when it had got too much. Henley had reciprocated in kind when Eloise had suddenly found herself with the unwelcome title of widow.

'Before you ask, no, I'm not stalking you. I'm here for the usual bureaucratic nonsense that could have been dealt with by email,' Eloise said.

'I didn't think you were stalking me at all, but I wouldn't blame you if you were. I know it's been a few months, and I haven't returned your—'

'I'm asking a lot of you. I know that,' Eloise cut her off, tenderly taking hold of Henley's hand. 'Harry was my husband, but he was also your friend, not just your boss. Bloody hell, *now* it sounds like I'm trying to guilt trip you. I promise you that's not what I'm doing.'

'You want answers,' Henley said, feeling very guilty.

'Not want, *need* answers.'

'And you'll get them. You'll know as soon as I do.'

Eloise nodded, watching a news crew unpacking their van. 'I'll let you get on. I've got a trial starting this afternoon and you've got whatever this lunacy is.'

*

'Oi, oi, sunshine,' said Stanford, peeling himself away from the grey stone brick that formed the walls of the court building.

'The last thing I feel is sunny and bright.' Henley drained the last of her coffee and threw the cup into a nearby bin. She moved aside as a trio of barristers, black gowns flapping around them, horsehair wigs tucked under their arms, descended from the stone staircase.

'Still not over your jetlag?'

'No, my body clock is all over the place and I could think of a million other things I'd rather be doing on a Monday morning.' Henley lifted up her head and inhaled deeply. The sun broke through the heavy rain clouds. 'I should have stayed in Grenada. Transferred to CID in the Royal Grenada Police Force.'

'For the love of God, get over yourself, woman,' said Stanford, patting Henley affectionately on her arm. 'Let's go in. You can vent to the judge.'

Tension tightened the muscles in Henley's neck. They entered the court building and cleared security. 'I still can't believe this is happening,' she said.

'We didn't do anything wrong, with Fox-Carnell, I mean.' Stanford had read Henley's mind.

'I know that,' Henley replied, their footsteps echoing through the hallways. 'But you know what the media and the public are like. It's easier to blame us if something goes wrong and a murderer is put back on the streets.'

'The judge may not even let her out.' Stanford adjusted his tie. 'How do I look?'

'You're fine,' Henley said distractedly as she caught sight of Leonard Calgary's widow, Deborah, and Fox-Carnell's last victim, Jorge Menjivar, being escorted to the courtroom by an usher. 'Come on, let's go.'

The courtroom buzzed with excitement and anxiety. Counsel, reporters, family members, and curious onlookers who'd managed to snag seats in the public gallery, waited for the woman who'd been called the angel of death. Henley and Stanford both declined the invitation to sit behind prosecution counsel and sat at the bench usually reserved for probation, close to the Judge's own bench but also with an unrestricted view of the dock. Stanford nudged Henley as the sound of metal clanging against metal rang out from the direction of the dock. Loud chatter lowered into whispers as Sian Fox-Carnell, flanked by two officers, entered. She was a pale-skinned, slim woman whose dark blonde hair hung in waves down her back. Fox-Carnell's barrister scurried forward. Henley watched as Fox-Carnell walked to the corner of the dock, leaned towards the slim gap in the window and nodded in response to her barrister's advice.

'She looks . . .' Stanford paused. 'Surprisingly well.'

'Wouldn't you be looking well if a court of appeal had overturned all your murder convictions and ordered a retrial?'

Henley asked, frustrated. She adjusted her blazer which suddenly felt too tight in the warm courtroom.

'Even so. I would expect her to look a bit more, I don't know . . . Broken.'

Henley didn't reply as Fox-Carnell's barrister returned to counsel's row. Fox-Carnell remained standing and locked eyes with Henley. She was taken back in time to the moment she and Rhimes had sat across from Fox-Carnell in the interview room questioning her over the course of eighty-seven hours. Every single negative emotion that Henley could think of had swam in Fox-Carnell's eyes: contempt, selfishness, smugness, arrogance, malevolence, boredom, hate, and Henley would swear blind that she saw evil.

'That woman is anything but broken,' Henley said as a loud knock reverberated around the courtroom and the door at the front opened. Everyone rose to their feet for the judge.

'She's enjoying every single minute of this,' Henley said and Fox-Carnell smirked cruelly at her and winked.

'Ms Fox-Carnell, do you understand that the Crown Prosecution Service have submitted that you will be retried for two counts of murder, two counts of attempted murder and that they have offered no evidence to count five; arson with intent to endanger life and count six, attempted murder?' the judge asked.

'Yes, I do,' Sian replied, wiping her eyes with a tissue that had been handed to her. Henley wasn't moved by Sian's crying, she knew that they were well-rehearsed crocodile tears. Performing to the gallery.

The judge cleared his throat. 'All that leaves is the matter of setting a trial date with a time estimate of twelve weeks which we will fix once we've dealt with the issue of bail. Mr Beckworth?'

'M'lord, yes.' Mr Beckworth placed his hands on the lectern. 'A notice of application for the court to consider bail with supporting documentation was submitted to both the court and my learned friend.'

'Yes, I've had sight of the application,' the judge replied and gave a subtle nod to another court officer who had been standing silently by the door. 'And you wish for the matter of bail to be heard in chambers?'

Stanford leaned towards Henley and whispered, 'That won't go down well.'

'That's correct, m'lord,' confirmed Mr Beckworth. 'I have discussed the matter with my learned friend and there is no objection.'

'This court is now sitting in chambers,' said the judge. 'That means everyone in the public gallery must now leave.'

Disgruntled murmuring rose from the public gallery.

The gallery's palpable anger made it difficult for Henley to compartmentalise and lock away her own emotions. She caught the look of arrogance on Fox-Carnell's face as her victim's family members weakly threatened to stage sit-ins. A slow three minutes passed until the courtroom suddenly felt cavernous.

An hour after he'd started his argument for Sian Fox-Carnell to be granted bail, Mr Beckworth said, 'That was my final submission, m'lord, so unless I can assist you any further?'

'No, you have been most helpful. My thanks to both yourself and Ms Reese. Ms Fox-Carnell, will you please stand,' the judge said.

Fox-Carnell made a show of shakily rising from her seat and pulling her cardigan tightly around her.

'I have heard a very detailed application that was put forward by your counsel and also objections to bail from the prosecution's counsel, Ms Reese,' the judge continued. 'Listen to me very carefully. I will be granting bail but subject to very stringent bail conditions.'

'Shit, shit, shit,' Stanford muttered. Henley released her tight grip on the armrest and pulled out her phone. Her hands shook as she texted Pellacia with an update.

'Ms Fox-Carnell,' the judge said firmly. 'You are to live and sleep at the address that has been submitted to the court by your counsel. You will be subject to electronic monitoring with an additional doorstep condition. You must report three times a week to Colindale police station. You are to surrender your passport, which I understand is still valid and you are not to apply for any travel documents. You are not to contact any witnesses directly or indirectly. You are not to enter any hospital without prior arrangement and must be accompanied by another adult unless, of course, it is an emergency. You will be subject to a curfew which means that you must be at your residence between the hours of 9 p.m. to 7 a.m.. The monitoring equipment will be installed by a representative from Soteria this evening. A security of £100,000 must be deposited to Her Majesty's Court and Tribunal Service before you are released from custody. Do you understand your bail conditions?'

An intense heat pulsed through Henley. She turned away from the dock but heard Fox-Carnell splutter that she understood in between her sobs.

'Nah, she'll never get out,' Stanford whispered stubbornly as the judge directed Fox-Carnell to sit and he proceeded to fix a trial date. 'Do you really think her dad is going to stump up a hundred grand?'

The judge rose quickly to his feet and left the courtroom. 'This is so wrong. So very wrong,' Henley said as they walked towards the court door.

'Inspector Henley.'

'Keep moving,' Stanford hissed as Henley's name was called out for a second time with insistence.

Henley stopped and turned around. She felt sick when she saw the wide and monstrous grin on Fox-Carnell's face. Fox-Carnell spoke softly, as though she was reassuring a patient.

'I'm coming for you next.'

*

Henley leaned against her car door, waiting for Stanford to complete the debrief with the prosecutor. Watching a small crowd, made up of nearly everyone who'd sat in the public gallery, gathered in a huddle in the court car park, she sensed danger. Stanford emerged from the court building and jogged down the steps, ignoring the shouts of the reporters.

'You're not going to believe it. They're releasing her in about fifteen minutes. Her brief must have messaged her dad the second the judge spoke because, according to the police liaison officer, the bail money was paid before we'd made it down the corridor.' Stanford shook his head in disbelief.

'There are two entrances to this building,' Henley said, scanning the crowd that showed no sign of breaking up. 'They can't release her from the front. It would make more sense to have her use the rear entrance.'

'What do you want to do? Talk to security?'

If Stanford was right with his timings then they had minutes to convince security and the court staff to release Fox-Carnell away from public view. 'Let's do that,' she said. 'I really don't like the look of the crowd.'

The dark clouds released drops of rain. Henley could feel the hostility from the crowd intensifying, their anger amplified and impatient murmurings growing louder. Suddenly, the murmurings transitioned to shouts as the public and the waiting reporters surged forward. Henley was pushed to the side.

'Bollocks,' muttered Stanford, joining Henley behind the throng of reporters and cameramen. 'She's already here.'

Sian Fox-Carnell stood defiantly at the top of the stairs. Her solicitor looked anxious as the crowd screamed obscenities and reporters shouted questions.

'*Murderer.*'

'Sian, do you have anything to say to the families?'
'You bitch.'
'How does it feel to be out of prison?'
'Is this a miscarriage of justice?'
'I'm going to kill you!'

A couple of court security guards exited, looking out of their depths as they surveyed the crowd. 'We need to help them,' Henley said.

Stanford sighed begrudgingly but pushed through the crowd with Henley close behind him.

'Police! Move to the side now,' Henley shouted to no avail, an elbow jabbing her side.

'I will bloody arrest you if you don't move right now,' Henley shouted. Stanford surged forward and was able to form a small space between Fox-Carnell and her attackers. Henley cursed as the rain began to fall harder and she saw someone in the crowd throw a bottle. Two reporters quickly crouched down as it soared over their heads and smashed on the wall behind them. A stocky white man, wearing a brown suit, stepped out in front of Sian and drew back his fist. There was a cacophony of screams as a security guard pushed in front of Sian and the man's fist slammed into his cheek. The security guard stumbled back causing Sian to fall to the ground, her face scraping against the stone step, her solicitor stumbling against the railings.

'Police,' Henley yelled again, lowering herself and grabbing hold of Sian's arm. Disgust pumped through her at the feel of Sian's skin. Stanford manoeuvred to restrain the man who'd thrown the punch.

Henley pulled Sian to her feet and her solicitor picked up his case from the floor. 'Where to?' she shouted.

'My car. The black Focus,' the solicitor called back.

A cup hit Henley's chest.

Cold milky coffee dripped down her neck and she dragged Sian through the crowd to the sound of police sirens.

'Get your hands off me, you fucking bitch,' Sian said aggressively.

'Either shut up or I'll leave you to the mob.' Henley dragged her towards the car.

Sian ran her hand across her mouth, smearing the blood that ran from her split lip. 'This should be your blood.'

Henley didn't reply. She pushed Sian down onto the passenger seat and slammed the door.

4

DS Eastwood stood at the bank of lifts having lost two hours of her life in a performance development review at New Scotland Yard. She stepped back with surprise when the doors opened and she saw Pellacia, his forehead crinkled with annoyance.

'Eastie,' Pellacia exclaimed as she stepped into the lift and the doors closed. 'What are you doing . . . oh,' he clicked his fingers with the arrival of the memory, 'PDR. How did it go?'

'Completely pointless, although they did suggest that I should think about my career beyond the SCU,' Eastwood said candidly.

Pellacia went to respond but three others stepped into the lift and they fell silent, both keeping their thoughts to themselves until they reached the ground floor and walked out of New Scotland Yard. The sky was the colour of gun-metal grey and the wind whipped up around them.

'Fancy taking the river bus?' Pellacia asked. 'Less faff than trains and they've got a half decent bar on board.'

'Yeah, why not,' Eastwood replied. 'If you're buying.'

The river bus was less than a third full as it left Westminster Pier, towards Greenwich. It was a different view of London. Townhouses, rowing clubs and warehouses, that had once been used to store tea, coffee, spices and other legal – and illegal – commodities, converted into apartments and office spaces bordered the riverfront.

'Bad day?' Eastwood deadpanned when Pellacia placed cans of gin and tonic, Jack Daniel's and Coke and a bottle of Peroni on the table.

Pellacia laughed sardonically, pushing the gin and tonic towards her. 'You first,' he said.

'It was suggested, no suggested is wrong. I was *told* that they want me to transfer to LOCU.'

'Organised crime?' Pellacia opened his Jack Daniel's and Coke.

Eastwood nodded. 'I would be acting DI and have my own team but I don't get it. Why would they want me to leave the SCU?'

'Are you not tempted? I wouldn't be doing my job as your boss if I didn't ask. This unit has been through a lot, and no one would blame you if you wanted to leave and take up the opportunity to lead your own unit.'

'Look, guv,' Eastwood said, leaning forward. 'I do want to be an Inspector, maybe even DCI and take your job.'

Pellacia smiled. 'One day.'

'But let's be honest. Henley would probably get there first.'

'Truth is, she should have been the one sitting in Rhimes's chair, not me. If it wasn't for Olivier nearly killing her and . . .' Pellacia paused as the memories of the serial killer, Peter Olivier, carving a crescent and double cross into the skin on his chest, flashed in his mind. 'The point is, it should have been her.'

'Punished for doing her job,' Eastwood snorted. 'But as I was saying. I want the position of DI because I've earned it and not because someone handed it to me on a plate.'

'Who exactly was making the offer?'

'Irene from HR didn't say, but what she did say was that she wasn't sure if the SCU would still be around in six months.'

'They've got this annoying habit of talking out of both sides of their mouth,' said Pellacia as the boat came to a brief stop at Blackfriars. 'I've spent the entire morning in a budgetary meeting and there wasn't one hint of the SCU being shut down. In fact, it was the opposite; practically falling over themselves to commend me and the SCU for our results.'

'It's the art of deflection, isn't it?' Eastwood sipped her gin and tonic. 'You think that they're giving you a pat on the back without realising that they're holding a knife.'

'I shouldn't be surprised. They're not happy that we exposed their golden boy and his corruption.'

'You mean that this is payback for exposing Larsen?'

Pellacia nodded. He'd spent the summer sitting in endless meetings, first with the Independent Office for Police Conduct and the CPS explaining, ad nauseum, how ex-police commissioner James Larsen had bribed witnesses and destroyed evidence. Larsen did everything possible to undermine the credibility of their boss, DCSI Rhimes and the SCU. It was more than just misconduct. Larsen's actions had led to the wrongful conviction of Andrew Streeter for the murder of five people. There had been no happy endings when Streeter's convictions were overturned. Streeter had been killed by the real killer, Scott Beckett, who'd been allowed to freely walk the streets for twenty-five years. As far as Pellacia was concerned, Larsen had a lot of blood on his hands.

'But if you look up corrupt officers in the dictionary, there would be a picture of Larsen. Are you trying to tell me that the higher-ups would have been happier if we'd just left Larsen to disappear quietly into early retirement and leave Rhimes with a question mark on his grave?' Eastwood asked.

'I'm not going to sit here and tell you that you're wrong.'

There was nothing said for a few moments. The silence between them comfortable as the boat sped away from Blackfriars.

'I never expected it to be easy, running the SCU I mean,' said Pellacia. 'But I never expected—'

'Them to be so underhand.'

'Exactly that,' Pellacia agreed. He crushed the empty can in his hand before picking up the bottle of beer and settling back into his seat.

'It probably doesn't help that Sian Fox-Carnell is now out on bail.'

Pellacia leaned his head back and sighed. 'It doesn't bloody help at all. I know that we're not at fault with Fox-Carnell and we've got the support of the borough commander but that's the equivalent of having a lone lieutenant attempting to go to war against a battalion.'

'So, what's the plan?'

'We keep doing what we're doing,' Pellacia answered 'But we're also going to have to go through every request that we've received in the past six months, not only from the Met but from every other police force. We need to make sure that the numbers don't lie. That we have a substantial caseload. We can't give the higher-ups any reason to think that we're acting like a bunch of prima donnas and refusing to designate cases as serial crimes.'

'Guv, there are forty-three police forces in England and Wales. Forty-six if you include the British Transport Police, Scotland and Northern Ireland.'

'And I'm pretty sure that every single one of them has contacted us at some point.'

'Fine.' Eastwood drained her gin and tonic. 'No disrespect to you, guv, but there are only four of us who are actively working cases. I'm not saying that all you do is sit behind a desk—'

'That is exactly what you're saying and you're right. I spend more time deflecting cannons than doing what I was trained to do.'

'You've really got a thing with the war metaphors today, haven't you?'

'What can I say, they've put me in that kind of mood. So, you're good with this plan?'

'I could say that I'm not,' Eastwood answered with a laugh. 'But I'm not prepared to let them take down the SCU without a good fight.'

5

'I cannot believe they let that evil woman go free!' Joanna said, dumping a file on Henley's desk. 'It's diabolical and unbelievable. Didn't you say anything?'

'I'm thrilled about it. I want to take her out to dinner,' Henley snapped, folding her coffee-stained shirt and blazer into the plastic bag on her desk.

'There's no need to be sarky.'

'Jo, if you knew the day that I've had . . .'

'I saw the day that you had. Your little kick-off outside court was all over the news. And to really make your day, Fox-Carnell will be recording an exclusive interview to be shown on *Newsnight* tonight and will be on *Good Morning Britain* tomorrow.'

'Tell me that you're taking the mick,' said Stanford who was perched on Eastwood's empty desk.

Jo tutted and slowly shook her head, 'Detective Sergeant Paul Stanford,' she said in a tone that you would normally use for chastising a small disobedient child. 'When have you ever known me to take the mick?' She picked up the carrier bag on Henley's desk.

'Point taken.'

'Right,' said Jo brightly. 'I'm off to the post office and I'll drop this off at the dry cleaners on my way but, one more thing: I don't want you thinking that you did anything wrong in court today. No matter what that evil cow says on the telly tonight.'

'I'm not thinking that.' Henley watched Ramouter making a

cup of tea in the kitchen area. 'She's only out because her parents are crazy enough to put up a hundred grand.'

'It's a parent's love, innit?' said Stanford as Jo walked out. 'Who's to say that any of us wouldn't do the same thing if that was our kid. Fast forward ten or fifteen years and it's, God forbid, Emma sitting in a prison cell. Wouldn't you do everything to get her out?'

Henley chewed her lower lip not wanting to give voice to her answer. Yes, she would do everything and anything for her daughter, but she was unsure whether her love for her daughter would override the pursuit of justice.

'I promise you that she'll end up back inside. She's evil. She's a monster and she'll get what's coming to her.'

Ramouter finally made his way to his desk and asked, 'Are you ready for a catch up, boss?'

'I haven't had a chance to go through the progress report for our home invasions investigation,' Henley said. She scratched absentmindedly at a mosquito bite on her elbow. 'I'm hoping that your day has been more productive than mine.'

'I'm not sure if it's been productive but it's definitely been interesting.' Ramouter reached into his pocket and pulled out his notebook. 'We had a lot of units referring their aggravated burglary cases to us. The majority of them didn't fit the modus operandi of our home invasions, except this one case in Dulwich.'

'Is that where you were this morning?'

'Aye. On paper it fits so the guv asked me to assess the crime scene and speak to the OIC.'

'And does it belong on the board?' Henley asked. They walked towards the two whiteboards. On the first board was a map where red magnets had been placed on twelve different aggravated home invasion locations in South London and the outskirts of East London. The MO for each home invasion was the same. They took place on either a Wednesday or Thursday between 1 a.m.

and 3 a.m.. The occupants were grabbed from their bed, stripped to their underwear and tied up. Each victim was then locked in either their bedroom, bathroom or a cupboard. Jewellery, money, computers and bank cards were stolen.

'This is the thing.' Ramouter approached the map, picked up a yellow magnet and placed it on Dulwich Village. 'I'm not convinced that this belongs to us. It's nasty but it doesn't fit.'

'Explain to me why.'

'Our home invasions have all the elements of a traditional aggravated burglary. Entry as a trespasser with an intention to commit theft, possession of a firearm or other offensive weapon and every home was ransacked.'

'What's the problem with this burglary, other than it taking place on a weekend? This happened last night, right?'

'Possibly. There was an incident recorded just after midnight, but the exact timing of the burglary hasn't been confirmed. The problem is that nothing was stolen. Also, this Dulwich burglary was too violent.'

Henley stepped back and faced Ramouter. 'How can an aggravated burglary be too violent?' she asked.

'I'll show you. Just give me a sec,' Ramouter replied as he turned on his laptop, opened his email account and scrolled down. 'Ah, here it is. Watch.'

'Our burglary takes place at number 24 Cullen Lane,' Ramouter explained. 'There's only one way in and out because the council implemented traffic calming measures and blocked the junction with planters. This footage is taken from the last house on the lane.'

Henley leaned forward and watched as a video showed a man run into view. The sound was muted but it didn't lessen the impact of him being intentionally hit by a speeding car.

'Jesus Christ.'

'That wasn't an accident,' said Ramouter.

'So, the driver picks him up and takes him where?' Henley asked.

'Back to the property,' Ramouter answered. He opened the photos that had been forwarded to him by the CSI photographer. 'A postwoman found him in the middle of his driveway at 8.36 this morning.'

'Forced entry?'

'No evidence of any, but the attack starts in the kitchen, carries on along the hallway and onto the doorstep. There's blood tracking from inside to the driveway. The victim is injured but not seriously enough to stop him making an initial run for it. He's then hit by the car. The driver picks him up and dumps him bleeding on the driveway. Not one of the victims in our home invasion cases were able to escape.'

'Where's the victim now?'

'King's College Hospital,' Ramouter replied. 'I have no idea of his prognosis.'

'And who is he?'

Ramouter leaned back and raised his head to the ceiling. 'Dr Graham Ashcroft. Fifty-two years old. Married to Tabitha Ashcroft and they have one child, a daughter.'

'And where were they, the wife and daughter, when all of this was taking place?'

'According to the officer on scene, his daughter is studying in Canada. His wife wasn't at the property and the OIC hasn't been able to get hold of her,' Ramouter said as he stood up and walked back to the whiteboard.

'You're right. It's too violent,' Henley conceded, joining him. 'The extent of it and the targeting of the victim as opposed to his possessions.'

'That's it. Ashcroft was the target. Not whatever was in his house or even the car that was on the driveway. The car keys were still on the kitchen counter.'

Henley picked up a marker and wrote Graham Ashcroft's name on the board and added a question mark. 'There's a significant deviation from the MO of the other burglaries. From timing to the assault. Do you really want to devote our limited resources investigating something that is nothing to do with us?'

Henley watched Ramouter closely as she waited for him to answer. When they'd first met, his quiet thoughtfulness was more attached to his newness and his uncertainty as to how he would fit in the close-knit team. Now, it was a sign of how secure he felt with his position.

'Catch-22,' he said after a long beat. 'If we say no, and it turns out that the people who committed our series of burglaries are responsible then we'll be criticised for passing the buck but we're still at risk of criticism for taking time and resources away from the home invasions by adding a case that doesn't fit the MO.'

'So, what do *you* want to do?' Henley repeated.

'Isn't this above my paygrade?' he finally asked. 'Making decisions like this.'

Henley could sense Ramouter's unease. 'Yes, it is, but one day it won't be, so you might as well familiarise yourself now with the feeling of making a decision that can change the trajectory of a case.'

Ramouter shook his head and turned his back to the whiteboard. 'Boss, I really don't think that I should be making a decision like this.'

'Tell me what you want to do with the case.'

Ramouter exhaled with resignation. 'Can I have a bit of time? Let me have another chat with the OIC, DC Copeland, and go through the preliminary CSI reports. I also want to speak to Graham Ashcroft, that's if he's up to it.'

'Fine,' said Henley. 'You've got forty-eight hours.'

6

Sian Fox-Carnell pulled at the cuff of her tracksuit bottoms. She huffed and tutted in disappointment when the material failed to cover the electronic tag on her right ankle. The tag – and the restrictions on her life – angered her, but she'd hidden that when she sat next to Susanna Reid on *Good Morning Britain*, looking every inch like a woman who had been let down by a *not fit for purpose* justice system. She'd hooked strands of unwashed hair behind her ears, winced when she'd touched the bruise on her cheek and had fiddled nervously with the buttons on her dress. She'd worn the same dress when she'd appeared on *Newsnight* the night before and had dabbed Vicks VapoRub in the corners of her eyes. She'd cried when she said that she wished she'd been there when Leonard Calgary had died and that she blamed herself. Sian knew what she was doing. She was appealing to the public, to that man and woman who may be a potential juror on her trial in twelve months. The sounds of the train departing Brockley train station rumbled behind her as she checked the map app on her phone. Her destination was a twelve-minute walk away. Sian pushed her phone back into her bag, adjusted her headphones and walked along Coulgate Street. She felt her heartbeat increase as she obeyed the guided instructions and turned onto Foxberry Street.

*

'When is Daddy coming home?' Emma asked as she held on firmly to Henley's hand.

'Daddy will be home on Friday night,' Henley replied.

'Can't he come home now?'

'No, sweetie. I told you this before. Daddy has to go away to work so there are going to be days when it's going to be just you, me and Luna.'

Emma stopped abruptly in the road, snatching her small hand away. Henley groaned at the well-known signs of an emerging tantrum. Emma's tantrums had become more frequent since Rob had started his new job, and their routine had been disrupted. Rob now worked in Manchester every Thursday and Friday but today was forced to go in for a Tuesday morning meeting which had not made life any easier. Henley had not been prepared for a three-and-a-half-year-old's determination not to eat the breakfast that was put in front of her, even though it was the exact same breakfast that her dad made for her most mornings.

'Ems, come on, we're nearly home,' Henley said wearily. 'Give me your hand and let's go.'

'I don't want to go home. I want Daddy.'

'I'm not in the mood for this. Give me your hand now.'

'No!' Emma turned around and started to walk in the opposite direction.

'Where are you going?'

'The bus stop.'

Henley's annoyance quickly gave way to bemusement as she watched her daughter walk determinedly along the pavement. 'What's wrong?' Henley asked when Emma stopped and looked at her, a mixture of confusion and annoyance on her young face.

'I don't know where the bus stop is,' Emma admitted.

Henley did her best not to laugh. 'Come on, let's go home. Luna is on her own.'

'Can we have pizza?' Emma asked, running to keep up with her mum's pace.

Henley didn't get a chance to admit that she'd already placed the order because something caught her eye. There were five roads that separated Henley's street from the main road. Henley's street didn't experience a steady stream of traffic, she'd lost count of the number of times that a visitor or a cab driver had told her *'It's so quiet around here'*. Both Brockley train station and the nearest bus stop were a good walk away.

As a figure wearing a long camel coat and black tracksuit walked towards them, maternal and detective instincts combined, and Henley picked up her daughter

Henley sped up as her hypervigilance and anxiety – symptoms of her PTSD – kicked in. A Tesco delivery van turned onto the road and blocked her field of vision. She placed Emma down at her front gate.

'Hello.'

Sian's voice sent tremors of anger and fear through Henley's body. The acidic aroma of cheap wine was heavy on Sian's breath.

'Baby girl. We're going to play a game,' Henley said to her daughter. She opened the gate with her free hand and gently pushed her into the front garden. 'I want you to run to the front door as fast as you can, and then cover your eyes and count to ten. Now.'

For the first time that afternoon Emma listened to her mum and ran, her Spider-Man rucksack bouncing against her back, to the front door, stopped and covered her eyes.

'I missed seeing my daughter and my son at that age.' Sian's face darkened with fury. 'It's such an important time. You really see their personalities shine through. My daughter Penny is ten years old now and my little boy, Lyle is seven. The last time you would have seen them both was when you arrested me at my house that Saturday morning. I'd just finished breastfeeding Lyle, and I'd planned to take them both to the park. Six years is a long time to be away from your babies. Their father refuses to let me see them.'

'You can't blame him,' Henley said, fighting to keep her voice steady.

'You stole my children from me.'

'No, Sian. You did that to yourself. Now leave.'

'I don't have to do anything except make sure that I'm home by 9 p.m. which means that I'm free to . . .' Sian stepped back and spread out her arms as though she was about to take flight. 'I can do what I like. Take long walks. Refamiliarise myself with the area,' she said.

'Your area is on the other side of the river.' Henley's pulse gathered pace when she heard the sound of footsteps running across gravel. She saw Emma tapping at the large bay windows as Luna pressed her nose against the glass.

'My bail conditions don't stop me from travelling,' said Sian, placing her hands on the gate.

'Leave, Sian. Right now.' Henley's tone was firm. 'I promise you that I will find a way to throw your arse back inside if I see you near my home again. Do you understand me?'

Sian tapped her fingers against the wooden slats of the gate as a moped turned the corner and came to a stop at the kerb.

'Pizza,' Sian said disapprovingly. 'It's not the best food choice for a child, but I suppose it's hard, working to put the wrong people away and also finding the time to raise a family.'

'Mummy, I thought that we were playing a game?' Emma shouted, running back towards Henley.

'Your mother lied,' Sian shouted as Henley accepted two boxes from the deliveryman.

'We are, sweetie. We're going inside now to finish the game,' she answered, handing Emma the smaller box. 'Go on. Be a big girl and carry this for Mummy. Fast as you can.'

'Enjoy your dinner. If you can call it that. It must kill you,' Sian said. 'All of that hard work to put me away for life and here I am. Standing in front of you.'

'I've already warned you. And I'm not in the habit of repeating myself. Do not come near me or my daughter again or—'

'Or what? What can you do, Inspector Henley? What can you really do?' Sian taunted. She turned her back on Henley and walked away.

7

Sian had felt self-conscious from the minute she'd walked into a local Co-op. The security guard had looked her dead in the eye and then turned his attention to the rack of newspapers on his right. Her photograph was on the front of the *Daily Mail* with the headline, 'Monster Unleashed'.

She kept her head lowered as she paid with her mum's debit card, quickly packed her bag and left the shop. Her chest tightened with anger as the image of Henley holding her daughter's hand flooded her mind. Sian forced a new picture into her head. She felt the familiar buzz of excitement in her body picturing Henley begging for forgiveness before Sian pushed a syringe filled with fentanyl into her jugular vein.

'Hey!' Sian exclaimed as a sharp elbow to her side dragged her out of her dark thoughts. She turned around to see a man in a black parka with the hood over his head, hands stuffed in pockets walking hurriedly away. She pushed her hand into her right pocket and felt a sense of relief as her fingers curled around the freshly cut door key, ready to use as a weapon. She increased her pace and jogged towards her parents' house.

Sian was disorientated by the bright lights of a van's full beams. She didn't even see the figure heading towards her until he gave her a sharp push to the chest. Before she could react, she was thrown hard against the van, forcing all air from her chest. There was a smash as her bag fell to the floor, her red wine mixing with the rain running across the pavement. Rage and adrenaline flooded through Sian's body and she grabbed her attacker's wrists, her nails tearing through his skin. The punch to her bruised face was swift and she fell to the ground, tasting blood. Her attacker roughly snatched her phone from her pocket. Struggling, Sian turned over, pushed her hands against the ground screaming as shards of glass pressed into the palm of her hand. She rose shakily to her feet, attempting to find someone who could help her or to find a way to safety but the small window of opportunity disappeared as Sian felt a pair of muscular arms around her.

'No. Please, no,' Sian shouted as she was thrown into the back of the van, landing hard against the metal bulkhead. A few seconds later, the van jolted forward and made a sharp U-turn. Sian rolled onto her back, her hands raking through her hair as the sound of Coldplay's song, 'Paradise', filtered through the van's speakers.

8

'Fox-Carnell was at your house?' asked Stanford.

'I'm sure she'll say it was just a coincidence.' Henley switched to speaker, placed her phone on the coffee table and reached for the last slice of cold pizza.

'A coincidence? Please. She sought you out.'

'Of course she did. I've been sitting here trying to figure out how she found my address. I'm ex-directory and I'm not on social media.'

'But Rob is.'

'He is, but he doesn't expose our lives on there, it's just work-related stuff.'

'Let's be honest. You can find anyone if you really put your mind to it. All she would need to do is go online, get a copy of the electoral register and Bob's your uncle, she's at your front door.'

'I don't want her turning up at my house or talking to my child again,' Henley said angrily. 'My family has been through enough.'

'Are you going to tell Rob?'

Luna bought her some time by barking at the sharp whistle of the stormy wind outside.

'You remember how Rob got when Olivier sent me that . . .'

The skin on the back of her neck broke out in goosebumps at the memory of a decapitated head being left at her front door. An unwanted gift from a killer making his presence known.

'It would be easier not to tell him and save myself from another argument about the dangers of my job, but it wouldn't be right,' Henley said. She looked down at her hand and saw that her fingertips were slightly stained with pizza sauce.

'Do you want me to come over,' Stanford asked his voice filled with concern. 'Gene won't mind at all.'

'No. You don't need to put yourself out.' She dropped the half-eaten pizza slice into the box and closed the lid. 'Fox-Carnell's curfew will kick in soon and she's on tag. She would be a fool to even think about putting a foot outside her front door. The alarm is on, I've triple checked the doors and windows and Ems is sleeping in my bed. We're going to be fine.'

'Even so, I'm going to make a call to Colindale police station and tell them to carry out a doorstep check on Fox-Carnell. In fact, I might just do it myself.'

'Stanford,' Henley said sternly. 'I'm not having you driving across London in this weather. Don't put yourself out.'

'I hear you but I'm not making any promises.'

```
PRINTED AT 23:28 19OCT.   PC K Quinlan
SINGLE INCIDENT PRINTOUT
INCIDENT No. 315: 19OCT
Location Based Comments
**Attendance and Incident and Caller Location**
HAROLAZE TERRACE, NW9
BETWEEN COLINDALE AVENUE AND AJAX AENUE
WARNING **OFFICER SAFETY ISSUE**


Remarks:
Time          Date
              19 OCT


21:28:46   CALLER - PC GRAYS 89274- STATED THAT A
           DOORSTEP CHECK WAS ATTEMPTED AT SIAN
```

	FOX-CARNELL'S BAIL ADDRESS IN COLINDALE. FEMALE OCCUPANT REFUSES TO OPEN THE DOOR. LINE CLEARED
22:19:56	CALLER – PC GRAYS 89274 – CONFIRMS SECOND DOORSTEP CHECK ATTEMPTED AT SIAN FOX-CARNELL'S BAIL ADDRESS IN COLINDALE. ENTRY OBTAINED. SIAN FOX-CARNELL NOT ON THE PREMISES
	HEARD A MALE IN B/G FAINTLY
	FEMALE CAME TO THE LINE – APPEARED UPSET – SHE SAID THAT THE POLICE NEED TO LEAVE HER HOUSE.
	HEARD PC GRAYS 89274 WARN FEMALE THAT HE WILL ARREST HER FOR ASSAULT IF SHE TOUCHES HIM AGAIN.
	PC GRAYS 89274 CONFIRMS THAT PROPERTY HAS BEEN CHECKED. F0X-CARNELL IS NOT PRESENT. PHONE NUMBER ENDING 924 IS SWITCHED OFF.
	LINE CLEARED
22:32:56	CALLER DS PAUL STANFORD 37195 ATTACHED TO SERIAL CRIMES UNIT, SE10
	STATES THAT SIAN FOX-CARNELL HAS HARASSED DI ANJELICA HENLEY AT SE4 ADDRESS. LAST SEEN EST 17.00-17.15 IN SE4
22:52:45	DS STANFORD 37195 PRESENT AT FOX-CARNELL BAIL ADDRESS. STATES THAT FOX-CARNELL IS NOT PRESENT.
23.24:16	S. FOX-CARNELL IN BREACH OF CROWN COURT BAIL CONDITIONS – CURFEW 21.00 – 7.00. Consider contacting MIB Intelligence Support
	GPC Supervisor – All Alert Point Bulletin.

Inform PLO - Central Criminal Court in AM.

Please note that Fox-Carnell has been categorised as dangerous. OFFICERS AT RISK OF PHYSICAL ABUSE

SUBJECT TO FREEDOM OF INFORMATION
ACT AND PROTECTION ACT.
NO UNAUTHORISED DISCLOSURE-DISPOSE OF
AS CONFIDENTIAL WASTE

9

Henley's reflection in the dented and scuffed lift door was distorted by the aging yellow and white 'Meet the Met' sticker. She sighed wearily. The dark and puffy circles under her eyes were in stark contrast to the rest of her skin which was still benefiting from three weeks of Caribbean sunshine. It had been a restless night, the rain ferocious against her windows and filled with toxic dreams of home invasions and Sian Fox-Carnell stealing her child. Henley walked into the office with her dripping umbrella. The motion sensor lights had stopped detecting activity months ago and the facilities team had shown no urgency in replacing them. It saddened her that she felt safer in the dark, empty SCU than she did in her home.

Fifteen minutes later, Henley was standing in front of the map on the whiteboard, holding a steaming cup of coffee. She picked up the yellow magnet that had been placed on Cullen Lane and rolled it in her free hand. She'd given Ramouter forty-eight hours to decide to keep the case or not, but her gut told her the Ashcroft case did not fit. As Ramouter had said, 'There was too much violence.'

'Why didn't you call me?'

The yellow magnet fell out of Henley's hand and coffee sloshed from her cup as she spun around. She'd been so lost in her thoughts that she hadn't heard the sound of the SCU becoming alive with activity.

Pellacia bent down and picked up the magnet.

'Call you about what?' she asked.

'Sian Fox-Carnell. She turned up at your home, harassed you and I had to find out about it from a PC at Colindale.'

'Fox-Carnell turning up on my street isn't work related,' said Henley.

'Why are you down playing this?' Pellacia exclaimed. 'She was at your house, travelled across London to find you, to—'

'To gloat. That's all she wanted to do. Gloat and make it seem as though she'd got one over on me.'

'You can't see the danger?'

'I was never in danger.' Stanford and Eastwood's chatter suddenly became audible in the office hallway. 'And I can take care of myself.'

'Christ, you make it sound as though I'm not allowed to be concerned about your welfare. I do have a duty of care when you're inside these four walls and, whether you like it or not, outside of them too.'

Henley turned to face the far wall, unable to handle the hurt and concern that was etched on Pellacia's face.

'There must be a good reason why she missed curfew.' Henley was eager to turn the conversation away from her. 'I can't imagine her willingly sacrificing the hundred grand that her parents gave the court and her freedom.'

'I'm not really interested in what the reason is,' Pellacia said coldly. 'But I can't ignore the fact that she came after you which means that all of us in the SCU have a target on our backs.'

'It's not just us though,' said Stanford, shaking the rain off his mac and hanging it on the coat rack in the corner. 'The woman turned up at Henley's door when she was with her kid, and—'

'Stanford, stop,' Henley pleaded.

'Emma was with you?' Pellacia asked, shaking his head with disbelief.

'Emma was . . . is fine,' said Henley. 'Fox-Carnell breached for a reason. That's not just a problem for her lawyers and the CPS. It's a concern for us too.'

'I like the fighting spirit but what are we supposed to do?' asked Stanford.

'Are you worried that she's going to rock up at your house next?' Eastwood asked, sitting down at her desk and switching on her computer.

'If she does, she better bring milk, because I'm out.'

'All right enough,' said Pellacia, his face stern and unyielding to Stanford's attempt at levity. He took a chair and brought it towards Eastwood's desk. 'We've got a lot to get through this morning. You're going to find on your desks a list of our current caseload and Eastwood should have a list of case transfer requests.'

'Just give me a sec.' Eastwood ran to the printer and collected a large bundle.

'Where's the boy wonder?' Stanford asked as he pointed at Ramouter's empty desk.

'En-route to King's . . .' Henley paused as she scanned the first page of the bundle that Eastwood had just placed in her hand. 'Avon and Somerset, Cleveland Police?'

'Police Scotland?' Stanford exclaimed as he flicked through the pages in his hand. 'These seriously haven't just come in this week?'

'No,' said Eastwood as the sound of the intercom buzzer rang out. 'These are all the requests we've received since January of this year.'

'As you know, there was an internal review of the SCU after the Streeter case,' said Pellacia. 'You would have thought that having it in writing and I quote *"the SCU's performance, efficiency and effectiveness exceeds expectations"* would have made some people happy but it wasn't enough. I was ordered to the Yard on Monday for a bollocking. I was told that the SCU was being too selective and ignored legitimate transfer requests.'

Stanford picked up a red pen and struck it dramatically across the page. 'I'm sorry but a dirty nonce flashing in service station toilets in Bury St Edmunds is not a case for the SCU. Bunch of jokers.'

'I agree but—' Pellacia stopped midsentence as the office door suddenly swung open, slammed against the wall and Ezra ran into the office.

'Ezra what's going on?' Henley asked.

'I wanted to warn you,' Ezra answered. 'Two officers from the Met Intelligence Bureau are on their way to see you now. Right now.' They could hear the lift hydraulics as it ascended. 'I'd literally just walked in, when the buzzer went,' Ezra's eyes darted towards the door, 'I opened it and there they were, looking like the Men in Black and they said they wanted to see you, Henley. I said that I didn't know if you were in and that I wanted to see their cards. The man accused me of obstructing so I dashed off as soon as I heard the lift open and—'

The door to the unit swung open for a second time. Pellacia stood and straightened himself to his full height. A white, stocky-built, bald-headed man in his late thirties, dressed sharply in a navy suit, walked in. His partner, a tall Asian woman, her dark hair pulled tight into a bun and dressed similarly in a charcoal trouser suit with her white shirt buttoned up to the collar, was close behind.

Pellacia crossed quickly to the middle of the room, effectively blocking both officers from proceeding any further. 'You are?' he demanded. The male officer pressed his lips together as he shoved his hands into pockets and rolled back his shoulders.

'DS Liam McLaren and this is DC Dao,' he said.

'It seems that you've both forgotten how to address a senior officer,' Pellacia said sternly, taking a step towards McLaren.

'I have no idea who you are,' McLaren answered smugly.

'I find that very difficult to believe, considering that you're standing here in my unit. No one finds themselves here by accident.'

'Ah, DCI Pellacia,' DS McLaren replied with a tut and an overdramatic shake of the head.

'What can I do for you and why have you turned up without notice?'

'We're dealing with the disappearance of Sian Fox-Carnell, sir,' DC Dao replied in a clear effort to diffuse the tension.

'And they sent you from the Met Intelligence Bureau to deal with some scrote breaching bail? Someone doesn't like you two much,' said Stanford.

DC Dao glanced over at Stanford, subtly gave him a side-eye and turned towards Henley who had remained in her seat, quietly observing the exchange.

'The last recorded GPS entry from Fox-Carnell's tag places her outside your home yesterday afternoon,' DC Dao said to Henley. 'We would like to discuss that meeting with you, ma'am.'

'It wasn't a meeting,' Henley replied.

'You may not call it a meeting but clearly something took place between the two of you that may have triggered her disappearance,' said McLaren who clearly wasn't used to sitting quietly on the sidelines.

'Clearly something took place,' Henley repeated disapprovingly. 'But you should know better than to make assumptions and jump to conclusions.'

'What I do know is that due to someone's—'

'Aren't you forgetting something, sergeant,' Henley cut in. She stepped away from Ezra and joined Pellacia. It had been a long time since Henley had found herself in a pissing match with an officer who didn't respect her rank and her unit. She wasn't having it.

'Ma'am.' The skin on DS McLaren's neck flushed red, his contempt of Henley clear. 'As I was saying, we're—'

'Assuming,' Pellacia interrupted this time. 'And that's where investigations usually falter when detectives, out of their depth, fail to assess the facts.'

'Ma'am,' said DC Dao, almost apologetically. 'As you can appreciate, the first seventy-two hours—'

'Of a person's disappearance are the most critical,' recited Henley. 'Maybe next time you'll remember that when you decide to make statements and not ask actual questions.'

DS McLaren quietly fumed as DC Dao looked at him for instruction.

'Unbelievable,' muttered Pellacia, glaring at the two officers.

'DS McLaren. DC Dao. Follow me,' Henley ordered, stepping away from Pellacia, she picked up her phone from her desk and made her way towards the door.

The overhead light caught the dust particles in the air as Henley opened the greying blinds and pushed the windows open. The paint was flaking off the walls of the former multi-faith prayer room.

'Ma'am,' DS McLaren sat down on a chair that had seen better days, 'Sian Fox-Carnell failed to return home. There has been no sighting of her, and no one has heard from her.'

'What have her parents said about her disappearance?' Henley asked.

'Not much,' said DC Dao. 'Her mother is, I suppose, understandably quite frantic but if I'm honest, slightly paranoid, ma'am. She's convinced that someone has taken her daughter.'

'Why would she think that. Have there been threats?'

DC Dao shook her head.

'According to Soteria, the electronic monitoring company, Fox-Carnell's last movements were recorded at 5.03 p.m. at Brockley overground station, 5.14 p.m. at Joe's coffee shop on Coulgate Road, 5.24 p.m. on Breakspears Road, which is where you live, and 5.41 p.m. on Mantle Road,' said McLaren.

Henley pulled out her notebook and wrote down the times.

'So, what happened?' McLaren asked.

'I was with my daughter when I was approached by Fox-Carnell,' said Henley. 'We weren't far from home. Maybe three houses away.'

'I wasn't aware that you had a kid,' McLaren said his features softening slightly. 'How old is she?'

'She's three.'

'If Soteria is correct, Fox-Carnell spent twenty-one minutes in your area,' said McLaren. 'Twenty-one minutes is a long time to spend with someone.'

'I didn't spend twenty-one minutes with her,' Henley replied. 'I spoke to her for no more than five minutes.'

'What did you and Fox-Carnell talk about?' said DC Dao.

'My main priority was to protect my daughter,' Henley said, clenching her right hand into a tight fist. 'It's not exactly a secret that this isn't the first time that someone I've investigated has paid me a visit. I told Fox-Carnell to leave,' said Henley. 'I warned her.'

'Warned her or threatened her?' the DS asked.

Henley leaned forward in her chair. 'What are you suggesting, DS McLaren?'

McLaren stared back at Henley wide-eyed with mock innocence. 'I'm just asking the question, ma'am,' he said. 'I've got four kids, and I wouldn't blame you if you'd been, what's the best way to put it, physically forceful.'

'I didn't touch her. I warned her that she would find herself back inside if she came near me again. I then took my daughter and went inside my house.'

'And you haven't seen or had any communication from her since?' McLaren asked.

'No,' Henley replied bluntly. 'Now let me ask you a question. Do you seriously have no idea where Fox-Carnell is?'

McLaren's face reddened. 'No,' he admitted.

'Mantle Road at 5.48 p.m. was her last location?'

'Presumably she was making her way back to Brockley station.'

'I still don't understand why you can't track her or to be precise, her tag,' said Henley. 'Mantle Road shouldn't be her last location?'

Henley caught the look that DC Dao gave DS McLaren as though she was requesting permission to speak.

'DC Dao,' Henley said sternly. 'There's a reason why MIB are involved in this case, and it's got nothing to do with Fox-Carnell breaching her curfew.'

'Yesterday, at 6.02 p.m., Soteria, the electronic monitoring company reached its data storage capacity,' said DC Dao.

'What does that mean?'

'It means that for the past fifteen hours and thirty minutes, Soteria haven't been able to record or view the movements of 12,892 people who are currently on tag, including Fox-Carnell.'

Henley leaned back in her seat, momentarily lost for words as she processed the enormity of DC Dao's statement. The fact that there was an IT explanation for the fact that Sian's current location was unknown didn't appease Henley.

'Fox-Carnell doesn't know that Soteria has IT problems so it doesn't stop her from complying with her bail conditions, which means that she's either disappeared of her own volition or—' said Henley.

'Or something happened to her,' McLaren concluded as he intensified his gaze on Henley. 'Or someone *did* something to her, ma'am.'

10

Ramouter hesitated as he waited outside the locked entrance to the intensive care unit. His only good hospital memory had been the birth of his son, Ethan, but he had plenty of bad ones. The pain of discovering that his wife, Michelle, had been diagnosed with early onset dementia and the pain of being stabbed by the serial killer Peter Olivier. Ramouter pressed the intercom buzzer for a second time when a doctor, dressed in dark blue scrubs, appeared behind him.

'They're a bit short staffed,' the doctor said, his gaze drifting to the warrant card around Ramouter's neck. 'Who are you here to see?' he asked.

'Graham Ashcroft. He was admitted two days ago.'

'Come on through,' the doctor said, pressing his staff ID card against the security panel. 'He's doing well considering that he took a bloody battering. We would have moved him down to the general ward but we're waiting for a bed to become free.'

'What were his injuries?'

'What weren't his injuries? Stab wounds in his right bicep, back and hands. Broken ribs. Broken leg, cheek and collarbone and we had to perform a splenectomy. Do you want to know the odd thing though?'

'What's that?' asked Ramouter.

'He's been here for two days and you're the first person who's been to see him.' The doctor stopped at the nursing station and tapped the shoulder of the nurse who was sitting at the computer. 'Mabel, has Ashcroft, bed nine, had any visitors since I've been on break?'

'Nope. Not one and he's been asking.'

'Who has he been asking for?' Ramouter asked.

Mabel looked up and stared at Ramouter for a brief moment before turning her head towards the doctor.

'Police,' the doctor answered in response to her unspoken question.

'Right,' said Mabel as she stood up and reached for a file on the side of her desk. 'He's been asking for his wife, but she hasn't responded to any of our messages. Bed nine. Straight ahead on your right.'

Graham Ashcroft slowly raised his head and squinted at Ramouter through heavily bruised eyes. The disappointment on his swollen face was hard to miss. He lowered his head and turned his gaze towards the window.

'Hi, Graham. I'm Detective Salim Ramouter.' He closed the door behind him. 'I'm from the Serial Crime Unit.'

Graham coughed as he turned his head. 'Sorry,' he croaked. 'My throat. Could you . . . water.'

Ramouter quickly made his way to the tray on the side, filled up a tumbler with water and held the paper straw to Graham's mouth. He waited patiently as Graham drank.

'Thank you,' Graham said when he was finished.

Ramouter placed the empty glass back on the tray and sat down on a chair next to Graham's bed. 'You've been through the wars a bit. How are you feeling?'

'Everything hurts. I'm not even sure if the morphine pump is doing anything.'

'It must be hard for a doctor to be the patient.'

'Understatement of the year.'

'When I came in you looked as though you were expecting someone else.'

'I thought that you were— I was expecting my wife but . . . I don't know.' Graham touched his forehead as though he was trying to activate a memory.

'I got a message last night from the senior investigating officer who attended the scene, DC Copeland. She informed me that she'd spoken to your wife—'

'Tabitha. She—' Graham stopped abruptly, groaning in pain and clutching his side as he tried to sit up.

'Hey, hey, relax,' said Ramouter as he placed his hand gently on Graham's shoulder. 'You're going to rip out your stitches if you move around like that.'

'You spoke to my wife?' Graham asked as he reached for the morphine and rapidly pressed the neon green button.

'No, I didn't speak to her. DC Copeland did,' said Ramouter. He watched the morphine descend from the drip and travel down the IV into the vein in Graham's arm.

'Is she ok?' Graham asked anxiously, he sighed heavily, dropped his head back against the pillows and squeezed his eyes shut.

Ramouter gave Graham a few minutes and then picked up the bed remote control and adjusted it slowly until Graham was sitting up.

'You got quite agitated when I mentioned your wife,' said Ramouter. 'I was told by the doctor that you haven't had any visitors since you were admitted.'

Graham took hold of the morphine pump again. 'That can't be right,' he said. 'Tabitha must have been to see me when I was sleeping or something.'

'No, she hasn't.' Ramouter glanced around the room. It looked like his room had before his wife had arrived. She brought bags of fruit, bottles of energy drinks and water which cluttered the table. Henley, knowing that the hospital menu had little to be desired, had arrived with a bag of homemade meals. Ramouter bent down and opened the cupboard on the bedside table. It was empty. There was nothing in Graham's room to show that anyone cared about him.

'Can you remember anything about the night you were attacked?' he asked, straightening up.

'No. Not really, but I think I was upstairs when I heard a noise,' said Graham.

'What sort of noise was it?'

'She screamed.'

Ramouter tried to keep the surprise out of his voice as he asked, 'Who screamed?'

It was hard not to miss the look on Graham's swollen and bruised face. It was the look of someone who had been caught out.

'"Scream". I don't . . . I never said that.'

'You said that "She screamed". Who was screaming? Was it your wife?'

'No. No, I didn't say that.'

'Was Tabitha in the house?'

Graham shook his head as if the memory of what he'd gone through was too much for him.

'Dr Ashcroft, when your wife spoke to DC Copeland, she said that she was in Bath and that she'd been there since Friday.'

Graham withered on the bed. 'No. You're confusing me.'

'I don't think you're confused at all. Did you hear Tabitha scream before you were attacked?'

'No.'

'Did you have another woman in the house? Was she the one screaming?'

'I don't know.'

Ramouter watched Graham growing more agitated as he searched the folds of his blanket with his hand. 'What are you looking for?' he asked.

'The alarm. I need the nurse. I'm not feeling good.'

'Don't worry. I'll get the nurse for you,' Ramouter said, heading out of the room convinced that Graham's request for a nurse was just a ploy to avoid answering a hard but straightforward question. Where was his wife when the attack happened? What was Graham hiding?

'Can't say that I'm surprised to see you here.'

Ramouter turned towards the direction of the voice. 'DC Copeland,' he said as a nurse rushed past him and entered Graham's room.

DC Copeland smiled broadly as she approached Ramouter. She looked different now that she was out of the shapeless protective oversuit. The aggressive overhead lights bounced off her red hair which hung loosely down her back and contrasted sharply with her black blazer. She had the long and lean look of a marathon runner. Ramouter felt his cheeks grow warm with shame as he realised that he was actually pleased to see her.

'I don't want you thinking that I'm interfering with your case,' he said. 'I just had some questions.'

'Please,' Copeland said, waving her hand dismissively. 'I was the one who called you first remember? And I don't think we were properly introduced when we first met.'

'Salim Ramouter.'

'Nice to meet you, Salim. I'm Xania Copeland,' she replied.

'Xania,' Ramouter said with a slight grin.

'You can stop right there. I've heard it all. It's not Xena warrior princess, its Xania. Nia for short.'

'Got it.'

'So, how's Graham? I take it you saw him just before the nurse rushed in?' asked Copeland.

'Aye and it was . . . maybe we should talk about this somewhere else?' Ramouter suggested.

'Let's talk in there,' Copeland said as she pointed in the direction of a small and empty family room. 'So how is he?'

Ramouter sat down on a worn green chair. 'Physically he's an absolute mess.'

'They told me that they'd removed his spleen,' said Copeland, sitting down opposite him with only a small, white coffee table between them.

'Yeah, they did. Obviously, he's in pain but he's lucid. Upset that his wife hasn't been to see him.'

'She *hasn't* been to see him?' asked Copeland with surprise.

Ramouter shook his head. 'She hasn't visited even though she told you she was on her way, right?'

'Right. Surely that's not correct. The poor man must be high as a kite on painkillers.'

'No, it's right,' Ramouter was adamant. 'The doctor told me I'm his first visitor.'

'That doesn't make any sense. She specifically told me on Monday afternoon that she was on her way. I could hear the traffic because she'd just pulled into a petrol station and then she texted me yesterday morning and said that she'd seen him,' said Copeland. She took her phone out of her pocket and quickly tapped and swiped the screen.

'Look,' she said, holding the phone to Ramouter.

'"Sorry to bother you. I just wanted to let you know that I've just seen Graham. Please keep me updated on the investigation."' Ramouter read out loud. 'Why would she lie and say that she's seen him when she hasn't?' he asked.

'Good bloody question. I'm going to ask her,' Copeland replied, her face fixed with determination as she tapped the phone again and turned on the speaker.

'This is Tabitha Ashcroft. Please leave a message and I'll return your call as soon as possible. Please call my office if this is a work-related matter or send an email to Tabitha@TabithaAshcroft.com'

'Where the hell is she?' Copeland asked as she ended the call without leaving a message and began to type furiously. 'I'm telling her that there's no record of her visiting her husband and to call me asap. Why on earth would she lie to me?'

'There's something else,' Ramouter said once Copeland had finished. 'Granted, he's been through a lot, but he was a bit cagey with his answers. Well, I didn't get any answers.'

'Cagey? How so?'

Ramouter explained about Ashcroft's misstep. 'He started calling for the nurse once I tried pressing him. I don't want to say that he's lying but something isn't adding up.'

'Maybe he's concussed. You saw how hard he was hit by that car and how the driver picked him up like a rag doll.'

'I'm not saying it's not concussion,' said Ramouter. 'But he specifically asked if his wife was ok before I asked him where she was and yes, he'd been hitting that morphine pump hard, but he knew and understood what I was asking him.'

'You think that his wife was in the house when he was attacked?'

'I do.'

'But I spoke to her, and she was driving. She said that she got my message and was on her way.'

'So, she called you back after your first message?'

'No, no,' Copeland said as she stood up, peeled off the hair band on her wrist and tied her hair back as if the discussions in the room were irritating her. 'She never called me back. I had to chase her. I called her office first, she owns a cosmetic clinic in Dulwich Village, Botox, fillers, that sort of thing. The manager gave me her mobile number. It went straight to voicemail the first time. I left a message and then I called her again a few hours later and the phone rang out. It must have been another twenty minutes or so before she called me back.'

'Just because you heard traffic in the background, and she told you she'd just pulled into a petrol station doesn't mean she was driving back to London.'

'What are you saying?'

'She lied to you twice, Copeland,' said Ramouter. 'I reckon when you spoke to her, she was probably driving away from London. Away from a crime scene.'

11

Sian collapsed wearily against the van door. Her throat was raw after hours of screaming and no water for days. She'd crawled around the small space searching in the dark for anything to use as a weapon or a tool but had come up empty. The van was cold and smelt of Sian's sweat and urine. She crawled to the front of the van and pressed her face to the grill, where she was able to see the clock on the dashboard. She didn't have the energy to cry when she saw the date and time. Thursday 21 October, 11.38 p.m., two days since she was kidnapped. Suddenly the sliding door was pulled open. Sian's scream lodged in her throat as a pair of hands grabbed her tightly under her armpits and dragged her out of the van. She landed heavily on the floor. Fight mode was activated in Sian's brain. She contorted her body and kicked out. Her right leg connected heavily with something unseen, and she yelled out in pain as sharp jagged edges bit into the skin on her shin.

Sian bit down hard on the rough hand pressed against her mouth. She could taste stale sweat, salt and vinegar as her teeth sank into the calloused flesh. She tasted blood.

'You stupid bitch,' a voice rang out sharply in Sian's ear. His hot breath prickling her skin.

Sian tried to scramble to her feet but stumbled, falling sideways against the van and down to the floor. A pair of hands grabbed her shoulders, flipped her on to her stomach and pushed her face firmly against the ground, scraping on the concrete. Sian choked on the pungent scent of engine oil. Then, she felt something worse than fear as her hands were pulled behind her back and cable ties were zipped tightly around her wrists. Her hoarse scream muffled by the ground as she felt hands travel down her legs and a second tie was wrapped and tightened around her ankles.

'Here,' a second voice said. Softer but commanding.

Sian twisted her head away but was unable to stop the thick tape from being pressed hard against her mouth. She lay still and prostrate as the man who had restrained her stood up. She had been so consumed with fear-infused adrenalin that she hadn't taken in her surroundings. The naked dim light bulb overhead gave enough light for her to see that she was in someone's garage. The muscles in her stomach tightened when she saw the coils of beige rope spilling out of a blue bag.

Sian could hear the sounds of the room and life outside; the dull thrum of a passing car and the slow dripping of water. She could hear the deep breathing of the person who'd gagged and bound her like a wild animal and then there was her heart, beating erratically and fearfully in her chest.

'Stupid, evil bitch.'

Sian's eyes widened as a phone was put in her face. The bright light of the flash almost blinding her as she heard the voices say:

'You're going to suffer the same way that your victims suffered.'

'You have no right to redemption. Justice should always be in the hands of the people.'

The kick to her temple was quick and hard. White light of pain obscured her vision as intense pressure and heat built inside her head and bile crept up her throat. Minutes felt like hours as Sian cried, her body withering like a fish out of water, gasping for air.

'You deserve everything that is going to happen to you,' the softer voice said. 'You probably thought you were going to walk away from all the pain you caused and live a great life. That is not going to happen.'

A sharp and bony knee pressed into the bruised and tender flesh of her lower back, which sent an electric shock down her sciatic nerve. A hand grabbed a clump of her hair and cold metal touched her tender scalp on the crown of her head. The skin on her face grew taut as the fine hairs of her hairline were ripped out. Sian's blood-tinged saliva softened the glue on the tape across her mouth and she released a guttural scream as the sharp blade pierced the thin skin, inched down her scalp and scraped her skull. Hot spilled blood dampened her hair and ran into her eyes.

'I don't feel sorry for her,' the first voice said followed by the sound of a throat clearing. Sian cried pitifully as her body grew cold with shock. She writhed on the floor, turning onto her back, as footsteps approached. Sian was helpless as a hand grabbed her face, squeezed and turned her head so that her eyes met her punisher.

'Do you know what this is?' the man asked, holding a small glass vial in his thick fingers.

Sian could neither shake nor nod her head as the small words on the bottle swam in front of her.

'You should know what it is. It's what you gave to your patients. Those poor people who thought you were there to help them.'

For a fleeting moment there was clarity in Sian's mind as she watched the man place the bottle carefully onto the floor.

'What is it they say when you go to the hospital for a blood test?' asked the man. He removed a syringe from his shirt pocket and pulled off the orange safety cap. 'You're going to feel a sharp scratch.'

Sian couldn't move as the needle entered her neck and the cold, poisonous liquid was forced through her skin and absorbed into her bloodstream. She knew what was coming but she wasn't ready for the violent convulsions as blood continued to fall into her eyes.

*

'Not again. How many times do you need to take a bloody piss?' Eric said to his West Highland terrier when she stopped at the bench and squatted.

'As long as you're not taking a shit because I'm out of bags.' Fifteen seconds later his dog gave a satisfied yap, and he threw her a treat. As much as Eric moaned about being the one stuck walking the dog – that his kids had promised to walk – he enjoyed this time of the morning. He'd left the house at 6.30 a.m. with a freshly brewed cup of coffee, popped in his Airpods, pressed play on his favourite podcast and started his walk along the riverfront. He watched a flock of seagulls take flight across the sky which was a wash of purples and pinks as the sun slowly ascended. Eric raised his cup but it never met his lips. It slipped out of Eric's hand and landed on the ground, causing the dog to yelp. Eric stepped closer to the railings to make sure that he wasn't seeing things. Eric knew what he should do, but confusion and disbelief had him frozen. A woman, hanging from the pier, her body twisting slowly in the breeze, as a seagull pecked at her feet.

12

'Are you saying you think that this doctor's wife, Tabitha, may have had something to do with his attack?' Henley asked as she put aside a disclosure request from the CPS and turned to Ramouter.

'I mean I can't say for certain that yes, she had something to do with her husband's attack, but . . .'

'Their behaviour is off,' Henley concluded. 'Have you tried to contact the wife yourself?'

'No. I thought that if she is involved then having another officer from a completely different unit might spook her.'

'Good point. What about anyone else? Family members. Friends.'

Ramouter shook his head.

Henley picked up markers from her desk and walked over to the whiteboard. She drew a vertical line in red down the middle of the blank whiteboard and wrote Graham Ashcroft's name. 'What do you know about him?'

'He's fifty-two years old and the director of a fertility clinic. Married to Tabitha Ashcroft. They have one daughter. Colette. twenty years old and studying at the University of Toronto. He has a clean criminal record now but there was a drink driving conviction seventeen years ago for which he got a twelve-month driving ban. He got his licence back and there's a speeding ticket from three years ago.'

'On the surface you can't see why anyone would have it in for him?'

'Not unless he owes someone money. I can ask Ezra to have a dig around and see what his personal finances are like, but I went on Companies House and from the accounts that they filed they're doing more than all right.'

'Fertility is a lucrative business. What about social media?' said Henley.

'He's on Instagram and he's . . . a bit annoying really. He runs marathons, volunteers for his local food bank, looks to be a good and very proud dad and even officiated a friend's wedding last summer in San Francisco. He's perfect.'

'No one's perfect, Ramouter,' Henley said, tapping the marker against her palm. 'Ok, if there's nothing on the surface to explain why someone would want to take this man out, what about the wife?'

'She's not so perfect. Dr Tabitha Ashcroft. Owns an equally lucrative beauty clinic. Again, good financials. She's forty-eight years old and has no presence on social media. Her clinic has an Instagram and TikTok page, but she personally doesn't.'

'Why is she a blackout on social media?'

'Previous convictions.' Ramouter handed her a printout.

Croydon Gazette
Monday 6 September 2021
Sharon Weaver and Kate Linton

Careless driver avoids prison after Thornton Heath schoolteacher's death

A woman has narrowly avoided a prison sentence after pleading guilty to causing death by careless driving.

Tabitha Ashcroft, aged forty-eight, hit sixty-year-old Sherri Durant on Thornton Heath High Street.

The crash took place at around 7.30 p.m. on 16 April, last

year, and Sherri Durant died later at Croydon University Hospital from a head injury.

Ashcroft, of Dulwich, London, was given a fifteen-month prison sentence suspended for two years at Croydon Crown Court on Monday after pleading guilty to causing death by careless driving.

The court was told that Ashcroft was six miles over the 30mph speed limit and that she was on her phone when the collision took place.

The court heard that the prosecution had dropped the original charge of death by dangerous driving after receiving evidence that Durant had run out into the road and that Ashcroft's view had been partially obscured by a bus.

In addition to her fifteen-month suspended prison term, Ashcroft was banned from driving for two years and seven months and ordered to perform 200 hours of unpaid work, a driver awareness course and made to pay £1,250 in costs.

Barrister Grant Dodd said his client would never forgive herself for her role in the tragic accident.

The family of Sherri Durant sat through the proceedings in the public gallery. A spokesman for the family said: 'We are devasted and will never get over the loss of Sherri. The legal system has failed us. There has been no justice here today.'

'She killed someone,' Henley said, instantly feeling the sense of loss and despair that would forever be part of their life.

'And all she got was a suspended sentence and a ban,' added Ramouter.

'Didn't Tabitha Ashcroft tell DC Copeland that she was driving back from Bath to see her husband?'

'Yep.'

'Even though she's on a two-year ban and has a suspended prison sentence?' Henley wrote Tabitha Ashcroft on the whiteboard with an exclamation mark. 'Why would you risk driving on a ban and going to prison for two years unless you're running from something?'

'Or because you did something.'

Henley's desk phone started ringing but Stanford walked over and answered it.

'So, husband is a saint, but the wife isn't,' Henley continued. 'Husband is attacked, first by stabbing and then, ironically, being run off the road. Wife is on a driving ban but is blatantly ignoring the ban and unless something has changed in the last hour, she's still a no-show at the hospital. Do you have any more updates about the burglary? Forensics? Independent witnesses?'

Ramouter shook his head. 'DC Copeland didn't update me on forensics and Graham was less than forthcoming.'

Henley bit her lip and nodded to the second whiteboard. She tapped the board with her marker. 'I gave you forty-eight hours; you've already gone over the clock. What's your decision?'

'It doesn't fit. Which means that I have to let it go. I'll call DC Copeland and tell—'

'No, don't call her just yet. There's something not right about the wife,' Henley said as she drew a circle around Tabitha Ashcroft's name followed by an arrow and wrote the following questions:

WHERE IS SHE? WHY IS SHE RUNNING?

'Oi, Henley. You fancy a trip down the road?' said Stanford as he strolled over towards Henley and Ramouter.

'For what?' Henley asked.

'That was the control room on the phone. A woman's body was found hanging on the old Deptford Pier on Glaisher Street. Lewisham CID haven't got the manpower to deal with it so they're passing it on to us, as though we don't have enough on our plates.'

'I've had enough of Lewisham passing—'

'You might want to hold off from calling their DI and cussing them out though,' Stanford interrupted. 'I was scanning HOLMES and there was an update with Sian Fox-Carnell's missing person's case. Soteria managed to get their systems back up and running and twenty minutes ago they got a GPS alert as to Fox-Carnell's location.'

Ramouter looked across at Henley and then back to Stanford. 'Glaisher Street?'

'Give the boy wonder a prize.'

'I'll get my coat,' said Henley.

13

A police helicopter hovered overhead while boats from the marine policing unit bobbed on the low tide of the river. A crowd had gathered at the edges of the large, cordoned area which stretched from the riverside entrance of the Ahoy sailing club and fifty metres past the entrance to the underground car park that faced the rotting pier.

'Brings me back to the day we first met, and you made me walk along the riverbank in my new shoes,' said Ramouter as he and Henley ducked under the police tape. The CSI team and uniformed officers were staggered around the periphery of the staircase that led to the pier unsure of what their next move should be.

'New and wrong shoes,' Henley replied, watching a fire engine enter the cordoned area and stop. Wild purple flowering bushes and barbed wire bordered a crumbling concrete staircase that had been reinforced with sheaves of rusting black metal. Security hoarding – the black paint peeling off the rotting wood – had been erected along the perimeter at the top of the staircase. A bright yellow warning sign had clearly been ignored. The door in the middle of the hoarding swung back and forth, exposing the metal gangway that had taken on a green hue after decades of neglect and exposure.

Ramouter stepped around Henley and moved closer to the black safety railings. 'Is that her?' he asked.

Henley craned her neck to get a better view of the body that was hanging over the river, 'It's impossible to tell. She's facing the wrong way, but there's a tag on her ankle.'

'How the hell did someone manage to get her up there? Look at the pier, it's on the verge of collapse.'

'Someone with a lot of determination and hatred,' she answered.

'So, what now?' Ramouter asked.

Henley turned around and spotted a police sergeant that she recognised from Plumstead police station. 'Miller,' she called.

The officer smiled thinly. 'I would say it's nice to see you but, you know, I would have preferred better circumstances.'

'Yeah, me too. This is my partner, DC Ramouter. This is PS Ted Miller.'

'Pleasure,' said Miller.

'How fucked up is this?' Miller said, pushing his hands behind his stab vest and turning his gaze towards the body twisting in the breeze. 'I don't know how they even got her up there without falling headfirst into the river.'

'Whoever did this is obviously looking for attention,' said Ramouter. He pointed behind him at the eight-storey apartment blocks that overlooked the riverside. Most balconies were filled with people watching the activity below.

'I counted,' said Miller. 'Twenty-four balconies that have a prime river view and unfortunately, there's no way to stop them from looking and taking pictures. I made myself hoarse screaming at them to go back inside. Not that that would stop them. Do you see that thing flying around up there?'

Henley and Ramouter looked up to where Miller was pointing. The sun's rays bounced off the propellers and the slim body of the drone.

'Our boys in the helicopter are doing their best to obstruct it but it's like trying to catch a fly. We've scanned the crowds looking for anyone with the bloody remote but no luck. Who knows how long it will be before this is all over the internet.'

'This is not good. Not good at all,' said Henley.

'No, it's not,' agreed Miller as a second forensic service van entered the scene. 'So, I suppose you want the usual?'

Henley nodded.

Anthony, the senior crime scene investigator, exited his van and made his way towards a firefighter.

'Call came in at 6.47 a.m.. Me and my partner, PC Eldridge, had the stupid luck of just leaving the scene of a domestic on Maze Hill and were diverted down here.'

'Who made the call?'

'A dog walker, Eric Hall. Lives in one of the townhouses just through the courtyard behind you. While the dog's taking a piss, owner looks up and sees her.'

'Where's Eric now?' asked Ramouter.

'Home. I've got a couple of police community support officers sitting with him. As you can imagine, he's not in the best shape.'

'Did he see anything suspicious, other than her?' Henley asked.

'Simple answer: no,' Miller answered as Anthony approached but sat down on the nearby bench that faced the river and opened his notebook. 'You're probably wondering how we're going to get her down and search for any evidence,' he said.

'It had crossed my mind,' Henley replied. 'Are you going up there?'

'You're having a laugh, aren't you?'

'I take it that's where our fire crew come in?'

'That's the reason for the delay. These lot are the water rescue specialists. The plan is that once the fire crew are satisfied that no one is going to plunge to their watery deaths, they're going to escort two of my guys up there to do their jobs,' explained Anthony.

'I don't envy them,' said Henley.

An officer from the marine unit made his way towards them.

'Believe it or not I've got a couple of daredevils in my team who are looking for a story to tell when they're down at the pub tonight.'

'And it looks like they'll be adding me to their story too.'

'You're going up there?' Ramouter asked with surprise.

'We're *both* going up there,' said Henley. 'Don't you want to see the body in-situ for yourself?'

Drew, a firefighter, double checked Henley's life jacket and safety harness. 'I'm right in front of you,' he said. 'Despite how the pier looks, it's not about to collapse under your feet. It's been standing there since the seventeenth century.'

'Unfortunately, I don't share your confidence,' Henley answered, watching Ramouter, secured to his own firefighter escort, make his way up the stairs and step carefully onto the unstable-looking gantry.

'Ready?'

Henley nodded and Drew turned his back and confidently walked up the concrete steps and waited for her and Ramouter at the top. 'You're going to hear a lot of creaking and other strange noises as you walk along the gantry. Try to ignore it. Keep as far to the left as possible and whatever you do, don't let go of me.'

Henley tried to ignore the shakiness in her legs as she grabbed hold of the yellow safety belt that had been attached to Drew's own life jacket. Despite his advice, Henley couldn't ignore the sound of the aged wood creaking under their weight. The sound of the river grew louder as she walked, occasionally looking down through the gaps in the planks at the dark waters swirling. Seagulls, pigeons and crows circled overhead, occasionally landing and perching on the green and blue rusting support beams. Henley kept her mind focused on what she could see and who would have been motivated to carry a dead body along a perilous path beyond the river's edge.

'You made it then?' Ramouter said with a grin on his face and his hands clasped firmly behind his back.

Henley stopped a foot away from the body. 'This is absolutely terrifying.'

'It's not that bad, as the firefighters said, it's more stable than it looks.'

'The plan is to give you guys as long as you need to do whatever it is you do,' said Drew, keeping his distance from the body. 'We'll then escort you back, forensics will come and do what they need to do and then we'll bring the body down. And it's ok to let go of me now,' he said with a grin.

Henley reluctantly released the safety belt. She carefully stepped closer to Ramouter and around the body. She looked up. 'It's her,' she confirmed.

Sian Fox-Carnell's dark blonde hair blew lazily in the wind that swept along the river, fresh bird droppings were visible on her skin. The left side of her face was covered with bruises and there was visible swelling along her jaw and cut lips. She'd been stripped almost naked, with only a pair of sky-blue knickers keeping her modesty. Henley grimaced at the succession of red, harsh scratches and dried blood on her dead alabaster skin and the noose around her neck. There was more bruising on her torso, back, her right thigh and a large gash on her shin. The thick black cable ties, that held her hands together in front of her, were almost lost in the folds of her swollen wrists. The red light on the electronic monitoring tag on her ankle flashed furiously, signalling that the battery was low.

Ramouter took a step around Sian. 'I'm thinking that she was already dead when she got here?'

'What makes you say that?' Henley asked.

'I can see chafing but I can't see any fresh bruising on her neck. I don't know how long she's been hanging here, but the rope looks quite slack.' Ramouter walked slowly around the body, the wood creaking. 'And, let's be honest, it would be easier to carry a dead person up here instead of someone fighting for her life.'

'What are we thinking, that she's taken off the street . . .'

'Held somewhere for what, forty-eight hours or so, killed wherever she's being held, brought here and hanged.'

'By someone who has knowledge of the area,' said Henley as she remained rooted to the spot.

'Why here though? Why take the crazy risk of coming up here when they could have just dumped her anywhere.'

Henley did her best to ground herself feeling the wind swirl around them. The bridge shuddered and she tried not to grab hold of the railings. The last thing she wanted to do was to accidentally remove any trace of forensic evidence. 'She must have a head wound but I can't see the top of her head. There's a lot of blood on the back of her neck but I can't see any other visible wounds other than her leg, which isn't fatal,' said Henley once the wind settled down.

Henley looked down at her feet. She couldn't see any blood on the wooden planks – another indication that there were two crime scenes.

'Let's go,' Henley said quickly, turning to Drew who'd been patiently observing the pair. 'I really don't like bridges, and I want CSI to get on with their job.'

'I'm thinking that it won't be too hard to find people who would want her dead.' Ramouter followed Henley back along the bridge, supported by his own firefighter escort.

'Wanting someone dead and doing it are two different things,' Henley replied. She placed her feet on solid ground and felt the rhythm of her breath start to return to normal.

'I agree. This is all performative,' answered Ramouter. 'Putting her up there on a platform for the world to see.'

'Whoever it was has a personal vendetta against her.' Henley was tearing off her gloves and removing her oversuit.

'The crowd looks as though it's thinned out a bit.'

Henley scanned the area. All of the activity was now at the riverside as the CSI team gathered evidence and police vans reversed closer to the railings in an effort to block the view of Sian Fox-Carnell's body from members of the public. 'People have to go to work,' she said.

'Who's that?' Ramouter pointed in the direction of the fire engine in the cordoned off area. 'Boss, can you see him?'

Henley nodded, and they both began to walk towards the white man who was dressed in jeans, a black bomber jacket and wearing a baseball cap who was moving casually towards the riverfront. As Henley and Ramouter got closer they could see that he was holding a smartphone stabiliser with a microphone on top which was pointed towards the river.

'Hey,' Ramouter shouted, sprinting towards the man with Henley close behind 'Stop right now and put down the phone.'

The man stopped but turned the phone towards Ramouter.

'For God's sake,' Henley muttered when she saw a yellow press lanyard hanging around the man's neck.

'Can I have your name please, officer,' the man asked, turning the camera towards Henley.

'No, you cannot have our bloody names,' Henley said, taking hold of his arm and marching him away.

'You have no right to remove a member of the free and independent press,' the man said.

'Name,' Henley demanded as she placed him against the side of a police van.

The man smiled, reached into his pocket and held out his business card to Ramouter.

'Ben Trezeguet. Reporter. *Freedom News*,' said Ramouter. 'This looks like you made it yourself. If you're legit, where's your National Union of Journalists ID card?'

'I am a free man and do not wish to be constrained by the bias and lies of the mainstream media,' answered Ben.

'Jesus Christ,' Henley muttered but released his arm.

'I'm part of the independent press,' Ben continued.

'You're a nuisance with a phone and a YouTube channel,' corrected Ramouter, placing the card in his pocket.

Ben pointed his phone at Henley and said, 'I report the news. And a body hanging over the Thames first thing in the morning is news. So, officers, can you give me your names and your initial views on the case?'

Henley reached for her police radio. 'What I'm going to do is have an officer escort you away from here. If you come back, I'll have you arrested for obstructing the course of justice and trespassing. Do you understand me?'

'I have a right to free speech and there's freedom of the press. You're breaching my human rights and my first amendment right.'

'First amendment,' Ramouter said with a laugh as a police officer approached them. 'Lad, this isn't America.'

'I have a right to—'

'Is that anything to do with you?' Henley asked, pointing at the drone which was still hovering in the sky but now closer to where they were positioned.

'Am I under arrest?' Ben demanded. 'I'm not obligated to answer your questions unless—'

'Please get him away from here and if you see him again, arrest him,' Henley said to the officer.

They watched him get led away.

'Do you think he'll be back?' Ramouter asked Henley.

'Probably not, but I'm more concerned about the bloody drone and what it's already seen,' she replied, her gaze fixed on the firemen who were untangling the rope from which Sian Fox-Carnell hung.

14

'The little shit,' said Ramouter, turning his phone around so that it was in landscape mode.

'Who's a little shit?' asked Henley, switching off the car engine.

'Ben Trezeguet. I checked out his YouTube. Take a look.'

Ramouter scrolled back to the beginning of the video and held up his phone. An aerial view of Fox-Carnell's body swaying gently filled the screen with firemen and CSI officers milling below.

'Who is the woman on the pier? That is the question that the police officers from the elite Serial Crimes Unit refused to answer this morning. My name is Ben Trezeguet and welcome to this special edition of Freedom News. *Deptford has transformed itself into an "up and coming" area full of young families so you can imagine the shock that a local resident had when he discovered a woman's body hanging by a bloody noose over the River Thames on Glaisher Street, while walking his dog. The arrival of officers from the Serial Crime Unit, which you may recall were responsible for the investigation into The Jigsaw Man copycat case a few years ago, can only mean one thing: there's a serial killer at large in South-East London'*

'He's not working alone,' Henley said. 'I didn't see him with a remote control for the drone when I dragged him away. The last thing we need is for that footage to be all over the internet when we haven't even spoken to the family yet.'

'Too late for that,' Ramouter replied. 'It's not so easy to put the toothpaste back in the tube. He's already shared it to all his social media channels and people are speculating in the comments.'

'I suppose we should count our blessings that this Ben idiot wasn't able to get any footage of Fox-Carnell's face, but that's not the only thing that concerns me,' Henley said.

'How did he get the information?' said Ramouter and they began to walk along the pavement. 'Some he could have guessed but to specifically name the SCU? Either he has a contact at the 999 control room or he has a police scanner.'

Henley stopped outside the last house on the terrace. She pushed the gate open and walked up a black-and-white checkered pathway towards the Victorian building. The wooden blinds inside the window were closed and a thick film of grey dust coated the slats.

'What's wrong?' asked Ramouter as Henley moved closer to the window.

'Take a look,' Henley answered, pointing at the red smears on the window frame and paving stones.

'If the paint matched the window frames or even the planter, I would have said that it was an accident. But red paint. Bright red paint?'

'Red is a warning,' Ramouter replied. He moved away from the window and pressed the doorbell.

Henley took out her phone and took a photograph of the frame. 'A warning to whom?' she asked. 'The people inside or outside?'

'Could be both,' Ramouter went quiet when the door was answered.

Disappointment was etched in every wrinkle and crease on the face of the woman standing in the doorway.

'Hello, Linda,' said Henley, stepping towards the door. 'I'm not sure if you remember me, I'm—'

'I do and I bet you're loving every minute of this,' Linda replied coldly, her hands gripping the side of the door. 'You lot kept my baby away from me. For so many years. And now you've got your bloody wish.'

'This is my partner, Detective Constable Ramouter,' said Henley as a man made his way down the hallway.

'I don't give a toss who he is,' Linda replied angrily. Her swollen eyes reddened and filled with tears. 'Just piss—'

Linda stopped herself but the anger on her face remained. The man behind her reached out and squeezed her shoulder.

'Hello, Keith,' Henley said to Sian's stepfather.

'Come in,' he said, gently manoeuvring his wife away from the door.

Keith sat down in an armchair as Linda looked on disapprovingly, her features hardening as the minutes passed and the tea in her hand cooled. 'We haven't seen her yet,' he said. 'Linda doesn't want to formally identify her because that will mean that it's true. That our girl isn't coming back to us, but I need . . . need to see her for myself.'

Linda shakily brought her chipped cup to her lips and Keith fiddled with a remote control.

'The police officers who were here earlier. They sounded as though they were still unsure. That it could be any ol' Tom, Dick or Henrietta lying there in the morgue. That it may not be our kid,' said Keith. 'They give you hope. But it's not true. Everyone knows that it's your kid.'

The room was dark and oppressive. The only light came from the flashing images on the television in the corner of the room. An old modular wall unit was filled to bursting with books, DVDs and family photos but the wall to Henley's right was a photographic journal dedicated to Sian. Henley watched Sian's life progress from birth, to school, graduation, her first day as a nurse outside Guy's Hospital and finally a photograph of Sian sitting on a sun lounger holding a wine glass. Sian wasn't Linda and Keith's only child, but she'd clearly been the favourite.

'I'm sorry for what you're going through,' Henley said, pulling herself forward on her chair, closing the space between her and the grieving couple. Ramouter remained seated on an unstable dining room chair.

'You're not sorry,' Linda spat. She placed her mug heavily onto the floor, spilling tea that disappeared into the carpet pile. 'You hated Sian. Hated her! She told me what you were like in court. Begging the judge to keep her locked up.'

'That isn't what she said, love,' Keith said wearily.

'Look at her,' Linda continued. 'She's gloating. She's got what she wanted. My Sian. My—'

Keith stayed in his seat as Linda sprang from hers, kicking over the remainder of the tea as she ran out of the room.

'I'm sorry about that,' Keith said, wincing when a door, somewhere upstairs, slammed shut.

'You should have someone with you, when you attend the identification,' Henley said gently. 'You shouldn't be alone.'

'Linda's brother, Alfie, is going to come with me. Better to get it over with.'

'Keith, I'm not going keep you,' Henley added. 'We just wanted to ask you a few questions about Sian. How she was when she came home and her last movements before she went missing.'

'The officers who were here when she didn't come home that night said that Sian had been to see you. Been to your house,' said Keith.

'Not at my house exactly, but yes she was on my street.'

'Did she threaten you?'

Henley hesitated.

'You don't have to spare my feelings, Inspector Henley. She wanted to throw it in your face, that she was out,' Keith said matter-of-factly. He looked at Sian's wall. 'I don't know where she gets it from. That need to see how far she can push people.'

'Whose idea was it to put the money up for Sian's bail?' Ramouter asked.

'That was her mum. She wanted her girl home. Linda and I had bought a flat donkey's years ago. We moved out when our first son was born but we kept it and rented it out. We sold it four years ago and we did well on it. Really well. I didn't want to put our money at risk because who knows what the hell might happen.'

'But Linda insisted?'

'Threatened to leave me if I didn't get our girl home.'

'Did you want her home?'

'No,' Keith replied his voice breaking. He sniffed and rubbed roughly at his tear-filled eyes. 'No, I didn't. We ... the family. My grandkids have been through enough.'

Henley raised her head at the sound of creaking floorboards. 'When did you last speak to Sian?' she asked.

'Tuesday morning. I wake up early. Always have done. I was a train driver and can't break the habit of being up at 4 a.m.,' said Keith. 'Sian must have come downstairs at about quarter to seven. She was already dressed and impatient, counting down the minutes until her curfew ended. She was pissed off. Throwing a strop. Just like when she was a teenager but worse.'

Henley asked the question she already knew the answer to, 'She knew that you didn't want her bailed to your house?'

Keith nodded. 'As soon as the clock hit 7 a.m., she was out the door.'

'She left early because she had to be on the telly. *Good Morning Britain*,' Linda said, reappearing in the doorway. She sat next to her husband. 'She was also on *Newsnight* on Monday, but they pre-recorded that early because of her bail conditions.'

'I offered to drive her to the studios, but she wasn't interested,' said Keith.

'How did she get there?' asked Henley.

Keith shrugged. 'Bus, or maybe she took a cab. She had Linda's card.'

'We're still waiting for the monitoring company to give us a full report of Sian's movements, but did she tell either of you if she was meeting anyone? Her legal team, friends, any—'

'Sian didn't have any friends,' Keith said firmly. 'No one wanted to be associated with her, not after what she did.'

Henley glanced at Ramouter. It wasn't lost on them that Keith wasn't jumping out of his seat to defend his daughter and protest her innocence.

'What about her husband? Her children? Did she have any contact with them?' Henley asked.

'Ex-husband, Charlie. No. Absolutely not,' Keith clarified. 'Sian only kept his surname because she wanted to punish him for not supporting her. Linda was trying to convince him to let Sian see the kids, but he point-blank refused.'

'You last saw Sian on Tuesday morning. What about Monday, when she came home from court?'

'We were told at 11.15 a.m. that the court had the bail money. We thought she was going to come straight home, but she didn't. She went back to her solicitor's office because the *Newsnight* people were interviewing her there. Her solicitor then brought her home at around 4 p.m.. But she went out again almost immediately and came back home a few minutes before her curfew started. She had a bath, something to eat and stayed in her room until the Soteria people turned up just after ten. They fitted her tag, and she went back upstairs to her room.'

'Did she have any visitors? Had there been any trouble?'

'No one knew she'd been bailed here. We moved into this house after the first trial, and we keep ourselves to ourselves. We didn't go around broadcasting that we were the parents of Sian Fox-Carnell who was in prison for killing her patients, for trying to kill a kid.'

Keith took hold of Linda's hand as she looked at him expectantly. 'Wrongly convicted of course,' he added.

Henley looked across at Ramouter, wondering if the same thought had also crossed his mind, that Keith hadn't answered the question: had there been any trouble?

'Keith, why have you got the blinds and curtains closed?' Ramouter asked.

'No one was supposed to know that Sian was here,' Keith said. He stood up and rubbed the base of his back. 'We told no one. We didn't even tell Charlie that she'd been bailed here in case he stopped us seeing the grandkids.' Keith sat back down, and lowered his voice, as though he was worried that someone was listening.

'But on Tuesday morning, I came downstairs to put the coffee on, but I didn't even make it to the kitchen because there was a smell in the air. I could smell it as soon as I stepped out of the bedroom.'

'What was the smell?'

'It smelt like shit and when I turned on the hallway light, I could see it.' Keith wrinkled his nose as though the smell was still in the room. 'And it wasn't dog shit either. It was disgusting.'

'Has anything like that ever happened before?'

Keith shook his head. 'Never. Not even when we had Sandy, our dog. She knew that she had to do her business outside. It was revolting. I cleaned it up as best as I could. Washed the door down, threw the door mat out. Bleached out the entire hallway. Of course, I had to explain to Linda why the entire downstairs stank of Domestos and why I had to go and buy a new doormat.'

'Did you tell Sian what had happened?' asked Henley. 'To warn her? Did she say anything about the smell of bleach?'

Keith shook his head. 'I was going to tell her, but she was angry and out the door as soon as the clock struck seven. She didn't look back,' Keith said sadly. 'But that wasn't all.' He took a deep breath. 'On Wednesday morning, something else happened. I saw drops of red paint on the floor outside the front door. I thought it was blood at first, but then I stepped back and looked at the door and there was paint everywhere and all our plants had been destroyed.'

'Do you have any idea who might have done it?' Henley asked. 'The damage I mean.'

'Ain't got a clue. But whoever it was knew that Sian was staying here. Which doesn't make sense because no one was supposed to know.' Keith pulled out his phone and handed it to Henley.

Henley felt the breath constrict in her throat at the photo on Keith's phone: an image painted on the front window. A noose.

15

Ezra plopped himself down in the chair next to Henley's desk and turned around so that he had his back to the whiteboard.

Henley looked up from her computer screen on which she'd been updating the CRIS – the crime reporting information system that was used by every police force in the country to record every development in an investigation. 'What are you doing up here?' she asked. 'You never want to be in this room.'

'True, but I'm making a run to the bakery, and you weren't picking up your phone. Do you want anything?' Ezra asked.

'No, I'm good.'

'If you're sure, but on your head be it when I walk in with cinnamon rolls,' Ezra said dramatically as he jumped up from the chair.

'I'm sure I'll survive, but before you go, I wanted to ask you about—' Henley lowered her voice as she scanned the room. Ramouter was with Pellacia in his office, Eastwood had her headphones on and Stanford had walked out of the office five minutes ago with his phone pinned to his ear.

'Are you asking about?' Ezra whispered.

Henley nodded.

'Ok, cool. Yeah, there is stuff. Do you want to come to my room later?'

Henley shook her head, ignoring the voice in her head telling her that keeping Stanford and Eastwood in the dark was wrong. 'Can you come to my house? Tonight. Is that ok?'

'Cool as a cucumber,' Ezra said. He left the room passing Stanford as he walked back in.

'Everything all right?' Henley asked, noticing the look on Stanford's face.

Stanford stopped at Henley's desk but didn't sit down. 'That was Gene. We've been matched with a kid. Our social worker wants us to meet him this weekend.'

'Isn't this a good thing?' Henley replied warmly. 'This is what you and Gene have wanted for God knows how long.'

'That's the thing. Each time we've gotten close it's all fallen through. It's a bit hard for me to get my hopes up.'

'But you *should* get your hopes up. Meeting your potential child for the first time is a big step. I doubt that the social worker would be arranging for you to meet if this wasn't going to be a thing.'

'Hmm,' Stanford replied noncommittally.

'What do you know about them? The child I mean?'

'He's eighteen months old. White. The poor kid has been in care since he was nine months old. His mum has drug issues and was using when she was pregnant with him, so he's got developmental delay, and the father isn't in the picture.'

'Poor kid,' Henley said, pushing her chair back and standing up. 'But he's going to have a good life with you and Gene. The best. So be positive. It's ok to make plans.'

'Yeah, I'll do my best.' Stanford gave a smile and Henley pulled him into a hug.

'I promise you; it will be fine. I have a good feeling,' Henley told him. Pellacia's office door opened and Ramouter strode out with an unmissable grin on his face.

'Boy wonder looks like he must have got a good review from the big man,' Stanford commented.

'So, he should, he's doing well,' Henley said proudly.

'Look at you. You're beaming like he's your own kid.'

'He'll be a DS before you know it. He'll probably end up taking your spot.'

'Let's not get too carried away. He's boy wonder, not Superman.'

Henley laughed. 'You're so easy to wind up.'

'Right, back to work. I need to keep my mind off things. What's going on with the new murder case?'

'I'll update everyone once Pellacia's done,' Henley answered. 'But I wish that it wasn't her, Fox-Carnell, not that I wish death on anyone, but for it to be her . . .'

'It comes with a whole host of problems, doesn't it? It means that we can't deal with this investigation in the dark so to speak.'

'No, all eyes are going to be on us.'

Pellacia took his usual position, standing in front of the window, with a wide view of the whiteboard and his team. He nodded at Henley to start.

'This is where we're at.' Henley pressed a button on the presentation pointer and three images of Sian Fox-Carnell appeared on the screen. The first was her custody picture that had been taken when she was first arrested in 2014 showing her with dark blonde hair, the second was a screenshot taken from her recent appearance on *Good Morning Britain* and the third was a photograph of the woman hanging over the river.

'Jesus Christ,' said Eastwood. 'How the hell did anyone manage to get her up there?'

'No bloody idea,' Henley answered. 'But I can confirm that the woman hanging from the pier *is* Sian Fox-Carnell. Anthony emailed me with the DNA match about an hour ago. Her stepfather, Keith Fox, should already be at the mortuary with his brother-in-law to view the body.'

'How were the family?' Pellacia asked.

'We've only spoken to the parents so far. Her biological father has been out of the picture since Fox-Carnell was three years old.

Her mother Linda is angry, very angry. She blames us, the police, for both her daughter's disappearance and her death.'

Stanford snorted disapprovingly.

'The stepfather, Keith Fox, although upset was a bit more amenable to our presence and he made some interesting points.' Henley continued, pressing the remote again, bringing up a timeline. 'Fox-Carnell was released on Monday afternoon at 12.03 p.m. with stringent bail conditions which included residence at her parents' address and an electronically monitored curfew. The initial bail application was made in chambers. No press or members of the public. The dad swears blind that no one knew that Fox-Carnell was bailed to their address.'

'Not even her ex-husband?' Eastwood asked.

'No. They didn't tell him, and they didn't tell their other kids either. They have a son who lives in Putney and a daughter in Ashford, Kent. I'm going to need you, Eastie and Stanford, to talk to the ex-husband and the siblings. Anyway, Fox-Carnell returns home on Monday afternoon and on Tuesday morning a short campaign of harassment begins.'

Henley pressed the remote again. The images Keith showed her appeared on the screen. 'These photographs were taken by Sian's stepfather on Wednesday morning. He also said that shit was pushed through the letterbox the day before, on Tuesday.'

'Did he report it to the police?' Pellacia asked.

'No, he didn't, but he told his wife. I don't think that it's too far-fetched to believe that the harassment was aimed at Fox-Carnell, which begs the question, how did anyone know that she was there? The only people who knew her bail address were the court staff, lawyers and us. Who knew?'

'I'm thinking that the mum must have talked,' said Ramouter. 'She was anxious for Fox-Carnell to see her kids, but her ex-husband was having none of it, maybe she let it slip to him that Fox-Carnell was home.'

'Or he worked it out for himself.' Eastwood scribbled a note down. 'But if the people who murdered Fox-Carnell are responsible for the harassment, why bother coming back on Wednesday morning to throw paint at the house, if they already had her? It's possible that the harassment and the murder aren't related at all.'

'Eastie's got a point,' said Stanford.

'She does, and that brings us to the next question: who was following Fox-Carnell?' said Henley. 'Fox-Carnell's tag's last location before it went dark was my street early Tuesday evening. Her body was found just before 7 a.m. this morning and her tracker went back online at 8.43 a.m.. We've got sixty hours where Fox-Carnell could have been anywhere or with anyone. She wouldn't want to risk losing her freedom after all these years so it's safe to assume that she was on her way home when she left my street. Someone took her between Brockley and Colindale.'

'How was she getting about?' Stanford asked.

'Her dad said she was using public transport and that her mum had given Fox-Carnell her debit card. I'm assuming she was using that to pay for her fares. She also had an old phone her mum gave her with a pay-as-you go sim card.'

'Even if her tracker went dark her phone wouldn't have done,' said Ezra who had entered the room with his shopping. 'Unless she had an absolutely brick of a non-smartphone, her location services would have been on. I mean how would she find her way to your house if she didn't have a map? Anyway, the point is that I can tell you where she went and who she may have spoken to before the phone company even starts to process your application for cell site data.'

'Ezra, you're right,' said Henley. 'I've been in touch with MIB and they're still waiting on the phone company, but they were able to confirm that her phone's last location was on Archway Road in Highgate.'

'If that's her last location, she either switched off her phone or her battery died,' said Ezra. 'But she could also have switched off her location services but that would be a bit pointless because her phone would still connect to a cell site tower.'

'Are you sure you don't want to join the Met officially?' asked Pellacia.

'Absolutely not,' Ezra replied.

'Ezra, I'll email you Fox-Carnell's phone number,' said Henley. 'In regard to the mum's credit card, I've given Linda Fox until the end of the day to send me a copy of pending transactions.'

'But in case she's not compliant – and she probably won't be,' said Ramouter, 'I've already submitted a request to her bank for confirmation of all transactions from Monday.'

'What about MIB?' asked Pellacia. 'Surely they've done a lot more than make a phone call and traipse up here to have a pissing match with us.'

Henley shook her head. 'They've given us what they've got, which is not a lot, but, that's not all. We need to get a statement or call a press conference as soon as possible. There are images of Fox-Carnell's body circulating all over social media. We had drones at the crime scene and people filming from their balconies. We need to be the ones putting out Sian Fox-Carnell's name and not some random who managed to work out that one plus one does in fact equal two.'

'I'll contact the press office as soon as we're done here,' said Pellacia. 'Where are we on forensics?' he asked as Ramouter's phone rang on his desk. Ramouter mouthed sorry as he turned his back to pick up his phone, speaking in hushed whispers.

'At the moment, nowhere. It's early days,' answered Henley. 'Anthony said that he's going to fast track the results because of who we're dealing with and in terms of the post—'

'Henley,' Ramouter shouted out, his face serious. 'It's Dr Linh Choi. It's about Fox-Carnell. Pick up line three.'

Henley turned to the nearest desk and picked up the phone. 'Linh, it's me,' she said.

Linh, the senior pathologist at Greenwich mortuary, let out a laugh. 'You know, sometimes it would be nice to have a simple, *he died in his sleep* case but with the SCU never.'

'What's going on?' Henley asked cautiously.

'I've got Sian Fox-Carnell on my table. The dad and uncle viewed her and left about forty minutes ago. Bear in mind this is the first time that I've seen the body because I sent Theresa down to confirm death.'

Henley remained quiet as she listened to Linh take a deep inhale.

'She was scalped,' Linh said.

Henley shook her head to make sense of what she'd just heard. Ramouter frowned at her, in question. 'She was what?' she asked.

'Scalped. From skin to skull. 324mm across and 584mm down. I can see the knife marks on the bone.'

'Right. Right.' Henley pulled out a chair and sat down, suddenly weary by the savagery of the violence that Fox-Carnell had been subjected to. 'How soon can you complete the post-mortem?'

'As soon as I'm done with you, I'm opening her up.'

16

'Do you know this is the first time that I've been to your house?' said Ezra, following Henley into the kitchen.

'Are you sure? I would have sworn you've been here before.'

'Nope. I'm not saying you haven't invited me, like when you had that barbecue back in the summer, but it was on the same day as my Grandad's birthday. It's nice in here.'

'Thank you very much. So, what can I get you to drink?'

Ezra walked up to the counter and tapped the side of the coffee machine. 'I'll have a cappuccino from this fancy machine of yours.'

'Of course you would.' Henley opened the dishwasher and removed a couple of cups. 'Biscuits are in the bread bin next to you. And whatever you do, do not feed the dog,' she warned as Luna walked in from the living room, making her way towards Ezra.

'So, are you ready?' Ezra asked.

'Shoot.' Henley placed Ezra's cappuccino in front of him and sat down with her own cup of tea. She hoped that Ezra could see past her fake confidence. She'd always prided herself on her ability to compartmentalise, but something had cracked inside her that night when Peter Olivier had stabbed her. Her professional life had finally intersected with her personal life, and she hadn't slept through the night since. During those challenging times she'd always been able to rely on her old boss Rhimes, but the Streeter and Beckett case had forced her to question if she'd ever known the real Rhimes. The allegation was that he'd been corrupt and had sent an innocent man to prison for twenty-five years. When Rhimes's widow, Eloise, asked Henley to investigate his death, Henley had hoped that she'd successfully exonerate him and close the door on the many questions that had circulated around his life and that he could finally rest in peace, but the opposite had happened. With each passing day of the Streeter investigation, Henley became more convinced he'd been murdered. Now Henley wondered if involving Ezra had been a mistake.

'I think that Rhimes may have been working undercover or investigating someone in the Met,' Ezra said.

'Undercover?' Henley repeated as she tried to process what Ezra was telling her. 'Why would he be working undercover? Also, it doesn't make any sense for—'

'Boss. I'm just telling you what I've found so far. The first thing I did was look at the money. That's what they did with me when I was being investigated. Start with the money and work backwards.'

Henley settled back in her chair as Ezra opened his laptop. He didn't often speak about the events that led to him serving a three-year prison sentence for fraud. He'd insisted more than once that he wanted to forget about that part of his life, but his computer hacking skills and the fact that experts during his trial had been in awe of his talents was the reason why he'd ended up working for the SCU in the first place.

'Rhimes had three bank accounts. A current and savings account that he held jointly with Eloise and his own current account which he had with Barclays for decades and a credit card. His salary went into his Barclays account,' Ezra explained.

'Nothing about that sounds in the slightest bit dodgy.'

'Rhimes told me more than once that he was a simple man, not interested in "new-fangled ideas",' Ezra mocked. 'So it doesn't make sense that the man who refused to get a banking app on his phone had an account with Novafin Bank.'

'Who the hell is Novafin Bank?'

'Another one of these online banks that seem to be popping up every five minutes,' said Ezra, spinning his laptop round. 'What you're looking at is seven months' worth of Novafin bank statements.'

Henley scanned the statements. 'Deposits but no withdrawals,' she said. 'Five grand deposited every two months from a Kit Walker.'

Ezra sniggered. 'Whoever it is thought that they were being clever,' he said. 'I bet you don't know who Kit Walker is?'

'No. But I suspect that you're going to tell me.'

'It's the real name of a comic book character called "Phantom". My dad used to read the comics to me as a kid. The account name may be fake, but the sort code isn't. The account is held with another online bank called Stellar Banking.'

'No one is going to pay you five grand a month just for the fun of it,' said Henley.

'Or go through all the trouble of setting up accounts in fake names and bouncing all the money around.'

'How do you know that they're bouncing all the money around?'

Ezra shrugged. 'I don't but I'm thinking that if you're using online bank accounts based in Iceland you must be bouncing the money.'

'What about these payments? £1800 in April. £870 in May. £109 in August. £339 in June. They're all from the same account. Innowave Solutions.'

'That's where the undercover bit comes in. Innowave Solutions doesn't exist. I mean, it does, but it doesn't do anything. They're a shell business that I tracked back to the NCA.'

Henley remained quiet as she stared back at Ezra. There was

no joviality or humour in Ezra's eyes. She felt sick as anxiety prickled her nerves.

'The National Crime Agency,' she finally said.

'Yeah. They've got quite a few of these accounts set up which I think they use to—'

'Pay their undercover agents.'

'But what were the random payments for?' Ezra asked quietly.

'A salary. Expenses maybe,' Henley said, picking up the empty cups and bringing them over to the sink. She stood facing the window, looking out to the dark garden as she searched her memories for her last interactions with Rhimes. The SCU back then had been busy. It wasn't unusual for Rhimes not to be in his office, as he was summoned for another meeting at New Scotland Yard. She felt her chest filling with both disappointment and betrayal. She willed herself not to cry.

'Boss,' said Ezra softly. 'Are you ok?'

'Yeah, yeah,' Henley sniffed, picking up a tea towel and dabbing the corner of her eyes. 'I'm fine but I'm not going to pretend I'm not surprised.'

'You must have thought something was up if you were asking me to look into his. . . well all of this?'

'It's one thing to think it but it's another thing to know it.'

'I suppose it's not the sort of thing you can talk about when you're on a SCU curry night out. "Oi, Ezra, pass over the tandoori chicken and by the way did I tell you that I was going undercover?".'

'No, you're right,' Henley replied.

'You told me to start with the investigation into his death, right?'

'But you started with the money, which was a good strategy,' said Henley. 'But what about the investigation into his death?'

'I've got the postmortem and CRIS report that was opened when they found him.'

'What about his emails?'

'His work email was shut down, but they should have archived it.'

'Don't do anything that will get you—'

'You panic too much, boss. He also had a Yahoo email account but there was honestly nothing in there that looked suspicious.'

Ezra handed a memory stick to Henley. 'Everything is on there. The bank accounts. His Yahoo account if you want to go through the emails for yourself. I'm going to move onto his phone records.'

'Thank you, Ezra.' Henley turned the memory stick around with her fingers. Its weight didn't convey the gravity of Ezra's revelations. She took her free hand and rubbed the throbbing vein in her temple. In that moment she wished she could have gone back. Back to that moment when Eloise had told her she believed that someone murdered her husband. She would have been stronger and told Eloise she was wrong. That it was time to move on.

'I know what I'm asking of you is a lot,' said Henley.

'Don't worry about it. I'm doing it because it's for you and it's him,' Ezra said sadly. 'Grief is the strangest of things.'

'Yes, it is,' agreed Henley as she looked across at the black-and-white photograph of her mum that had been taken a year before she died. The time that had passed didn't lessen the loss.

'Oh yeah, you're going to find one more thing that doesn't make sense on that memory stick,' said Ezra.

'Like what?'

'The conclusion on the post-mortem report doesn't match the cause of death on the death certificate.'

'That can't be right. I saw the death certificate myself because Eloise was in no fit state to register Rhimes's death. Their son, Nicholas, agreed to do it but on the day, he was in bits and Pellacia and I took him to Bromley Registry office. The registrar even gave me a copy of Rhimes's death certificate, not that I've got a clue what I've done with it, but I clearly remember what was in the cause of death box: carbon monoxide poisoning. The registrar had the conclusion of the post-mortem report and that's what she told us.'

'That's not what's written in the post-mortem report I've got,' said Ezra.

'What does it say?' Henley asked with slight irritation.

'See for yourself,' Ezra replied as he opened a PDF file and scrolled down to the conclusion of the report.

'Asphyxiation,' Henley said. 'That's not right. Where did you find this report?'

'Archived files in the coroner's office digital case system. Remember how I say nothing's ever deleted.'

'I know what you say, but there has to—' Henley was interrupted by the doorbell ringing. 'That has to be my dad with Emma. Just give me a sec.'

Henley ran through the possible scenarios that would explain the errors on the post-mortem report as she made her way to the front door. Had the author cut and pasted the wrong information into Rhimes's post-mortem report? Had Ezra downloaded the report for a different Harry Rhimes? Neither scenario sat right with her.

'Mummy,' Emma squealed, holding up a small bunch of tulips. 'We bought you flowers.'

'I can see that.' Henley smiled tightly as she took the flowers from Emma. 'Thank you, sweetie.'

'What's wrong?' Henley's dad, Richard, asked as he closed the front door.

'Nothing's wrong, Dad.'

'Your face doesn't agree. You look, what's the word? Pensive.'

'It's been a long day, that's—' Henley paused when she heard Emma's excited screams at the discovery of Ezra in the kitchen.

'Every day is a long day in your work. You're not supposed to take this job home with you,' said Richard.

'I try not to,' Henley said, giving her dad a hug. 'You look good,' she told him.

'Hmm. My new meds seem to be fixing my head and my complexion,' Richard joked.

Henley watched her dad. His mental journey had seen more downs than ups over the years but there was always a strong sense of relief when she saw her dad in control and in good spirits.

'Dad, can you do me a favour and keep Emma occupied for a bit? I just need to finish my chat with Ezra.'

'Of course. I'm sure I can sit through another episode of *Pingu*,' said Richard.

'I'm not an expert in death and stuff,' said Ezra, once Henley had returned. 'Maybe Dr Choi can explain what it means to you.'

'Yeah, maybe she can,' said Henley, putting the memory stick into her pocket, instead of the bin which had been her second thought. 'You've done good, Ez.'

'I don't feel good.'

'If you want to walk away from this, then that's fine. Honestly, you're not obligated to do anything just because I'm your boss.'

'I know that but its Rhimes innit? How can I walk away from him? He was miserable sometimes and stubborn, but he gave me a chance when he didn't have to. He could have said "Stephen, nah".' Ezra shook his head and grinned. 'It feels odd calling the boss by his first name, but the point is Rhimes could have told Pellacia to do one when he told him to give me a job, but he didn't.'

'He had a lot of respect for you,' said Henley. 'His exact words when we were investigating you were "He's not a devious little git, just misguided".'

'Sounds about right, but I hope I'm wrong here. I hope I've made a mistake.'

'You and I both know that you don't make mistakes.'

Emma's hysterical laughter travelled through the kitchen.

'I know that Rhimes had depression,' said Ezra.

'You knew about that?' Henley was surprised. Rhimes had never been one to talk openly about his feelings and it pleased her that he'd trusted and confided in Ezra.

'Yeah. He took me to lunch one day and told me. I used to go out for walks with him when he felt like—'

'The walls were closing in,' Henley said sadly.

'Exactly, but I don't know. The gassing himself in the garage never felt right to me.'

'I keep thinking about the last thing that we said to each other and there's nothing there.'

'No signs that he would take his life?'

'And no signs that he was in fear for his life either, but look at what you found, Ez. If the post-mortem isn't a mistake and asphyxiation was the real cause of death . . . it's a cover-up.'

'And that means that Mrs R was right. Someone killed Rhimes.'

17

'Who gets justice?' she asked, rising from her seat and anchoring herself in front of her audience.

'They do,' Josh and Don replied in unison.

'Who deserves justice?'

'They do.'

'Who delivers justice?'

'We do.'

'That's right. We do. We deliver justice and the deliverance of justice is sweet and gives final victory to those who've had justice denied.' She held the Ziplock bag aloft and walked towards the man on her right. She twisted her wrist slowly so that the light caught the contents of the bag: a clump of dark blonde hair that was streaked with dried blood.

'This was a job well done. You should have been there.' She prised the bag apart and turned it upside down.

Josh yelped and jumped back in his seat, pushing the piece of Sian Fox-Carnell's scalp off his lap as though it was a lump of hot coal.

'What *is* that?' Josh asked.

'That belongs to her,' the woman said. She bent down, picked up the scalp and placed it back in the bag. 'Where were you, Josh?' she asked.

'I'm sorry, but . . . but last night,' Josh stuttered as he looked down at the bloodied stain on his jeans. 'My kid. I had . . . it was a family issue. I would have been there if I could, but my kid. You understand, don't you?'

'I understand that I'm questioning your commitment to us. You can't just pick and choose how you want to contribute to our mission to deliver justice,' she told him. 'You need to be with us every step of the way and you have to accept that you're going to get blood on your hands. Despite our name, you cannot exist in the shadows.'

Josh licked his dry lips, trying to focus on something else in the room and avoid her gaze that bore into him. 'I am with you. Of course I am,' he grovelled. 'I thought I'd proven that.'

The woman turned around, leaving the statement hanging in the air. She walked over to the table in the middle of the room, on which sat her tote bag. She put the Ziplock bag into the zipped compartment and then removed two green document wallets, each containing identical documents. She lifted the flap and pulled out the top sheet and read through the ten names. She nodded to herself, satisfied that she had chosen the right people.

'I'm hoping that the system does the right thing, and the right decision is made. But, in the event that it's not, I want us to be ready,' she said, handing the wallet to Josh.

Josh cleared his throat and placed the wallet on the floor. 'I think,' he coughed and tried to dislodge the frog in his throat. 'I think that maybe we're going too far.'

She looked directly into Josh's eyes and waited as the seconds ticked by. It was the simplest way to intimidate someone. To make them wait. To sweat.

'Say that again Josh,' her voice was calm and steady. There was no need for performative displays of authority – not with this group. She was the one in charge. She'd made that crystal clear from day one.

'Say that again,' she repeated.

Josh ran his hand across his hairline, wiping away the beads of sweat. He looked across at the man on his right. Searching for support. Looking for a saviour.

'It . . . it wasn't just me,' Josh swallowed hard. 'We were both—'

'No, no,' Don cut in forcefully. 'I didn't say a word. I promise you, that is not what I said.'

She sighed with disappointment as she watched the pair in front of her. They used to be larger in numbers when the group was first formed. They'd found each other in an online chatroom in the darker corners of the internet where each echoed the same mantra of 'This is not justice' after they trawled through the latest criminal court news. Online meetings and the trolling of leftist, liberal supporters with their unrealistic notions of how the world should be, turned into meeting in person in shady pubs and now, finally, here, in a garden office in deepest South-East London. The numbers dwindled from eight, to five, to four, to now three once the chatter changed from 'This is what should be done' to 'This is what we're going to do.'

'You're bang out of order, Josh,' said Don. 'Why are you questioning things now when you knew that this was the plan?'

'I didn't know that killing her was part of the plan!' Josh's voice was rising and falling like disturbed waves in the ocean. 'Just punish her. Scare her.'

Don laughed. 'Oh, she was scared all right.'

'She's dead,' Josh said. His eyes cast to the window as the lights in the house, at the opposite end of the garden, switched on.

'And what exactly is the problem?' Don asked. 'What exactly is wrong with doing what those who call themselves the holders of justice have failed to do?'

'Nothing. There's nothing wrong with that. I mean that's why we're here. That's why we're doing what we're doing. Making them accountable for their actions. But—'

'But what, Josh?'

Josh looked away.

'There's no buts,' Josh said unconvincingly. 'I'm not saying that we shouldn't have punished her. We—'

Don moved quickly for a man of his size. Swift on his feet with a dangerous right hook was how they'd spoken about him at the boxing club when he was a kid, before life got in the way, before everything changed. He kicked Josh hard in the chest. The metal folding chair collapsed and skidded across the floor. Josh yelped as he fell hard on the floor and banged his head against the edge of the metal filing cabinet.

'I'm sorry. I should have been there,' said Josh. He pressed his hand against the back of his scalp. The flickering images from the TV screen briefly spotlighted the blood on his fingers.

The woman said nothing as Don grabbed Josh by the collar of his polo shirt and dragged him into the middle of the room.

Don straddled Josh, placing his full weight on his chest. 'This is just a warning. You don't want me to start making promises.'

'I'm sorry. I'm sorry,' spluttered Josh. 'I shouldn't have questioned you. You were right. She deserved it. She deserved it all.'

18

5 February 2019

Douglas Mantell, walked out of Manchester Crown Court with the arrogance of a man who had got away with it all. Almost three years ago to the day he'd been dragged out of his bed at 6 a.m., thrown into a police van and taken to Weatherfield police station. The detectives, especially the woman who he wouldn't have touched with a bargepole, looked at him as though he was a piece of shit under their shoes. He didn't ask for a solicitor. Why would he? Only people with something to hide asked for a solicitor. They said that he'd abused his daughter from the age of five. He paused for a moment. He wasn't sure how she would have remembered that afternoon, but he denied it all, repeatedly and tearfully during a three-hour police interview. Four weeks later they'd charged him with eight counts of historical sex offences against his daughter and three counts of possession of indecent images.

Douglas was convinced he was going to be found guilty. He'd thought about faking a heart attack halfway through the trial. Against his barrister's advice, he gave evidence and so did his wife, against her own daughter no less. His barrister had warned him, saying:

'In my experience, Mr Mantell, a short deliberation period usually means a guilty verdict and, as I've advised you, a guilty verdict means prison. You're looking at eight to ten years. You should pack a bag with the essentials.'

The jury took three days to think about the counts against him. They sent notes to the judge. The first couple of notes were about the evidence they had seen and heard but the third note was about numbers. They were not all in agreement. His barrister advised him that the judge would give a majority direction and explain to the jury that he could accept a decision where at least ten of them agreed on the verdict. Douglas asked what would happen if only nine of the jury agreed that he was guilty. The barrister had taken a deep breath and looked away as though the possibility disgusted her.

'If only nine of the jury agree that you're guilty or not guilty, that's a hung jury and we will have to do it all again. A retrial.'

The jury had taken three days, seven hours and eighteen minutes to reach a verdict. One person wanted to convict him. Eleven couldn't be sure.

Douglas walked unsteadily out of the pub and raised his face towards the night sky as he fished in the pocket of his thinning coat for his cigarettes. He was drunk but he was a happy drunk. A free drunk. The temperature had dropped, the pavement glistened with frost and there was a stillness that promised the arrival of snow. Ashton canal was just around the corner and Douglas knew that as long as he followed the canal, he could find his way home. He pulled up the collar of his coat, inserted the buttons into the wrong holes and began to walk.

'Shit,' Douglas said, slipping on the icy tarmac as he walked toward the steps that descended towards the canal. He frantically grabbed the frosted metal of the railings and took a moment to straighten up. The cold air had sobered him up a little bit. He took hold of the railing and descended, pausing briefly when he saw that no light was emanating from the next two lampposts ahead of him and that his path was shrouded in darkness.

'Stupid council,' Douglas muttered, slipping again. He moved onto the small grassy patch that was close to the water's edge.

'You got to be careful, mate. The last thing you want is to end up in that water.'

Douglas turned towards the direction of the voice that was not Mancunian. The person walking towards him was dressed for the weather with a fitted navy parka, navy beanie on his head and leather gloves. The man lowered his head and pulled up his grey, striped scarf around his lower jaw.

'I most definitely do not want that,' Douglas sang as the man walked quickly past him, disappearing into the darkness.

'Should have gone to my local,' Douglas grumbled. He looked around, unsure if he was heading in the right direction and the light flurry of snow that began to fall didn't help. He pulled up his sleeve and squinted at his watch but there wasn't enough light to illuminate the cheap dial. His head felt a bit clearer and he followed the man's advice and stepped away from the water's edge, continuing to walk along the icy path.

Someone bumped into him. Douglas stumbled and fell flat onto his back.

'Aw, mate. I'm sorry. I didn't see you,' said the man. He leaned forward and reached out his arm. 'Are you all right?'

Douglas begrudgingly accepted the man's gloved hand and was pulled to his feet. 'Fucking idiot,' he said.

'No need for that sort of language. I warned you to be careful.'

'Be careful? You bumped into me. I could have . . . ow, what are you—'

Douglas looked into the eyes of the man who was squeezing his hand so tight he could have sworn he could feel his fingers break.

Despite what he told himself, Douglas was a physically weak man, and he couldn't stop the man from forcefully grabbing his coat.

'You are disgusting. A piece of fucking shit,' said the stranger.

Douglas yelled out as the man turned him around and pushed him hard against a brick wall and let go. Douglas fell hard onto dirty syringes and makeshift crack pipes made from Coke cans. The man pulled a whimpering Douglas back up, turned him around and rammed his face into the black wall breaking his nose and his front teeth. His knees buckled and his face was dragged across the wall, scraping the skin from his cheek.

The man turned Douglas around and pushed his hand against Douglas's broken nose. 'Look at me,' he demanded.

'No,' Douglas squeaked as the nerves in his face ignited. The man pushed his thumb and forefinger against Douglas's right eye and prised it open.

Embers of recognition briefly dulled Douglas's pain as the man who'd assaulted him let go and lowered his scarf. Douglas put his hand to his face, his fingers sticking to his bloodied and shredded skin.

'I know you,' Douglas said.

Before his trial started, Douglas's barrister had told him that the jury would be watching his every move and that he should keep looking forward. He had done what he was told, he kept his gaze away from the jury, but he'd watched the courtroom and noticed who came in and out of the heavy wooden doors of Courtroom Seven. He knew this man.

'You sicken me,' the man said, unzipping his jacket and reaching into an inner pocket.

'I didn't do anything,' Douglas cried, his tears mixing with his blood as they ran down his face, stinging his broken skin.

The man's laugh echoed in the silent night. 'Is that what you tell yourself?'

Douglas felt the air leave his body when he saw the blade of a knife catch the light. The man pushed him and he landed heavily on his stomach.

'You're a disgusting, wicked pervert,' the man said, digging the knife into Douglas's flesh. 'You destroyed her. Your own daughter.'

'I'm sorry,' Douglas screamed out again as the man plunged the knife into his left calf, his back, his right buttock and his neck. He was soon silent and still.

The man looked down at his gloved hands and grimaced. Blood had seeped through the seams and his skin was sticking to the fake fur lining. He dropped to his knees and grabbed a fistful of Douglas's thinning grey hair. The man held the blade against Douglas's scalp and carefully ran the knife against the skin as though he was filleting a fish. When he was done, he placed the piece of scalp in a plastic bag that he'd removed from his pocket. He stood up, took hold of Douglas's legs and dragged him to the water's edge. Douglas's body hit the dark, freezing canal waters with a dull and heavy splash. The man picked up the bloodied knife and dipped it into the water. He kept his eyes on the spot where Douglas's body had landed. Once his knife was clean, he walked away satisfied that Douglas was at the bottom of the canal with the rest of the rubbish.

19

'Is everything all right?' Ramouter asked as they stopped at the wrought iron gates that blocked the public from entering the ironically named Greenwich Public Mortuary. 'You just don't seem like yourself.'

'Yeah, I'm fine,' Henley lied. She focused on entering the security code but could feel the strain from the lack of sleep pulling at the skin around her eyes. She'd lain restless beside a snoring Rob, replaying Ezra's revelations about Rhimes like a record stuck on repeat in her head. She was now second guessing every interaction and trying to find double meaning in every word that Rhimes had said to her in the twelve months before he died. She was also performing mental gymnastics in order to justify her decision to keep Stanford and Eastwood in the dark. She'd written and deleted three text messages, explaining to them both what Eloise had asked her to do. *I'll them when I have evidence* is what she'd told herself, but her words sounded hollow and did nothing to erase her shame.

'I'm sorry that I'm bringing you out here on a Saturday,' Henley said. The hum from the axial fans in the refrigeration storage units drifted in the air as they walked towards the mortuary.

'No, it's fine. Ethan is on half term and Michelle has taken him to Bradford for a few days. All you're doing is interrupting a day of me on the sofa eating crisps and waiting for Netflix to ask me if I'm still watching.'

Henley smiled. 'Did they get there ok?'

'Yeah, they did,' Ramouter replied with a touch of sadness staining his voice. 'The doctor put Michelle on a new medication. Memantine. It helps her to deal with the normal daily stuff. She's doing so well that it's easy to forget that she's got dementia.' Ramouter stopped, puffed out his cheeks and shook his head. 'Sorry. It's just that word "forget". It has a heavier meaning now.'

'You don't have to carry all this weight on your own. You know we're all here for you,' said Henley, stopping outside the examination room. 'And don't punish yourself for worrying.'

'Easier said than done,' said Ramouter. 'I keep telling myself that this is our new normal, but it's anything but normal. I try and focus on what we have now and those happy moments we have as a family, watching Ethan play football or just me and Michelle watching an awful Christmas movie in the middle of October, but—' Ramouter exhaled sharply. 'Then I'll catch Michelle standing in the middle of the bedroom and I'll have all these questions running in my mind. Is she standing there because she's having one of those moments that we all have? You've forgotten what you went into a room for. Or is it something more? Is her dementia advancing? Am I losing her already?'

Henley put a hand on Ramouter's shoulder as he turned his back to her.

'Sorry,' he said.

'Ramouter. Don't ever apologise. Not for this.' Henley walked around and faced him. 'What you're going through is shit. I'm sorry I can't dress it up for you, but that's all I've got. It's a horrible situation and no way to live but, right now, you've got to find a way to focus on the positive. Celebrate the small wins. Take up something new with Michelle.'

'She wants to try indoor climbing. She's been going on about it ever since she watched it in the Olympics.'

'I take it that you have no interest in indoor climbing.'

'Absolutely not.'

'Ramouter if you can climb a collapsing pier over the river, then you can climb a wall,' Henley said.

'Yes, boss.'

'Good. Let's go in and if Linh asks why your eyes are red, tell her it's hay fever.'

'Hay fever. In October?' Ramouter asked opening the door into the mortuary.

'It's either that or you can tell her that you became overcome with emotion at the thought of seeing her.'

'I'll tell her that it's hay fever.'

'I was thinking about the strange circularity of this case,' said Dr Linh Choi as she removed the sterile surgical drape that covered the body of Sian Fox-Carnell. 'I completed the post-mortem on her first two victims and now look, here she is on my examination table.'

'You sound as though you're having an existential crisis,' said Ramouter.

'Nah, I had one of those way back in medical school but this? This is what I would call karma.'

The harsh fluorescent light placed a luminous sheen on the naked body of Sian Fox-Carnell which, from her forehead to her feet, was a patchwork of bruises, cuts and grazes. Henley had long trained herself not to have an emotional reaction to the bodies that ended up on Linh's table, but the crescent shaped caesarean scar on Fox-Carnell's body violently triggered her maternal instincts. She tried to rationalise the feelings by reminding herself that Fox-Carnell had been separated from her children due to her murderous actions and that she'd been a threat to Henley's own daughter, but the sympathy and regret swam strongly through her.

'It's such a quick turnaround, isn't it?' said Henley in an effort to cut off the unwarranted emotions that she was feeling. 'Monday morning, she was sitting in a cell in Bronzefield Prison and five days later she was hanging from a rope over the River Thames.'

'And now she's here on my table,' Linh said.

'So, what happened to her?' asked Ramouter. 'She wasn't killed by the hanging?'

'No, she was already dead before she was hanged,' Linh replied as she placed her hands under Fox-Carnell's chin and gently raised it. 'All of this abrasion around her neck was caused post-mortem.'

'When exactly did she die?' asked Henley.

'I've estimated time of death to be between 10 p.m. and midnight, Thursday night.' Linh replied. 'And she took a lot of hits before she died. She has significant bruising along the left side of her torso, left buttock and her left thigh which was all caused pre-mortem. You can see the cut on her right shin. I removed grass and soil from the wound.'

'What happened to her face?' Ramouter asked, stepping closer to the body.

'Blunt force impact,' said Linh. 'She has a broken nose, jaw and several of her teeth are broken. She was either hit hard in the face or fell onto something hard like a floor but an interesting thing about the bruises is that they're a good time map.'

'What do you mean?' Henley asked.

'You can split her last, let's say last thirty hours to three significant events,' said Linh as she picked up Fox-Carnell's right hand and turned it over to reveal two cuts on her palm. 'Event one: I removed debris and glass from the wounds. The shards were deeply embedded which suggests to me that she must have pressed her hand down on the ground and if we look at her jaw.' Linh ran her finger along the blue and purple bruising. 'This colouring is consistent with a bruise that's one to two days old. And if you look at the top of her arms.'

Henley and Ramouter stood on opposite sides of the examination table.

Ramouter pointed at the four circular bruises on Fox-Carnell's biceps. 'Are those finger marks?' he asked.

'Yes,' replied Linh. 'She was grabbed tightly.'

'Restrained,' Henley said.

'Agreed and then when we turn her over,' Linh placed her hand on top of Fox-Carnell's torso, pulled her towards her and turned the body on its front. 'She has significant bruising on her lower back and a row of small circular bruising on her buttocks. Same purple colouring, suggesting to me that she's been thrown or landed heavily onto something sharp.'

'Fox-Carnell never made it home, which means that between 5.45 p.m. and 9 p.m. she's taken off the street. She's punched, falls to the ground and is then restrained and maybe thrown into a van,' said Henley.

Ramouter nodded in agreement.

'Event two,' said Linh as she moved to the top of the body and pulled apart the remaining hair on Fox-Carnell's head revealing a rectangular patch of missing scalp. Scrape marks left behind by the knife could be seen on the exposed skull. The edges of the wound were uneven and jagged as though a piece of material had been ripped in two.

'Bloody hell. Was she alive when this happened?' asked Ramouter.

'Very much alive,' said Linh. 'The cuts and bruising to her right shin, restraint bruising around her wrists and ankles are reddish in colour. That suggests that the injuries were sustained in the twenty-four hours before she was found; so, between the hours of 6 a.m. on Thursday and 6 a.m. Friday. Finally, event three.'

Linh dragged her finger along the bruising around Fox-Carnell's neck. 'This is caused post-mortem. She was already dead when hung.'

Henley stepped back from the table and scanned Fox-Carnell's body as she recalled the elements of all three events. 'What killed her, Linh?' she asked.

'Asphyxiation and organ failure, but it was due to an overdose and not because she had a rope around her neck. There are signs of a pulmonary edema which is where fluid leaks into the lungs. There was bloody phlegm and vomit in her oesophagus, nose and throat. Also, her veins showed signs of collapse and there's evidence of a cardiac arrest. There are no track marks in her forearms or any of the usual places that a drug user would inject, but if you look at her neck.'

Linh reached for the magnifying lamp and placed it above Fox-Carnell's neck. She then lifted her head and turned the neck to the right. Swelling and a reddish hue surrounded a small puncture wound.

'Didn't Fox-Carnell kill and attempt to kill her patients by injecting them with poison?' Ramouter asked Henley.

Henley nodded. 'She used strychnine. It's a poison that was banned in 2006, but they still use it as a pesticide in the States. Is that what killed her?'

Linh covered Fox-Carnell's body with the surgical drape. 'I don't know yet. I only sent samples to toxicology this morning but, from the look of her, I didn't see any of the usual signs of poisoning.'

'Someone wanted to punish her before she died,' said Henley.

'It's more than a punishment. It's torture.' Ramouter's phone was ringing. 'It's Anthony. Must have an answer on forensics for Fox-Carnell. I'll take it outside.'

'I don't envy you,' said Linh as she peeled off her gloves, threw them into the yellow wastebin and washed her hands. 'I've never seen anyone scalped before.'

'Neither have I,' said Henley, following Linh into her office.

'You know that the images are all over social media, right?'

Henley sighed. 'I know. It turns our investigation into a spectacle and makes our jobs harder.'

'Speaking of your job,' Linh said with a noticeable glint in her eye. 'How are things with you and Pellacia?'

Henley rolled her eyes and groaned. 'Do you know what, I'm more than aware that I've put myself in this stupid position but I'm doing my best to move on. Focus on family and on my job, but he makes it hard.'

'What do you expect. You keep playing with his heartstrings and his d—'

'Linh!'

Linh laughed. 'You take away all my fun, but I seriously don't know what you expect. The way that you two go back and forth. It's not healthy and, if I'm honest, it's not fair.'

'Fair to whom?'

It was hard to miss the defensiveness in Henley's tone. Linh raised her eyebrows in warning.

'To him,' Linh said firmly. 'He's the single one, pining away and waiting for you.'

'Are you saying that I'm leading him on?'

'I didn't say that. I'm just saying that this back and forth is a dangerous game.'

Henley felt her shoulders slump. The energy it took to defend herself – especially when she knew that she was in the wrong – was exhausting.

'Bloody hell, you don't have to look so dejected,' said Linh.

'It's hard not to, especially when Rob has been working really hard on—'

'Not being a twat?'

'Linh!'

'Where's the lie?' Linh asked with a laugh.

'Rob's doing better and also, Pellacia has moved on.'

'With Laura Halifax MP?' Linh snorted. 'The poor cow doesn't realise that she's only getting a piece of him. It'll never last.'

Henley bristled. 'Enough about him. I need to ask a favour. An unofficial request.'

'What is it?'

Henley removed the memory stick from her pocket. Linh's facial expressions changed from surprise to stone cold seriousness as Henley explained what Eloise had asked her to do and what Ezra had discovered.

'Why are you indulging Eloise?' Linh asked. 'It's not good for you. It's not good for anybody.'

'I'm regretting saying yes,' Henley admitted. 'But I need you to go over the full post-mortem report for Rhimes that Ezra found. We only ever had sight of his death certificate. I'm praying that Ezra made a mistake and that there's a good reason for the discrepancy.'

'Ezra make a mistake? Really?'

'Yeah, I know. It's unlikely.'

Henley felt a panicked flutter in her chest. This request was another step closer to confirming Rhimes's murder. She wondered if it was too late to take it all back. To tell Linh to ignore her.

'Fine. I'll do it,' said Linh. 'Have you told the others? Pellacia, Stanford?'

'No.'

'Don't you think they have a right to know?'

'They do, but not right now. Only if there's something to tell them,' said Henley as the door swung open and Ramouter re-entered the room.

'What did Anthony have to say?' Henley asked.

'He took DNA swabs from Fox-Carnell and there was a match,' Ramouter explained.

'Why are you standing there with a face like a slapped arse. A match is good news,' Linh exclaimed. 'That means you've got a suspect, right?'

Ramouter rubbed his forehead. 'No, it doesn't. The DNA retrieved from Fox-Carnell matched DNA samples retrieved from Graham Ashcroft's clothing and the blood found in the kitchen.'

'Excuse me,' Henley said. She stepped towards Ramouter forcing him to look up at her.

'That's not all. There was a lot of blood on that kitchen floor and DNA analysis produced matches for three people.'

'Don't tell me.'

'The third DNA profile is a match for Tabitha Ashcroft,' Ramouter confirmed.

Henley closed her eyes, raised her face and cursed the sky. 'For fuck's sake.'

'I know. I know.'

'The person who nearly killed Graham Ashcroft is involved in the murder of Fox-Carnell. Shit,' Henley said. 'You always said from the beginning that the Ashcrofts' aggravated burglary was too violent.'

'I just can't figure out why Ashcroft would be a target. There's no such thing as a perfect victim but I could understand why someone would seek Fox-Carnell out,' Ramouter replied, just as his phone started ringing again. 'Oh.'

'What's wrong?'

'Nothing, there's no caller ID. But. What if . . . what if it's—'

'I'm sure that everything's fine,' Henley said reassuringly. 'It's probably nothing to do with Michelle.'

'Most likely someone trying to sell life insurance,' said Linh.

Ramouter gave a tight smile as he accepted the call. 'Hello. Oh. DC Copeland. Sorry, yeah. Nia. What can I . . . seriously? How long? Right. Right. Ok. Thank you for letting me know. Of course. Not a problem. Thanks again. Bye.'

'Nia?' Henley asked. She folded her arms when she caught the slight flush on Ramouter's cheek.

'That was . . . well you heard who it was,' Ramouter said, putting his phone away. 'Tabitha Ashcroft just called DC Copeland and told her she's on her way to the hospital.'

'It's been nearly a week since someone used her husband as

a human target and she's just turning up now?' said Henley incredulously.

'Copeland said that Tabitha should be there in forty minutes.'

'Graham Ashcroft is at King's, right?'

'Yes, he is.'

'Denmark Hill. We'll get the train,' said Henley, grabbing her coat. 'If we leave now, we might catch her before she has a sweet reunion with her husband.'

20

DC Copeland's smile dissipated when she saw that DC Ramouter was not alone. She adjusted her hoodie.

Henley could see a hint of annoyance in Copeland's eyes as she extended her hand. 'DI Henley.'

Copeland shook her hand firmly. 'It's good to meet you, guv, sorry I mean ma'am.'

'I'm surprised to see you here,' said Henley.

'Oh.' Copeland was clearly caught off guard by the abruptness of Henley's statement. 'I was already out, and I just thought it might be a good idea for Tabitha Ashcroft to put a face to the name so to speak. Also, I realised I hadn't told her DC Ramouter was now the senior investigating officer on her husband's case.'

Henley kept her face passive as Ramouter, who had been standing silently next to her, stifled an embarrassed cough.

'That would have been incorrect,' said Henley as she walked towards the bank of lifts and pressed the button. 'I'm the SIO on the case.'

They stepped into the lift together. The silence grew uncomfortable as they ascended.

'Do you know where she is now? Tabitha Ashcroft, I mean?' asked Henley. 'She told you it would take her forty minutes to get here.'

'I have a feeling that was a lie,' answered Copeland.

*

Henley knocked twice on the door and then pushed it open. Graham Ashcroft was sitting up in bed, but his wife wasn't by his side. A woman was on the other side of the room, standing with her back against the large window. The oversized black hoodie she was wearing drowned her and she was wearing a black beanie. If Henley didn't know better, she would have sworn that the woman was attempting to conceal her identity. She looked up at Henley with fearful eyes and pulled the collar of her hoodie towards her chin, but it was too late. Henley had already seen the fading rainbow of bruises along her jaw. Henley scanned the couple. The space between them felt charged with an emotion that Henley couldn't yet name.

'Sorry to barge in like this,' Henley said softening her tone 'I'm Detective Inspector Henley and Graham you already know DC Ramouter and DC Copeland.'

'Yes, yes I do,' Graham replied, his voice barely a whisper.

'And you must be his wife, Tabitha?'

Tabitha nodded, keeping her eyes not on her husband but on the door as though she was mentally navigating the gauntlet of three police officers in order to get out of the room.

'How are you feeling?' Henley asked.

'Not the best. They took away my morphine pump,' Graham smiled unconvincingly, 'and as you can imagine, it's a bit of an adjustment to be the patient and not the doctor.'

'I understand that. And how are you Mrs Ashcroft?'

Tabitha looked past Henley as she spoke. 'Tired, stressed. It's so hard to see Graham like this.'

'It can't be easy for you at all,' said Henley. 'Even though Graham is the one in hospital, it probably feels as though it's happened to both of you.'

Henley caught the look that passed between the couple,

and finally she was able to attach a word to the emotion that was squeezing the air out of the room. It was an emotion she recognised. Guilt.

'Graham, I'm going to leave you with DCs Ramouter and Copeland,' said Henley as she stepped away from the bed. 'We had a quick word with your doctor before we came in and he was confident that you should be able to give a more detailed statement about what happened to you.'

'I don't think that I'll be able to,' Graham said. 'I'm a bit tired.'

'We'll take it easy,' said Ramouter. 'No pressure. We'll go at your pace.'

'Mrs Ashcroft. Tabitha,' Henley said as she moved around the bed and faced her. 'You're coming with me.'

'No. I should stay with my husband,' Tabitha said quickly.

'Your husband is in really good hands. Let's go,' Henley said in a tone that suggested there was no room for negotiation or argument.

Tabitha's shoulders sank with resignation as she picked up her bag, placed the strap on her shoulder and audibly sucked the air through her gritted teeth. Henley watched intently as Tabitha dropped her bag into the crook of her arm.

'Are you ok?' Henley asked.

'I'm fine. I'm fine,' Tabitha replied but when she walked out of the room she did so with a visible limp.

'It must be difficult, seeing your husband like that,' Henley said, stopping for the second time in the corridor for Tabitha to catch up with her. 'Are you sure you're ok?'

'I'm fine. I twisted my ankle when I was coming out of the shower this morning,' Tabitha said quietly.

'I broke my ankle last year and it still plays up,' Henley replied, unconvinced by Tabitha's explanation. She opened the door to the empty family room. 'This should be fine. Unless you'd prefer to go downstairs to the café and get a cup of coffee?'

'Here is fine,' said Tabitha. She lowered herself onto a chair and sat ramrod on the edge of the seat.

Henley sat down on the chair opposite Tabitha. 'Why did it take you so long to come and see your husband?'

'I was in Bath,' Tabitha said quickly, twisting her bag straps.

'It doesn't take a week to travel from Bath to London.'

'I . . . I didn't want to disturb Graham. He'd been through a lot. Surgery and he needed to rest.'

'Your husband has been asking for you.'

'I'm here now but what I don't understand is why I'm talking to you and not DC Copeland.'

'Because this is my investigation and I'm trying to find the person who nearly killed your husband.'

'Kill him?' Tabitha exclaimed. She squinted her eyes as though she'd experienced a jolt of pain. 'Why would anyone want to kill him. He's a good man. It was a burglary.'

'Tabitha,' Henley said firmly. 'There are no signs that whoever entered your house was attempting to steal anything. Everything, all your jewellery, bags, laptops were untouched, but your husband was violently assaulted. Someone entered your home and stabbed him. His blood was found in the hallway and outside on the doorstep.'

Henley paused as Tabitha sniffed noisily and ran her hands across her face to wipe away the tears.

'And then he was attacked again,' Henley continued.

Tabitha heaved as though she'd been thrown into the sea and was gasping for breath. Henley steeled herself as she pushed away the feeling of wanting to comfort a woman who was reliving a painful experience.

'They ran your husband over Tabitha and then picked him up and dumped him like rubbish back on your doorstep.'

'I don't . . . I don't know why anyone would do this to Graham. He's a good person,' Tabitha repeated. She opened her bag and rummaged inside, eventually retrieving a box of ibuprofen. She pushed out two caplets and swallowed them whole.

'You keep saying that Graham is a good person, but that doesn't explain why someone tried to kill him.'

Tabitha inhaled sharply and squeezed her eyes shut. 'I don't know,' she said.

'You're not ok,' said Henley. 'You're in pain.'

Tabitha rocked back and forth. 'I'm fine,' she said.

'Where were you when your husband was attacked Tabitha?' asked Henley as she leaned in closer.

'I was in Bath.'

'I don't believe you. Where were you?'

'I told you already.'

'Someone tried to kill your husband, and you disappeared for six days. You must understand that there are going to be questions.'

Tabitha nodded and then shook her head as though the need for denial was stronger than telling the truth.

'Your house was examined by the crime scene investigators,' Henley said. 'They found blood. Graham's blood, blood belonging to an unknown person and your blood.'

Tabitha's face whitened as Henley held her gaze, daring her to blink first.

'Why would your blood be on your kitchen floor when, at the time of the attack, you were apparently in Bath?'

Tabitha pursed her lips and stubbornly shook her head.

'What happened?'

'I can't . . . I can't.'

'You were in the house when your husband was attacked, weren't you?'

'No,' Tabitha whispered.

'You know who attacked your husband.'

'No. No, I don't. I don't know what he—'

'He?' Henley said as Tabitha placed her hand over her mouth and shook her head again.

'Did you see who attacked Graham?'

'No. I wasn't there. I don't know who hurt him.'

'Was Graham protecting you?'

'I can't . . . you've made a mistake.'

Henley watched Tabitha become more agitated as her face grew even paler which made the bruises on her jaw appear even brighter.

'What happened to you? I can help you if you—'

A loud bang interrupted Henley as the door to the family room swung open and hit the wall. Tabitha jumped back and cried out as the back of her head hit the wall. She doubled over in pain, her hands cradling the side of her head.

'I am so sorry,' said the man who stood in the doorway, equally stunned and embarrassed. 'I didn't realise . . .'

Tabitha's face was twisted in pain. This was more than a bump to the head.

'Tabitha, talk to me. What's wrong?' Henley asked, ignoring the man. She kneeled in front of Tabitha and gently took hold of her arm.

'Is she all right?' the man asked cautiously.

'No, she's not. Get someone in here. A nurse,' Henley commanded.

Henley felt dread fill her stomach as she looked at the black beanie on Tabitha's head. 'Is it your head?' she asked. 'Is that where you're hurt?'

Tabitha's reply was barely audible.

'Is it your head?' Henley asked again.

'Yes,' Tabitha replied painfully.

'Let me take a look.'

Henley carefully placed her hands on the hem of the beanie. 'I promise, I'll be careful,' she said. 'I won't hurt you.'

Tabitha's body grew rigid as Henley pushed the beanie and slid it slowly back. Her breath caught in her throat. Bloodied pus coated the strands of Tabitha's hair that was sticking to the wool of the hat. Henley gently pulled the hairs away and a clump of cotton wool, stained yellowish green and red, fell from Tabitha's head and onto the floor.

'Turn your head, Tabitha,' Henley instructed gently as the putrid smell of an infected wound filled her nose. Henley bit her lip to stop herself from gagging as a nurse entered the room.

'Is everything ok?' the nurse asked.

'No,' Henley answered, staring at the large seeping wound on the back of Tabitha's head.

A scalping that a killer hadn't been able to complete.

21

DI Henley, 14.20

TA was at the house. Has head injuries. Tell him we know!!

Ramouter reread the text message from Henley as Graham grew more agitated in his bed, constantly shifting his attention to the door as though he expected his wife to walk in at any minute.

'I understand that this is difficult for you,' said Ramouter, putting his phone away. 'To say that you've been through a lot is an understatement.'

Graham turned his head away. 'Do you know when my wife will be back?' he asked Copeland.

'Graham, look at me.' Ramouter said firmly. 'I'm going to ask you a question and I want you to think very carefully about the answer that you give me.'

Graham did what he was told, his Adam's apple bobbing as he swallowed.

'Why didn't you tell me that Tabitha was in the house with you the night that you were attacked?'

'Hold on, what?' Copeland exclaimed. She turned towards Ramouter with both question and fury in her eyes at the realisation that she'd been excluded from a conversation between colleagues.

'I don't know what you're talking about,' Graham said. 'Tabitha wasn't home. She was—'

'Don't say she was in Bath. We know she wasn't. We have forensic evidence and forensics don't lie. I saw your house. There were no signs of a burglary. No ransacking of your property. Nothing was stolen. No forced entry. Did Tabitha let someone in? Who?'

Graham's fingers curled around the bedsheets as he tightened his fists. Ramouter glanced over at the patient monitor that was recording Graham's vitals. His pulse and blood pressure had increased.

Graham lowered his head and finally spoke, but his words were lost in the folds of his bedding.

'You're going to have to repeat that, Graham,' Ramouter said.

Graham raised his head. 'Tabitha opened the door,' he admitted.

'What happened?'

'Oh god. I can't.'

'If you want us to find who did this to you, and why, then you will.'

Graham took a pained breath and wiped his bruised face with the corner of the sheet. 'I'd gone upstairs to get the charger for my laptop, and to use the bathroom. Tabitha was downstairs. We ate late and she was going to clean up. I heard the doorbell and I . . . I'm sorry. I can't do it.'

'What happened Graham?' Ramouter pushed.

'I heard a scream,' he said. 'Tabitha was screaming for help. I ran out of the bathroom and down the stairs and it—'

Graham put his hands on his ears as though he was hearing his wife's screams again. 'She was in the kitchen and there was a man, dressed in black and he was sitting on top of Tabitha, and she was screaming.'

'What did you do?' asked Ramouter.

'I can't really remember. I grabbed something and I hit him. I remember seeing a knife and I pulled him off Tabitha. Tabitha was screaming but this man, he . . . I lost my grip, and he picked up the knife and,' Graham held up his injured hand. 'I tried to grab it and then he stabbed me.'

'Where was Tabitha?' asked Copeland.

'I told her to get out. To run. I think she ran out of the back door. I managed to get up, but the man attacked me again and I fell against the mirror. I remember slipping in the hallway being stabbed in the arm. It's all . . . I don't know what happened next. The next thing I remember is waking up here.'

'You don't remember running outside and being hit by a car?' Copeland asked as Graham sank back against the pillows.

Graham looked shocked at this. 'No. No, I don't remember that.'

'What about the man?' asked Ramouter. 'Can you remember anything about him?'

Graham shook his head. 'No. I don't remember anything about him except that he was big and . . . he smelled. His body odour . . . yes, I remember that. The smell.'

'Can you describe the smell?'

'Beer. Cigarettes and vinegar.'

'Graham. Why was this man trying to hurt Tabitha?' Ramouter asked. 'And why didn't you tell us the truth in the first place?'

'I knew she was safe. You told me DC Copeland had spoken to her so I . . . I knew that she was ok.'

'What aren't you telling us?' Ramouter asked as the door opened and Henley stepped into the room. 'There's a reason why this man was attacking your wife. There's a reason why Tabitha was a target.'

Graham looked at Henley and sighed deeply as though he'd resigned himself to the inevitable. 'Tabitha had a car accident. It wasn't her fault. Tabitha was arrested and they charged her. It nearly broke her, broke us. She pleaded not guilty but then the prosecution offered a deal, and she changed her plea. I didn't want her to take the deal, because she'd done nothing wrong, but Tabitha wanted it to be over.'

Graham took a breath as his eyes filled with tears. 'We thought that would be the end of it when she was sentenced but that was just the start.'

'The start of what?' Ramouter asked.

'The harassment. The first letter arrived the day after Tabitha was sentenced. Hand delivered.'

'What did the letter say?' Ramouter asked.

'That she would always be guilty. The following week someone keyed our cars, threw red paint on our windows and posted negative reviews about our businesses.'

'And the second letter?'

'It arrived last week,' Graham grimaced. 'It was a demand for money with bank details. I threw it away. I didn't hear anything more until a couple of days later and I woke up to find that someone had slashed my tyres.'

'Did you report it to the police?' Ramouter asked even though he knew the answer.

'No. Tabitha didn't want me to. She'd been through enough.'

'Were there any more demands for money?'

'Yes. Last Thursday. A letter was sent to my office. They wanted £10,000.'

'And did you pay it?'

Graham pulled himself up, grimacing slightly as he reached for the glass of water. He took a long drink. 'I did,' he finally answered. 'I paid it all, but I didn't tell Tabitha. I thought that the harassment would stop if I paid but then . . . well, look at me now.'

'Can you remember the name on the bank details?' Copeland asked.

'Oh my god,' Graham said as his eyes widened. 'Everything is so out of order in my head that I . . . Durant. I don't know the first name because it was just initials but it was Durant.'

Ramouter turned and looked at Henley. 'Durant,' he said. 'It's the surname of the woman that Tabitha killed.'

22

The sharp rapping on his office door pulled Pellacia away from his screen. He looked up to see Joanna standing there.

'Not like you to knock. What's going on?' Pellacia asked suspiciously.

Joanna placed a cup of coffee on his desk. 'DC Copeland is waiting outside,' she said. 'I haven't buzzed her through yet.'

'The same Copeland who was the SIO on the Ashcroft case?'

'Yep, and I reckon that she wants in,' Joanna said, her eyes wandering around the organised chaos in Pellacia's office.

'Maybe she's got some additional papers to hand over,' said Pellacia as Jo picked up a file from a chair.

'At 7.30 on a Monday morning? And you call yourself a detective. She wants in. So, what do you want me to do with her? Tell her to piss off?'

'No. Don't do that. Do you mind bringing her up?'

'You want *me* to go and get her?' Joanna sneered.

'I'd be very grateful,' Pellacia said, overdoing the gratitude.

'Fine. But there's one thing you should know before DC Copeland attempts to sweet talk you. She made two transfer requests to the SCU and Rhimes knocked her back each time. I bet you any money that there's probably another transfer request in your inbox.'

Pellacia sighed wearily. He opened his inbox as Joanna left the office. He scrolled through endless emails until he stopped at the one that had landed in his inbox on Friday afternoon. He usually received at least three transfer requests a month from detectives eager to join a specialist department that was rumoured to run by their own rules. Pellacia usually forwarded each request to Joanna who would send the pro-forma rejection email. Pellacia noted the time that DC Copeland had pressed send on her transfer request. She'd made the request an hour after he'd informed her DCI that they would accept the Graham Ashcroft case. He opened his drawer, pulled out a packet of paracetamol and popped three into his mouth when Joanna appeared at his doorway with DC Copeland at his side.

'Thank you very much, Jo,' said Pellacia 'And I've just printed out a document; can you bring it for me.'

'Of course, sir, and should I bring DC Copeland a cup of tea?' Joanna asked sweetly, glaring at him.

'There's no need,' Pellacia answered before Copeland had even had the opportunity to ponder her beverage decision. 'We won't be long. Take a seat, DC Copeland.'

'Thank you. I really appreciate you seeing me, sir, considering the time.'

'I did wonder if you'd camped outside.' Pellacia caught the flush rising on Copeland's neck and wondered how close to the truth he'd been with his quip. Jo quickly handed him the printout and left.

'It's not the way I usually do things. We have a procedure for a reason,' he said.

'I know I should have waited for a formal response, but I know how long the transfer requests can take and I didn't want to wait,' Copeland replied.

'You are aware that I've closed this unit to requests?'

'Yes, sir. I am, but I'm a firm believer in creating the opportunity and not simply sitting back and waiting for one that may never arise.'

'This is now your third transfer request to the SCU. DCSI Rhimes turned you down. Twice.'

'Not because he didn't think I was qualified, because I am, sir. I am more than qualified. It's just that back then, DCSI Rhimes said that he had more than enough bodies on his team.'

'So even though every unit in the Met knows that I'm not taking any transfers, you thought it would be wise to come to me personally in the hope that I would change my mind?'

'With all due respect, sir, the SCU took my case. Graham Ashcroft is only here because of me.'

Pellacia leaned back as he observed Copeland's face to see if she was aware of the audaciousness of her statement.

'We took your case because, and you'll correct me if I'm wrong, you made the call for the SCU to attend because you believed that the Ashcroft case fitted the MO of our series of home invasions,' said Pellacia.

Copeland's mouth twisted as she clasped her hands in her lap.

'Am I wrong?' Pellacia asked.

'No, no, you're not,' Copeland relinquished. 'All units are told to assess their cases to see if they would qualify as a serial crime and that's what I did. I wouldn't have been doing my job if I'd just ignored the possibility that the Ashcroft case might qualify as an SCU home invasion. I don't mean to get ahead of myself, but I don't think that would be a fair reason to knock back my transfer request.'

'I'm not using that as a reason. I'm simply explaining to you that the Ashcroft case came to my unit because of a decision you made and—'

'I'm very much aware of that, sir, and I don't regret that decision, but I know that the Ashcroft case is big,' Copeland said enthusiastically. 'Much bigger than I ever anticipated, and I want to be . . . sorry, sorry, sir. I interrupted you.'

Pellacia bristled. He instinctively knew that Copeland's next words would have been 'I want to be a part of it'. He knew from experience that it was never a good sign when a detective placed their ego first and case resolution second.

'Sir, I'm sure that you know how it feels to want to see an investigation through to the end. It's not about me. It's about doing what I can to make sure that we stop any more names being added to your whiteboard.' Copeland changed tack.

Pellacia internally rolled his eyes at this well-rehearsed line. 'I would question any detective who didn't want to see a case through to the end,' he said.

'Of course you would. I would question it too,' Copeland replied, the voices of Stanford and Eastwood drifting through the office.

'I've got a small but tight and committed team,' said Pellacia. 'We've been burnt before by detectives transferring to us and then realising that they can't cut it after six weeks. In addition to that, my budget won't stretch to a new team member.'

'You don't have to worry about the budget if I join the SCU on secondment,' Copeland pointed out 'You won't be searching under your desk looking for pennies. You'll be getting me for free. Once the investigation is concluded I'll go back to Lewisham CID. If you haven't worked it out already, I'm quite determined, sir. I want this.'

Pellacia looked past Copeland as his ears picked up the voices of Henley and Ramouter. He may be in charge of the SCU, but Henley was the senior investigating officer in charge of the Fox-Carnell murder and the attempted murders of the Ashcrofts, and she was the one who managed the team.

'It's not just my decision,' he said.

'Detective Inspector Henley,' Copeland stated understanding Pellacia's meaning. She stood up with her feet hips' width apart and clasped her hands behind her back, grounding herself as though preparing herself for an attack.

Pellacia scanned Copeland's face, attempting to read her but Copeland was pokerfaced.

'No. The borough commander,' said Pellacia. He opened his

office door. 'Can I help you?' he said sarcastically to Stanford who hadn't been quick enough to leave his prime eavesdropping position.

'Not at all, guv,' said Stanford as he held up his mug. 'Just passing.'

'Well, keep passing,' said Pellacia. He closed the door and turned back to Copeland. 'I'll get back to you in a couple of days about your transfer request, but I wouldn't get your hopes up.'

'Of course,' said Copeland as she seemed to momentarily deepen her stance in defiance.

'And I would appreciate it if you didn't have any further contact with the Ashcrofts,' Pellacia added. 'We don't need any crossed wires.'

'That goes without saying, sir,' she said, her bright tone not matching the darkness in her eyes. 'Thank you for seeing me. I'll see myself out.'

Henley tapped her pen against her monitor as she watched Copeland stride out of Pellacia's office.

'Why have you got your "I think you're talking shit" face on?' asked Stanford as he placed an egg and bacon roll on Henley's desk. 'You normally save that for when you're interviewing a suspect.'

'I don't have my "you're talking shit" face on,' Henley replied unconvincingly as she watched Copeland stop at the kitchen area where Ramouter was taking his bowl of porridge out of the microwave.

'Now you've got your "why are you talking to my man" face on.'

'How many faces do I have? Shut up, Stanford.' Henley was keeping a close eye on Copeland. She felt a sense of unease watching Copeland finally leave but leaving the door open, as though she was making a not-so-subtle point.

'So, what did you hear?' Henley asked Stanford.

'Not much to be honest, but I heard your name mentioned by her and guv said something about decisions.'

'She wants in,' Henley concluded.

'Wants in on the case or all in with the SCU?' Stanford asked as Ezra bounced into the room with his laptop in one hand and a large purple smoothie in the other. 'Joining is a big ask but, saying that, look at us. It's not as if we don't need the help.'

'Hmm, I'm not saying that we don't but let's not waste our time on something that may never happen.' Henley balled up her greasy wrapper and threw it into the bin under her desk.

Pellacia came out of his office. 'Right, team, we've got a lot to get through. So, let's get started.' He picked up the whiteboard eraser and removed Graham and Tabitha Ashcroft's names from the home invasion case board.

'So, it's confirmed then?' asked Eastwood as Pellacia wrote the names of Sian Fox-Carnell and the Ashcrofts on the mobile whiteboard. 'These two cases are linked?'

'Forensics link them,' Pellacia answered. 'The third DNA profile found on Sian Fox-Carnell's body matches the DNA that was recovered from blood found in the Ashcrofts' house.'

'Is there any prior association between the Ashcrofts and Fox-Carnell?' asked Stanford.

'No associations,' he continued. 'I spent the weekend going through the original Sian Fox-Carnell murder investigation file and I couldn't find anything to link the two either in terms of evidence, victims or location.'

'But they do share something in common,' said Henley as a notification signalled the arrival of the email that she'd been waiting for. 'Wait. I've just received the toxicology report for Fox-Carnell.'

'What killed her?' Ramouter asked as Henley left her desk and joined Pellacia at the front, taking over.

'Fentanyl. It's a schedule two controlled drug in the UK but that doesn't mean that it's not lethal,' said Henley. 'Most people who die of a fentanyl overdose have levels that range from 3 to 58 micrograms per litre of blood.'

'How much did Fox-Carnell have in her blood?' asked Eastwood.

'75.3 micrograms,' Henley replied as Stanford released a low whistle. 'She also had traces of alcohol and cannabis in her system. The levels are low, which is to be expected considering that she was held captive for two days before she was killed. That's not to say that she may not have been drinking heavily before she was taken. I could smell the alcohol on her breath when she approached me.' Henley turned her back and drew a red arrow between Fox-Carnell and Tabitha Ashcroft. 'So, there are two things they have in common. First, the scalping.'

'What?' Ezra asked wide eyed.

'Turn around,' Henley instructed, aware that Ezra didn't have the stomach for the images of a brutal death that she faced daily. Ezra did what he was told and she picked up the photograph of the back of Fox-Carnell's head and placed it on the board.

'Christ,' Pellacia muttered as his hand involuntarily went to the area on his chest where the serial killer, Peter Olivier, had left scars.

'Fox-Carnell was scalped before she died. Tabitha Ashcroft too,' said Henley. She placed a second photograph, with two images, on the board. The first image was the left side profile of Tabitha Ashcroft, showing bruising along her jawline and a large cut with a thin segment of skin laying against her scalp like an unopened envelope. The second image was a close up.

Stanford shook his head. 'How is she?'

'Understandably a mess. She was admitted because the wound was infected and she was on the verge of developing sepsis,' said Henley. 'The only reason she's not in the morgue is because her husband saved her.'

'I also don't think we can ignore the fact that both Fox-Carnell and Tabitha Ashcroft had appeared in court recently,' said Ramouter. 'It seems to be more than just a coincidence.'

'I agree, which leads me on to where we go next. The other link is that both victims suffered instances of harassment at their homes before they were attacked. Fox-Carnell's parents had a noose painted on their window and shit pushed through their letter box.'

'How pleasant,' Eastwood said as she screwed her face.

'The Ashcrofts also suffered harassment. Slashed tyres and demands for money.'

'Blackmail?' asked Stanford.

'Yes,' said Henley. 'Which Graham Ashcroft paid. Fortunately, our blackmailer wasn't smart. We've got a name. Laurence Durant. Husband of Sherri Durant, the woman who Tabitha Ashcroft killed. Stanford and Eastwood, can you pay him a visit?'

Eastwood was already standing and picking up her jacket from the back of the chair. 'Sure. But, to be honest, boss, blackmail to murder – it's a leap.'

'It is. It could be something, or it could be nothing, but that doesn't mean that we sit and wait to see,' answered Henley. Stanford took a sheet of paper containing Laurence Durant's details from her outstretched hand 'But before you both go; Ezra, are you ready?' Henley spun the whiteboard around so that the photographs faced the wall.

'Finally,' Ezra said, jumping off the desk and making his way to the front. 'I don't come down here often and you kept man waiting for ages. I haven't got any fancy graphics to show you because, well, you wouldn't understand 'em. I'll get straight to the point. Soteria lied about the reason why their systems went down.' He paused, took a breath before continuing. 'In their press release Soteria said the reason they lost contact with everyone who was on tag was because they'd reached their data storage capacity, and they couldn't track anyone. That just struck me as dodgy. When I was given early release from prison, they put me on tag, do you remember, boss?' Ezra said, turning to Pellacia.

'I remember that a couple of officers turned up here to question you about breaching your curfew.'

'Exactly, anyway, the point is back then Soteria were constantly maxing out their data storage because they were cheap. All that meant was that they couldn't send notifications to probation the minute you weren't home on time. But the minute they increased their data storage; notifications would be pinging all over the place.'

'So, you're saying that even if they're out of data your movements are still being recorded?' asked Stanford.

'Exactly. And these new trackers, they're a million times better than what I had; they can tell you the seat you're in at the cinema. Now that Soteria's systems are up and running, they should have sent you a log of her movements from the minute they tagged her but they haven't, so I went digging on the parts of the web that you shouldn't really go.'

'I don't know why you're being so melodramatic. He means the dark web,' said Stanford.

'What are you saying, Ez, that they were hacked?' asked Pellacia. 'They wouldn't be the first company to be a victim of ransomware.'

'Keyword there is ransom,' said Ezra 'Usually when big companies like this are hacked there is a group asking for something stupid. Acer got a ransomware demand for $50 million, there was another gang who demanded £60 million worth of bitcoin after they hacked a couple of IT companies in Amsterdam and Germany. The point is, they all do the same thing: hack the system, make it unusable, copy all the data and then ask for stupid money otherwise they'll release the data. From what I can see, there is not one hacker, cybercriminal or whatever you want to call them demanding a ransom from Soteria. There is no evidence that they were hacked'

'If they weren't hacked and it wasn't a data storage issue then what was it?' Ramouter asked.

'I think it was an inside job,' said Ezra.

'We're assuming that this is all about Fox-Carnell. Soteria is monitoring over 12,000 people and all of their tags were down. Why would anyone in Soteria want to make just one person disappear into the wind?' asked Eastwood. 'Unless they were in on it.'

'That's another leap. A big leap,' Stanford commented.

Pellacia looked at Ezra. 'Can you confirm if what you're suggesting is true?'

'I can,' Ezra said slowly, 'but I'd rather do it through the front door as opposed to the back door, if you know what I mean.'

'We need a warrant or an invitation,' said Henley.

'I don't think that we've got strong enough grounds to convince a judge to give us a warrant,' Pellacia mused. 'And even if we did, we'll be wasting time drafting an application and then hanging around Bromley magistrates waiting for an available judge on the off chance that they'll sign off on a warrant for us to search Soteria's computer systems.'

'That settles it,' said Henley. 'Eastwood and Stanford will go and speak to Laurence Durant and Ramouter and I are heading to Soteria.'

'Can I come?' Ezra said excitedly. 'I'm not being funny, but you two would be like bunnies in the headlights the minute they showed you their servers.'

'Ezra, despite your brilliant work you're a civilian. I'm not having you out on the street,' said Pellacia.

'Oh, come on, guv, you know it makes sense. You lot don't just keep me around because of my good looks.'

Ramouter laughed. 'He has a point. The boss and I go down to

Soteria and they agree that we can look around, but what exactly are we looking for?'

'It will be the equivalent of standing in the middle of Greenwich Park and being asked to find a squirrel named Derek,' said Ezra.

'That makes absolutely no sense.' Eastwood shook her head.

'Of course it doesn't and that's my point. Look, all I'm doing is looking at their systems, that's if they let me and if they so no, I'll just come back here or maybe the boss will buy me a burger to console me,' Ezra said with a shrug.

'I don't like it,' said Pellacia.

'Me neither,' agreed Stanford.

'But I don't think we have a choice,' countered Henley. 'We've got three options. Waste time applying and waiting for the inevitable rejection of our warrant application, plead our case to the NCA Cyber Security unit and again waste time waiting for them to authorise sending an agent who – and I will put money on it – will be less qualified than Ezra or—'

'Fine, fine. It may not be the worst thing,' said Pellacia, raising his hands in defeat. 'But Ramouter I want you to stay here. I need someone by my side for the press conference at 1 p.m..'

'That's good with me. I'll use the time to go through the council CCTV footage,' said Ramouter.

'And, Ezra, I don't even want you turning left unless Henley tells you to, do you understand me?' Pellacia asked.

'Crystal,' Ezra said as he gave a salute.

23

Stanford pulled up his coat collar, insulating himself against the chill in the air. 'I heard Oprah say once that your home should rise up to meet you.' The garden gate was missing and tall weeds that had begun to flower grew through the multiple cracks in the stained paving stone. 'This house looks like it's about to drag you down to the pits of hell.'

'Yeah, it's not the best is it?' Eastwood wrinkled her nose at piles of cat litter that had spilled from the multiple bags in the corner of the small garden. She pressed the doorbell.

The outline of a figure appeared in the frosted panels of the front door. There was the sound of a lock turning and then the door cracked open, a silver chain still secured to the wall cut across the man's face on the other side.

'Laurence Durant?' Eastwood asked.

'Who's asking?' the man's voice was low and hoarse as though he was recovering from a cold.

'I'm DS Eastwood and this is my colleague DS Stanford. We'd like to have a word,' she held up her warrant card to the gap.

The chain pressed against the man's cheek as he pushed his face closer against it to squint at Eastwood's ID. A second later, the door closed shut and they heard the distinct sound of the chain sliding back and the door reopened.

'Laurence Durant?' Eastwood repeated.

'Larry,' he said. 'Come in but watch where you step. The kittens are roaming.'

Inside, the house contrasted with the exterior. It was clean and looked to have been recently decorated but Larry himself looked neglected. His greying beard was unkempt and there were visible stains on his misshapen navy T-shirt. The smell of burnt bacon lingered in the air.

'So, what can I do for you?' He picked up the remote control from the sofa and lowered the TV volume.

'We're here to ask you some questions about Graham and Tabitha Ashcroft,' Eastwood explained as she picked up a tortoiseshell kitten that had dug their claws into her jeans and was attempting to climb.

'I don't have anything to say about *them*.' Larry took the kitten from Eastwood's hand and placed it in a cage.

'I'm afraid it doesn't quite work like that,' said Stanford as he walked across the room and sat down at the table, gently pushing aside a towering pile of papers.

'It looks like we interrupted you,' he commented.

'You did,' said Larry. 'I'm marking exam papers and the last thing I want to do is talk about those people.'

'I'm afraid you're going to have to and, to be honest, I'd rather do it here as opposed to going through the trouble of taking you down to the local station.'

Larry stared at Eastwood through narrowed eyes as he lowered himself into an armchair.

'What happened to your hand?' Eastwood asked, pointing at the scabs and bruises on his knuckles.

Larry turned his hand and looked at his knuckles as though he'd just realised that the wounds were there. 'I had an accident in the back. Gardening. Ask me your questions because as I said—'

'We know. You're busy,' Eastwood replied. 'So, let's get to it. I know that you've been through a lot and the last thing you want to do is talk about the Ashcrofts.'

'They ruined my life. I don't my want their names spoken in my house.'

'If there was a way I could ask you these questions without mentioning their names then I would, but that's not possible,' Eastwood was sympathetic. 'Take a moment. Steady yourself and listen carefully to what I ask you.'

Larry stared intensely at Eastwood, the muscles flexing in his arms as he gripped the armrest. After a few seconds he nodded at her.

'Thank you,' said Eastwood. 'Someone tried to kill Tabitha and—'

'Tried to kill?' Larry interrupted abruptly. He huffed and shook his head. 'You've knocked the wrong door if you're expecting me to feel sorry for her.'

'Tried to kill her and her husband,' Eastwood continued. 'We've checked your record, and we can see that you were arrested for threatening words and behaviour on the date that Mrs Ashcroft was sentenced.'

'That woman killed my wife, and she walked out of court with a slap on a bloody wrist. She should have been sent to jail to rot so I—'

Larry stopped, his chest rising and dropping as anger visibly swarmed him. 'I had a few things to say outside of court.'

'You threatened to kill Tabitha Ashcroft,' said Stanford.

'How many times have you said that you want to kill someone?' asked Larry, turning to Stanford. 'It doesn't mean that I would actually do it. I was just angry.'

'And are you still angry?' asked Eastwood.

'What do you think? I'm sitting here with you two and my wife is in Croydon Cemetery.'

'Last Sunday night, Tabitha and Graham were attacked in their home. Tabitha managed to escape but Graham wasn't so lucky. He was stabbed and was run over by a car.'

'I don't have a car,' Larry said quickly.

'DVLA records say you own a 2012 Skoda Octavia,' said Stanford.

'That's a mistake. I sold it.'

'When?'

'When Sherri was killed by a car.'

'Before the attack, the Ashcrofts had their car tyres slashed and had been receiving threatening letters,' Eastwood added.

'That wasn't me,' Larry replied as his eyes cast to the left. 'If that's what you're trying to suggest.'

'I'm not going to suggest it, but I am going to ask if you've been to the Ashcrofts' house?'

Larry shook his head. 'I don't even know where they live.'

'They've also alleged that you blackmailed them.'

'I did what?'

'Blackmailed them. Asked for money. £10,000 which they paid to you.'

Eastwood and Stanford kept their eyes on Larry as he placed his hands on his legs and straightened his back. The TV played quietly as the kittens meowed and Larry breathed heavily.

'That is. A. Lie,' Larry said calmly. 'A bloody lie.'

'Did you send them letters and demands for money?' asked Stanford.

'Are you really going to believe the words of a murderer?' Larry asked.

'Where were you last Sunday, late in the evening, just before midnight?'

'I was here, at home. I went to my son's house for Sunday lunch. I was back by five – five-thirty. I spent the evening doing my lesson prep and I fell asleep right here, in front of *Match of the Day 2*. I woke up about 2 a.m. and went upstairs to bed,' Larry replied, his tone becoming angrier.

'Were you home alone?'

'My wife is dead.'

Stanford looked across at Eastwood who was studying Larry intently.

'Do I need a lawyer?' Larry asked, breaking the silence. 'Because these questions you're asking me, I don't like it.'

'How long were you and your wife married?' Eastwood asked, leaving Larry's question unanswered.

'We met in school, but we didn't get married until we were in our early twenties. We were about to celebrate our fortieth wedding anniversary when that woman murdered Sherri.'

'Have you ever been to the Ashcrofts' home or their place of work?' asked Eastwood as Stanford stood up and walked over to the mantelpiece. He picked up Sherri Durant's funeral programme, the edges dirty and curling as though it'd been picked up and read numerous times.

'No, I haven't been to their house or anywhere else,' Larry stood up, took two long strides across the living room and snatched the funeral programme out of Stanford's hand. 'Tabitha Ashcroft killed my wife,' he said through gritted teeth as though her name was cauterising his flesh.

'We're not expecting you to like the questions we ask,' said Stanford, eyeballing Larry.

Larry turned his back as he carefully placed the programme back on the mantelpiece.

'I don't like them and I'm not answering any more. So, if you want answers, you'll have to arrest me and speak to my lawyer.'

'Do you believe him?' asked Eastwood as they walked away from Larry's house. 'That he got the injuries on his hands from gardening?'

'The only thing he didn't lie about was marking exam papers,' Stanford replied.

'Maybe we should— Where on earth are you going?' Eastwood

asked as Stanford left her side and jogged across the road. She turned to follow, but had to stop as a bus drove past.

'Why did you run off like that?' Eastwood asked once she'd joined Stanford.

'Something caught my eye when I picked up his missus's funeral programme from the mantelpiece.' Stanford took out his phone and opened his email. 'Explain to me why you would have a resident parking permit, if you don't own a car.'

'You wouldn't,' Eastwood said.

'And why would a Skoda Octavia that you said you don't own be parked on the other side of the street.'

'The lying little—'

'Read out the number plate. I'll check it matches the DVLA records.'

'SB12 LKW.'

'Snap,' said Stanford, walking to the front of the car. 'Eastie take a look at this.'

'I think the old man in there did more than just lie,' said Eastwood as Stanford took photos of the large spider-webbed crack on the windscreen and the dented bumper.

24

'This is a very nice building,' said Ezra as he and Henley stepped into the lift that would take them to Soteria's offices on the twelfth floor.

'Are you thinking of leaving us?' Henley asked. She looked stressed and could easily have blamed her appearance on the cause and effect of working an intense case, but it was more than that. The internal debate that Eastwood, Pellacia and Stanford had a right to know the truth about Rhimes's death was exhausting her.

'Why, do you want me to leave?' Ezra replied.

'Fishing for a compliment much,' Henley said in jest as they exited and began to walk down a carpeted hallway. 'Didn't think you cared.'

'I do have a heart,' Ezra replied.

'Of course you do and, for my own selfish reasons, I would hate for you to leave,' Henley admitted, heading for the empty reception desk. 'Let's be honest, you're brilliant. You could be working somewhere like this and earning double the money the SCU pays you.'

'Triple and benefits.'

'Triple! Are you serious?'

'Serious as a heart attack. Every couple of months I get an email from a head-hunter or the NCA cyberunit wanting to talk to me about exciting opportunities. You'd think they'd give up asking.'

'They want you because you're good, Ez. Best of the best.'

'Thanks, boss,' Ezra said with both embarrassment and pride. 'I thought I'd really messed up my life when I got sent to prison. Do you know that I fainted in the dock when the judge said I was going down for five years?'

'No, I didn't know that.'

'Banged my head on the stupid chair and knocked myself out. I was proper convinced that my life was over, but the worse thing was knowing that I'd disappointed not just my mum and dad but my entire family. You know what it's like, boss, there's a bunch of people out there who think we're all from broken homes, don't know our dads and that we're in gangs stabbing each other up and then what do I go and do? Get myself a stretch in Coldingley. Became a big ol' stereotype.'

'Don't ever think of yourself as a stereotype. You made a mistake, but you did your time and, most importantly, you didn't give up on yourself,' Henley said as a door behind Ezra opened and a man stepped out, his hands still wet.

'I am so sorry,' the man said, stepping behind the desk, wiping his hands along the side of his legs before picking up a headset and placing it around his neck. 'I was in the . . . do you know what? Never mind. How can I help you?'

'Detective Inspector Henley,' she said as she presented her warrant card. 'This is my colleague, Ezra Williams and you are?'

'Ada Payne.' He peered at the warrant card and then at Ezra with suspicion. 'And what about your colleague. I need to see his credentials.'

'He's with me,' Henley said in a tone that made it clear the question was moot.

'Fine. So, how can I help you? There's nothing in the diary to show an appointment.'

'I'm investigating a murder, and the victim was being monitored by Soteria. I need to see your director of cybersecurity.'

'Kaiden Longley,' Ezra whispered behind her.

'He's in a meeting but that should be wrapping up now,' Ada replied as left his position, with his ID card in hand. 'I'll take you through.'

Ada led them through an open plan office that had views of the city of London on both sides.

Henley could feel it as she walked, tension hung heavy in the air, phones were ringing and people raised their heads to watch the unscheduled visitors on parade.

'Here he is,' Ada said as a tall man in his mid-forties stormed out of a conference.

'Kaiden,' Ada stopped him, leaned in and whispered. Kaiden looked up at Henley, tiredness evident all over his face, and nodded to Ada.

'Kaiden Longley,' he had an American accent. He shook Henley's hand firmly. 'I don't have much time. I'm in between . . . there's a lot going on. I'll take you through to my office.'

Henley sat down on a chair that had not been created for comfort while Ezra sat equally uncomfortable next to her.

'I'm sorry, I should have asked if you wanted one,' Kaiden said as he pushed a coffee pod into the machine behind him.

Henley shook her head no, instead asking, 'How long have you been working for Soteria?'

'It will be four years next month,' Kaiden replied. 'I moved here from Boston because my wife wanted to come home.'

'So, you know Soteria's IT system well?'

'Like the back of my hand.'

'This is my colleague, Ezra Williams. He's our . . .' Henley paused, suddenly realising that she wasn't sure what Ezra's official title was with the SCU as he seemed to change it each week.

'Senior forensic computer analyst for the SCU,' Ezra said proudly. 'Specialist in cybersecurity and network security.'

'We're investigating the murder of Sian Fox-Carnell who was being electronically monitored by Soteria,' Henley explained.

Kaiden's face paled. 'Murder,' he said. 'I thought she was just missing?'

'How can you not know?' Henley asked incredulously. 'Her tag came back online last Friday morning.'

'It came online but then it went off again once the battery died, but the point is I wasn't informed the offender had been found and that she was—'

Kaiden paused and watched through the glass as a small group exited the conference room he'd been in earlier. 'Ever get the feeling that you're being hung out to dry? Sorry, you're not here to talk about office politics.'

'No, we're not,' said Henley. 'When Fox-Carnell first went missing we were told that you were unable to track her because your systems had exceeded their data storage capacity, but it turns out that was wrong.'

'But that's what happened. We had a server migration issue which in turn led to the data storage issue.'

'How come you weren't able to produce the electronic monitoring reports for Fox-Carnell?' Ezra demanded. 'The only reason you couldn't do that was because someone who works for you, shut down your systems and made it look like you were hacked. You didn't have a server migration or data storage issue.'

Kaiden opened his mouth and closed it again as Henley shot Ezra a warning look.

'Why are there two different versions of events?' Henley asked, watching Kaiden sip his coffee, buying time.

'I was on annual leave when the systems went down,' Kaiden said eventually. 'No one told me what happened with the systems until I came back.'

'That's not an explanation.'

'Soteria secured a six-year contract to deliver electronic monitoring services to England and Wales for the Ministry of Justice,' said Kaiden. 'That contract is worth £200 million with a two-year extension available worth another £75 million. The contract is up for renewal in nine months. I can only assume that it would be better for the company to say that the systems went down because of a data capacity issue.'

'Are you saying that this company released a statement blaming the issue on data storage because they didn't want to lose a government contract?' asked Henley.

Kaiden nodded. 'It wouldn't be the first time.'

'So, what do you know?'

'The systems went down on Tuesday afternoon when I was on the Eurostar to Paris. I was aware of the issues but the Wi-Fi on the train was terrible, and it was difficult to send and receive emails. I did see the messages telling me we had a data issue but when I came back to work on Friday morning, I knew that couldn't have been right because all of our offenders' movements would still be recorded.'

'Did you think you'd been hacked or that it was an internal error?'

'I thought it was an internal error initially,' said Kaiden. 'The network was compromised from 3 a.m. Tuesday morning which is, for lack of a better word, the dead zone. 95 per cent of curfews start between 6 p.m. and 9 p.m. and we usually start receiving breach alerts from 6 p.m. to about midnight. After midnight, it's dead, there might be the odd one or two breaches, but no one is usually breaching at 1 a.m. and no one is in the office monitoring server activity after hours. The network then went back online at 3.18 a.m.. At 6.02 p.m. on Tuesday afternoon the entire network was compromised. I thought it was a hack because compromising the network for a short period of time, a few minutes or an hour, is the reconnaissance stage of a cyber-attack.'

'You said you *thought* it was hacked? What made you unsure?'

'There was no command and control of the network, which is stage six of a cyber-attack. Usually, when someone hacks a network like this, they download everything they can, release malware into the system, lock us out of the network and start demanding eyewatering sums as ransom but that didn't happen here. No obvious control of the network. No mass download. No ransom.'

'Told you,' Ezra muttered.

'So, what were they doing in the system, other than shutting it down?' asked Henley.

'I'm not entirely sure,' Kaiden admitted.

'I'll be able to tell you, if you let me take a look at your systems,' Ezra said excitedly.

'I don't think that would be wise,' Kaiden answered warily. 'Our systems have already been compromised, and you don't have the authorisation'

'We're the police, well the boss is, and the fact is someone out there,' Ezra spun around in his chair and pointed at the office, 'has been poking around in your system and getting up to no good.'

'How long would it take you?' Henley asked Ezra, before Kaiden could voice any further objections.

'Not long, once I get access from the big man here. Also, if you think they're setting you up to take the fall, you'd have ammunition.'

Kaiden tapped his fingers against his empty cup as he watched Ezra, a wry smile spreading across his lips. 'Let's go,' he said.

Ezra released a low whistle as Kaiden pushed open the doors to the room that housed his cyber-security team. Half of the team were wearing noise cancelling headphones and didn't look up when they entered the room and were led to an empty desk. Kaiden leaned over the keyboard, inserted his ID card and typed in his password. 'All yours.'

'I'm not being funny, but your cyber-security is lax,' said Ezra five minutes later as he stared intently at the screen, his fingers dancing across the keyboard.

'I have no idea what I'm looking at,' Henley admitted as she watched the expressions on Kaiden's face morph from intrigue to impressed as Ezra worked.

'Neither do I,' Kaiden confessed.

'Ok, it looks as though I was wrong, and your systems were accessed externally which doesn't quite make . . . do you mind if I copy data?' Ezra asked. He reached for his rucksack and pulled out a memory stick. 'Most hackers leave some kind of digital footprint, think of it like a graffiti artist leaving a tag. They just can't help themselves.'

'Go ahead,' Kaiden replied.

'Bingo!' Ezra said a few minutes later. 'There it is. Your hacker placed a digital tracker on the Sian Fox-Carnell equipment, which means that the GPS data was being sent to a third party. They also shut down the system, placed the shutdown on a timer and installed malware that made it look like you had exceeded the data storage system.'

'Are you saying the systems were still monitoring the offenders?'

'That's exactly what they were doing. Look, all the reporting information from Tuesday morning at 3 a.m. until 9 a.m. on Friday was being diverted to this encrypted folder which was then sent to a virtual drive.'

Kaiden crouched down and scrolled through the data on the screen. 'Can you tell where the hack originated from?'

'It's the usual rerouting the IP address and bouncing it around,' Ezra said. 'I could tell you, but you know how it is.'

'It would take a while.'

'Exactly and me and the boss have another appointment we have to get to.'

Henley raised her eyebrows at the sudden revelation of their second appointment, but instead of questioning it she asked, 'Ezra, were you able to download all of the reporting information for Fox-Carnell?'

Ezra removed the memory stick from the computer. 'It's all here,' he said. 'And I've decrypted the file that contained the monitoring information for everyone on tag and moved it to your main server.'

'Thanks for that. Is there anything else you need?' Kaiden asked, taking Ezra's place at the screen.

'Nope,' Ezra replied. He turned to Henley and pointed at his watch. 'We're going to be late.'

'Why did you want to get out of there so quickly?' Henley asked once they were out on Cannon Street and a safe distance away from the Soteria offices.

Ezra blew out his cheeks and headed to an empty table outside a café. 'Ok, those lot up there were hacked but the weird thing is that the hack originated from within that building.'

'I thought you said their servers were accessed externally. You also said that it would take you too long to find out that information.'

'Boss, seriously, it's me and I'm not an amateur. The hacker rerouted the IP address and made it look as though it originated from San Francisco. They bounced it all over the place, China, Japan and Brazil, but I tracked it back and guess where I tracked it back to?'

Henley turned around and looked up at the building that they'd just left. 'Someone in Kaiden's team hacked the system?'

Ezra shrugged. 'Could have been Kaiden or it could have been Ada from reception for all I know.'

'It doesn't make any sense,' said Henley. 'Why would anyone go through all of the trouble of hacking the system and diverting all of Fox-Carnell's reporting information. Why not just shut the entire thing down?'

'They wouldn't be able to find her if they shut the entire thing down.' Ezra picked up a menu. 'It makes sense to me. Track her movements. Follow her and grab her. And by the time the police are called no one knows where to start looking because to you she's disappeared into the wind.'

'Pellacia was right. You really should think about joining the force.'

Ezra smiled. 'No, thanks.'

'Hmm,' Henley leaned back, processing it all, 'I'm just thinking, what if Fox-Carnell wasn't the only offender they put a digital tracker on?'

'I'll start looking as soon as we get back to the SCU, after you buy me lunch.'

'It's not even midday.'

'Call it brunch then.'

'You're worse than Eastwood,' Henley laughed, picking up a menu. 'Anything else I need to know?'

'Remember when I said that some hackers like to leave a tag?'

Henley nodded as she beckoned a waitress over.

'This hacker – or Soteria employee – did exactly that. It's like they couldn't help themselves, boss.'

'What's their tag?'

'SpecterCipher393, but give me a few days and I'll be able to tell you their real name.'

25

The rumoured death of a convicted serial murderer turned innocent until proven guilty defendant had commanded an audience. Reporters and photographers had turned up early for the press conference that would finally confirm that the woman seen hanging from the pier all over social media was indeed Sian Fox-Carnell. The queue had been diverted from the main entrance on Lewisham High Street and into Lewisham police station car park. Mounted police, their horses still but on alert, watched the crowd as they waited for the rear gates to open.

'We're going to have to use the room next door as an overflow,' Pellacia said.

'It would have made more sense to have the press conference at the Yard,' Ramouter answered, flicking through the file that contained his case notes.

'The Yard want to keep this case at arm's length. Fox-Carnell is a pariah. You can't ask people for sympathy for a woman who has already been convicted of multiple murders and attempting to murder a kid. Much better to have us sitting in front of the cameras appealing for help and making a fool of ourselves and not the assistant commissioner.'

'Fox-Carnell is hardly the perfect victim,' Pellacia continued. 'And neither is Tabitha Ashcroft. We've got two victims who, in the public's eyes, have got away with murder.'

Ramouter saw a familiar but unwanted face. 'You have got to be joking,' he sighed. 'I'll meet you inside, guv.'

'I am a member of the free and independent press,' intoned Ben. 'I have a right to be here and a right to report the news.'

'And I've told you before that you are not on the list. Just because you ordered an ID card with press written on it from the internet doesn't mean you can just walk in here,' said the civilian officer at the signing in desk. 'Now leave voluntarily or I'm going to have you escorted out.'

'You're breaching my rights,' Ben insisted.

'No one is breaching your rights,' said Ramouter, taking hold of Ben's arm and escorting him away.

'Mate, what are you doing?' Ben protested as he unwittingly allowed himself to be pulled out of the queue and back into the car park.

'Stopping you from getting arrested,' Ramouter replied, opening the gate. 'You are going to get into a lot of trouble if you keep pushing yourself into uninvited spaces. Do you understand me?'

Ben shook off Ramouter's hand. 'Do you know who I am?' he asked. 'Do you know how many followers I have.'

'398,000.'

'So, you've seen my channel then?' Ben smirked. 'Impressive, isn't it?'

'No, it's not. It's dangerous and full of misinformation.'

'I'm giving the people what they want because you lot are no longer the good guys.'

Ramouter felt a low burning rage swell inside of him as Ben's words touched a nerve. The battle of showing that the police were for the people was proving much harder to fight these days. He shut the gate.

'You can't stop us,' Ben shouted.

Ramouter turned around and found himself facing DC Copeland, her face flushed as though she'd just run a race.

'Looks like you had your hands full just then,' she said, removing her jacket and unclipping her covert police vest.

'Just a pain in my arse who tried to blag his way into the press conference, that I need to get to actually,' Ramouter replied.

'Is this for the Ashcrofts?' Copeland asked in a tone that suggested to Ramouter that she knew exactly what the press conference was about.

'And Fox-Carnell,' he said, pushing the main door open. He checked that the corridor was empty of any reporters before continuing. 'There are similarities, both forensically and evidentially that suggest the person who attacked the Ashcrofts also killed Fox-Carnell.'

Copeland's mouth formed a wide O as her eyes brightened. 'I need to sit in. In the conference I mean.'

'I think it's standing room only.'

'I'll just come with you and hang out at the back.'

'Won't your DCI be wondering where you are?' Ramouter asked as they turned a corner and saw Pellacia talking with the borough commander, Geraldine Barker.

'Yeah, you're right.' Copeland backed into an alcove in the hallway, out of Pellacia's view. 'But you know, why don't you tell me all about it later. Maybe a drink after work? I should finish my shift by six.'

Ramouter looked across at Pellacia who had raised his arm and was pointing at his watch.

'Sure, why not,' he said. 'The Gypsy Moth in Greenwich good for you?'

'Perfect,' Copeland replied.

'I thought the press conference went well,' said Barker, who oversaw the police stations and specialist units that operated in

South-East London. 'The questions from the press weren't too painful.'

'That's because we've withheld information,' said Pellacia, loosening his tie and taking a seat on the grey sofa in the corner of the room. 'The last thing that I or DC Ramouter needed was to mention the scalping . . . I know,' he said as Barker wrinkled her nose in disgust.

'Scalping,' she said. 'It's the stuff you read about in history books or see in Westerns. Makes my blood run cold. Where are you in terms of suspects?'

'When it comes to Fox-Carnell there's a long list. From the victims who somehow survived and the family members of the ones who didn't,' answered Pellacia. 'Her stepfather reported incidents of harassment to Henley and Ramouter. There are photographs but no evidence as to who was responsible.'

'You've got your hands full.'

'Which brings me to why I wanted to see you, ma'am.'

'You'll have more luck standing outside waving a tincan on the high street if you're thinking of asking me for money.'

'No, I know that would be a fool's errand,' said Pellacia. 'But what I'm asking for is for you to agree to a secondment. I was planning to discuss it with Henley.'

'And have you?'

'Not yet. There are a lot of moving parts to this investigation and it's all hands on deck. I'll be honest I wasn't particularly keen on the idea of expanding the team, but I had to have a word with myself when I agreed for Ezra to accompany Henley to Soteria.'

'You sent a civilian. Someone with no police training out on an investigation and you're only telling me now?' Barker exclaimed.

'Ma'am, as I explained, there's a lot going on with this case and the computer evidence is an important part of it. Unfortunately, my *Red Dead Redemption* Xbox skills are of no use here.'

'DCI Pellacia, please don't try to avoid the seriousness of what you did with poor humour. You'll need to give me a full report as to why Ezra accompanied Henley and how his experience is integral to the digital component of this case.'

'Of course, ma'am, and my apologies.'

Barker sighed. 'Honestly, as if I don't have enough on my plate, but back to your secondment proposal. Do you have anyone in mind or would you like HR to distribute a notice to the usual unit heads?'

Pellacia picked up the slim blue folder that was on top of his Fox-Carnell and Ashcroft case notes. 'In the past three months I've received five transfer requests. You're obviously privy to a lot more information about the applicants than I am, so I would appreciate your input.'

Barker drank her coffee as she flicked through the file. After a moment, she said, 'DC Xania Copeland. I can't say that I'm surprised to see her request.'

'She submitted her request an hour after the Ashcroft case was reallocated to the SCU and then she came to my office at 7.30 this morning and repeated her request in person,' said Pellacia.

'She's keen.'

'There's another word for it.'

'Let's hope that word is tenacious.'

'It wasn't tenacity. It was an attempt to ambush me.'

'She's ambitious, which in itself isn't a bad thing, but she tends to get ahead of herself and not necessarily respect the chain of command. I think her DCI's exact words were "She walks around like she owns the place".'

'She left that out of her transfer request,' Pellacia said drily.

'Can hardly blame her. Much better to put "I work well on my own but I'm also a team player" in your request,' Barker sniggered. 'A secondment wouldn't cost you or me a penny.'

'Are you saying that I should take her on?'

'No, that's not what I'm saying but, at first glance, Copeland has a head start on the applicants. She was the SIO on the Ashcroft case before it came to you. Did the secondment idea come from you or her?'

'It was all her,' Pellacia confirmed.

'The problem is that the SCU is no different to any other unit that's under my command. Some cases can be solved in a matter of days and others remain unsolved for years,' Barker said, disappointment coating her words. 'You can't attach a time limit to these things.'

Pellacia merely nodded.

'I feel that you would all benefit from the addition of someone clean – and by clean, I mean no associations with Rhimes.'

Pellacia sat straighter in his chair, the muscles in his jaw tensing as he gritted his teeth. He focused on adjusting the cuffs of his suit, to stop himself from saying the wrong thing in defence of himself. 'It feels as though you're suggesting that I can't control my unit,' he finally said.

'You know full well that you wouldn't be sitting here in my office discussing the future of the SCU if I thought that. Your success is my success.' Barker stood up, signalling that their meeting was drawing to a close. 'The SCU is a close-knit team. That obviously has its benefits, but it can also create its own set of complex issues. Hierarchical lines become blurred, and you can become your own fiefdom with your own set of rules like sending civilians out on operations, for example.'

'Ma'am, again, I apologise for that.'

'Apology accepted. Look, you've gone to hell and back with the SCU, both professionally and personally and that hasn't gone unnoticed by me, so I'm going to make sure that I have an answer for you about this secondment before the start of the night shift.' Pellacia felt as though he could finally breathe as he walked out of Lewisham police station. It wasn't until Barker had mentioned blurred lines that he'd realised how much the melding of his professional and personal lives was impacting him. Pellacia took out his phone and sent a message to Laura Halifax, his on and off again girlfriend. If he could finally define his relationship with Laura, then maybe he could finally close the door on his relationship with Henley and give 100 per cent to the SCU.

26

The body heat of fifty-two people had made the air in Courtroom Six leaden and stale. The judge and the barristers in counsel's row, weighted by their woollen robes and horsehair wigs, were uncomfortable and sweating but Nathan Hall, premier league footballer with sixteen caps for England, was not sweating. He'd thought very carefully about what he should wear for the last day of trial. No obvious designer labels. Nothing that would make him seem arrogant. In the end he'd settled on a soft navy Ralph Lauren suit and a crisp white shirt. No tie. He'd explained to the jury on Thursday that it had been a running joke in his family that he couldn't tie a tie. He'd then gone on to say that it would have been impossible for him to tie the men who'd accused him of rape to his bed because he didn't own any ties. He'd gratefully accepted the tissues from the court usher when he'd told the jury that he wasn't ashamed of being gay, but the world of football wasn't ready to have an openly gay footballer. He'd sat in the witness box and denied it all. No, he hadn't threatened the men. No, he hadn't held a knife to their throats and forced them into the bedroom. No, he didn't give them money to keep quiet. These men were his lovers and everything they'd done was consensual.

He'd thought that his lawyer's fees were daylight robbery,

but he had to admit that every penny had been worth it when he'd listened to his barrister's closing speech:

'The complainants – not victims but three complainants – orchestrated a plan to destroy Nathan Hall. They were complainants, complaining because Nathan Hall was not yet ready to make his private life public. Angry that Nathan Hall had decided not to give in to their demands for money to pay for their silence. Nathan Hall, a footballer who famously never received a yellow card in his professional career, a man who was hailed as a hero after he stopped a woman from being sexually assaulted in the street. Nathan Hall, a man held in high regard by his team, his family, the local school where he acted as a mentor to the students, is being targeted by the complainants because he was the one who had said no. Nathan Hall withdrew his consent to sex, to a relationship and to making his private life public.'

Fucking hell, Nathan thought to himself when his barrister sat down forty minutes later. *He's convinced me that I didn't do it.* He'd managed to cry when the judge had finished summing up the case to the jury. He'd even caught the eyes of the woman on the jury who he knew wanted him, and thought that she could change him, and the man on the front row who wanted to be him. *Look remorseful. Show pain. Show innocence. Show regret and remorse for putting your family, friends and the jury through this campaign to destroy an innocent man.*

Nathan took a deep breath and smiled apologetically at his mum in the public gallery as the judge handed a note to his clerk and then nodded at the usher, who quickly left the court through a side door. Nathan watched his mum gather herself as she mouthed 'I love you'. *The papers will love that*, he thought. His mum was a newspaper's dream, always available to deliver a soundbite about the persecution of her son. She'd ignored the truth when the men had given evidence. They'd all told the same story, about meeting Nathan on a dating app and being invited to his house for a good time. Yes, there had been drugs, and they'd agreed to have sex, but they'd all told Nathan to stop when he started to get rough, to strangle them, to tie them up. Nathan had heard the word 'no' loud and clear, but he didn't like it when people told him no.

The courtroom hummed as the door leading to the jury room opened and the usher stepped out. Seven women and five men followed and made their way to the seats they'd been occupying for six weeks, but something was different; Nathan could see it. The body language was off with three members of the jury. Juror number three, a black man, looked at Nathan as though he was a piece of shit floating in the toilet, juror number four, the white man next to him, kept his eyes to the floor as though he'd done something he was ashamed of and juror number eight, the white woman with the pixie cut who'd folded her arms and sighed impatiently every time his barrister had opened his mouth was scowling at the foreperson.

Nathan lowered his head as the clerk's voice crackled loudly through the speakers in the dock.

'Could the defendant please stand.'

Nathan did so as an icy hush descended. He raised his head. He wanted the court sketch artist to see him. To capture the anguish on his face.

The clerk turned towards the jury. 'Could the foreperson of the jury please stand.'

A light-skinned black man, who looked as though he'd just finished school, stood in the middle of the front row and unfolded a single sheet of paper.

'Count One. Have you reached a verdict on which you all agree?' asked the clerk.

'No.'

Nathan felt hope.

'Has the jury reached a verdict on which a majority of ten to two have agreed?'

'Yes.'

Nathan felt sick.

'Do you find the defendant guilty or not guilty of the rape of Michael Cannon?'

'Not Guilty.'

'Do you find the defendant guilty or not guilty of the false imprisonment of Michael Cannon?'

'Not guilty.'

Nathan felt as though he were swimming underwater as he listened to the clerk ask the same questions and receive the same answers four more times.

27

'You did good,' said Stanford as Ramouter entered the room and Eastwood stood up and gave a slow clap.

'Yes, Ramouter. Well done for being able to read from a script,' Eastwood teased.

'All words, no pictures. Like a proper grown up,' Ramouter replied. 'Has there been much of a response since the conference?'

'Response is an understatement,' said Henley from her desk. 'Jo hasn't been off the phone since the conference started. Unfortunately, the calls have been less than helpful. Nine times out of ten it's people calling to say they're glad Fox-Carnell is dead.'

'I can't say that I disagree with them.' Stanford picked up the notebook on his desk. 'I hated every single minute of that original investigation and was glad to see the back of her and now she's back on my bloody desk.'

'What made her case so bad?' asked Ramouter. 'It's not as if it was your first serial murder case.'

'But it was the first one with kids. Fox-Carnell was charged with two murders and two attempted murders, but we'd originally arrested her for eight murders. There were three more children. The youngest was six years old.'

'We all know she did it, but the CPS said the evidential test hadn't been met.' Henley's tone was bitter. She'd thought the passage of time would have subsided the anger, but it was still there, like lava in a dormant volcano.

'I can still remember Rhimes's reaction,' said Eastwood.

'I can still hear the sound of the glass breaking when Rhimes put his fist through the window in his office,' remembered Stanford.

Henley found herself drifting in and out of the conversation as she felt the full weight of carrying Rhimes's secrets. She knew telling the team was the right thing to do but the question was, what would it do to them? It could strengthen or fracture the SCU.

'We need to focus on the here and now,' said Henley. 'Fox-Carnell is our victim. Our case. Whether we like it or not. Stanford and Eastie, tell us how you got on with Durant and where he fits.'

'We can find no links or associations between Durant and Fox-Carnell,' said Eastwood as she jogged over to the smartboard with her laptop in hand.

'With the exception of a caution for threatening words and behaviour, he's as clean as a whistle,' added Stanford. 'Teaches economics at London South Bank University. Four kids, who I'm in the middle of checking out, and a crateful of kittens.'

'We asked him about his whereabouts last Sunday, when the Ashcrofts were attacked, and he says that he was home,' Eastwood continued.

'Any way to verify that?'

'Unless you're Doctor Dolittle and can talk to his cats, then no,' Stanford confirmed. 'He denied harassment and blackmail and then refused to answer any more questions without a lawyer.'

'So, we left.' Eastwood turned to the smartboard and switched it on. 'But the thing is, Durant lied to us when we asked him about his car. He said he sold his car, a 2012 Skoda Octavia, when his wife died. That was a lie.'

Eastwood tapped the screen, and a photograph of the car appeared. 'This is the car Durant said he no longer owned, and these are photographs of the damage to the windscreen and bumper.'

'It can't be a coincidence,' said Ramouter.

'It's impossible to say until we get forensics verified one way or the other,' said Eastwood. 'I also observed scratches to his hand and on the side of his face.'

'We need to get him in.' Henley walked over to the whiteboard and wrote 'suspect' and 'Laurence Durant' on the board. 'The only problem is that I don't want him sitting in an interview when we don't have anything evidential to put to him. Any half decent legal rep or solicitor will advise him to keep his mouth shut and accuse us of fishing and they'd be right.'

'I'm halfway through making an application for seizure,' said Eastwood. 'I should be done in an hour which means we could have the vehicle in our yard this evening if the application is granted.'

'Great. If we get a hit with the car then I'll be happy with our grounds for arrest.' Henley turned to Ramouter. 'Where are you with CCTV?'

'Progress was slow because Southwark Council decided to dump us with footage that we don't need. But it's going to seem less like looking for a needle in a haystack now I've got Durant's car details. I'm also waiting for the enhanced footage that we took from the neighbour to come back. I'll chase them up.'

Henley felt herself relax a bit. 'We seem to be making good progress. Ezra's currently going through the data we downloaded from Soteria. He's suggesting that a Soteria employee was responsible for the monitoring system being disabled.'

'Was Tabitha Ashcroft electronically monitored?' Eastwood asked.

'I don't know,' Ramouter answered. 'But I'll check the CRIS reports and see. If she was on tag and her address wasn't in the public domain then it would mean that Durant, if he is involved, was possibly in contact with a Soteria employee.'

'And that means that it's not just a murder and an attempted murder investigation but a conspiracy,' said Henley. 'We've got evidence that he lied about his car, blackmailed the Ashcrofts and he has what looks like defensive injuries. His prints and DNA were expunged from the database when he was NFA'd for threatening words and behaviour, so we need to get DNA swabs from Durant as soon as possible.'

'Are you suggesting that the third DNA profile recovered from the Ashcrofts' kitchen and on Graham Ashcroft's clothing could belong to Laurance Durant?' asked Ramouter.

'We've got no evidence to suggest that it doesn't.' Henley shrugged.

Henley breathed a sigh of relief. Not quite believing that she was leaving the SCU before 6 p.m.. Her plan had been to go home but Linh's text had put a stop to those plans. She checked her phone. She had four minutes until her Uber arrived.

'Nice to finally escape from here, isn't it?'

Henley looked up to see Pellacia making his way towards her. There was the distinct clink of glass bottles in the bag that he was carrying. Henley felt the familiar pinch of jealousy when she saw roses in Pellacia's other hand. She chastised herself.

'You shouldn't sneak up on people,' Henley said.

'Sorry, about that. What are you doing out here?' Pellacia asked.

'Waiting for a cab. I'm off to Linh's and I suspect alcohol will be involved.'

'I'd be surprised if it wasn't. Anyway, I'm glad I caught you. I wanted to talk to you about something. I had a meeting with Barker, about expanding the team.'

'Jo told me that Copeland was here this morning. Are you taking her on?'

'She's not the only option.'

'Do you want my thoughts on Copeland?' Henley asked.

Pellacia laughed. 'I can pretty much guess your thoughts.'

'You always could.'

Pellacia stepped towards her and placed his hand on her cheek.

'We don't talk anymore,' he said, removing his hand. 'I don't mean about work . . . I mean . . . you. I miss you.'

'We talk,' Henley said as a car approached the entrance. 'And we've spoken about this. We need to be better than this. This back and forth.'

Pellacia said nothing but glanced at the roses. 'I thought I knew exactly what I was doing earlier today. That I'd made the right decision.'

'My cab is here,' Henley said wearily.

Pellacia's expression was blank. 'Of course. Barker said she'll let me know by the end of play today whether the secondment will be Copeland or someone else. As soon as I know, you'll know.'

'Let's hope it's the right choice,' Henley said as she got into the cab.

The end of tourist season and the fact that parents had finally taken their exhausted children home after a day of half-term activities meant that Copeland was the only person sitting in the beer garden of the Gypsy Moth pub on a Monday evening. Ramouter paused for a second as he took another look at the WhatsApp message he'd received a few minutes earlier:

Michelle, 18.38

Mum is doing my head in! But your brother Dal has rescued us 😂 Eat proper food!

Ramouter felt guilt prickling his skin as he put his phone away and he saw Copeland waving him over.

He sat down opposite her. 'I'm so sorry I kept you waiting.'

'Don't worry about it.' Copeland picked up her glass of red wine and took a sip. 'Are you all right sitting outside? They've got heaters. It's just I've been cooped up in the office all afternoon and you know how it is.'

'No, it's fine. I've spent hours staring at CCTV footage since I came back from the press conference. It's good to be out.'

'How's it going? But before you answer, what are you drinking? First round is on me.'

'Thanks. A pint of Guinness.'

'Do you want anything to eat?' Copeland asked, picking up the menu.

'Oh, I'm not really—'

'Oh, bollocks. You probably have to get home to your—' she asked hesitantly.

'Wife,' Ramouter said. 'She's actually away with my son. It's half term and she took him up to Bradford. They'll be back on Friday.'

'She won't mind you being out with another woman?'

Ramouter felt as though a vice had gripped his stomach as it dawned on him that Copeland's invitation for after work drinks may not be innocent.

'Oh my god! Your face,' Copeland laughed. She reached out and touched Ramouter's arm. 'I'm so sorry. This is what happens when you grow up with a football team's worth of brothers. I have extremely poor taste in jokes, and I don't know how to read the room.'

'It's fine,' Ramouter relaxed. 'It's been a long day and, if I'm honest, it's probably just a bit of guilt. The only women I've gone to drinks with are Henley, DC Eastwood and Joanna.'

'Doesn't your wife like you being out with people she doesn't know?'

'No. Michelle – that's my wife's – she's . . .'

'Can she be a bit clingy? My ex-husband was like that.'

'Clingy? No. It's not like that. She's—'

Ramouter picked up the menu. Not feeling comfortable with talking about his wife's condition with this woman he'd just met.

'Sorry. I did it again. Not reading the room,' Copeland said sincerely. 'I need to be better with words. Let me get your drink.'

'Are you going to tell me why you were at the SCU this morning?' Ramouter asked when she returned, keen to keep conversation away from his family.

Copeland ran her finger along the stem of her wine glass and smiled. 'I thought I would take the initiative and ask your guvnor in person if I could transfer to the SCU. This case – the Ashcrofts – it's got under my skin. Do you know what I mean?'

'You're invested,' Ramouter nodded.

'Exactly. I'm not saying I want to take it back, but I want to be a part of it.'

'What did he say. Pellacia?'

'He wasn't exactly jumping up and down with enthusiasm about me joining the team.'

Ramouter laughed sardonically. 'You'll find that jumping up and down is not in his nature.'

'Yeah, I gathered that, and I don't think I helped my case by turning up out of the blue this morning.'

'I think he'll respect you for it. He and the boss, Henley, I mean. They value people who don't necessarily wait for things to happen.'

'Sounds as though they're a package deal,' said Copeland. She stretched her leg and brushed against Ramouter's calf. 'Do you think I should have a word with Henley?'

'I don't think that would be a good idea. She values independence but I don't think she'd like to be ambushed.'

'Ah, that makes sense,' Copeland said as she bit her lip. 'I thought she was a bit off with me at the hospital on Saturday.'

'Not off, just surprised, maybe.'

'Ok, I'll try not to take it personally. So how long have you been with the SCU?'

'Just over a year, but sometimes it feels as though I've been there forever.'

'Was it hard to join the team?'

Ramouter took another sip of his Guinness as he thought back to the night before his first day at the SCU. He'd agonised over the decision of leaving his wife and child in Bradford whilst trying to settle his nerves about joining one of the most specialist units in the Metropolitan Police Force. He hadn't been at the station for thirty minutes when DCI Pellacia had told him that the SCU had a case and that he was to meet DI Henley in Deptford. Ramouter had assured Pellacia that he wouldn't get lost. That was a lie. He'd got lost twice and hadn't been prepared to see dismembered body parts on his first day on the job.

'Let's just say that I was definitely thrown into the deep end,' Ramouter finally said.

'Any regrets?'

'About joining the SCU?'

'Yeah. It couldn't have been easy leaving . . . where are you from again?'

'Bradford.'

'That's it. I came down here from Newport in Wales when I was twenty-one. Big lights, big city sort of thing and following my older sister.'

'Ah, I thought I heard an accent.'

'It only really comes out when I'm tired, angry or when I'm back—'Copeland stopped as her phone began to vibrate on the table. 'No Caller ID,' she sighed with annoyance. 'I bet it's the CPS calling with a charging decision. I told them I was off duty . . . you know what, never mind. I'll be back in a sec.'

Ramouter looked at Copeland's empty wine glass and wondered if being out with her was innocent. Michelle had always told him that it was a miracle they'd even had a first date, let alone got married, because he was so useless at noticing when someone was interested in him. It had taken Ramouter three years before he'd realised that Michelle wanted out of the friendzone.

Copeland reappeared five minutes later.

'Shall I get another round in?' Ramouter asked.

'Most definitely. We need to celebrate.'

'Why's that?'

'That was your guvnor, well I suppose my guvnor now – Pellacia. I'm in. The borough commander confirmed it. I'm transferring to the SCU.'

28

'Does this look like a small glass to you?' Henley asked, shaking her head at the wine glass that Linh had handed her.

'Did you really expect anything less,' said Linh as she filled her own glass.

'I would be a fool to expect anything less,' Henley conceded. 'It's a good thing I'm not driving. I'll definitely be over the limit after drinking one of your measures.'

'How about I feed you? I was at my parents' yesterday for Sunday dinner and mum gave me loads of food.'

'How is your mum?' Henley asked, knowing that Linh's relationship with her mother was dysfunctional at best.

'A complete pain in my arse as per usual, but back to you. You look like shit Anj.'

'That's because I hardly slept.'

'Did Rob keep you up by trying to get his leg over.'

'Shut up, Linh.'

'You are so miserable.'

'The point is, I couldn't sleep,' said Henley, taking a long drink of the Pinot Noir. 'I can't stop thinking about Rhimes and every time I closed my eyes, I kept seeing Fox-Carnell hanging over the pier. I then made the mistake of going on YouTube and watching these idiots who think they're detectives and their ludicrous conspiracy theories.'

'Your first mistake was going online.' Linh pulled out her iPad.

'So, let's cut to the chase and then we can spend the rest of the evening talking about our mummy issues and the rubbish men in our lives. You ready?'

Henley felt that she was anything but ready. She gripped the stem of her wine glass as nervous energy travelled through her arm. All she wanted was for Linh to tell her that Ezra was wrong.

Linh carried on regardless. 'The post-mortem report that Ezra found is not the same one that was included in the case file that was opened when Rhimes's death was being investigated. The official cause of death as we know was carbon monoxide poisoning as a result of him gassing himself in his garage.'

Henley was never usually bothered by Linh's blunt approach but this time it hit a nerve. She was brought back to the moment when she'd received the phone call from Rhimes's son, Nicholas. She'd arrived at the house at the same time as the ambulance in the early hours, the toxic fumes still hanging thick in the air.

'When you look here at the death certificate, the cause of death is the same.' Linh continued to swipe the screen. 'I thought that Ezra had simply made a mistake, put in the wrong date of birth and got a post-mortem report for someone else but something didn't sit right with me when I was looking at the report in the case file. In my experience, whenever I've had someone on my table whose gassed themselves, they usually have a cocktail of drugs or alcohol in their system, but Rhimes had nothing. Not a thing.'

'That can't be right. He was on anti-depressants but not even that, the night before, we'd all been in the pub, and he'd definitely been drinking.'

'The official toxicology screening on file was clean. No anti-depressants, no alcohol. Not even an aspirin,' said Linh. 'I called Ezra and asked him where exactly he'd found this second post-mortem report. Bless him, he tried to explain it to me, but I got confused. In simple terms Ezra found the report deep in the equivalent of the bin within an archive file. He said that it'd been deleted but—'

'Ezra says that nothing is really deleted.' Henley gulped down her wine.

'He's not wrong here. Long story short, I pulled the same report and found the addendum files. Name, date of birth, weight, height. Basically, everything matches but the report that Ezra found pre-dates the report that was filed. Take a look at this,' said Linh, zooming in on the conclusion on the report.

'Death by asphyxiation,' Henley read. 'I don't understand the problem.'

'The question is why is it "Death" and not "suicide by asphyxiation"? Furthermore—' Linh paused as she looked up at Henley, the tone in her voice become gentler. 'I'm going to show you some photographs. Don't worry, they're not the full autopsy photo.'

Henley tried to steel herself, but nausea swept through her as Rhimes's face, fixed forever in death, filled the screen. She took a breath and focused on what she did best. Compartmentalise. 'What am I looking at?' she asked.

'His neck.'

Henley saw it before Linh could explain it. Purple bruising, half an inch in width around the circumference of Rhimes's neck. Ligature marks.

'The report details vagal inhibition, fracture dislocation of the cervical vertebrae, hypoxia, bleeding in the neck muscles and a tracheal rupture,' said Linh. 'Which is what you expect for a strangulation.'

'They found him in the back seat of his car,' Henley said quietly.

'A first-year medical student could tell you it would have been impossible for him to do this himself,' said Linh.

Henley could feel her resolve and calm collapse within her as she took the iPad from Linh and recalibrated the photograph so that she was looking at Rhimes's face. 'Who signed off on this?' she asked.

'Doctor Heath Wright. I've never heard of him but that's not unusual. It's not as if every pathologist in London meets up for Taco Tuesday, but I checked him out.' Linh faced Henley, her faced fixed with concern.

'I'm wondering if it would be a good idea to talk to him,' said Henley still looking at the iPad.

'Good luck with that,' Linh replied 'You can visit him, but you better take flowers.'

'What do you mean?' Henley said, trying to process all of the information.

'He's in Mortlake Cemetery. Knocked off his bike in Elephant and Castle. Make of that what you will but there are other questions. Doctor Wright was based at Haringey Mortuary. But Rhimes died in Lee which is Lewisham Council, which means his body should have gone to the mortuary in Ladywell or Greenwich. Why was his post-mortem performed all the way in Haringey? It doesn't make sense.'

'There's only one thing that does make sense,' said Henley, opening the door that led to the back garden. Her head was swimming, and she needed air. She raised her head and inhaled deeply. 'Rhimes was murdered and someone covered it up.'

'Have you spoken to anyone else about this yet? Pellacia, Stanford. Your husband?'

'No.' Henley shook her head. 'Just you and Ezra.'

'The way I see it, you've got two choices.' Linh joined Henley at the door and placed her arm around her. 'You forget everything that you asked me and Ezra to do and what you learnt, and you walk away.'

Henley wiped her eye and pushed away the tear that had been threatening to fall. 'But I made a promise to Eloise.'

'Then that leaves you with the second choice.'

Henley couldn't handle the wave of emotions crashing over her. It felt as though she was losing Rhimes all over again, but now the grief was also accompanied with guilt. She'd been angry with Rhimes for not just taking his life but abandoning his family. Trying to pick up the pieces after his death, whilst also dealing with the death of her mum had felt like walking barefooted in the rain on broken glass while holding a live wire. She drained the rest of her wine as the image of the ligature marks on Rhimes's neck flashed in front of her eyes. The guilt quickly gave way to a fury and a determination to uncover the truth. She owed Rhimes and Eloise that.

'You've made a decision, haven't you?' asked Linh, topping up Henley's glass.

'I'll be careful,' said Henley.

'You'll have to do more than that,' said Linh. 'Remember there's nothing stopping whoever killed Rhimes from coming after you next.'

29

@Shep9783
Disgusting verdict. Where's the support for the victims? No justice in this country.

@CY_Belle
Not guilty doesn't mean that you're innocent. It just means that the prosecution couldn't prove it. HE DID IT!

@phil87
to @NathanHallOfficial - you're a dirty rapist!

@JA.fanzine
Dirty player. Dirty rapist. Cancelling my season ticket if they re-sign him. 38,120 have signed my petition. Click the link to sign. Petition.Com - Do not re-sign Nathan Hall.

@Dan-PTExeter
to @NathanHallOfficial - Hope someone takes your knees out.

'Fucking cunts!' Nathan shouted. He threw his phone across the room and watched it land on the armchair on the other side of the room. The acquittal this afternoon and his impassioned speech on the steps of Southwark Crown Court, where he'd thanked the jury and his family for their support had fallen on deaf ears. His appeal that victims of sexual assault should always be heard, and that justice should run its course had done nothing to quell the shouts of rapist that filled the air. He couldn't see how he was going to get his life back. He'd sat in the back of the car, listening to his agent fob him off when he'd asked when talks would resume about his transfer to Valencia CF. It was all well and good to be paid £75,000 per week to sit at home but he needed to be on the pitch and not – as he was currently doing – playing FIFA. He needed to play real football even it meant listening to the supporters in the stands baying for his blood.

The doorbell rang sharply and echoed around the house that he'd rented to escape the so-called activists who'd doxxed his home. Nathan pulled himself up from the sofa, crossed the room and picked up his phone. A notification confirmed that his kebab order was at the gate. Nathan opened the security app and unlocked the main gate, and headed to the front door.

He opened it and stood confused. There was no one there or making their way along the drive from the gate. He opened the security app and checked the last recording. Two minutes ago, the delivery person had been at his gate. He stepped onto the doorstep and looked out onto the driveway that was softly illuminated by the solar lamps. He could see nothing, but he could hear someone breathing.

The blows to his legs came in quick succession. First his right knee and then his left shin. The bones in his legs disintegrated like broken eggshells.

Through his piercing screams, Nathan could hear a man's voice, his words fractured but clearly angry.

Nathan tried to turn onto his front to crawl back into the house, but every movement sent shards of bone deeper into the damaged tissue and muscle of his leg.

'Not such the big man now,' the man said as Nathan lay on his back, weeping, his breathing laboured. Resigned to his fate. He tried to raise his head to look down and see the damage, but his vision was blocked by the forged steel head of a sledgehammer.

'Help me bring the dirty fucker in,' the man muttered.

Nathan weakly pulled his right arm to his chest to protect himself, hearing the steel head of the hammer being dragged along the tiles. He cried out in pain when a pair of strong hands grabbed his arms and dragged him back.

30

Henley stood in front of her mirror and watched her naked body as she massaged cocoa butter into her stomach. She closed her eyes as her fingers ran along the scar that had been left behind by a killer's knife, but it didn't make a difference. The scar was etched in her mind. Half an inch of smooth, discoloured skin that morphed into an inch of raised, staggered, dark and thick skin where the scar tissue had grown excessively. There were times when the scar itched sending her a message that Peter Olivier would always be with her.

'I'm ok,' Henley whispered to herself as she fell back onto the bed. She closed her eyes and concentrated on her breathing. Her attempted meditation was interrupted by her phone signalling the arrival of a message. She sat up and stared at the screen. It was Eloise. The message preview was innocent enough: 'Morning Anjelica', but she knew that the rest of the message would contain questions she wasn't ready to answer.

Rob entered the bedroom and placed a cup of coffee on the bedside table. 'Everything all right?'

'Everything is fine.' Henley reached for her bra and put it on.

'You need an outlet.' Rob sat down next to Henley and untwisted her bra strap.

'It's quarter past seven. We've got to get Emma ready and take her to my dad.'

'I wasn't talking about sex,' said Rob. 'Not that it wouldn't be a bad thing. I mean you need something outside of us.'

Henley faced Rob, her eyes narrowed, and asked, 'What do you mean, "Outside of us"?'

Rob saw her reaction and laughed softly. 'I'm talking about self-care, not an open marriage. I have running and mountain biking with the boys.'

'The same mountain biking where you end up at the pub, have a skinful and then spend Sunday morning nursing a hangover?'

'The point is that I have something to channel my frustrations into.'

'I'm not going running. I hate running.'

'Find something else then. Tennis. Swimming. You used to do kickboxing once upon a time.'

'Back when I was twenty-one. But, also, where am I going to find the time?'

'Just think about it.'

Henley's phone began to ring, Rob picked it up. His mouth twisted slightly as though he'd tasted something bitter and he handed it over.

'I'll get Emma ready,' he said and left their bedroom.

Rob's demeanour made sense when Henley saw who was calling.

'Are you still at home?' asked Pellacia.

'Yes,' said Henley. She got up and opened her wardrobe. 'Why, what's going on?'

'Nathan Hall,' Pellacia said with clear disbelief. 'He hasn't been formally identified but—'

'Nathan Hall, the footballer?' Henley's brain kicked into gear. 'Didn't he—'

Henley stopped as Emma ran into the bedroom, followed by Rob.

'Come on, chipmunk. This isn't the time for games,' Rob told her. Emma squealed with delight as Rob picked her up, held her aloft in the air and left.

'Sorry about that,' said Henley.

'It's fine,' answered Pellacia. 'I'm sending you the details. Ramouter will meet you at the address.'

'Can you say why the SCU?' Henley asked.

She couldn't see him, but she knew what Pellacia was doing: closing his eyes whilst he massaged his forehead.

'Head injuries . . . that look like a scalping.'

'Morning,' Henley greeted Ramouter as they both put on their protective clothing and gloves.

Haverstock Road in Beckenham was flanked by large, detached houses barred from public view by high brick walls and black security gates. The occupants – from hedge fund managers to social media influencers – had woken up to find their peace disturbed by police sirens.

'I've got some updates,' she continued. 'We got confirmation from the property management company that the house was rented by Nathan Hall.'

'Shit. He got acquitted yesterday,' said Ramouter.

'Yes, he did, and the majority of social media are not very happy about that.'

'Who found the body?'

'Odette Pinto. The housekeeper employed by the property management company.'

Gravel crunched under their feet as they passed a brand-new black Mercedes G-class and a blue McLaren 570S parked side by side.

'Where's the housekeeper now?' Ramouter asked.

'No idea. The call handler told her to wait for the police but when they arrived, she'd gone. Whatever she found must have scared the shit out of her. We've got a couple of officers looking for her.'

Ramouter and Henley stopped by a torn white plastic bag and food container on the floor. Pieces of kebab meat, chips, browning salad and a half-eaten pitta bread were scattered on the ground.

'Looks like foxes got to it,' commented Ramouter.

'I didn't notice any damage on the gate,' said Henley. 'Hall – if it's definitely him inside that house – must have let his attacker in. The attacker was someone he knew, or the attacker possibly intercepted the delivery person.'

'Reminds me of the Ashcroft crime scene. Violence outside and inside the house.' Ramouter pointed at the yellow marker on the doorstep.

Henley looked at the blood staining the pale sandstone doorstep. A Rolex watch, the face cracked, and bracelet links broken, was on the doorstep next to a dying olive tree.

'We need to check if there were any reports of a disturbance last night. An attack like this, I would be surprised if someone didn't hear something,' said Henley. She stepped around the blood and entered the house. Bloodied footprints tracked in and out of the house. Henley could feel the heavy weight of death as she breathed in the nauseating combined odours of metallic-spilled blood, human faeces and urine. The dull sound of a mobile phone ringing in a room somewhere on the ground floor, the rhythmic beep of the dying battery of a smoke alarm and Ramouter talking on his police radio, penetrated the silence. Henley followed the bloody footprints that faded as they progressed up the cream and black bordered runner on the staircase. She could feel Ramouter's presence at her side as they both stared at the man hanging from the twisted polished chrome balusters of the staircase.

'Is that him?' Ramouter asked. 'I can't tell. His face.'

The man had been hanged from near the top of the staircase. A thick, tight knot connected two navy ties together. The end of the first tie had been secured tightly around the bottom of the third highest baluster. The second tie was around his neck. His eyes bulged out and his tongue hung out of the side of his mouth. His face and naked torso were bloodied, bruised and swollen. His dark blond hair was stained with blood. His legs were uneven and disjointed. Broken bone piercing through the material of the tracksuit bottoms. Henley had no idea whether she was looking at Nathan Hall or not but there was no question that she was adding another victim to her whiteboard.

Henley watched the housekeeper, Odette Pinto's, quivering fingers tap a cup of overly sweet tea on the table. An officer had located her in a small café on Kelsey Park Road. The owner had called the police after Odette walked into the café with blood on her hands and trainers. 'I thought she was hurt or that she'd hurt someone,' he'd said. Two officers stood guard outside the café where the only people seated were Henley, Ramouter and Odette.

'I can't believe that Mr Hall is dead,' Odette said, her Portuguese accent made her words sound more mournful.

'It hasn't been confirmed that the body you found is Nathan Hall,' Henley told her gently although she knew it was only a matter of time before his identity would be confirmed.

'Who else could it be?' Odette replied.

'What time did you arrive at the address?' Henley asked.

'7 a.m.. That's the time I always arrive except on the weekend. I don't work then. Mr Hall is always awake when I arrive, and he makes me a cup of coffee. He is a very nice man.' Odette picked up a napkin and wiped her eyes. 'I didn't believe the things that they were saying about him.'

'And how did you get in?'

'I have a code for the gate and a key for the house. But I should have known that something was wrong because the front door was open when I arrived, and Mr Hall never did that. He was careful. Always careful.'

'Did you notice anyone hanging around outside before you entered the house?' asked Ramouter.

Odette leaned forward as tears continued to stream down her face. 'A couple of cars drove past and a young man, he had a rucksack and was on a bike. Not a cycle, but not a *motocicleta*, the other one, a small one.'

'A moped?' Ramouter guessed.

'*Si*, a ciclomotor. He was outside but that was it.'

'And what about when you went into the house?' asked Henley.

'I knew something was wrong,' Odette said softly. 'As soon as I walked in . . . it was quiet. Mr Hall always had the sport station playing on the radio and there was no smell of coffee. It was too quiet except for that stupid smoke alarm. And then I saw him, hanging there.'

'You didn't notice the blood on the floor outside and on the floor?' Ramouter asked.

'I didn't realise that I'd even stepped in the . . . no, I didn't know. I just saw Mr Hall.'

'Did you go further into the house. Upstairs? Look around or—'

'No. No. I went in, saw . . . saw him and I ran out. You can check the cameras.'

'Cameras. What cameras?' Ramouter asked, looking at Henley. They were both thinking the same thing. That they hadn't noticed any CCTV cameras outside the house or even a video doorbell. 'Are there cameras inside the house?'

'Not inside, but outside. You can hardly see it, but Mr Hall showed it to me, it's in the wall but it wasn't working properly but there's another one in the keypad on the front gate. Sometimes Mr Hall would see me and open the gate before I'd even put in the code.'

'You said the front door was open when you arrived this morning, but what about the gate?' Henley asked.

'It was locked,' said Odette.

'You need to call Ezra,' Henley told Ramouter as the police officers escorted Odette out of the café. 'If the camera caught Odette going in, then it would have caught whoever Nathan Hall let in last night.'

31

Stanford stood in front of Eastwood's desk searching for a clear space to place the cup of tea that he was holding. 'Hello. Earth to DS Eastwood,' he said loudly.

Eastwood looked up from her computer screen. 'Why are you shouting at me?' she asked.

'I thought you might have been one of those people who literally drop dead at their desk.'

'Not dead, just deep in thought about Fox-Carnell,' she said, taking the tea from Stanford's hand.

'Thinking that there won't be many people who will mourn her, but that there will be a lot of people saying she got what she deserved?' Stanford pulled up a chair and sat down.

'Last week, before Fox-Carnell turned up on our active cases pile, the guv asked me to go through all the applications that we've received from the other forces to see if any of them qualified as serial cases,' Eastwood continued. 'The majority of them were just other departments looking for an excuse to reduce their caseload but Sussex, Cleveland, West Midlands and Greater Manchester have all had a run of vigilante cases.'

'Vigilante. Like Batman?' Stanford sniggered.

Eastwood pursed her lips and fixed Stanford with a stare.

'Jesus Christ, it was just a joke.'

'No one has ever told you that you're funny,' Eastwood snapped. 'The point is, I went down a rabbit hole with these cases. A lot of them were just your usual gangs of disgruntled dads hunting down and entrapping suspected paedophiles and grooming gangs. Sometimes they were bang on the money and there were successful arrests but more often than not, they targeted the wrong person or completely fucked up ongoing investigations.'

'Fox-Carnell and Tabitha Ashcroft were neither paedophiles nor in a grooming gang. Fox-Carnell just had a penchant for knocking off her patients.'

'But someone targeted her, Ashcroft and – from the looks of things – Nathan Hall. My point is that all three have something in common.'

'The court verdicts,' said Stanford.

Eastwood handed Stanford a printout. 'February 2019, a man called Douglas Mantell was reported missing,' said Eastwood. 'He was last seen at a pub in Fairfield, Manchester. Two and a half months after his disappearance Mantell's body was found in the Ashton Canal.'

'Drunk man falls into canal. What's that got to do with us?' Stanford asked as the office door opened and Henley and Ramouter walked in.

'Post-mortem report concluded that Mantell died from multiple stab wounds so Greater Manchester Police's investigation went from a missing person to a murder. One that had no further leads until—' Eastwood raised her wrist and checked her watch, 'ninety-five minutes ago, when you were still in bed.'

'What did you find, or shall I just call the boss over and you can do a big reveal?' Stanford folded his arms.

'Call her over,' said Eastwood.

'Douglas Mantell was acquitted of historical sexual offences on the day he went missing,' Eastwood told them.

Henley stepped back and took in the full body photograph of Mantell's waterlogged and slightly decomposing body on an examination table like a macabre museum exhibit. 'Who was he alleged to have sexually assaulted?' she asked.

'His daughter,' Eastwood replied.

Ramouter tutted loudly with disgust.

'How long was he in the canal for?' Henley asked

'Nearly three months but it was a record-breaking winter when Mantell disappeared. Temperatures dropped to −8°C, the canal was frozen over and he was basically entombed in ice. Post-mortem details multiple stab wounds but more importantly for us a 2.36 inch by 1.37 inch wound on his head.' The image of the back of Mantell's head filled the screen, the wound visible in the middle of his scalp. 'Pathologist concluded that the wound was caused by a knife, but that's not all.' Eastwood tapped the board several times. 'I found another case.'

A custody photograph of an Asian woman in her fifties filled the screen. The harsh, unflattering light brought out the anger in the woman's eyes, her mouth fixed in a thin, unamused line.

'This is Gong Bo Hyoo,' said Eastwood. 'Murdered in September 2019. Her throat had been cut, and she was found in an alleyway in Sheffield.'

'Sheffield?' repeated Ramouter. 'First Manchester, now Sheffield. What have we got? A travelling salesman of a killer?'

'Not quite,' said Eastwood. 'Two weeks before her murder, Gong Bo Hyoo had been acquitted of attempted murder and fraud.'

'Who did she attempt to kill?' asked Stanford.

'According to the CRIS reports, a friend, Cynthia Onslo who was seventy-five years old and lived in Ancoats in Manchester.'

'Ah, Manchester. Maybe not a travelling killer. So how did she try to kill her?' asked Ramouter.

'Pushed her down the stairs and the fraud was faking her will so that she would inherit her house. Hyoo denied both charges and had a trial. Technically she had two trials, both at Manchester Crown Court.'

'The same court as Mantell,' pointed out Stanford.

'Hyoo had moved back to Sheffield because she'd been evicted from her flat in Ancoats,' Eastwood said as she flicked through the crime scene photographs. 'The jury couldn't reach a verdict in the first trial in May 2019 or the retrial. The prosecution decided that the third time wouldn't be the charm after two hung juries and threw in the towel. Two weeks later, Hyoo is dead. In addition to the cut throat, she also has a large wound on her scalp.'

Henley sat on the desk nearby as the photograph of Hyoo's upper back filled the screen. Her skin was discoloured and covered with raised scars. The wound on her scalp was raw and vicious.

'So many similarities and yet no one on the murder teams saw a link?' Henley was angry. 'How in this day and age and the fact that we have HOLMES, is that possible?'

'It shouldn't be possible,' said Eastwood. 'But someone wasn't paying attention. I only found them because I was paying attention.'

'None of this is a coincidence.'

The door opened and Pellacia walked in with DC Copeland by his side. Henley paused and watched the pair as Pellacia directed Copeland to sit at an empty desk. Henley picked up a marker and walked to the whiteboard. She added Douglas Mantell and Gong Bo Hyoo's names and the dates they went missing to the board. 'Both walked free, both scalped. Just like Fox-Carnell.' she tapped Sian's name on the board. 'Tabitha Ashcroft the same but the only reason why her name isn't in red is because her husband intervened.'

'And now we have Nathan Hall,' added Ramouter.

'Is that confirmed?' asked Pellacia as Copeland picked up an unused notepad from the desk and began to make notes.

'His DNA and prints were already on the database because of his recent arrests and charges of rape. Anthony confirmed an hour ago that there was a match. We've sent officers round to inform his next of kin.'

'Where are we on cause of death?' Copeland asked.

'And who are you exactly?' asked Stanford.

'I was going to wait until Henley had finished,' said Pellacia. 'But this is DC Xania Copeland from Lewisham CID.'

'You're the one who palmed the case onto us,' Stanford stated.

'DC Copeland is joining the SCU on secondment to help with this case,' Pellacia explained.

'I'm looking forward to being part of the team,' said Copeland.

'Ramouter, carry on,' Pellacia instructed.

'We won't have an answer about cause of death until earliest later this evening or first thing tomorrow morning,' said Ramouter. 'But Dr Choi—'

'Based at Greenwich mortuary,' Copeland interrupted as she nodded to herself. 'I've met her before.'

'Right,' said Ramouter, catching the look of disapproval in Henley's eyes, knowing she wasn't impressed with interruptions. 'Dr Choi has given a time of death of between 10.30 p.m. last night and midnight, but we think that it's closer to 10.30 p.m.. There was a kebab takeaway – well, the leftovers after the foxes got their way with it – all over the driveway. The restaurant's logo was on the bag. They received the order at 10.02 p.m., it was picked up at 10.13 p.m. by Uber Eats and delivery was confirmed at 10.31 p.m.. We spoke to the courier, who said that he met the owner outside the gate, and handed over the order.'

'Just like that,' said Copeland. 'Don't you usually have to give a code before you get your order?'

'Not always and, in this instance, the courier didn't ask for one,' Henley said bluntly. 'CSI also found Nathan Hall's mobile phone in the hallway. We'll get it to Ezra once they're done with it. Hopefully he'll be able to retrieve security footage.'

'Sorry to jump around but I've got a question about Tabitha

Ashcroft,' said Stanford. 'You can call me a pessimist, but I'd be surprised if whoever attacked her wasn't determined to finish the job. I'm just thinking of Fox-Carnell.'

'Why is Fox-Carnell relevant?' Copeland asked as she turned and faced Stanford.

'She's dead, isn't she?' Stanford said sarcastically. 'I'm thinking that Tabitha and Graham Ashcroft could be at risk. Where are they now?'

'Graham Ashcroft is still at King's,' answered Henley. 'But I need to check when Tabitha—'

'Tabitha discharged herself from King's yesterday afternoon,' Copeland interrupted. 'I told her to stay but she was adamant that she wanted to leave. Her parents picked her up and she's staying with them in Margate.'

Henley folded her arms and turned to face Copeland. 'You spoke to the Ashcrofts even though until five minutes ago you weren't on this case?' The iron in her voice was impossible to ignore.

'It wasn't like that. Tabitha already has a relationship with me, and she—'

'Stop,' Henley said, holding up her hand and inwardly counting to ten to quell her frustration with Copeland stepping out of bounds. She turned her back and faced Pellacia. 'What can we do about getting Tabitha Ashcroft some form of protection?' she asked.

'I'll speak to Kent police and also the NCA if she's moved to Margate, but you know how it works, they won't provide as much as a panic alarm unless Tabitha Ashcroft agrees to co-operate,' Pellacia pointed out.

'I think that we may have some difficulty with that,' said Ramouter. 'The Ashcrofts are refusing to sign their witness statements.'

'Even though they told us what happened to them?' asked Pellacia.

Ramouter nodded. 'We had to really push for them to do that.'

'I can talk to Tabitha,' said Copeland. 'Convince her that we can—'

'Ramouter will speak to the Ashcrofts,' Henley cut in. 'Make sure that you pass on the Margate details to him. Let's move on. The vigilante angle?'

'I think that it may be more than one person. This is the problem with these people – these vigilante groups. They do more harm than good,' said Eastwood.

'That's not strictly true,' DC Copeland jumped in. 'Some of these vigilante groups have been successful in stopping men grooming young people and attempting to commit sexual offences. Their actions have resulted in successful criminal prosecution.'

'Pretending to be a fourteen-year-old kid and arranging to meet a disgusting pervert is a lot different to dragging people off the street, pumping them full of fentanyl and hanging them over the river,' said Eastwood coldly.

'DC Eastwood, I wasn't sa—'

'It's DS,' said Eastwood.

'I'm sorry, DS Eastwood,' Copeland said warmly. 'I don't agree with the idea of vigilantism, but we can't ignore that their actions have been helpful. Of course, that's not the case here.'

'That's an understatement,' Eastwood bit back.

'Let's get back to the case,' Henley said, joining Eastwood at the front in a show of solidarity. 'Unless Eastwood has discovered any other cases preceding Mantell or anything between Hyoo's murder and the Ashcrofts' attack?'

'None with the distinctive MO of the scalping,' Eastwood confirmed.

'But that's not to say there may not have been any attempts,' Ramouter added. 'Tabitha Ashcroft got away but only because her husband was home. What if she wasn't the only one?'

Eastwood sighed as she reached for her notebook. 'You're right. I'll take a look.'

'I'll take London, and you take Manchester,' offered Stanford supportively.

'That's great,' said Henley. 'We also can't dismiss the family and friends of Fox-Carnell's victims and the men who accused Nathan Hall of rape. Where are we with Laurence Durant?'

'His car was seized last night but I don't think CSI have got round to examining it yet. I'd rather not drag him into an interview until I've got something solid to put to him,' answered Stanford.

'I agree.' Henley took her phone out. 'I'll text Anthony and ask him if he can pull some strings to get us higher up the priority list. Right, let's go back to the location of these attacks. There has to be a good reason why the attacks started in Manchester and then migrated to London.'

'The London cases start with Tabitha Ashcroft but why her? It wasn't as though the case made national news,' said Ramouter.

'Liverpool, Sheffield, Leeds. All three are big cities and at least forty miles from Manchester. Depending on the traffic it would take you no more than ninety minutes to get there,' said Copeland. 'But to come to London, that's a ten-hour round trip. I think maybe our vigilantes had a specific reason to be here that had nothing to do with the Ashcrofts or even Nathan Hall.'

The image of Henley's husband Rob, booking his train tickets to Manchester Piccadilly popped in her head. 'Work,' she said. 'If Stanford and Eastwood don't find any more similar cases in North-West England then I'm thinking that whoever we're dealing with may have moved down to London for work.'

'That's a bit of stretch,' said Pellacia.

'I don't think that it's a stretch at all,' said Henley. 'They could have moved down here for work or followed a partner who has moved for work. If Eastwood and Stanford don't find any more cases north of the M25 then I think it's safe to assume that whoever is responsible has set up base in London.'

'Fair enough,' Pellacia conceded as he shuffled in his seat. 'How about the elephant in the room? The scalping.'

Henley brought up the photographs of the injuries on each of the victims onto the smartboard.

'Oh god,' Copeland said, putting her hand to her mouth. 'That's horrific. I had no idea.'

'No, you wouldn't,' Henley replied. She picked up a marker and added Nathan Hall to the victim board. 'Obviously we need to see the full investigation file for Mantell and Hyoo.'

'Five victims,' said Pellacia.

'Five *targeted* victims. I'm not including Graham Ashcroft. He wasn't a target. He just got in the way.' Henley paused. 'I think we need to bring Mark on board.'

'Who's Mark?' Copeland asked as Pellacia shook his head no.

'Mark is a criminal profiler,' Stanford intoned monotonously.

'Dr Mark Ryan is a forensic psychologist and a consultant for the SCU,' Henley said sternly. 'We need him to explain the motivation behind the scalping. It's extreme and I've never seen anything like it before.'

'Forensic psychologist, criminal behaviour analyst. Whatever you want to call him, it's all a bit woowoo. You don't need a degree to tell you why a madman is killing people,' Stanford gave his well-rehearsed speech.

'We've used him on a number of cases where the case circumstances and the MO were unique,' Henley explained.

'We won't be using him on this one,' said Pellacia. 'We can't afford him.'

'I'll call in a favour. He'll do it for me,' Henley said.

Ezra walked into the room with a smile on his face. Henley quickly tapped the screen and turned it blank.

'I have— you're new?' Ezra asked, pointing his laptop in Copeland's direction.

'I'll explain later. What is it?' Henley asked.

'The phone company finally came through with the cell site report for Fox-Carnell's phone and I'm done with the Soteria data,' said Ezra. 'Can you turn on the smartboard please.'

'Because I know you lot like pictures, I've got a map,' Ezra said proudly. 'These are Fox-Carnell's movements. After she left your house boss—'

'Left your house. What does he mean?' Copeland asked.

'Carry on, Ez.' Henley turned her back to Copeland.

'Her phone and tracker places her at New Cross Gate at 6.04 p.m. and at London Bridge at 6.12 p.m.. I'm assuming she goes on the tube because her phone connects to a phone mast and her tracker places her thirty-five minutes later at 6.47 p.m., Colindale tube station,' Ezra continued.

'She's got a little more than two hours before her curfew kicks in,' said Ramouter. 'So where does she go?'

'I think she's walking because the tracker information next places her at Colindale Park. She doesn't move for about thirty minutes. It next tracks her to the Co-op on Colindale Avenue.'

'Stanford, I need you to get hold of the manager for that branch. We need details of CCTV and anyone who was working there at that time,' said Henley before turning back to Ezra. 'Where did she go after that?'

'Her tag and her phone next place her near Mornington Close but that's where the information ends,' said Ezra. 'Whoever was receiving the monitoring information was able to switch it off.'

'I'll find out which council covers Colindale and see if they've got CCTV available for the area,' said Ramouter.

'Thank you. There's one more thing. Is there any way that you can check if the monitoring information for anyone else was being diverted?' Henley asked Ezra.

'Yeah, I can do that,' Ezra replied. 'Anyone in particular or just see what turns up?'

'Look for Nathan Hall first.'

Ezra left the room, and Henley took a deep breath, finally feeling as though she was getting control of the case.

'I'm going to talk to the victims of Fox-Carnell who survived. DC Copeland, I want you to familiarise yourself with the serial crimes investigation manual,' said Henley.

'Wouldn't it be more useful to investigate Nathan Hall,' asked Copeland, flipping the page of her notebook. 'I can check for any instances of recorded harassment against him and look into the backgrounds of his complainants.'

'No,' said Henley. 'This is your day one. An SCU investigation doesn't work in the same way as your usual major crime.'

'I didn't expect it to, but I have worked on a murder investigation before.'

'Oh god. She's going to get a lesson,' Eastwood muttered. She opened her desk drawer and pulled out a bag of Maltesers.

'DC Copeland, a homicide is investigated by a major investigation team that usually includes at least four Detective Sergeants and eighteen Detective Constables.' Henley bit her lip to stop herself from adding that she was sure that Copeland was on the lowest rung of the ladder. Instead, she said, 'We're a smaller, specialised unit and you don't work until you understand how we work. Is that understood?'

'Yes, guv,' Copeland replied, her Welsh accent prominent.

'Once you've completed that task, I want you to go through the Fox-Carnell and Ashcroft CRIS reports, witness and forensic statements so far. And you . . .' Henley said, turning to Pellacia. She stared at him, the anger visible in her eyes.

'You forgot to say guv,' Pellacia said icily.

'I need to talk to you. Outside. In the yard, *guv*,' Henley said.

*

'That really is no way to talk to me, especially in front of the rest of the team,' said Pellacia.

'I don't appreciate being left in the dark,' said Henley. She pulled the hairband off her right wrist and tied back her hair. Despite the blue sky interrupting the sequence of clouds, she could smell rain in the air.

'How have I left you in the dark?' Pellacia asked.

'DC bloody Copeland. You just sprung her on us. You've never done that before when you've brought someone new into the team. You didn't do that with Ramouter. You consulted all of us and you didn't do that with DC Kemble who was here for all of five minutes. Why didn't you call me last night?'

'Because I try my best not to disturb your home life unless it's serious and two, when I think about it, not everything I do, as your boss, needs your input *Detective Inspector Henley*.'

Stunned, Henley took a short step back. She wasn't used to Pellacia calling her by her full title when it wasn't official business, in front of their superiors or discussing a case in a news conference.

'We shouldn't have found out the way we did,' said Henley. 'And Copeland of all people.'

'That was Barker's decision not mine. Copeland isn't costing us any money and she's invested in the case.'

'Please,' Henley muttered as Pellacia paced the yard 'She's not interested in this bloody case. She's interested in Ramouter.'

'Don't you think you're seeing something that isn't there?'

'No, I do not. Her behaviour. Putting herself in places where she has no right to be. I've seen what she's like with him. Her interest isn't just this case. Trust me on this one.'

'I do. Trust you, that is.'

'Do you really Stephen? Because honestly it doesn't feel like it. I don't know whether I'm coming or going with you.'

'It works both ways Anj.'

Henley closed her eyes, turned her back and walked towards

the railings. She could sense that Pellacia was hurt, and she hated the fact that she was the cause of it. She held her breath and she listened to his steps as he moved closer to her. The last thing she wanted was for him to touch her.

'I would have liked to have been given a bit of notice before Copeland walked through the door,' she said, turning around and finding herself far too close to Pellacia. She stepped back. 'I'm leading this investigation, and I can't do my job properly if things are being hidden from me.'

'What else am I hiding from you?'

'A lot. You don't tell me everything that's said in those meetings you're constantly being called to. I know you're under pressure, Stephen, but you don't usually keep things from me – especially when it comes to the SCU.'

'I'm not going to pretend this job is easy because it bloody isn't and there are times when I walk into our office and I see you and . . . trust that I always try and make the right decision for the SCU,' Pellacia said. 'But speaking of hiding things. When were you going to tell me about your secret investigation into Rhimes?'

Pellacia's question hit Henley like a punch to her stomach. 'What are you—'

'Don't. Don't do that, Anj. You've never lied to me. Don't start now.'

Henley looked away and faced the wall. 'How did you find out?' she asked.

'How do you think? Eloise. She's worried about you. You're ignoring her calls and texts.'

'It's not like that. I've been busy.'

'Don't give me that. You're not known for leaving people hanging. You left Eloise unread and now she's got it into her head that digging into Rhimes's death has triggered your PTSD.'

'When did she tell you?'

'A couple of weeks ago.'

'A couple of weeks?!' Henley exclaimed. 'So, what were you waiting for? For me to have a complete breakdown at your front door?'

'Don't be ridiculous. Of course I wasn't,' Pellacia said, visibly hurt. 'What I was waiting for was for Eloise to tell me that she'd put an end to it and was getting on with her life. When she called me last night I thought it was over but it's not. You haven't stopped, have you?'

Henley said nothing but walked away and opened the back door that led to the old custody suite.

Pellacia stepped in front of Henley and pushed the door shut. 'Who's helping you?' he demanded.

'What are you doing? Get out of my way,' Henley voice was raised as she pulled on the handle.

'Stanford? Eastie?'

'Stephen! Let me through.'

'You haven't asked Ezra, have you?' Pellacia placed his hands on Henley's shoulders and turned her towards him.

'It's not what you think.' Henley was unable to form a lie.

'That's *exactly* what I think, and I want you to stop.'

'Stephen. He's not—'

'It's like telling a kid not to touch the cooker because it's hot. It's obvious you won't listen to me, so I'm going to have to tell Ezra myself. That he's to stay out of it. '

'He's not involved. Not anymore,' Henley said with resignation. 'Don't say anything to him. It's done.'

'Why are you putting yourself through this?'

'I'm not doing anything to myself. Eloise asked me to help her, so I'm helping her.'

'But why keep it to yourself? Why not let me, Stanford or even Eastie help you?'

'We don't all need to be involved and distracted with Rhimes when we have this vigilante case going on. I'm protecting the SCU and I'm protecting you. You act as if you haven't suffered too, when I know you have.'

Pellacia stared at Henley as though he was searching for the truth.

'Remember what you said,' said Henley. 'I've never lied to you.'

'I feel as though you enjoy manipulating me,' Pellacia answered sadly.

'What are you talking about?'

'You. Us. I follow you blindly and then you let me down.'

Henley felt her breath catch in her throat.

'I'm not doing this with you,' she eventually said. 'This has nothing to do with us.'

'Your actions don't match your words, Anj. They never have.'

'You want to go through all this again? You want me to tell you again why I can't leave my family? I'm not going to do that, Stephen. I'm not going to take precious time away from this investigation to talk about something that doesn't exist anymore.'

'Would it make a difference if I told you that Laura and I . . . she wants something that I can't give her,' Pellacia spoke as though he hadn't heard Henley's words. As though he knew that this time she *was* lying.

'No, it wouldn't make a difference,' Henley's voice broke.

'And you're content to be in an unhappy marriage with a man who doesn't understand you or support you?'

'Just because Rob and I have problems like any other married couple doesn't mean that it's unhappy.'

Pellacia snorted with displeasure. 'Keep telling yourself that.'

'Why don't you focus more on the SCU and less on what happens outside of it? What I do in my spare time has absolutely nothing to do with you.'

'Are you serious? You've dragged Ezra into this, and you really think that what you're doing doesn't impact me? I don't understand why you're being so selfish.'

'How am I being selfish?'

'By taking advantage of a widow's grief and giving her hope when there isn't any. Let it rest and focus on what you've got to do in this building. Stop thinking of yourself for once.'

'Wow.' Henley shook her head with disbelief. 'Anything else you'd like to share?'

'Yes. Do your job or I'll think nothing of getting someone else in to do it for you.' Pellacia snapped. He walked back into the building slamming the door behind him, leaving Henley outside alone.

32

Ramouter had thought that playing The Verve loudly would have made the car journey bearable, but he was wrong. Henley had barely said two words to him since they'd left the office. When they stopped at the traffic lights on Blackfriars Bridge, Ramouter broke.

'Is everything all right, boss?' he asked. 'You just seem . . . a bit annoyed.'

Henley released her foot off the brake and turned onto Farringdon Street. 'Did you know that Copeland was going to be joining the SCU?' she asked.

'Why do you think I knew?' Ramouter asked, turning his face towards the window.

'Because you're the only one who wasn't surprised when she walked in.'

Ramouter put a hand to his chin and rubbed at his beard. 'It's not what you think,' he eventually said. 'We were out for a drink last night. She told me then it was a possibility.'

'A drink? I didn't realise you were that close.'

'We're not close. I bumped into her when I was at Lewisham for the press conference, and she suggested drinks. It just happened that I was there when she got the call from the borough commander that her transfer had gone through.'

'And you didn't think to tell me?' Henley asked, her tone sharp.

'To be honest, I assumed you already knew, and you'd agreed to it.'

'I didn't know it was approved, and I can't say I'm pleased about it.'

'I think it could be a good thing she's here, DC Copeland that it is,' said Ramouter as Henley parked the car. 'It can never hurt to have an extra pair of hands.'

'This restaurant. The Itria,' Henley said, pointing to it. 'I've been here a couple of times with Rob. You should take your wife.'

Ramouter opened his mouth to respond but then thought better of it.

Henley scanned the posters on the walls of the Starlight Community Centre. The elderly woman on reception had directed them to room four which had been booked for the legal clinic and victim support group.

'I'm surprised a place like this is still going,' Ramouter commented, stopping outside a community library. Every table in the room was occupied with people, either reading on their own or being taught to read. A young mother and her child sat with an older woman as they conversed in Swahili.

'There would be more of them if the government wasn't intent on shutting every good thing down,' said Henley. She thought back to the moments when her sanity had been saved by the mother and baby groups at her local library. 'Here we are.' She pushed a door open.

A couple sitting on a sofa in the corner looked up, their chatter immediately silenced. The room was set up for a meeting with the chairs arranged in a semi-circle.

'Can I help you? You look a bit lost.'

Both Henley and Ramouter turned around to find themselves facing a woman in her mid-forties. Her long, thick brown hair framed her face, but it couldn't hide the visible scars that stretched like a road map across rugged terrain from her throat, along the lower right side of her face and ended at her temples. She adjusted the pink and grey chiffon scarf that had been draped loosely around her neck.

'I'm Detective Inspector Henley and this is Detective Constable Ramouter.'

Ramouter flinched when he realised that Henley omitted the words 'my partner' from her introduction. She was still pissed.

'I'm looking for Jorge Menjivar,' said Henley. She put her warrant card away and scanned the room. The last time she'd seen Jorge was when she'd sat in his parents' living room and taken his victim impact statement. She'd been impressed by his resilience and his determination not to be defined by Fox-Carnell's attempt on his life.

'He popped out to grab a coffee. He's not a fan of the coffee in here, not that I can blame him.' The woman led them to the office at the back of the room. 'You can wait for him in here.'

She walked off quickly, phone in hand, before Henley had a chance to ask for her name.

'I'm sorry I didn't tell you about DC Copeland,' said Ramouter. 'I just assumed.'

'You should know better than to assume anything.'

'I know,' answered Ramouter. His phone began to vibrate in his pocket. He pulled it out, grateful for the opportunity not to push the matter further with Henley. 'That was Ezra,' he said. 'Anthony couriered Nathan Hall's phone over and he was able to get into it.'

'Anything useful?' she asked.

'He's sent some files but the reception in here is rubbish. I've barely got one bar.'

'We'll deal with it later,' said Henley, extending her hand to the man who had just arrived. 'Jorge Menjivar. I'm not sure if you remember me. I'm DI Anjelica Henley.'

'Your face looks familiar,' Jorge said, switching the coffee to his left hand so that he could shake hers. 'But I can't think how we would have met.'

'You were very ill at the time, but I took your statement,' Henley reminded him. She released Jorge's hand and closed the door behind him.

'How could I forget. You came to my parents' house with the other detective, the tall one,' Jorge said, taking a seat.

'That would have been Stephen Pellacia.' Henley remained standing.

'I take it this is about her, the nurse?'

'Sian Fox-Carnell. Yes,' said Henley. 'And sorry, I forgot to introduce you to my partner, DC Ramouter.'

Jorge nodded in Ramouter's direction. 'If I'm honest, I'm not sure how I can help you.'

'What do you do here?' asked Henley.

'I run a victim support group. After everything that happened to me, I knew I had to give something back. I completed my degrees in psychology and neuroscience of mental health a couple of years ago at Middlesex University. I have group sessions a couple of days a week. I appreciate that therapy isn't cheap, and trauma isn't means tested. It affects everyone and everyone should have access to help. Sorry, I can get on my soap box a bit,' Jorge apologised.

'I understand completely,' said Henley. 'It's a good way to give back.'

'That woman. The nurse. She tried to kill me, but I survived. It would be wrong of me not to use my life to be of service,' said Jorge.

'I notice that you don't say her name.'

'To call her by her name gives her humanity. No,' said Jorge shaking his head, 'she doesn't deserve that. I'm not even sorry that she's dead.' Jorge took a breath. 'The right thing to say is that I'm sorry but—'

'I'm not expecting you to be sorry,' said Henley. 'But you understand that we have to investigate her murder. To find out who was responsible.'

'I can't say that I have much faith in the justice system. They put her back on the street after all.'

Henley ignored the statement, not wanting to get into a debate. She indicated to Ramouter to take over.

'Jorge, you may or may not be aware, but Sian Fox-Carnell was being electronically monitored.' Ramouter unfolded several sheets of paper that he had in his pocket. 'The day before she went missing her tag placed her at a number of locations including the Williams Therapy Practice in Aldgate, last Tuesday at 11.36 a.m..'

'The Williams Therapy Practice,' Jorge repeated, his voice shaking. 'That's where I work.'

'We've got CCTV footage showing Fox-Carnell going into the building where your practice is based,' said Ramouter. He turned the page and showed a screenshot of Fox-Carnell entering the building. 'Did you see her?'

Jorge didn't look at the picture. He kept his eyes focused on a space behind Henley.

'Jorge, did you see her?' Ramouter repeated, shifting his position forcing Jorge to look at him.

Jorge placed the coffee on the table behind him and stood up. 'I've got my session starting soon.'

'You didn't answer the question, Jorge,' Henley pressed gently.

Jorge looked across at Henley and saw that she was blocking the door.

'I did. I did see her,' Jorge admitted finally.

'What happened?' Ramouter asked.

'She called me, not by my full name but JV. That was her nickname for me when she was looking after me. She would call me JV.' Jorge inhaled deeply and when he looked up his eyes were dark with fury. 'It brought it all back. Seeing her standing over me. Telling my parents that she would look after me as though I was her own.'

'Did you talk to her?'

'I told her to leave otherwise I would call the police.'

'And what did she do or say?'

Jorge snorted with disgust. 'She said I had grown up well. Such an evil . . . I went back inside. I don't know where she went after that.'

'Why didn't you call the police? She would have been arrested and remanded in custody immediately,' said Henley.

'In custody but alive but I didn't call the police and now she's dead,' Jorge said with a shrug. 'Some would call that a win-win.'

Henley stepped aside and opened the door.

'Thank you very much for your help, Jorge,' said Ramouter. 'We'll leave you to it.'

'Are you speaking to her other victims and the families of the ones who didn't make it?' Jorge asked.

'We're talking to everyone. But we will contact you again if we have more questions.' Henley looked around the room. A trio were standing at the beverage table, and a few others had already taken their seats. They looked up but continued with their conversations.

'Seems like a full group,' Henley commented.

'We usually are,' answered Jorge. 'A lot of them have been coming here for years. We all need support.'

'Yeah, we do,' Henley agreed as a man reached for his jacket on the back of his chair and quickly left. 'Who was that?' she asked.

'I can't say. Confidentiality. This is a safe place,' Jorge said.

Henley smiled tightly. 'We'll let you get on.'

'What do you think that was all about?' Ramouter asked as they headed out of the room.

'The man ran out as soon as that woman told him who we were,' said Henley, looking up and down the hallway.

'Do you think that's what happened?' Ramouter asked.

Henley spotted the man stepping out of an alcove in the corridor with a woman and then push through the double doors.

'That's exactly what happened. Stay here,' Henley said. She took out her phone and jogged towards the woman who was walking towards her.

'I'm sorry, this is my first time here and I was just in the group with that guy you were talking to, and he left his phone,' Henley said, holding up her own phone. 'He told me his name, but I've forgotten.'

'Oh. You mean Larry,' the woman said, turning around as though expecting him to still be there.

'That's it. Thank you so much. Hopefully I can catch him up. You don't know his last name, do you?' Henley asked gratefully.

'Durant.'

'Thank you so much,' Henley said as she ran down the corridor.

'Where did he go?' Ramouter asked as he joined Henley outside on the steps of the community centre.

'The number sixty-two,' Henley said, pointing at the single decker bus that had just pulled away from the bus stop. 'It was Durant. Larry Durant. I think we've been looking at this case all wrong,' said Henley. 'We've been looking at outside vigilantes, people with no links to Fox-Carnell and the others but what if it's a little bit closer to home?'

33

Henley stood at her front garden gate watching her house and wondering if it was still a place of safety. She'd done everything to protect her family refuge, made herself ex-directory and had no social media presence to speak of, yet Sian Fox-Carnell had found her. She looked over her shoulder at the street. A jogger ran by and the family who lived three doors down – the young twins dressed in their judo gis – walked home. Life looked normal but Henley knew that it was an illusion. Sian Fox-Carnell wasn't the only one to breach the wall and cross her boundary. Peter Olivier had been the first one to show her that she and her family were not untouchable. Henley could feel sharp splinters pushing through the soft flesh of her palm as she gripped the garden gate. Most of the time she could convince herself that she was ok and that she had survived but that wasn't the truth. Her PTSD wasn't gone but was just buried in a shallow grave in her body. The anxiety was silent to the external world, but it was like a pneumatic drill in her chest, she was irritable, the hours she slept were getting shorter and she wanted to hide, to avoid the world. The pace of her heart was erratic, her breathing laboured, as she approached her front door.

'For god's sake,' she said under her breath, her hand shaking too much to unlock the door. She jerked back as the lock pulled away from her and the door opened. She looked up to see Rob standing in front of her with a tea-towel over his shoulder.

'What's wrong, what's happened?' he asked.

Her answer was swallowed by choke-filled tears as she fell against him.

'I didn't know you were going to be home. I thought you'd changed your Manchester days this week,' Henley said as she walked back into the warm kitchen an hour later. Despite the hot shower, her body ached with exhaustion.

'I texted you.' Rob took a shepherd's pie out of the oven and placed it on the counter. 'There was another change of plans at work. The journalist who was covering the crypto conference at the Excel this week is sick, so I said I'd cover it.'

Henley reached for her bag that Rob had hung on the back of the chair. 'Crypto? I thought you said it's all a scam.' She took out her phone, scrolled through the text messages including another text from Eloise, until she found the message that Rob had sent her at 11.14 a.m..

'It is all a scam,' Rob said, dishing up.

'How did you know that I was at the door?' She was grateful that Rob had decided to come home early and cook comfort food.

'The doorbell app. I keep forgetting to turn off notifications for motion. I looked and I could see your face. It brought back memories of when you were home on sick leave just after we found out you were pregnant. You looked broken. As though the world was about to come crashing down on you.'

It wasn't lost on Henley that Rob had avoided saying 'When you were on sick leave after you were stabbed.' She knew that time had been just as painful for him as it had been for her.

'The problem with my job is that death isn't the end, it's the beginning,' Henley said. 'And it's never straightforward. When we're dealing with a person's death it comes with all of these complexities and emotions that aren't even your own. You don't have room for yourself, and you can't close the door at 5.30 p.m. and leave it all behind. That person's death follows you.'

Rob ate silently for a few minutes, the news drifting from the TV next door. 'It doesn't have to be this way for you,' he said.

'Rob, don't—'

'No, don't worry. I'm not going to start banging on about you leaving the SCU or the force. We've gone up and down that road and we end up in the same place. A stalemate. I'm just saying I want you to know that you're not on your own. I'm your safe place.'

'I'm sorry for making our marriage hard.' Henley reached out and touched his face.

'It's not all on you. Sitting on a train travelling up and down to Manchester every week has given me a lot of time to think and . . . it won't be easy, but it will be better, after all it's not just us. We've got Emma and Luna.'

'Yes, we do, and it would make her day if you were the one to pick her up from Dad's tomorrow.'

'That won't be a problem. I'm interviewing the keynote speaker at 3 p.m. and I'll leave straight after,' said Rob as Henley's phone began to vibrate across the kitchen table. 'Is there anything else going on with you or is it just the case?'

Henley groaned as her argument with Pellacia and the arrival of DC Copeland entered her head. 'My mum always said that half the battle when working in a team was managing people and their egos.'

'No, it's more than that,' said Rob. 'There's been something bothering you for a while. Even when we were on holiday there were times when you just seemed to disappear into yourself. You had the same look on your face that Emma gets when she's trying to work out a puzzle.'

Henley exhaled sharply. There were times where she was so focused on their marital problems that she forgot how well Rob understood her. Rob had an ability to see through her defences and to support her without being overbearing. She couldn't blame him for questioning her decisions to stay in a job which had brought danger to their front door on more than one occasion. She counted to five in her head and then she spoke. She told Rob all about Eloise's belief that Rhimes had been murdered. Rob let Henley talk, only interrupting to ask questions when the journalist in him took over.

'Fuck,' he said when Henley had finished. 'And you're sure in regard to the medical evidence that Rhimes was strangled and didn't die from—'

'Death from asphyxiation, not suicide from asphyxiation,' said Henley. 'Linh has the toxicology report and there was no carbon monoxide poisoning in his blood.'

'You can't breathe it in if you're already dead.'

'Exactly. Someone staged Rhimes's death to make it look like a suicide.'

Rob pressed his lips together as he leaned forward, placing his hands in a steeple. He was thinking, percolating his thoughts. 'What have the others said? Stanford, Eastwood, Pellacia.'

Henley flinched. Preparing herself to hear Pellacia's name followed by an accusation, but it never came.

'Stanford and Eastwood don't know about any of this. Eloise told Pellacia what I was doing but he doesn't know what I've found,' said Henley. 'I didn't want to burden them.'

'Anj, come on, man. I'm looking at my wife and *you* are burdened.'

'Rob, I can deal with this on my own.'

'Just because you can doesn't mean that you should. I don't want to see you—' Rob paused as Henley's phone began to vibrate across the kitchen table again. 'Maybe you should tell Pellacia everything. The one thing I know is that he won't let you break.'

Henley felt an anxious flutter in her chest. She had betrayed her husband on more than one occasion and he was entrusting another man with her well-being. She reached for her phone. It was Linh. She held it up, showing Rob. He pulled a face, stood up and cleared the table.

'I'm not sitting here listening to your mate talking about post-mortems or her latest escapades. Not tonight. I'll be in the front room.'

'I'll join you in a bit.' She accepted the call. 'What can I do for you, Dr Choi?'

'You sound bright, Detective Inspector Henley. What happened, did that husband of yours come home early and give you a good seeing to or was it the other one?'

'Thank God I don't have you on speaker. For the record, yes, he did come home early, and the second bit is none of your bloody business.'

'You're no fun. Well, let me give you some news about the case. Nathan Hall's legs were pulverised. In my opinion he was hit with a mallet of some kind. Both knees and shins smashed.'

'I can't even imagine the pain,' said Henley.

'Even if he had survived, there would have been no way to save those legs. He would have been looking at amputation,' explained Linh. 'Moving up. Broken pelvis, again looked to have been smashed with a mallet of some kind and then we have his face. Broken jaw, broken collarbone and fractures to his skull and, as you already know, he was scalped.'

'Are you able to say if all three victims were scalped with the same knife?'

'I won't know that until tomorrow. I've sent the photos of Nathan Hall and Tabitha Ashcroft to the knife expert to compare against Fox-Carnell,' Linh replied. 'But, what you really want to know is cause of death. Asphyxiation. He was still alive when he was hung from the top of the staircase. Hall also had cocaine and alcohol in his system, but it wasn't enough to impair him. He would have known exactly what was going on.'

'God,' Henley groaned. She got up and removed two wine glasses from the cupboard.

'Do you think there will be more? There's something about these scalpings that rub me the wrong way. It's not just wicked. It's cold, Anj. You have to put thought into that. It's not something you do on a whim.'

'That's what concerns me,' said Henley. 'Someone acting on the spur of the moment is going to be careless and make mistakes but when it's planned like this. It just seems more dangerous.'

'I don't envy you. In fact, I never envy you.'

Henley ended the call as the normality of home life continued around her. She could hear Rob flicking through TV channels and Luna licking the floor near the dishwasher. The sounds of her home should have been a comfort to Henley, but she couldn't settle. Linh's words swam in her head. She understood why Linh didn't envy her. This case was more than just a person committing murder. The scalping was vengeful and purposeful, but it also felt like an offering. Whoever wielded the knife wanted not only to punish but also to please someone. Henley shuddered. Whoever killed Fox-Carnell, Hall and attempted to kill Tabitha Ashcroft was trying to prove themselves, which meant that someone else was pulling the strings.

'Shall we do one more episode?' Rob asked Henley as the credits rolled.

'One more then bed,' Henley nodded, even though she knew she would probably spend half the night wide awake. The next episode had just begun when Henley's phone rang again. Pellacia's name appeared on the screen, and she steadied herself for the worse.

'It's work,' she said. 'I'll take it upstairs.'

Rob sighed and gently shifted Henley's legs off his lap. 'I'll put the kettle on.'

Henley accepted the call and went into the spare room. 'What's happened?' she asked.

'Nothing has happened,' said Pellacia. 'This isn't about the case.'

'Why are you calling me if this—'

'I didn't like how I left things with you,' Pellacia said hurriedly. 'I said things I had no right to say.'

'You told me that I was selfish and that you'd find someone else to do my job.'

'I was out of line. I'm sorry.'

Henley sat down on the bed and rubbed her temple. 'You're doing my head in.'

Pellacia laughed. 'I'm doing your head in. Imagine what you're doing to me?'

'Stephen.'

'I didn't mean . . . look, I didn't call to talk about us, well at least, not like that. I just want to know why?'

'Why what?' Henley asked as anxiety clawed at her chest. She opened the window and let the cold October air into the small room.

'Why you didn't come to me about Rhimes. Why you chose to do this on your own.'

'I don't need you to carry me, Stephen.'

'It's not about carrying you, it's about being by your side, Anj. This thing that Eloise asked you to do, it doesn't just affect you.'

'I know that.'

'So why not tell me? Why not let me in?'

'Eloise came to me,' Henley said with exhaustion. She didn't have the energy to fight.

'This has nothing to do with Eloise, not really. You're shutting me out. Building walls. That's not you, Anj. That's not us.'

Henley focused on the peeling wallpaper.

'You talk about me shutting you out, but what about you?' she asked.

'What are you talking about?'

'I'm talking about Copeland joining—'

'That's different and you know it,' Pellacia snapped.

'No, it's not. We've both been keeping things to ourselves. Not being honest with each other.'

'When have I ever not been honest with you?'

'I haven't got time for this. Rob is—'

Henley stopped as Pellacia tutted loudly with disapproval.

'You shouldn't have called,' Henley said.

'I just want you to talk to me,' Pellacia's tone softened. 'Let me know where your head is at with this Rhimes thing. You shouldn't – no, you don't have to do this on your own.'

'Was there anything else?' Henley asked stubbornly. She closed the window and made her way downstairs.

'Bloody hell. Don't treat me like the—'

'Is there anything else?' she repeated.

'It's funny,' Pellacia said sadly. 'I never thought that Rhimes would be the one who would actually break us.'

Henley opened her mouth to respond but Pellacia had already ended the call.

Ramouter leaned back and rubbed at his eyes. The match between West Bromwich and Derby was on TV but he wasn't paying attention. He'd spent the last two hours balancing his MacBook on his lap whilst he stared at CCTV footage of the night the Ashcrofts had been assaulted. 'I hate this case,' he said to himself as the Facetime notification appeared in the corner of his screen and he gratefully minimised the video player.

'You finally picked up,' said Michelle, her face only half filling the screen. 'The last time I heard from you was on Sunday night.'

'I am so sorry, babe,' said Ramouter, repositioning his laptop so that his wife didn't see the chaos. Empty takeaway containers he hadn't cleared from the table and clothes that had been removed from the dryer but dumped on the sofa. 'There's a lot going on.'

Michelle straightened her screen. 'So, you can't call your wife?'

Ramouter caught sight of the outside heater and Moroccan lanterns in the background and saw that Michelle was enveloped in a cream throw. 'Where are you?' he asked.

'In the garden. The kids are running around as though they're possessed and they're doing my head in. At this point I wouldn't mind forgetting them.'

'Oh my god, Michelle,' Ramouter groaned as his wife laughed. It was one of the things he'd always loved about her – her wry sense of humour and an ability not to take life too seriously as opposed to him. He'd been built to search for the cracks in the foundation and the holes in the roof. Early onset dementia had taken away her smile and humour for a year, but with the help of therapy and medication, Michelle's light – although slightly dimmer – had returned.

'How's Ethan doing?'

'He's champion,' said Michelle, drinking her tea. 'He's like a returning war hero. I would get him for you but—'

'Leave him be. I'll talk to him tomorrow. So, how are you doing?'

'I'm good. I'll be glad to come home to you though. It's nice being up here but my mother is suffocating. I'm surprised she's not here keeping watch.'

'That's because she loves you.'

'I know. So, tell me why didn't you pick up when I called yesterday? Were you out drinking with your crew on a school night?' Michelle asked with a smirk.

Ramouter looked away, not wanting to admit to his wife that he had been out drinking but with only one member of his team: DC Copeland. 'You know what it's like. You go for one and that turns into a few.'

'And the next thing you know you're forgetting to call your wife.'

'Aye, aye. I'll do better.'

'Make sure you do,' said Michelle. 'I need to go. That son of yours should be in bed.'

'I promise I'll call you tomorrow.'

'I'll hold you to that. And, Salim?'

'What is it, babe?'

'Make sure you put the washing away.'

'How did you even—'

Michelle laughed. 'It's my superpower. Love you. Night.'

Ramouter shook his head and laughed as the call ended. His wife never ceased to amaze him. 'Oh, bollocks,' he said when he saw that West Bromwich had conceded a goal. Also, on the sofa were printouts of Laurence Durant's previous convictions. He'd been arrested for threatening words and behaviour on the day that his wife's killer walked out of court but it hadn't risked his teaching career as the CPS had taken no further action against him.

'It can't just be you,' Ramouter muttered as he opened the video player again and pressed play. It was said that London was the most surveilled city in the world but that didn't mean there was a CCTV camera on every street, and video doorbells, although helpful, were limited in their view. The CCTV that Ramouter had been looking at was from Lordship Lane leading towards Cullen Lane. Even if Durant was involved, Ramouter couldn't believe that this was a grieving man acting alone. Thirty minutes later, Ramouter felt his eyelids droop, as he continued watching the passing traffic, and the referee blew the whistle on the game. West Bromwich Albion had lost 3-1.

'No, no way,' said Ramouter as he sat up, the empty beer bottle rolling onto the floor. He paused the footage and rewound it. He watched again, paused the video, watched it again. Paused, made a screenshot and texted it to Henley. The phone rang almost immediately.

'Is that what I think it is?' Henley asked.

'That's Laurence Durant's car on Lordship Lane twelve minutes after Graham Ashcroft was hit,' said Ramouter.

'That's good enough me,' said Henley. 'We'll arrest him first thing.'

34

'Thanks.' Josh took the pint of beer from Don's hand.

'You could sound a bit more appreciative than that,' Don said.

'Sorry. Thank you,' Josh replied quickly, wincing slightly at the pathetic tone of fear in his voice. He took a large swallow of beer as if to show how appreciative he was. He coughed loudly, his eyes watering as the beer went down the wrong way.

'What's wrong with you?' Don asked, his disgust clear. He pushed himself back against the stained fabric of the booth that he'd squeezed his solid frame into, as Josh wiped the spittle from the corner of his mouth.

'Nothing,' Josh answered, taking another sip of beer to show that he wasn't pathetic. Josh felt out of place in this bar on Bermondsey Street. The people around him, laughing and talking loudly about their latest deals and successes and couples sitting close together, knees touching as they talked intimately, overwhelmed him. He was grateful he'd chosen a booth that was like a cocoon. It was impossible for his neighbour to see that he was scared.

Don placed his thick fingers into the bowl of mixed nuts and picked out all the cashews. 'You wanted to talk,' he said.

'Aren't we going to wait for—'

'No,' Don cut him off. 'Whatever you need to say, you can say it to me.'

Josh drank his beer and tried to settle his nerves. The last time he'd seen Don, his hands had been around his neck. When he touched the back of his head, he could feel the flaking scab, the flesh still tender.

'I want out,' said Josh. He waited for a response, but there was nothing, just the sound of cashew nuts being pulverised in Don's mouth.

'Don't get me wrong. I agree with what we're doing. 100 per cent I agree with the cause,' he said. 'Giving the people what the police and courts aren't prepared to. Delivering justice.'

'So, what's your problem?'

Josh leaned on the table and put his left hand to his forehead. 'I can't do this,' he whispered. 'It was one thing, harassing people, putting shit through their door, exposing them on . . . but this—'

Josh caught Don's cold eyes and quickly lowered his head. He'd seen that look before – when Don had taken the sledgehammer to Nathan Hall's pelvis. Josh rubbed at his eyes. He couldn't remember the last time he'd slept through the night. He was constantly on edge, shouting at his children, sleeping in two-hour bursts. The over the counter sleeping tablets didn't work, neither did trying to silence the noise with alcohol. He could still hear Nathan's screams in his head as he slept, could still hear Graham Ashcroft hitting and smashing the windscreen. Almost worse were Don's shouts of delight.

'It's too much,' Josh said. 'I want to hold these arseholes accountable but not like this.'

'You know longer support our cause?' Don challenged.

'Of course, I support it but it's dangerous. The police. . . they came to my work.'

Don downed the remainder of his pint. 'We're going,' he said. He wriggled from the booth and walked briskly out of the bar.

'Who came?' Don demanded once Josh had joined him in the churchyard opposite.

'I picked it up from my boss's desk,' Josh said. He took a

crumpled business card from his jeans pocket and handed it to Don.

'Detective Inspector Anjelica Henley,' Don read. 'Serial Crimes Unit. When did she come by?'

'Yesterday morning.'

'And you're only telling me now.'

'I had . . . I had a lot on,' Josh stuttered. 'But I don't—'

'Shut the fuck up!' Don placed his hand on his hip and watched a kid on an electric scooter making his way through the park exit. 'Explain to me exactly what happened.'

'I don't know what was said but he gave them access to the Soteria network.'

'Them, you said them.'

'Yeah, she had this computer guy with her. Ezra Williams. I Googled him and found out that he was found guilty of fraud. He created phishing software for a gang that defrauded a bank. The prosecutor said that this Ezra kid was a prolific and highly skilled cyber-criminal.'

'I suppose the police will take anybody,' Don said, putting the business card in his pocket.

'You can see why I want out right? They're getting close,' Josh's voice rose in panic. 'What if she comes back?'

Don said nothing.

'I can't go to prison. I just can't. I've got my kids.'

'Fine.' Don slapped Josh hard on his shoulder. 'Consider yourself out.'

'What? Are . . . are you sure?'

'Absolutely.'

'You don't know what this means,' Josh said with relief. 'You have my word. I won't say—'

'I understand,' said Don, patting Josh's arm. 'Forget you ever met us.'

*

Don held the citrus vapour in his mouth for a few seconds as he read the witness statement. He could almost feel the pain of the victim, imagining how she felt as the liquid burned the skin on her face. She'd had no doubt about the identity of her attacker.

'Are you sure this is the one, Mika?' he asked, taking another inhale, desperate for the nicotine hit. He'd been careful not to use her name – not that he was even sure if it was her real name – when Josh had been around but now it was just the two of them, it was safe.

'Positive,' Mika confirmed as she adjusted the sleeves of her oversized cardigan. The heating was malfunctioning in the garden office and the night chill had settled in the room. 'Obviously this is a redundant discussion if the jury do the right thing, but we need to be prepared.'

'I think it would be better if we prepared for someone a little bit less high profile. Someone who hasn't been splashed all over the home page of *Sky News*.'

Don returned the witness statement back to the file and picked up the well-thumbed list from the table. He picked up a red sharpie and crossed out Nathan Hall's name.

'You're probably right, said Mika. 'It might throw the police off a bit. Speaking of the police, have you heard anything from Larry?'

'No,' Don replied. He tapped his pen against the list of names. 'Radio silence. I'm thinking that we scared him off.'

Mika snorted. 'I'd rather have him out than in if he can't handle the reality of what we do. You scream about wanting justice and then cry when we deliver it. Tea or coffee?'

'Tea, please. I've been thinking that it might be a good time to recruit another member, maybe two. I'm not saying I can't handle things myself, but two pairs of hands are better than one. I know a guy—'

'I'm not too keen on dragging anyone new into our business,' said Mika. She opened the fridge, pushing aside the Ziplock bags containing the scalps to get the milk.

'It wouldn't be anyone new, not really,' Don said. 'You already know him. His name's Frank, and he was a member of the Crawley Hunters. I met up with him last week and he's keen.'

Mika handed Don his tea. 'What's his background like and do you trust him?'

'I do. And he's clean. He's got a new job working security and he had to have an enhanced DBS check as part of the application,' said Don. He put his tea down and took out his phone. 'He's got an incentive to do what we do. His brother was robbed three years ago and had a knife put to his throat. The guy only got an eighteen-month sentence but was out in six. Frank showed him what he thought of that.'

Mika took the phone from Don and smiled at the photo of a man tied to a chair, his face bloody and bruised. The crutch of his blue jeans darkened from when he'd pissed himself.

'We can have a chat,' she said. 'We probably need someone to replace Josh.'

'That cunt,' Don said his face darkening with anger.

'I've been thinking about him a lot,' said Mika, taking a seat at the table. 'He didn't tell us about the police visiting Soteria and talking to his boss. Now all of a sudden he's out. I don't like it.'

'You thinking that he's talking to the police?'

'I wouldn't be surprised. We need to keep an eye on him. I want you to follow him.'

'Follow him. Mika, how am I supposed to do that?'

'You've shared locations with each other in the past. You shared yours with me when you came to Manchester.'

Don sighed and took out his phone.

'Well?' Mika asked as the motion sensor lights in the garden turned on. She smiled when she saw what was in her husband's hand. A fan heater and a file. She opened the door.

'You all right, Elliot?' asked Don.

'Not bad,' Elliot replied as he handed the heater to his wife. 'Don't stay out here too long – its freezing.'

'We won't be much longer. Is that the case you were telling me about?' Mika asked, pointing at the file in her husband's hand.

'Yeah. One to keep your eye on. I'll see you inside.'

'Thank you so much, darling.' Mika closed the door behind him.

'We could get your other half to join us.'

'Oh, no. He doesn't want to get his hands dirty. So, how did you get on?'

Don held up his phone, showing a map on his screen. A red pin had been placed on Cannon Street. 'Looks like he went back to the office.'

'Keep an eye on him and, if you can, follow him.'

'Mika, I've got work. Clients. I can't just take time off.'

Mika picked up a paring knife from the table and ran it along Don's cheek. 'I don't want to hear excuses. You need to think about the bigger picture.'

'You're right. Sorry, I wasn't . . . I'm sorry.'

'Don't be sorry, just do it and if it turns out that Josh is talking to the police, then you know what to do.'

Don smiled. 'I'll bring you his scalp.'

35

Laurence Durant was angry. The police arrived the moment he'd placed his duffle bag and the cat carrier into the back seat of an Uber. He'd stood, stony faced at the custody desk whilst the sergeant recorded that his property consisted of keys, passport, wallet, phone, cash total of £150, insulin, syringes, cigarettes, lighter and a duffle bag containing clothing. The only words that he'd spoken after he'd been booked in, and the body search was completed were 'where are my kittens?' The arresting officer had confirmed that his neighbour had agreed to look after the kittens until he returned.

Henley sat alone in interview room four at Lewisham police station watching the CCTV footage of Laurence Durant's car in Lordship Lane. It was times like this – when they had to book and interview a suspect – that she couldn't understand why the SCU was still housed in a run-down building in Greenwich and not the largest police station in Europe. Her ringing phone pulled her away from the screen. It was Anthony.

'Are you good to talk?' he asked.

'I'm good for the time being.' She checked the clock on the monitor to her left. 'Just waiting for Ramouter to bring in Durant for interview.'

'I've got news for you. Some of which will help you in your interview but the rest of it, well, it's going to give more questions than answers.'

'I hate it when you sound so ominous,' Henley replied. She put the phone in the crook of her neck and opened her notebook. 'Tell me what you've got.'

'First up, Durant's car. We obviously can't date the damage to the windscreen and the front bumper or tell you what caused the damage. Could have been an impact with a person, or it could've been a deer – there's no way to know. On the backseat, we recovered blood and hair that we matched with Graham Ashcroft.'

Henley felt excitable nerves in her stomach as she made a note. 'You're a superstar.'

Anthony chuckled. 'That's not all. We also recovered Graham Ashcroft's hair and blood from the broken glass. On the steering wheel we recovered prints belonging to Durant and prints and blood samples from, let's call them, person A.'

'I take it that person A is not on the database?' Henley asked as the door opened and Ramouter stepped in. She mouthed one minute.

'Yeah, person A is not in the database but the blood we recovered from the steering wheel matches not only blood that we recovered from the Ashcrofts' kitchen but also DNA recovered from Sian Fox-Carnell and Nathan Hall.'

'All three.'

'Yes. A nice little golden triangle. But the DNA from person A doesn't match the DNA that was recovered from under the fingernails of both Graham Ashcroft and Fox-Carnell.'

Henley could hear Anthony flicking through pages. 'I'm kind of somewhere but nowhere,' she said. 'Clear evidence of two suspects but no idea as to identification.'

'That's one way of putting it,' said Anthony. 'But I'm about to add a silver lining to your cloud. Nathan Hall's house. We recovered bloody footprints from the hallway and on the stairs. We've got three sets of prints. We originally had four, but we eliminated the housekeeper's. The first print is a size twelve, Men's Nike Air Max 90. Lot of wear on the outer edge of the heel, what you would expect with an overpronator. Second print, Vans Men's Ward sneaker, size ten and the third,' Anthony sighed. 'The third is a nosy guy.'

'What do you mean by nosy?'

'The second print we found halfway up the stairs, adjacent to where Nathan Hall was hanged. The first prints were on the hallway floor, twelve inches from the staircase, suggesting to me—'

'First prints held up Nathan Hall while the second print hanged him from the bannister.'

'Exactly, but the third print carries on up the staircase and we track them into the main bedroom, the bathroom and also the living room. We then recovered fingerprints from the bannister and also the wall going up the stairs and when we ran them through the database we got a match. A Ben Trezeguet.'

'Excuse me, say that again.' Henley's pen fell from her hand.

'Ben Trezeguet,' Anthony repeated. 'Fingerprints and samples were entered onto the database a year ago. Suspect three?'

Henley circled Ben's name twice and then got up and opened the door. 'Stay there,' she said to Laurence and his legal representative who were waiting in the hall. She pulled Ramouter into the room. 'Sorry, Anthony, you were saying.'

'Oh, nothing. Just that this Trezeguet geezer may be a suspect, or he could just be someone who's getting in the way,' Anthony opined. 'Anyway, I'll let you get on.'

'What the—' Ramouter stopped himself from swearing after listening to Henley's update. 'First the Fox-Carnell crime scene and then the press conference.'

'And now we've got him at the Hall crime scene,' nodded Henley.

'Are you saying that Ben is involved and is out there perving on his handiwork?'

'I don't know if it's exactly like that. Annoying as he is, my gut doesn't tell me he's involved in that way.'

Ramouter shook his head. 'We've got direct – not circumstantial – evidence of Ben's involvement. He was inside Nathan Hall's house, fingerprints and there was blood on his shoes. You know how this works, boss.'

'I do, but I have questions,' said Henley. 'Why would Ben make such a big mistake and incriminate himself by leaving his DNA behind in Hall's house? Mantell, Bo Hyoo, Fox-Carnell and the Ashcrofts. Nothing.'

'He got complacent. It wouldn't be the first time a criminal let his ego get in the way and he gets sloppy.'

'True,' said Henley.

'And even if we go with your theory, boss, why was Ben Trezeguet in Nathan Hall's house? How did he get in? And why didn't he call the police when he discovered the body hanging from the bannister?'

Henley smiled, both impressed with Ramouter's determination and analysis and that he wasn't afraid to challenge her.

'We also can't ignore that Ben's got previous convictions. He's not innocent,' Ramouter went on.

'No, he's not,' said Henley. 'We'll put him on the suspect board but, before we do that, let's deal with Durant. He's already lied to Stanford and Eastie. Let's see if he'll lie to our faces under caution.'

Henley kept her eyes on Laurence Durant as Ramouter completed the admin section of the interview. She had enough evidence to question Laurence but what she needed to move this case on was a confession.

Ramouter tapped the recording button on the touchscreen. 'We're good to go.'

'Before we start,' said the legal representative, a serious but young-looking woman, named Kalia Ghatak, whose black hair hung like silk curtains on her back. She kept her head down as she wrote her notes. 'Mr Durant is hearing impaired. You may not have noticed that he wears a hearing aid in his left ear. They failed to mention that on his custody record.'

As if on cue, Durant's hearing aid released a low whistle.

'I'm more than happy to put you back in the cell whilst we make arrangements to get a BSL interpreter here if that will assist you,' said Henley.

'No,' Durant answered quickly, putting a finger to his hearing aid. 'I can manage. Let's get on with it.'

'Fine,' said Henley. 'DC Ramouter, do you want to make the introductions?'

Henley checked the notes she'd made when talking to Anthony as Ramouter completed the introductions, explained to Laurence his entitlement to legal advice and the caution.

'Right, we'll start,' said Henley. 'Laurance Durant, you've been arrested for an offence of attempted—'

'I didn't do it.'

'Let the Inspector finish,' Kalia said.

'As I was saying, you were arrested this morning at 6.27 a.m. for the attempted murders of Tabitha and Graham Ashcroft on the twelfth October at their home on Cullen Lane in Dulwich Village. Your legal representative has received full disclosure about the allegations and now I'm going to ask you questions about your involvement. Do you understand?' asked Henley.

'I wasn't involved,' said Larry.

'Do you understand?' Henley repeated.

'Yes.'

'Good. So, let's start.'

Henley paused, allowing the silence to grow uncomfortable as she scanned the questions she'd prepared. She turned the page over and decided to change tack.

'We have no idea how we're going to respond to death do we, Larry?' she said.

'What do you mean?' Larry replied as he turned his head slightly, watching the door.

'It's one of the life events that we can never really prepare for. We tell ourselves that it's a fact of life and that we will be strong and won't break. We think we're going to be different and then the unimaginable happens and someone you love dies. I don't think it makes much difference if the person is sick, and you know they're going die or if it happens out of the blue. It hurts. You hurt. Do you agree?'

Larry cleared his throat. 'I do,' he eventually said.

'Some people break down straight away and with others, it's a very slow walk through denial until something innocuous sets them off. So, which was it for you when your wife was killed?'

Henley held her nerve despite Larry looking at her as though she were a piece of shit under his shoe. She was prepared to hit low and pinch all of the pressure points if it meant she would get what she wanted.

'I couldn't believe it at first. I thought they'd gone to the wrong house. My neighbour Tony is an alcoholic and spent last Christmas in hospital because he stepped out in traffic, drunk out of his skull. I didn't think they were coming for me,' said Larry.

'Were you angry?'

'Not at first. I didn't believe that . . . that she was gone. They drove me to the hospital, and I was running through all these different scenarios. Maybe someone stole her purse and the person who got hit had her credit cards or it was someone who just happened to have the same name, but then I got there.'

Kalia took out a tissue from her bag and handed it to Larry.

'It was her.' Larry rubbed roughly at his eyes, reddening the thin surrounding skin. 'The weird thing was that her face was fine, and she was still warm. I told her to wake up. Reminded her that we had a trip booked. But she didn't wake up.'

'When did you get angry?' Henley asked.

'I'm not sure really. I woke up one day and I was angry with everyone and then I went to the funeral director's the day before the funeral. Seeing Sherri in the coffin . . . it did something to me.'

'I'm not sure how making Mr Durant relive the loss of his wife is going to help you with your investigation. Are you going to actually ask any questions to do with the reason why you arrested Mr Durant?' Kalia cut in.

'Let's talk about the Ashcrofts,' said Henley. 'On the day Tabitha Ashcroft was sentenced you—'

'That wasn't a sentence,' Larry interrupted, his voice raised and angry. 'She walked away with a warning to behave herself. She committed murder. She killed my Sherri.'

'And you threatened to kill her too, didn't you?' Henley pulled a witness statement from a file. '"I'm going to kill you, you fucking bitch. I'm going to take everything from you."'

'They dropped the charges.'

'They may have dropped it but that doesn't erase the words that came out of your mouth. You held on to that anger, didn't you, Larry?'

'No, I didn't.'

'You were determined to get Tabitha Ashcroft back for ruining your life. For killing your wife.'

Larry tutted and shook his head. Henley pushed a sheet of paper towards him.

'What's this?' he asked.

'This is a copy of a bank transaction. A payment of £10,000 from Graham Ashcroft's bank account to Barclays account number 18740299, which is your bank account, right?'

'Yes, but I can explain.'

'Oh, I didn't realise there was an explanation for blackmail,' Henley said sarcastically .

'It wasn't . . . no, it wasn't blackmail.'

'Of course it was. After the police very kindly dropped the charges against you, you began a campaign of harassment against the Ashcrofts, didn't you?'

'Absolutely not. I wouldn't waste my time on those people.'

'You wrote them letters, made threats against them and then you started to demand money from them to make it all stop.'

'He offered me the money.'

'What, out of the blue Graham Ashcroft offered you money?' Henley asked with clear disbelief.

'To help with the funeral costs.'

'You're telling me that eighteen months after you buried your wife, Graham Ashcroft offered you ten grand?'

'It's not cheap to organise a funeral.'

'I know it's not cheap, but I also know that both you and your wife had funeral plans, so those costs were covered. So, you start with harassment and move on to blackmail. Told them things would get worse for them if they didn't pay you.'

'I didn't blackmail them,' Larry said weakly.

'But you weren't happy with the ten grand they sent you. You wanted more. You wanted revenge,' Henley said as she subtly elbowed Ramouter.

'Larry, you told our colleagues, DS Stanford and Eastwood that you didn't know where the Ashcrofts lived,' said Ramouter as he opened his laptop. 'Do you remember that?'

'That's right. I don't know where they live.'

'But that's not correct, is it?' Ramouter turned the laptop around. On the screen was a residential street. 'This is Cullen Lane. Do you recognise it?'

'No. Never heard of it,' Larry replied, his voice quavering.

'And this house belongs to the Ashcrofts.' Ramouter pointed on the screen.

'I want it on the record that this footage wasn't disclosed to me,' Kalia chipped in.

'We disclosed that we had video evidence,' Ramouter replied. 'Now, this is video doorbell footage from the house opposite. As you can see, its 9.18 a.m. on Tuesday 12 October.'

'I was teaching that day,' Larry said quickly.

'Keep watching.'

The minutes dragged painfully as the video footage played. A postman walked past pushing his trolley and a UPS van came into view followed by a Skoda Octavia.

'You own a Skoda Octavia, don't you, Larry?'

Larry didn't reply but he looked across at Kalia who had leaned forward in her seat, watching the screen intently. The Skoda disappeared from view.

The video continued to play. The UPS van now back but moving quickly down the street.

'You said you were teaching that day?'

'Um . . . yes, yes. I was,' Larry replied.

'What time?'

'Time?'

'Aye. What time did you start teaching?'

'I can't remember.'

'You can't remember?'

Larry didn't reply and Ramouter pressed pause.

'For the benefit of the tape, I'm showing Laurence Durant footage of himself outside the Ashcrofts' home on Tuesday twelfth October at 9.18 a.m.,' said Ramouter. 'Would you like to explain why you lied to my colleagues about not being at the Ashcrofts' house?'

'That's not me,' Larry said meekly.

'If I'm not mistaken, you're wearing the same jacket now that you were wearing on this video footage.'

Larry looked down at his arm as though realising for the first time that he was wearing a jacket.

'This is you going up to the Ashcrofts' front door. You then go across to the windows and then you go to their car and crouch down. You're out of view. Why did you slash the car tyres?'

'No. I didn't,' Larry said. 'That wasn't me. I wasn't there.'

'You're saying that this person, that we're all looking at, isn't you?' Ramouter clarified.

Larry shook his head.

'You need to speak,' Henley said. 'We're only recording the audio.'

'No, that's not me,' Larry said quietly.

'Fine,' Ramouter said brightly. 'Let's talk about your car then. You told my colleagues that you sold your car. A 2012 Skoda Octavia.'

'That's correct. It was my wife's car. I thought that it was time to get rid of it. To move on,' said Larry. He picked up his cup and water dribbled down his chin as he drank clumsily.

'When did you sell it?'

'Erm . . . a few months ago.'

'Did you advertise it, sell it to a car trader?'

'I just put a note in the window, and someone bought it.'

Ramouter took out two sheets of paper and placed them on the table. 'This is a DVLA printout of the registration details for your car. Make, model, stuff like that and, on the second page – the bit that I've highlighted – you will see the list of registered keepers, previous and current. The car was transferred to your name two months after your wife's death and it's still in your name.'

'I just haven't got round to letting them know, the DVLA that is,' said Larry.

'Why are you lying?' Ramouter asked. He brought up a series of photos on the screen. 'These are photographs of your car, on your street, taken last week by our colleagues. Exhibit PS/1.'

'They've made a mistake,' Larry said shakily.

'Are you suggesting that my officers are lying?' Henley jumped in, leaning forward on the table.

'I don't have the car, I sold it.'

'Stop lying and tell me what happened on the night of 17 October,' Henley said firmly.

'Nothing happened. I was home.'

'This is footage of your car on Lordship Lane, half a mile from the Ashcrofts' home,' said Ramouter. 'Your car is then seen turning into Cullen Lane at 11.38 p.m..'

'I sold the car,' Larry said, his voice breaking.

'Tabitha Ashcroft was attacked in her home,' Henley ploughed on, keeping her eyes on Larry as she produced photographs of Tabitha's injuries. 'She was pinned down in her kitchen and her attacker put a knife to the back of her head and scalped her.'

Larry paled, put his hands to his mouth and closed his eyes. 'Oh my god, oh my god.'

'Scalped her,' Henley repeated, tapping the table hard. 'You've got scratch marks on your hand and a mark on the side of your head. Did that happen when Tabitha was trying to defend herself?'

'It wasn't me.'

'If it wasn't you then who was it? Who did you drop off at the Ashcrofts' home, Larry?'

'I didn't do anything.' Larry lowered and shook his head.

'The only reason you weren't arrested for her murder is because her husband saved her,' said Ramouter as Henley leaned back in her seat. 'Not that he got away unscathed.'

'Look at the photographs, Larry,' Henley pushed. She placed more photographs on the table, this time of Graham. Half-naked on a hospital bed. His knife wounds visible.

'Stabbed multiple times because he was trying to save his wife,' Henley said slowly.

Larry breathed in deeply, clasping his hands tightly. 'I don't know anything about that.'

'Can you explain why Graham's blood was found in your car?'

'Again, you didn't disclose this to me,' said Kalia, pushing another tissue towards Larry.

'Check your disclosure,' Henley said coldly as Ramouter brought up the image of the shattered car windscreen. 'You were informed that we had forensic evidence. DNA.'

'Look, Larry, we're not asking you these questions because we're trying to hurt you or catch you out,' Ramouter said, his voice calm and warm as he switched the footage. 'We want to help you.'

'You can't help me,' Larry answered.

'Graham Ashcroft ran out of his house. He thought he was running away from danger,' said Ramouter. He pressed play on the footage that had been taken from the Ashcrofts' neighbour, Patsy Howe. The gasp from Kalia was audible as the footage showed Graham running into view, being hit by a car, landing heavily on the bonnet and then falling to the ground.

'I need a consultation with my client,' said Kalia.

'Interview suspended at 10.34 a.m.,' said Ramouter.

'We'll be waiting outside,' Henley told them. She and Ramouter gathered their things and left the interview room.

Ramouter leaned his forehead against the wall and exhaled as Henley began to pace the narrow hallway. 'So, what do you think?' he asked.

'He's definitely involved,' Henley replied. 'But I just don't think that he's got it in him to actually kill someone.'

'You said it yourself. Death can change us.'

'Or it reveals who you really are,' Henley countered.

The interview room door opened and Kalia poked her head out. She looked tired and fed up. 'We're ready.'

Henley entered the interview room and paused momentarily. She knew it was physically impossible, but Larry looked shrunken as though the burden he was carrying had made his body collapse. He rubbed the side of his face.

'Interview resumed at 10.46 a.m.,' Ramouter announced. 'I'm DC Salim Ramouter and also present is . . .'

'DI Anjelica Henley.'

'Legal Representative Kalia Ghatak.'

'Laurence Durant.'

'I must remind you Larry that you still remain under caution and again, you can let us know if you need a break for a further consultation, do you understand?' asked Ramouter.

'Yes,' Larry mumbled.

'Ok, so before the break, we were asking you questions about the night the Ashcrofts were attacked. Can you tell us where you were from 11 p.m. on the seventeenth October?'

'No comment,' said Larry.

Henley marked the question that Ramouter had asked with an X. She wasn't in the least bit surprised that Larry had decided to follow Kalia's new advice; to shut up.

'Who else was in the car with you?' asked Ramouter.

'No comment.'

'Whose idea was it to go to the Ashcrofts' home?'

'No comment.'

'Can you give me the name of the person who was seen dragging Graham Ashcroft into your car?'

'No comment.'

'Can you explain how Graham Ashcroft's blood got into your car?'

'No comment.'

'Did you attack and scalp Tabitha Ashcroft in her kitchen?'

Larry lowered head and shook it as he began to cry.

'Why are you shaking your head in a no gesture, Larry?' asked Henley. 'Are you shaking your head no because it wasn't you who hurt Tabitha, but you know who did?'

'No comment.' Larry replied, the words barely audible.

'Can you explain why you ran away from myself and DC Ramouter when you saw us at your victim support group?'

Larry didn't answer.

'Is the person you're covering up for a member of that victim support group?'

'Can you make them stop?' Larry whispered to Kalia who shook her head.

'Just follow my advice which is to answer all questions no comment,' she said softly.

'If it wasn't you driving your car then who was it?' asked Henley.

'No comment,' Larry continued as he hugged himself.

'We've seized your mobile phone as we believe that it contains information pertinent to our investigation,' said Henley. She placed an exhibit bag containing a Samsung Galaxy flip phone on the table. 'We want to examine it. Are you willing to give me your pin number?'

'No, no,' Larry said, turning to Kalia. 'You can't. They can't go in my phone, can they?

'Only if they serve you with a Section 49 RIPA notice and, even then, they will have to go before a judge who will decide if they can,' Kalia replied. 'Is that what you're doing Inspector. Serving a Section 49?'

'I will if Larry declines to provide his PIN,' answered Henley.

'No. I'm not doing it,' said Larry. 'No comment.'

'I've got to warn you that failing to provide your PIN is a criminal offence. You can go to prison.'

'No comment.'

'You do understand that you're potentially looking at two life sentences for the attempted murder of the Ashcrofts?' Henley asked. 'You and I both know that isn't what your wife Sherri would have wanted for you.'

Henley could see all the emotions in Larry's eyes as he raised his head and stared at her. Anger morphed into sadness, frustration and despair but it was the grief swimming in his eyes as he mouthed the name Sherri that gripped at the part of her soul that she hadn't locked away when she'd walked into the interview room.

Henley pushed aside the waves of compassion and strengthened her voice. 'Larry, do you have any questions for me?'

Larry opened and then closed his mouth as though he'd made a decision but had changed his mind.

'You look as though you want to say something,' said Ramouter. 'I just want to make sure before we stop the interview.'

'No,' said Larry as he pushed his hands in his pocket. 'I don't have anything to say. On the advice of my legal representative. No comment.'

'Fine. Interview concluded at 10.53 a.m.,' said Henley.

'Is that it. Can I . . .Can I go now?' Larry asked as Ramouter handed him a form to sign.

'No. You'll be taken back to your cell once you've finished your post interview consultation with Ms Ghatak,' said Henley. She stood up from the table, her back muscles protesting as they tightened in knots.

'Oh, I thought—'

'I'm sure that Ms Ghatak advised you that we can keep you here for twenty-four hours,' said Henley.

'Even longer if we apply for an extension. Up to ninety-six hours.' Ramouter opened the door and walked out.

Henley followed, but then she paused, turned around and stared at Larry.

'You said that we couldn't help you,' Henley said. 'But you need to think about how you can help yourself. Otherwise you'll be spending more time in a cell than Tabitha Ashcroft ever did for killing your wife.'

36

'This is a special edition of Freedom News *with your host Ben Trezeguet. Independent news is the only place to get the truth and I'm here to give it to you. Nathan Hall is dead. I was planning to reveal this information to you first, but the police released their statement shortly before I went live. Don't forget to leave your questions in the chat. Right, the statement reads "On Tuesday morning a twenty-eight-year-old man was found dead in his home. We can formally identify the victim as Nathan Hall. His next of kin has been informed, and a post-mortem has been carried out as part of the investigation. A murder investigation has been launched, and a team of detectives are making proactive CCTV and witness enquiries. No arrests have been made." Yeah, it's sad that he was killed but is anyone really sorry that a rapist is dead? No. This is exclusive footage of officers from the Serial Crime Unit entering Nathan Hall's house. You may recognise the female detective from my in-depth profile into the serial killer Peter Olivier. Dan092 asks in the chat. "Why would they hide that information?" Yeah, Dan, you're right. Why would the Met Police not reveal the involvement of the Serial Crime Unit?'*

Pellacia froze the video. 'How has this happened?' he asked Henley. 'And why isn't the little shit sitting in a cell?'

'For the record, I had no idea there was a drone hanging around when DI Henley and I were at the Hall crime scene,' said Ramouter.

'The fact that you had no idea is not going to help me when I'm sitting in front of the borough commander and the assistant commissioner in an hour,' Pellacia replied.

'Ben Trezeguet is in the wind somewhere,' said Henley, taking the control from Pellacia's hand. She rewound the footage, pausing at the drone footage of herself and Ramouter standing outside Nathan Lane's home with uniformed officers as a black private ambulance pulled into the driveway. 'Officers from Stoke Newington police went to Ben's address in Dalston an hour after Anthony gave me the update. There was no one there.'

'Does he work? I can't imagine that he's making a living from this YouTube thing?' said Pellacia.

'You'd be surprised,' said Stanford, dragging his chair towards Henley. 'The money rolls in once you get yourself monetised. That's what my niece Casey tells me.'

'I'm not thinking he's someone that needs to be on the suspect board,' said Pellacia.

'I didn't think that he's a suspect either,' Henley agreed. 'But Ramouter made some valid points. We can't just write him off. There's an argument for joint enterprise. His prints were in Nathan Hall's house, and he clearly has access to sensitive information.'

'He's got to be using a police scanner,' said Ramouter. 'It would explain why he was at the Fox-Carnell crime scene.'

'But it wouldn't explain how and why he ended up at Nathan Hall's house,' said Henley. 'What worries me is what he's going to release next. He thinks he's a detective and I don't trust him not to show Nathan Hall's dead body.'

'We need to get him arrested and charged with – if not murder – interfering with the course of justice and get him before a judge as soon as possible,' said Ramouter. 'He's a danger to this case and to himself.'

'What do we actually know about this Trezeguet geezer?' asked Stanford. 'I doubt he volunteered to put his DNA on the database.'

'He's twenty-six years old and he has previous for criminal damage, trespass and domestic burglary,' Copeland said, standing as she turned over the pages of Ben Trezeguet's PNC in her hands. 'Actually, two burglary convictions. He got a twelve-month community order for the first one and a suspended sentence for the second one.' Copeland sucked air through her teeth. 'Three strikes. He's looking at a minimum of three years in prison if he gets convicted of another domestic dwelling. Something he needs to be aware of if we ever get cuffs on him.'

'I don't believe this YouTube detective wannabe has just disappeared.' Pellacia checked his watch. 'He's invested in this case and not just as an observer, if Ramouter is right. He's been present at two crime scenes and he tried to get into the press conference. He either knows nothing or saw something and I can't see him not coming back to talk about it.'

'I'm always one for following your gut instinct,' Copeland said, looking pointedly at Henley. 'But we've got no evidence that he's not involved in these murders somehow.'

Henley folded her arms and cocked her head to the side.

'Where are we with Durant?' Pellacia asked quickly, manoeuvring his body slightly in front of Copeland. Shielding her.

'I'm going to release him under investigation at some point this afternoon, but I want to let him sweat in a cell for a bit. Give him a taste of the future if he doesn't start co-operating,' Henley said, her voice steady but filled with disdain. 'But I want to have eyes on him when he does get out. We need surveillance.'

'I've already told you, repeatedly, that we don't have the budget.' Pellacia was exasperated as he put on his coat.

'If you're off to see the bosses, talk to them. Tell them to find the money,' said Henley.

'Tell them?' Pellacia replied, his eyes sparkling with humour as the intercom buzzed.

'Remind them that we've got at least two crazy people running around South London scalping people.'

'Vigilantes,' Stanford offered as Joanna walked over.

'Mark is on his way up,' said Joanna as Stanford rolled his eyes.

'Thank god. Right, I'm off to beg for money,' said Pellacia. 'Keep me updated.'

'Before we move on, I spoke to the SIO of the Nathan Hall rape investigation earlier this morning,' said Copeland, facing Henley, the glare of defiance visible in her eyes. Copeland spoke quickly and forcefully, not giving Henley the opportunity to find a break in her speech and stop her. 'I know that we're focusing on the vigilante angle, but I think we can't ignore the fact that Nathan Hall was attacked by one of the complainants, Tyler Simmons, when he was leaving court after the verdict.'

'Physically or verbally?' Henley asked with cold steel in her voice as Dr Mark Ryan entered. He held up his bottle of water in greeting and took a seat.

'Physically,' Copeland replied. She took a step and turned her back on Henley to face the team. 'According to DI Knowles, Simmons rushed and punched Hall when he was leaving court and was restrained by security and arrested. Simmons was charged with common assault and was held overnight in custody. He appeared at Westminster Magistrates' Court yesterday morning and pleaded not guilty.'

'Eastwood,' Henley said loudly. 'I want you to see Simmons. Take the details from Copeland and you can also check with Anthony and ask him to run the DNA samples retrieved from Hall through the database. Simmons' samples may not have been uploaded when Anthony first did his checks.'

Copeland's neck flushed red as Eastwood tucked her pen behind her ear and raised her eyebrows at Stanford.

'Henley, I don't think that's fair,' said Copeland, a quiver in her voice. 'I did the—'

'You know how the rank system works, so make sure you address me accordingly and, secondly, I shouldn't have to explain to you what it means to be part of a team,' snapped Henley.

'No, of course not, guv, but—'

'We just don't go off and do whatever we want, when we want. Now, what you will do, once we've heard from Dr Ryan, is go through the prosecution case papers, unused material of the Douglas Mantell and Gong Bo Hyoo court cases and cross reference it against our investigation.'

'You want me to do paperwork.'

'You're working a case, Copeland. This unit is not about showboating. Is that understood?'

'Yes, guv,' Copeland replied bitterly as Henley walked away.

'Very formal – Dr Ryan,' Mark said with a grin as Henley joined him. He removed his glasses and cleaned the lens. 'I haven't seen you since before you went on holiday.'

'That holiday seems like a lifetime ago,' said Henley. 'The only reminder is the mosquito bites on my legs and the suitcases in the utility room. Let me introduce you to DC Copeland. She's joined us, temporarily, from Lewisham CID.'

Copeland shook Mark's hand. 'Pleasure to meet you,' she said with a tight smile.

'How come you're here?' asked Stanford. 'I thought we didn't have the cash.'

'Stanford, as always, it's a joy to see you too,' said Mark. He stopped at the whiteboard and pointed at the photographs of Douglas Mantell and Gong Bo Hyoo. 'I thought it was just three victims?' he asked.

'We thought so too,' said Eastwood. 'They're open murder investigations in Manchester and Sheffield. Similar MOs.'

'Five victims. Ok, let's start. The scalping. Popular culture makes it seem as though scalping, the act of cutting or tearing part of the human scalp off with the hair attached, is just unique to the indigenous people of the Americas but it's not. Europe, Asia, the colonial wars, the US civil war. I could go on.'

'The history lesson is all very well and good but that doesn't help us with what we're dealing with,' said Stanford.

'Stanford just let the man talk,' said Eastwood. 'Why the scalping? I'm assuming our killers are taking a trophy.'

'Or a souvenir – there's a difference. A souvenir is a memento whereas a trophy is proof of the killer's skill, but whether it's a trophy or a souvenir, keeping the victim's scalp allows your killer to both relive the thrill of committing the initial crime and allows them to feel powerful.'

'How common is it? To scalp your victim?' asked Ramouter.

'It's rare but it does happen. In fact, there are two recent cases,' said Mark. 'A man called Nyckk Visser was convicted of murdering three women in Holland two years ago but the bodies were found fifteen years ago. All three had been decapitated but Visser wasn't linked to their murders until he'd reported a burglary, and the police found their scalps in his bedroom.'

'That's crazy. He incriminated himself,' said Copeland, shifting away from Henley.

'There was also a case in Scotland last year. Bryce Schofield. Raped, murdered and scalped a male prostitute.'

'Two DNA profiles were found on our victims,' said Henley. 'Our vigilantes are, at a minimum, a pair. So, which one is taking the scalps?'

'Out of your group one of them has to be the leader, the alpha,' said Mark. 'Scalping in itself is so rare that I can't imagine it being a joint decision. Either the leader has requested it or someone in the group, the one who is most suggestible, eager to please. The trophy, their prize could be their gift to the leader.'

Henley grimaced.

'This isn't one of those cases where I can say that your vigilante is going to be a thirty to forty-year-old white man,' Mark continued. 'You're dealing with a group, a pack mentality but with all packs there is a leader. Your leader in this case may not be someone who has necessarily experienced an injustice. It's what we call a third-party role.'

'Do you mean they're taking on someone else's cause?' asked Copeland.

'Exactly that,' replied Mark. 'They haven't been directly impacted by what we would call a norm violation. They've either witnessed it or learned about it. You may also find that the pack leader works in a managerial position and that they have a heightened sense of moral self-worth.'

'They're taking advantage of the real victim. Exploiting their pain,' said Ramouter. 'There's no better example of that than Laurance Durant.'

'His wife was the one who was killed in the road traffic accident by Tabitha Ashcroft, right?' asked Mark.

'Yes, but her scalping wasn't complete. No kill. No trophy,' said Ramouter.

'The fact that she wasn't killed is fuel for them to keep continuing with their mission,' said Mark. 'This is all about control and exhibiting power and once someone has a taste for power,' he shrugged, 'it's hard to let go.'

'You really don't like her, do you?' said Mark as he pulled up his coat collar.

'I have no idea what you're talking about.' Henley fell into step with Mark as they walked away from Greenwich police station, the building grey, decaying and unwelcoming as it merged into the gun-metal overcast sky.

Mark laughed. 'You know exactly who I'm talking about,' he said. 'Your new team member. DC Copeland.'

'It's not that I don't like her it's just that I find her—'

'Too inna?'

Henley laughed at Mark's use of slang. 'Are you trying to keep up with your kids again?'

'The eleven-year-old told me this morning that I had no rizz. I had to Google it.'

'Ooh, that must have hurt.'

'I'll live. But am I right though? About Copeland.'

'I can understand why she would want to join the SCU but she's impulsive, sneaky and disingenuous.'

'That's quite a list, but I feel as though there's something missing,' said Mark

'Her intention. I don't think it's just the appeal of this case that's brought her to the SCU.'

'Ramouter?'

'How could you tell?' Henley asked with surprise.

'It's what I do. I'm a profiler after all.'

'And there I was thinking you were fussy about your title.'

'Nah, I just like winding Stanford up, but my advice is don't read too much into it. Ramouter has his family, but he still needs friends. It's probably no more than that. London can be a lonely place. You and I won't feel that because we were born and raised here.'

'Maybe I'll recommend him to my sister-in-law's book club.'

'Anjelica, come on.'

'Fine. Fine. I'll do better and thank you for coming by.'

'Tell Pellacia it's my last freebie,' said Mark. 'So where are you off to?'

'Bromley Mags. I'm hoping that the judge will grant my application to get into Laurence Durant's phone.'

'Looking for the pack leader?'

'Exactly. Find the pack and hopefully this whole vigilante group falls apart.'

'A group like that. It won't be easy for someone to just walk away. Your leader is someone who most likely has a narcissistic personality or borderline personality disorder and they'll have the hallmarks of coercive behaviour. They thrive on being able to control people, events and situations which means that they won't like it if a member of the pack attempts to break out. They'll want to reinforce their dominance. They'll do what some wolves do.'

Henley grimaced. 'Eat their own,' she said.

'Not just their own,' said Mark. 'Once they recognise the SCU as a threat, they'll snap. All of you are at risk.'

'You think that they would come after one of us?'

'I wouldn't put anything past them. These people, whoever they are, believe they're not just above the law, but better than it. As far as they're concerned, you, the SCU are stopping them in their pursuit of what they believe to be justice.'

Henley shivered as the wind nipped at her neck. 'You said the scalping made them feel powerful,' she said.

'And power is a drug,' replied Mark. 'But like all drugs, you can develop a tolerance.'

'What are you saying, that the scalping may not be a big enough high?'

'They'll be no different to any drug addict looking to recreate the buzz of their first high.'

'Nothing ever beats that first rush.'

'Imagine how frustrating that must be. Expecting the next scalp to placate you but instead you're left wanting,' Mark said, his face stern. 'There will come a point when taking their victim's scalp won't be enough and they'll make sure that they punish whoever gets in their way.'

Henley clasped her hands to the back of her neck and raised her head. She knew better than to underestimate a killer. 'They're going to want more,' she said. 'They'll come for us.'

Mark looked back at the station. 'And they'll want you to suffer,' he said.

37

'Guv, can I have a word?'

Pellacia looked up to see DC Copeland standing at his door. She looked pensive but also irritated.

'I won't take up much of your time. I can see you've got a lot on.' Copeland stepped further into Pellacia's office and placed her hands on the back of the chair. *A lot on* was an understatement. Pellacia's desk was overrun with copies of the investigation reports and statements from the cases that Eastwood had flagged as possible serial crimes.

'Close the door and take a seat,' Pellacia said, sticking a green Post-it note on a woman's statement alleging that her partner's kidneys had been harvested.

'I've always prided myself on being someone who doesn't let their personal feelings get in the way. I get on with the job,' said Copeland once she'd sat down. 'My priority has always been to do the best job I can.'

'I can hear a but,' said Pellacia.

'I only joined the SCU yesterday, and I understand that it can take time to fit in. To work out how a team moves and breathes.'

'I'm still waiting for the but,' said Pellacia as an email alert from Henley popped up on his computer screen.

Copeland pursed her lips and briefly closed her eyes, looking as though she was struggling internally with a decision. 'I'm not in the habit of making complaints, but the fact is that I'm being stopped from doing my job.'

'Excuse me?' Pellacia asked. He leaned forward folding his arms on his desk.

'I've been a DC for nearly four years. You know my history. I worked in the rape and serious sexual offences unit for two years and then I moved to homicide and major crimes. By the end of the year, I plan to sit my sergeant exams. The point is, guv, it may only have been a day but I'm not a probationary officer. I know how to do my job, but Inspector Henley isn't allowing me to do it. She's treating me like I'm a fifteen-year-old on work experience.'

Pellacia let the silence sit as he resisted the urge to immediately jump to Henley's defence.

'So, you are making a complaint?' he asked. 'One day in.'

'No, no,' Copeland said defensively, turning around as though checking that she wasn't being observed through the window in the door. 'I'm not here to rock the boat, but, guv, earlier after you'd left, when Henley did the briefing, she shot me down. I've been an SIO in a case before.'

Pellacia raised his eyebrows.

'Obviously not a murder investigation and definitely not something like this but I know how to work a major crime and the first thing you do, as an SIO, is to explore investigative strategies, provide investigative focus, co-ordinate, support and—'

'I really don't need you to quote sections of the major crime and investigation manual at me,' Pellacia said.

'The authorised professional practice for policing states that investigators need to be open to the ideas and experiences of others,' Copeland said determinedly. 'Inspector Henley should consult with her colleagues. Me, DS Stanford, Ramouter and Eastwood when trying to identify the most appropriate action to take in any given case.'

'You said it wasn't a complaint, but this is sounding very much like a complaint.'

Copeland shook her head. 'I'm not complaining. Just stating a fact.'

Pellacia picked up a notebook and began to make notes in the hope that the lack of eye contact would stop Copeland from digging a deeper hole for herself.

'Inspector Henley completely dismissed the enquiries I'd made that would progress the investigation, she talked down to me, embarrassed me in front of the team. I'm doing admin that, with all due respect, Joanna could do.'

Pellacia rubbed at his temple. 'Explain the admin part,' he said.

'Cross referencing CRIS reports instead of going out there and speaking to important witnesses.'

'You don't think that going through CRIS reports, identifying patterns and analysing information is police work, that it's important?'

Copeland sighed. 'Of course it's important,' she said firmly. 'I don't mind doing the work, but I would appreciate it if Henley, sorry Inspector Henley, afforded me the same respect that she gives to the rest of the team.'

'Is that it?'

'I just want to do my job, guv, but yes, that's it,' Copeland said, standing up. 'Thank you for hearing me.'

'Wonder what that was all about?' Ramouter asked Stanford as they both watched Copeland pick up her phone from her desk and walk out of the office from where they stood in the kitchenette.

Stanford threw the teaspoon into the sink. 'Probably having a moan about Henley,' he said.

'You don't really think that, do you?' Ramouter replied.

'I'd put money on it. The tension between Henley and Copeland is as thick as the custard that my nan used to make.'

'She's just keen,' Ramouter said. 'And let's be honest, it's not easy joining you lot. Remember you had a bet running that I wouldn't last six months in the SCU.'

'That's very true and also a reminder that I need to start a bet on Copeland. So, what do you reckon?' Stanford said, walking back to his desk. 'Twenty quid, she'll be kicked out by the end of the next week?'

'Wow? Ye of little faith,' Ramouter laughed, reaching for the doughnuts on top of the microwave. 'Fifty quid she'll be made permanent.'

'Bloody optimist. Just make sure your cash is in the tin by Friday,' Stanford said. His phone rang. It took a couple of seconds to realise that 0161 was the area code for Manchester. He quickly answered.

'This is DI Forfana. Serious sexual offences unit. Greater Manchester police. I've been on annual leave and came back to a bunch of messages on my desk. So, what can I help you with?'

'Douglas Mantell's murder is possibly linked to a series of murders that we're investigating.'

'Mantell was pulled from the canal well over a year ago, but even so, shouldn't you be talking to the SIO from the homicide team?'

'We already are but one of the unique features of our investigation is that all of our victims recently appeared in court and either walked away with an acquittal or a light sentence that wasn't worth the paper it was written on.'

'I'm assuming one of your line of enquiries is looking at anyone who would have been unhappy with the verdict?'

'Exactly. Someone like Mantell I doubt would have had an outpouring of support. So, are you good to go?'

'Fire away. I've got the case files open in front of me.'

'Ok,' Stanford said as he picked up a biro and smoothed out a page. 'When did you first open the investigation into Mantell?'

'Four years ago, Mantell's daughter Gia first reported the

allegations of sexual assault to her GP. She has a younger sister, Hazel who was nine years old at the time of the report. Gia said that she could see her dad looking at her sister the way he used to look at her and it unnerved her.'

There was a pause, where the only thing that Stanford could hear was the hum of office activity down the line. He heard Forfana kiss his teeth.

'Sorry,' Forfana said. 'There are some things that you just can't harden yourself to. Gia was five months pregnant when she made the allegations and had also found out that she was having girl.'

'Her sister and the baby. It triggered her.'

'Exactly. She broke down in front of her GP. Told him what her dad had done to her and what he'd made his friends do to her.'

'His friends?'

'Yeah, it's turned into a much bigger investigation than we initially thought. Still ongoing. Mantell was just the tip of the iceberg. Gia's GP directed her to SARC—'

'The Sexual Assault Referral Centre?'

'That's it. She went to SARC, and the case came through to me. She was understandably scared. She didn't want to be responsible for breaking up her family, but she came in and gave her statement over several months. I couldn't ask for anything more from her really,' Forfana's voice softened with empathy. 'We arrested and interviewed Mantell, hoping he'd break and give up the names of the others, but he didn't. He was charged and the court system being what it is, it took a while for the trial to come around and when it did . . . I don't know why the jury couldn't all agree that the dirty pervert was guilty.'

Forfana's disappointment and sense of failure permeated through the phone. Stanford let the silence sit for a while.

'Have you got kids?' Forfana asked.

'No. Well, nearly. We're adopting. He'll be with us in a couple of weeks.'

'Congratulations but to be fair it doesn't take having kids to feel that an injustice has been done. To feel angry.'

'Was anyone else angry? With Mantell I mean,' Stanford asked.

'Mantell's wife definitely wasn't angry. I still don't understand how she could stand by his side even after social services took Hazel. We had a lot of groups protesting outside court.'

'What about any attacks against Mantell personally?'

Forfana laughed. 'Take your pick,' he said. 'His trial was adjourned for a month because Mantell was attacked by his brother-in law. Can't say I was sorry to hear that. He was then harassed by a couple of paedophile hunters once his name got into the papers.'

'How bad was the harassment?'

'Pretty bad. Somehow they got a copy of the MG5 against him and posted it on Facebook.'

'How the hell did they get hold of the case summary?'

'No idea. The only decent thing they did was to redact Gia's name but everything else was out, his name, address, employer's details and the allegations.'

'Was that it, just the doxxing or was there more?'

'No. The hunters, Karim Messenger and Gareth Humphreys, livestreamed themselves following Mantell and abusing him, throwing rubbish at him, calling him a pervert but they went too far. They livestreamed themselves beating the shit out of him.'

'Absolute morons,' said Stanford as he wrote the names down.

'Why do you think his trial was adjourned for a month? Gareth Humphreys was Mantell's brother-in-law. Was I sorry that the sick pervert ended up with a broken wrist, and lost three of his teeth? Absolutely not. Was I annoyed that the trial was delayed? Definitely.'

'So, what happened to Messenger and Humphreys?'

'The irony is that they both spent more time in prison than

Mantell ever did. They both got eighteen months for Section 20 GBH.'

'Were there any more incidents like this with Mantell?'

'Not in regard to my case. I'm not sure if the team dealing with his murder discovered anything, although I doubt it, considering the case has gone cold.'

'You wouldn't happen to know where Messenger and Humphreys are now?'

'Those two seem to like prison. Back in Strangeways and, before you get too excited, they were already serving their sentence when Mantell was killed. The idiots were arrested and charged a couple of days after they livestreamed the assault on Mantell. Two weeks later they pleaded guilty at Manchester Crown Court and were given an immediate custodial sentence.'

'What are they inside for?'

'Four years for ABH and kidnapping.'

'Thank you. You've been a great help,' said Stanford, tapping his pen against the desk.

'As I said, I can't say I'm sorry that Mantell's dead but it's not right for people to take justice into their own hands.'

'No, you're right. Just one more thing before you go. Were Messenger and Gareth part of a larger group or were they out on their own?'

'I think they were out on their own but best to ask the SIOs for their cases. But there's one more thing. Humphreys just got an additional two years. You would think that being in prison would sober him up a bit.'

'What did he do?' Stanford asked.

'GBH,' said Forfana. 'Shanked his cell mate. Apparently, the injuries to his cellmate's head were so bad that the doctors said it looked like a scalping.'

38

At 4.21 p.m. the judge in Court Eight granted Henley's application to access Laurence Durant's phone. Henley had been so lost in her dark reverie, and guilt that she was still keeping Stanford and Eastwood in the dark, that she hadn't heard the judge call her name. She had a list of reasons to rationalise her decision. Stanford needed to focus on the impending adoption of his first child and Eastwood hadn't known Rhimes as long as the rest of the team. She'd walked out of the courtroom with no sense of euphoria but instead with a deepening sense of betrayal. Heading for her car, she was fishing around her bag looking for her parking ticket when she heard someone beeping their horn. Henley felt a flutter of panic as a Mercedes pulled up at her side but it quickly subsided when she saw who was sitting in the driver's seat. Eloise Rhimes.

'I was sitting at the traffic lights when I saw you cross the road,' said Eloise.

'I'm so sorry,' said Henley. 'I didn't even notice.'

'That's ok. Sometimes that building feels as though its sucking your soul, and you want to run away as far as possible but it's good to see you, Anjelica.'

'It's good to see you too, Eloise. I would have told—'

Henley stopped as a car appeared behind Eloise, the engine revving with annoyance.

'Let me park up and we'll have a quick drink,' said Eloise.

'Eloise, I really can't. I've got get back to the—'

'One cup of coffee,' Eloise said in the tone she reserved for the defendants appearing in her courtroom.

Henley closed her bag. There was no point fighting back. 'Ok.'

'If I'm honest, I'd rather be having a proper drink,' Eloise said, emptying the sugar sachet into her latte. 'But the last thing I need is a defendant to spot me knocking back a large gin and then getting into my car.'

'You'll be splashed over social media in a heartbeat,' Henley replied.

'Let's stop beating around the bush,' said Eloise. 'You've been avoiding me.'

Henley chewed her biscuit. She knew it had been coming. The moment when Eloise brought her to task.

'I wasn't ignoring you on purpose, but this—' Henley said.

'You can stop right there if you're about to use the "It's this case" line. I was married to a police officer for over thirty years. I've heard every excuse imaginable.'

'You're right,' Henley conceded. 'I have been avoiding you, but I have also been consumed with this case.'

'Fox-Carnell,' Eloise said, exhaling sharply. 'Harry hated that case. Hated her. Which was so unlike him, to hate a suspect. He always used to say, "I'm just doing my job. My emotions have got nothing to do with it," but her. He said you could see in her eyes that she was evil.'

'I'm not going to disagree but she's now my victim. My case. I can't treat her any differently just because I was in the room when she was charged with murder.'

'Harry would have said the exact thing,' Eloise said sadly.

They sat quietly in a moment of remembrance. Henley turned her face to the window, watching as the rush hour traffic stalled on London Road.

'You wouldn't have gone radio silent if you hadn't found

something,' Eloise said. 'I kept telling myself that no news is good news, but I know better than that.'

'Is that why you spoke to Stephen?' Henley asked Eloise. She felt a pang of regret at the sharpness of her tone when she saw the angst stretch the skin on Eloise's face.

'I didn't go behind your back,' Eloise said. She leaned back in her seat and hugged herself as though she was cold. 'Stephen came round to see me, and I was . . . you know what it's like. You're minding your own business doing something mindless, like throwing out the mouldy peppers from the fridge and then all of a sudden, the grief hits you.'

'The last time it happened I was putting petrol in my car and, out of nowhere, it came over me like a wave,' said Henley. 'I couldn't tell you who I was grieving for. Rhimes, mum or both.'

Eloise nodded with understanding. 'I only told Stephen because he was there in that moment. He asked how I was, and it came out. Asking you for help. That I thought—' Eloise lowered her voice. 'That he didn't do it himself.'

Henley knew she'd been living in a space of denial since Linh had confirmed that Rhimes hadn't killed himself and that someone had falsified his death certificate. She could see and feel Eloise's anguish and told herself that it would be kinder to lie, but knew she couldn't.

There was no easy way to rip off the plaster or to make the sting of lemon juice on a cut less painful. 'He didn't,' Henley said quickly.

Eloise's face crumpled as though she was hearing the news of her husband's death for the first time. 'How?' she asked quietly as Henley reached across the table and took hold of her hand, squeezing gently.

'Are you sure you want me to?' Henley asked softly.

'Yes,' Eloise said firmly, her eyes glistening as she pulled her hand away to wipe a tear, smearing her mascara.

'Asphyxiation,' said Henley. 'A cord of some kind.'

Eloise put her hands to her face and breathed in deeply three times. Henley leaned forward as Eloise spoke, but her words were muffled, lost in the flesh of her palms.

'I didn't catch that,' Henley said gently.

Eloise took her shaking hands away from her face and placed them on the table, the overhead light hitting the small diamonds in her eternity ring. 'Did he fight back?' she asked.

'Yes. Yes, he did,' Henley said as Rhimes's postmortem pictures, the scratch marks vivid on his neck, flashed in her mind.

'God, there are so many questions,' Eloise said.

Henley watched as Eloise bit her lip and nodded her head as though acknowledging the conclusion of a conversation in her head.

'Someone was in our house,' Eloise said, facing Henley. 'Whoever did it was watching us, tracking our movements. They knew that Harry always left for work before me. I was in that house whilst someone was downstairs killing my husband. Do you know how many murder cases I've seen in my career? The moments of passion, the loss of control. I understand that but when it's pre-meditated. It's cold. Harry was a problem that they wanted to get rid of.'

'I'm so sorry, Eloise. I'm sorry that—'

'No, don't be,' Eloise said vehemently. 'I don't know how to explain it but knowing that he was taken from me and didn't leave me . . . it's better. Does that make sense?'

'It does,' Henley agreed. 'But what doesn't make sense is—'

'The why,' Eloise concluded. 'It's the first thing that they teach you in law school when you're learning how to cross examine a witness. Not to ask the *why* question. The why opens a door, and you have no idea where that open door could take you.'

'I could just close the door and walk away but then I would go to bed every night wondering why.'

'No,' Eloise said defiantly. 'Whatever the why is, it put my husband in the ground. You have a family, Anjelica.'

'There's a reason why you came to me,' said Henley. 'Yes, you trust me, but you know that I can't walk past an open door. Even if that door is only cracked open, I will push it further. Even if this wasn't about Harry, if it was somebody else, a victim on my board, I would do the same thing. Keep digging and asking questions. You've shown me the opendoor, Eloise.'

Henley instantly regretted her words when she saw the crushed look on Eloise's face as she realised the full enormity of her actions.

'I've put you in a terrible position and for that I'm truly sorry,' Eloise said.

'Don't be. I was wrong to say that. You loved – no – *love* him. I would do the same thing.'

'Can I ask that you at least don't do it alone. Ask Stephen to help you.'

Henley picked up her bag and smiled. 'You and I both know full well that Stephen is extremely pissed off with me,' she said. 'What you want is for him to protect me.'

'And what's wrong with that?' Eloise asked, following Henley's lead and picking up her coat. 'Do you know the reason why Harry was so proud of the SCU? No egos. I don't want you out there like a lone wolf.'

'I can take care of myself.'

'Just because you can doesn't mean that you should.'

Henley stepped outside and held the door for Eloise. She knew she was letting her pride and stubbornness get in the way.

'Please have someone by your side if you're going to find the people responsible for ripping Harry from our lives,' said Eloise.

Henley hugged Eloise. 'I won't do this alone,' she promised.

*

Henley felt as though a weight was sitting in her chest as she walked back to her car. She'd made a promise to Eloise, and she needed to honour it. She wasn't ready to tell Stanford and Eastwood that she was looking into the why behind Rhimes's death, but she did need help.

'Fuck it,' she said as she took out a phone and texted her ex-colleague, Chris Snyder, who was now an agent for the National Crime Agency.

'Eastwood and I need to go to Manchester,' said Stanford as Henley walked in.

'What for?' she asked. It would take less than five minutes to tell them what she knew about Rhimes. To give them a choice to say 'yes, I'll help you' or just 'walk away', but the opportunity passed when she saw that Copeland was at her desk.

'Didn't you get my message?' Stanford asked as Ezra entered the room.

'I've been having problems with reception all afternoon,' Henley said. She checked her phone and saw that she was still missing signal bars.

'We believe we've got a viable link to our vigilante group. Two serving prisoners in Strangeways and also we have footage,' Stanford explained.

'Footage of what?'

'Nathan Hall,' said Eastwood. 'Both from his security gate camera and what Ezra found online.'

'Ok. Start with the prisoners. Who are they?' asked Henley.

'Karim Messenger and Gareth Humphreys,' said Stanford. 'They were both convicted of assaulting Douglas Mantell and were also members of a vigilante group called Iron Shadow.'

'Such a ridiculous name,' said Eastwood. 'No points for creativity.'

'What about Bo Hyoo?' asked Henley.

Eastwood swivelled her monitor towards Henley. 'Both charged with harassment after doxxing her and following her on the street, but for some inexplicable reason they were NFA'd on an assault charge.'

'What was the alleged assault?' Henley asked.

'They tarred and feathered her, and I do not mean that as some poorly disguised joke,' Eastwood said, clicking on a photograph icon.

Henley gasped and put her hand to her mouth as Bo Hyoo, sitting naked on a hospital bed, appeared on the screen. The skin on her neck, back and left arm had been stripped away and was red raw. White feathers were visible in her hair and on the back of her neck.

'They couldn't get hold of actual tar, so they used sulphuric acid,' Eastwood explained.

'You said that Messenger and Humphreys weren't charged,' said Henley tightly.

'DI Connors, the SIO for the Bo Hyoo GBH is adamant that it was Messenger and Humphreys but there was a problem with identification. Bo Hyoo couldn't describe her assailants, there were no independent witnesses and no forensics.'

'What about an alibi?'

'They didn't give one and they both went no comment,' said Eastwood. 'They were RUI and six weeks later NFA'd. Bo Hyoo spent a week in hospital and then moved to Sheffield to stay with her sister. Two months later she started reporting incidents of harassment. The same tactics: shit through her letterbox, paint on her sister's door.'

'So, they followed her to Sheffield?' Henley asked.

Eastwood nodded.

'Which leads to the question, how did they know she'd moved?' Stanford asked. 'Bo Hyoo was on strict bail conditions which meant her solicitors had to apply to Manchester Crown Court to amend her residence condition. The only people who knew she'd moved out of the city would have been the court, prosecutors and her own solicitors and, call me a prophet, I doubt Bo Hyoo was giving out her address to all and sundry.'

'You said she had strict bail conditions,' said Ramouter who had been listening quietly at his desk. 'She must have been on tag?'

'She was,' Eastwood confirmed. 'And guess which company was responsible for her electronic monitoring?'

'Soteria,' said Ramouter.

'Bingo.'

'There's something missing,' Henley said, catching Pellacia from the corner of her eye, inching closer towards them. 'You didn't say that Messenger and Humphreys were responsible or even thought to be involved in the murders of Hyoo and Mantell.'

Stanford shook his head. 'No, they were both serving at the time of the murders which is why we think it makes sense for Eastie and I to head up there and speak to them. They were a part of this Iron Shadow gang, so they should be able to tell us how they got hold of Hyoo's address and the MG5 for Mantell's sex offence case.'

'Before I agree to send you two up north, how do we know they were definitely part of this Iron Shadow gang and that they've got anything to do with our victims on the board?' Pellacia asked.

'Copeland. Go ahead,' said Eastwood.

'I can't take all of the credit for this. Ezra helped me a lot by showing me where to go online,' said Copeland. 'You've got two types of vigilante groups. Minor, non-violent groups who go around posting details of paedophiles on social media and then you've got the opposite end of the spectrum. There are groups out there who will hunt people down for a fee. I couldn't find any mention of the Iron Shadow group by doing a normal Google search, but I did find them on the dark web.'

Henley held her tongue as Copeland handed out printouts.

'These are transcripts from the vigilante forum and everyone is on there. Far-right radicals, incels and ultra left anarchists who just want to see the world burn.'

'Messenger and Humphreys' names are mentioned in this chat,' said Ramouter as he read through the pages. 'They're being celebrated.'

'Is that all they do. Just chat?' asked Henley as Pellacia's office phone rang.

'Carry on.' He returned to his office.

'No, they also like to show off their handiwork,' Copeland said. She walked up to the smartboard and pressed play.

'Shit,' Ramouter said as Fox-Carnell's face came into view. Whatever Fox-Carnell was trying to say was lost due to the tape that had been used to gag her. Fear radiated from her eyes as she watched whoever was holding the camera.

'You're going to suffer the exact same way that your victims suffered.'

'You have no right to redemption. Justice should always be in the hands of the people.'

'They've distorted the voices but that's not a problem as we can send the footage off to be analysed,' said Eastwood. 'But that's not all. The sound isn't the best, but we've got footage of Nathan Hall.'

Henley watched as two men, wearing balaclavas held Nathan's limp and broken body. Bubbles of blood were visible in his nose, his breathing guttural but audible as the men spoke.

'What I don't understand is why they've moved from doing their—' Henley paused, not wanting to use the word but lacking any alternative, 'hunting in Manchester and are now here in London?'

'It has to be what you said, boss,' said Ramouter. 'You only ever really move for work or family.'

Henley turned towards Eastwood. 'Did you find any more assaults with a similar MO?' she asked.

'The scalping? No,' said Eastwood. 'It seems as though Hyoo was the last one up north. There's nothing even remotely similar until Fox-Carnell.'

'Our vigilantes are sticking to London but that leads us to another problem,' said Henley. 'We have no idea who these vigilantes will be targeting next.'

'It can't be that difficult,' said Copeland. 'All of our victims recently had court cases.'

'There are ten crown courts in London, if you include Kingston,' said Henley. 'On average maybe four to five trials take place in each court per day. Some cases could finish in a day or – if it's Southwark Crown Court – months Also, it doesn't appear that our vigilantes are focused on defendants who were accused of committing a specific offence. Our victims were on trial for rape, murder and fraud. The point is that there is more chance of us hitting the bullseye on a dartboard blindfolded than we have at working out which defendant will be the target of our vigilantes.'

'So, what do we do?' asked Copeland. 'Sit and wait for another body to fall?'

'Hopefully not,' Henley said as Pellacia returned. 'The judge granted the application for us to access Laurence Durant's phone. I'll pick up the phone from Lewisham tomorrow morning.'

'Don't do that, boss,' said Ezra. 'I'll pick it up from Lewisham first thing tomorrow. Just let them know I'm coming.'

'Thanks, Ez,' Henley said gratefully.

'I know it doesn't feel like it but you're all doing a good job,' said Pellacia.

'Thanks for the gold star but what about our Manchester road trip?' asked Stanford, picking up his coat from the back of the chair.

'I'll get on it,' said Pellacia, looking up at the clock on the wall.

It was nearly 7 p.m.. 'Chances are that I won't get an answer until first thing in the morning, but I'll text you if the borough commander gets back to me tonight.'

'Great. I'm going home to crash in front of the match and ignore my other half banging on about mood boards for the nursery.'

'I'll walk out with you.' Eastwood shut down her computer. 'I've had enough for the day.

'Don't run off,' Pellacia said to Henley who was picking up her bag. 'I need a word.'

'Close the door,' Pellacia said.

Henley watched Pellacia position himself in the furthest corner of the office, creating distance between them. She closed his door and sat down.

'What's the problem?' she asked.

'Your attitude towards DC Copeland is the problem,' said Pellacia. 'She's only been here a couple of days, and you can see that she's earning her place on the team, but—'

'She's complained,' Henley said, slumping further into the seat. Too overwhelmed with exhaustion to put up the pretence of a fight.

'She's expressed concerns,'

'Call it what it is, Stephen. She's complained about me even though I haven't treated her any differently to anyone else in the team. I didn't give Ramouter any special treatment when he started. I don't know why she thinks that I have to treat her like—'

'Anj, it's late and I really haven't got the energy for this. She's raised concerns and I have to say that I agree with her. You're talking down to her. Giving her administrative tasks.'

'You think that I spoke down to her just now?'

'No, not now, but that was probably because I was there.'

'Oh, for fuck's sake,' Henley muttered. She straightened up and gripped the armrests. 'We are now a team of a grand total of eight people, no, scratch that, six people if you don't include Joanna and Ezra. For some inexplicable reason the higher-ups consider the SCU to be the runt of the litter when it comes to their specialist units.'

'You're acting as though I don't know this.'

'The point is that we're too small a unit to be giving anyone special treatment. I've told Copeland and I'm telling you again, she needs to understand how the SCU works.'

'She's been a DC for four years. It hasn't even been a year since Ramouter took off his training wheels.'

Henley sat back, settling into her anger. 'She's junior to the team. Rhimes did the exact same thing when Keith joined us for all of six weeks. He was three years more senior than Eastwood and I didn't see him complaining when Rhimes gave him tasks which you'd describe as admin.'

'I have to take into consideration the concerns that she's expressed to me.'

'They're not concerns. She's just pissed that I'm not kissing her arse. Am I grateful that we've got an extra pair of hands? Of course I bloody am.'

'Well, show it,' said Pellacia. 'Look, I'm not here to debate with you. It's too late and I'd like to have a life outside of this bloody place. Copeland is a full member of the SCU.'

'What happened to temporary?' Henley replied with disbelief as her phone vibrated in her pocket. She checked the screen. It was Rob.

'Something more important than this conversation?'

'My husband and unless you've got anything more to say, I'm going home to him and my child.'

Pellacia watched Henley. The hurt was evident in his eyes. He pushed his chair back and marched to his door. 'Treat Copeland with respect and not like a nuisance fly,' he said. 'Otherwise, I'm going to have to start making decisions that you're not going to like.'

'What is it with her?' Henley asked. 'Why are you bending over yourself to accommodate her nonsense?'

'What do you expect me to do when someone comes into my team and expresses concerns that most people could – and would – interpret as bullying.'

'Bullying?'

Pellacia bit his lip as the discomfort in the room swelled. 'That was the wrong word,' he said.

'That's an understatement,' said Henley. 'You allow someone who doesn't know this unit and most definitely doesn't know me, to question who I am.'

'That is not what is happening here. My obligation is to this unit. It doesn't start and end with you.'

'You're talking as if I expect special treatment.'

'Of course you don't, but maybe we were blinded to a lot of things. I've let *you* get away with a lot of things.'

Henley stood up. 'I do my job, and I expect other people to do their job,' she said. 'But instead of you recognising that, you're suggesting that I act like an entitled prima-donna.'

Pellacia huffed. 'What would you call your response to a new member expressing their genuine concerns if not entitled or privileged?' he asked.

Henley moved in front of Pellacia, closing the space between them. She was beyond angry, and she wanted him to feel it.

'If Copeland had complained about anyone else, you would have reacted differently. You would have reined her in and asked Copeland for more evidence than hurt bloody feelings, but it's not the others, it's me,' said Henley. 'You're the one who has a problem with seeing the line drawn in the sand. All of this – your warnings – is a poor attempt to prove something to yourself.'

Pellacia's jaw clenched as Henley stayed in place. She'd found a pressure point and she'd pressed hard.

'Treat Copeland with respect,' Pellacia said, the coldness in his voice freezing the air as he moved around her and to the door. 'Otherwise—'

'You're threatening me?' Henley said.

'You know me too well to know that I don't make threats,' Pellacia said quietly. 'Just know that I've got no problem at all with switching the partnerships around. You weren't that keen on having to partner up with Ramouter when he joined . . .'

'That was a completely different situation.'

'Maybe Copeland might be a better fit for you.'

Henley glared at Pellacia. She placed her hand on top of his and pushed it off the door handle. 'Carry on,' she said. 'If you want to lose me completely. To leave the SCU. Carry on.'

'Consider this a warning.'

'Then consider this my notice.'

Henley opened the door and walked out.

39

'You handed in your notice?' Stanford exclaimed, the last piece of his sausage and egg McMuffin suspended in mid-air as they stepped into the lift.

'That's what I said,' said Henley, pressing the fourth-floor button. She pulled a face as she caught sight of her exhausted reflection in the lift door.

'But you didn't mean it. Did you?'

Henley sighed. 'No, I was pissed off and running my mouth.'

'You've let Copeland get to you,' Stanford said.

'Which is not like me. I can usually rise above petty office politics but, I don't know, I feel as though she's purposely needling me.'

'Maybe she feels threatened by you,' said Stanford as the doors opened and they stepped out. 'You're quite a force you know.'

'If she's threatened by me then she should behave, keep herself quiet and not go whining to Pellacia just because I accidentally stood on her toe.'

'You really are miserable sometimes,' Stanford said, laughing as he pushed open the door into their room.

Henley paused and inhaled deeply when she saw that Copeland was already at her desk.

'You can't say that she's not diligent,' Stanford said, lowering his voice. 'Looks like she was the first one in.'

'I'll get her a bloody medal,' Henley muttered under breath.

'As I said, miserable,' said Stanford, picking up the internal post.

'Morning, guv,' said Copeland brightly.

'Morning,' Henley replied flatly. 'How are you?'

'Oh, I'm good, just going through the transcripts from the forum chatroom which reminds me, Ezra's been looking for you.'

'Ez is already here? It's not even 8.30 a.m.,' Henley said as the door opened and Pellacia walked into the room and passed her with no acknowledgement.

'He was here before me, and I arrived at 7.30 a.m.. I think he was just keen to get a start on Durant's phone.'

'Thanks,' Henley said, picking up a new notebook and pen from a desk. 'If anyone is looking for me, tell them I'm downstairs.'

Henley watched as Ramouter walked along the hallway, in his own world as he moved his head in time to the music being pumped through his headphones. He was almost nose to nose with Henley before he realised she was there.

'Morning, boss,' he said warmly. 'Looks like I'm not the only one who decided to have an early start.'

'We've got a full house,' Henley replied. 'Even Copeland was here before me.'

'She's keen.'

'Hmm,' Henley said non-committally.

'I've been working with you long enough to know what your hmm means,' Ramouter said, the jovial look on his face now replaced with one of concern.

'It doesn't mean anything,' Henley said, turning towards the staircase.

'I know that she can come on a bit strong, but she's got good intentions. She just wants to do a good job.'

'You're running to her defence a bit quickly.'

'I've spent time with her.'

Henley raised an eyebrow.

'Not like that,' Ramouter replied hurriedly, his cheeks flushed with embarrassment. 'There's nothing going on.'

'I never suggested that there was, but—'

'We're just friends,' Ramouter said adamantly. 'Really, it's nothing more than that. I don't think Copeland sees me that way. She's newly divorced and...'

'Even more reason for her to—'

'Boss, come on. You know me.'

'But I don't know her,' Henley said firmly. 'Be careful.'

'I know what it's like being the new guy and trying to fit in with a team that's tight. *Really tight*,' he said.

Henley recognised the truth of his words and nodded her head in agreement. 'What are you asking me to do, Ramouter?' she asked.

'Just give her a chance, like you did with me.'

Henley scanned Ramouter's face as she searched for suitable words to object to his more than reasonable request. 'I'll think about it,' was all she said.

Ramouter smiled with relief. 'For a minute there, I thought you were going to tell me to piss off,' he said.

Henley turned her back and as she walked downstairs shouted, 'I nearly did.'

'What time do you call this?' Ezra asked as Henley walked into his office.

'I call it far too early to be putting up with any cheek from you,' Henley replied, taking a seat next to him.

'Because I'm about to take myself out for a full English breakfast in a mo' and I'm feeling a bit smug with myself, I'm going to let that slide.'

'I take it you summoned me down here because you got something useful from Durant's phone?'

'Look at the monitor, boss,' Ezra said.

Henley found herself staring at an image of Durant's phone screen. His wallpaper was a photograph of his late wife smiling brightly as she held a cocktail.

'I've downloaded it all and sent it to your inbox, but this is what's really interesting.' Ezra clicked on a purple icon.

'What is that?' Henley asked.

'It's Discord. It's an instant messaging app but it's not just chatting to your mates. You can send videos, photos, can go live and watch livestreams,' Ezra explained.

'What's so special about that?'

'Well, you can also join different communities. Think of it like private member clubs because you have to be invited. It's also encrypted so no one can just listen in. So, what you're looking at are all the clubs that Durant has joined. Teaching, football, but these are the ones you're going to be interested in. A lot of vigilante groups. Most of them he hasn't participated in except for this one.'

'Shadow,' said Henley. 'Is that right? Only five members?'

'Small but active. Lots of chat, photos and documents,' said Ezra as he clicked on #target.

'Oh my God,' said Henley as Ezra opened a PDF titled, 'R v Tabitha Ashcroft'. 'Those are prosecution case papers.'

'I had a quick look, and everything is in there. Witness statements, schedule of unused material. Basically, everything I had when I was in court.'

'Is Tabitha Ashcroft's custody record on there and can you tell when these were uploaded?'

Ezra chewed his lip as he scrolled through the items. '6 September,' he said.

'That's the date that Tabitha Ashcroft was sentenced. Are there any names mentioned in the chat?'

'A couple. Someone called Don is mentioned a couple of times, but that's the only real name. The others have got random usernames and as good as I am, I can't reverse engineer that and find out who created it.'

'Don't worry, that's good enough for me to get Durant back into the interview room,' Henley said as Ezra's phone rang.

Ezra peered at the display screen. 'It's the guvnor,' he said. He picked up. 'Hello. Yeah, she's still here. Ok. He wants to talk to you.'

Ezra handed the phone to Henley and turned back to his computer.

'Hello,' Henley asked, struggling to keep the simple greeting balanced and nonconfrontational.

'Ben Trezeguet is at Bethnal Green police station' said Pellacia. 'He was arrested an hour ago. I'm sending Ramouter and Copeland to deal with him, are you ok with that?'

'That's fine. I'm going to reinterview Durant.'

'Ok. And we've got a problem with the Manchester visit. They're rioting in Strangeways. Prisoners on the roof.'

'So, they're in lockdown?'

'For the moment. The prison guvnor will let me know as soon as they've got the place under control and, when they do, Stanford and Eastwood are good to go. I'll let you get on.'

Henley felt a tremor in her stomach as she lowered the handset. She'd tried to get a sense of Pellacia's emotions as he spoke, but there'd been nothing. He'd spoken to her as though she were a stranger.

40

'If I didn't know better, I would say he looks pleased to be here,' said Copeland, moving away from the spyhole in the door.

'What do you mean?' asked Ramouter who was crouched on the floor sorting through the forensic reports that had been printed in the wrong order.

'What I mean is that he's calm, and I swear that he's got a smile on his face.'

Ramouter groaned as he straightened up. 'Maybe this is what he wants, to be involved. To have an angle for his so-called news reporting.'

'I've been in this job for so many years, and I keep thinking I'll get to a point where I'm no longer surprised by people but yet, here I am, surprised,' said Copeland.

'We need to keep being surprised, otherwise where's the incentive to keep going?'

'You're right. Being surprised is what makes me eager to get in there. So how do you want to play this? You're usually partnered with Henley, so you're probably used to taking her lead.'

'To be honest, she's always kept it 50/50.'

'Oh, that's a surprise. I saw her as being a bit more of a controller.'

Ramouter let the statement hang in the air, not wanting to get into a discussion about Henley. He could remember how quickly Stanford, Eastwood and Ezra had gathered the wagons when his poor attempt at small talk had been interpreted as him digging into her past. After working with her for over a year, he was now equally protective of her.

'Let's make a start,' Ramouter said. He reached past Copeland and opened the door, and gestured for her to enter. 'And you can follow my lead.'

'Of course,' Copeland said tersely. She walked in and sat down in the first chair, activated the touchscreen monitor and entered the interview details.

'Who's this?' asked Ben who had somehow positioned himself in the bolted down chair that enabled him to put his feet on the table. He was wearing no shoes, and the pilling was visible on his once-white socks. He looked relaxed as though he was at home.

'Sit up properly,' Ramouter ordered.

'I'm not going to lie, but I'm a bit disappointed.' Ben straightened up and smoothed down his unruly hair. 'I was expecting Inspector Henley.'

'I'll let her know she was missed,' said Ramouter. He turned the pages of the custody sheet printout and read through the log. 'Before we start, you were informed of your right to free legal advice and to have someone informed of your arrest, but you declined both.'

'I was dragged out of my boyfriend's bed at seven o'clock this morning so I would take that as him being informed, and I don't want to waste time waiting for a lawyer. So, let's get on with it.'

'Sounds good to me,' said Ramouter as Copeland pressed record.

They introduced themselves and Copeland asked Ben for his full name.

'Benjamin Sylvain Trezeguet.'

Ramouter repeated the caution and Ben confirmed he understood.

'And even though you've declined your right to legal advice, I will stop the interview if you change your mind.'

'I won't change my mind. Let's get things moving. Ask your questions.'

'You've been arrested for attempted burglary and the murder of Nathan Hall.'

'Am I able to get a copy of the video of this interview?' Ben asked as he pointed up at the black dome which concealed the camera in the corner of the room.

'You'll get a copy of the recording if the CPS decide to charge you with murder,' answered Ramouter. 'Now we've got evidence of you entering Nathan Hall's property on the night of his murder.'

'What sort of evidence?' Ben asked cautiously.

'These are screenshots taken from the security footage,' said Copeland. She laid out four A4 sized photographs on the table. 'Is that you?'

Ben pulled the photograph towards him, clicking his tongue against the roof of his mouth. 'It's going to be a bit hard to deny it. The only thing I didn't do was smile for the camera.'

'We also found your fingerprints in the property. How did you know where Nathan Hall lived?'

Ben snorted. 'Because he wasn't smart. I've been following him on social media since he was charged. I don't know what he thought he was going to achieve but he started posting these walking mindfulness videos. Just him chatting away about overcoming the odds and having faith when he was out on his morning walks. On one video, I saw a bus go past and I took a note of the number. Another video, you could see the street name. Put two and two together and bingo. A location.'

'How did you get past the security gate?'

'It was already open. Someone had jammed it.'

'This screenshot was taken at 11 p.m.. What were you doing there so late?'

'I'm a journalist. I wanted to ask him some questions about

the verdict, his victims and to also find out if he thought he was in danger.'

'Why would he be in danger?'

Ben looked across at Ramouter and Copeland open mouthed. 'Is it possible to be both smart and stupid at the same time?' he said.

'Watch your mouth,' Copeland warned. 'Stop with the attitude and answer the question.'

'Is she allowed to talk to me like that?' asked Ben.

'Answer the question. Why did you think he was in danger?' asked Ramouter.

'People think that because I'm running around the streets and make my living from YouTube that I'm an idiot, but I'm not. The serial crimes unit is investigating Fox-Carnell who was murdered after she basically got away with murder and Tabitha Ashcroft who was nearly killed because she got away with murder. Nathan Hall, if you ask me, got away with raping four men. Am I on the right track?'

Ramouter bit his cheek to stop himself from confirming that Ben was indeed right.

'Yeah, I'm on the right track,' Ben said smugly.

'What happened when you got through the gate?' Ramouter asked.

Ben shuffled down in his seat, the bravado disappearing as quickly as smoke in the wind. The photograph he was still holding tremored slightly in his hand.

'What happened when you went into the house, Ben?' Ramouter asked softly.

Ben sniffed, dropped the photograph and rubbed his face vigorously with both hands. 'If you watch enough true crime, you always hear that blood smells coppery but that makes it sound as though you're sniffing a handful of pennies but it's . . . it's worse than that,' he said.

'It sticks in your throat, doesn't it?'

'Yeah, that's exactly it,' said Ben as he finally looked up. His eyes red and wet with tears.

'What did you see when you got in the house?'

'He was on the floor. Nathan was on the floor.'

Copeland flashed a look of surprise at Ramouter. 'On the floor. Are you sure?' she asked Ben.

'Where else would he have been?' Ben asked as he looked quizzically at Copeland.

'What state was he in?' asked Ramouter.

'Alive. I could hear him breathing. I didn't touch him because that's what they tell you, isn't it? Not to touch someone if they're injured.'

'But you didn't call the police.'

'That's because I heard voices, and I ran upstairs.'

'What did they sound like?' said Ramouter.

'Men. Both men. One was definitely south London, and he sounded like he was in charge and the other, he had an accent. I couldn't really place it because the TV was on and I was too busy running for my life.'

'Where did you hide?' asked Copeland.

'In a cupboard.'

'How long were you there for?'

'I don't know maybe half an hour.'

'Half an hour in the cupboard. Knowing that Nathan Hall was still alive downstairs, and you didn't call the police. You're unbelievable.'

'Let's focus on what Ben did do and what he heard,' Ramouter intervened gently, not wanting to show Ben that he was annoyed with his partner's attitude. 'What happened after half an hour, Ben?'

'I came out of the cupboard, and I left.'

'You didn't check on Nathan Hall?' Copeland asked.

Ben twisted his mouth and looked away. 'No,' he said.

'Let me see if I understand this correctly. You illegally enter Nathan Hall's house, you see him on the floor, seriously injured, but you do nothing. You then tell us that you hear voices, and you hide upstairs for thirty minutes. I understand you were hiding so you wouldn't have called but you could have texted 999.'

'I didn't know that—'

'I haven't finished,' Copeland snapped. 'You then leave after thirty minutes, down the stairs, past Nathan Hall who is now hanging from the bannister—'

'Hanging from . . . No. I didn't see—'

'You didn't see this and this,' Copeland said as she slapped four photographs of Nathan Hall on the table.

Ben's face paled as he looked across at Ramouter as though pleading for help.

'Look at the photograph, Ben,' said Copeland. 'Do you see all that blood? His legs, face. Look at the floor. Do you know where all that blood came from?'

Ben shook his head.

'He was scalped. The skin peeled off his head and you walked past of all of that and did nothing.'

'I didn't see that. I would have called the police if I had,' Ben said as he began to cry.

'DC Copeland,' Ramouter said with warning as he rubbed his right ear.

'I don't believe you,' Copeland continued. 'You keep calling yourself a reporter. You returned the following morning with a drone. Did you film Nathan Hall?'

The room descended into silence as Ben raised his face to the ceiling.

'Don't worry about it. We're carrying out a Section 18 search in your mum's flat, your studio and have seized your equipment,' said Ramouter. 'But what I'm interested in is why you ran from your home and hid at your boyfriend's flat.'

'I want protection,' Ben blurted out.

Ramouter looked at Ben steadily. 'They saw you, didn't they?' he said. 'That's why you're here, because Nathan Hall's murderers saw you.'

Ben nodded.

'For the benefit of the tape, Mr Trezeguet nodded his head.'

'We found your prints in the bedroom and also trainer tread marks, Nike size nine, the same size as the ones we removed from you, with traces of blood on the carpet, facing the direction of the bathroom,' said Ramouter. 'You weren't just hiding in the cupboard.'

'I thought they were gone. I'd been in there for about twenty minutes. I left the cupboard and at the same time one of them came out of the bathroom.'

'He saw you?'

'Yeah,' Ben sniffed and wiped his nose.

'You got a good look at him?'

'Good enough. He was white, maybe six foot. Dressed all in black and he was about your size,' Ben said, pointing at Ramouter. 'He had brown hair, which was wet. In fact, his face was wet, and he looked . . . upset.'

'Upset.'

'Yeah, really upset. His face was wet, and he was heaving, you know, like a kid when they're crying.'

'Did he say anything to you?'

'Didn't get a chance. The other guy called him, and I ran into a bedroom and locked the door.'

'Did he follow you? Try to get into the room?'

Ben nodded. 'I saw the door handle turn. I thought he was going to break the door down but then he left.'

'The man who called him. Was he the one with an accent?'

'No, the Londoner.'

'Did he call him by name or . . .'

'Josh. He called him Josh.'

'And then what happened?'

'I gave it about half an hour and then I left too but I went out the back. The bedroom had a terrace and stairs that went into the garden. I went down that way.'

'And that's why you didn't see Nathan Hall hanging from the bannister, because you left through the back?'

'There was no way I was leaving through the front door. I would have jumped out the window if I had to.'

'And you still didn't call the police,' said Copeland. 'After all that. You knew Nathan Hall was dead. You saw the people responsible, but you saw it all as material for your ridiculous show.'

'DC Copeland!' said Ramouter. 'Ben has—'

'He came to my studio,' Ben shouted. 'The day after my report. I saw him . . . it . . . he's coming after me. So, you've got to protect me. You've got to.'

'Talk me through what happened?' Ramouter asked as Copeland leaned back in her seat, clearly annoyed at Ramouter's intervention.

'I was in my studio in Whitechapel. It's not hard to find me because my details are on my YouTube page. Seth, my boyfriend, dropped me off. He helps me sometimes with editing and—'

'Flying the drone?' asked Ramouter.

'He's better at it than me. I'd left the studio to go to the chicken shop, and I saw him in the car park. The guy who came out of the bathroom.'

'Are you sure it was him?'

'Positive. He clocked me and then he started to run after me, and I ran too.'

'Did he catch you?'

'No. I jumped the fence and ran into the estate. I heard someone shouting and I think they scared him off.'

'But again, you didn't call the police,' said Copeland. 'Which makes me think this is all a ploy. That you've watched too many true crime documentaries.'

'I was scared. What would you do if you were being chased by a serial killer?'

'As I said, I don't—'

Ramouter turned to Copeland and gave her a sharp look, silencing her before she had a chance to finish. 'This man. You've seen him twice. Could you give us a description?' he asked Ben.

'What about protection?' Ben asked as though he hadn't heard the question.

'It's unlikely,' Copeland said bitterly. 'You ran. You lied. You broke into property. Three strikes and you're out. I'm sure your lawyers explained that to you the last time you were in court.'

'Ben, I'll talk to my boss about the protection. It never hurts to ask, ok?' reassured Ramouter.

'Thank you,' Ben said.

'Now a description, do you think you could do that for us?'

'Yeah, I can.'

'That's good. We'll leave it there,' said Ramouter. 'Interview concluded at 10.46 a.m..'

'Do you believe him, that he saw one of the suspects?' Henley asked. She stopped outside the entrance of Croydon police station custody suite and looked through the sliding doors. Laurence Durant was sitting on the bench, his face pinched in deep concentration.

'He wasn't putting it on,' said Ramouter on the other end of the phone. 'He broke down crying towards the end. He's adamant he saw what he saw. We're just waiting for the police sketch artist to arrive.'

Henley could hear it. The hesitancy in Ramouter's voice. She could safely place a bet that if she was in the room with Ramouter, she would have seen him rubbing his ear. A sure sign of a temper on the rise.

'What happened in the interview?' Henley asked. 'What did Copeland do?'

Ramouter huffed. 'She went in too hard. Like a two-footed tackle. I had to intervene more than once. I know that she's more senior than—'

'Ramouter, it doesn't make a blind bit of difference how senior she is, she should know how to read the room. When it's time to treat a detainee as a witness and not a suspect. If you go in too hard, you undermine your position. I told you that on day one. This isn't a game.'

'Aye. I know.'

'I'm sorry, I'm not having a go at you. Tell me, what do you want to do with Ben?'

'RUI him with strict conditions not to post anything about this investigation on social media.'

'That sounds good to me. Keep me updated,' said Henley. She ended the call and stepped into the custody suite. 'Just give me one sec,' she said to Laurence as she spoke to the custody officer at the desk who pointed to Interview Room Three on his left and informed her that Laurence had declined legal representation.

'Are you going somewhere?' she asked as Laurence picked up the large duffle bag that had been resting on the seat next to him. She'd authorised his release under investigation thinking that showing a bit of empathy and allowing him to return home, would bring Laurence to his senses.

'I thought I should get some things together,' Laurence said quietly as though resigned to some unknown fate.

'You're not being charged,' Henley replied, realising that

Laurence believed he would be charged and remanded in custody. She motioned for him to follow her into the interview room.

'But I thought—'

'That doesn't mean the investigation against you is closed. I've got some questions for you, and I need to do that under caution,' Henley explained as she entered her details on the monitor. 'Just like last time I'm going to do my little speech and ask you to introduce yourself. Are you good with that?'

'Yeah,' Laurence replied, fiddling with his wedding band.

'So, I need to talk about the vigilante group known as Shadow or Iron Shadow,' Henley said after she'd made the standard introductions, cautioned and reminded Laurence about his right to a lawyer.

'I don't know anything about any groups.'

Henley sighed and placed a stack of printouts on the table. 'A judge gave us permission to access your phone. In front of you are copies of your WhatsApp messages and chats from the Discord app. So, I'm going to ask you again, Laurence, and I would appreciate it if you didn't lie to me. Tell me about the groups.'

Laurence sniffed and slid his ring off his finger. 'There was a time when I couldn't take the bloody thing off,' he said, holding it aloft. 'I was about a stone and a half heavier eighteen months ago and then Sherri was killed, and I couldn't eat. People kept bringing me food.'

'The groups Laurence.'

'I'm getting there. The point is that I needed help. To manage, not just the grief, but also the court process. You think that it would be straightforward. Someone kills your wife, that person gets arrested, convicted and then they go prison.'

'Unfortunately, it's not always that straightforward.'

'No, it's not. The victim support people at court referred me to a group for people affected by crime. I didn't want to go but my sister thought it would be a good idea.'

'Is this the group at the Starlight Community Centre?'

'Yeah. I started going and a couple of us would go to the pub afterwards and one of the guys started talking about justice and how to get it.'

'Do you have a name?'

'Don. He didn't give his surname.'

'How did he suggest getting justice?'

'Doxxing people, exposing what they've done on social media. That sort of thing. He stopped coming to the victim support group after a while, but we kept in touch, and he invited me to a group.'

'The Discord group?'

'That's the one. I didn't do anything at first. Just observed, have a bit of a chat and then, about a month ago, Don sent me the court file for Tabitha's case. Not just her case but her pre-sentence report. Everything. He then asked if I wanted justice, and I said yes.'

'Did you know what Don meant by justice?'

'I thought he meant scare her. Shake her up a bit. Get her to apologise for taking my wife from me.'

Henley could hear the whirl of the fans in the computer tower behind her as Laurence choked back tears. She passed him the box of tissues.

'She never apologised you know,' said Laurence. 'Not once. Her pre-sentencing report said that she was remorseful, but she never said, "I'm sorry for killing Sherri". And, at one point, she blamed Sherri. Said that she ran out into the road. That she was on her phone, not paying attention. Bitch.'

'You received a text message on Sunday 17 October at 9.28 p.m.. The number wasn't saved in your contacts,' said Henley. She tapped her pen against a highlighted message on the transcript. '"All good. On train now. Arriving at Forest Hill station. 10.04 p.m.". Who were you meeting?'

'Don. The plan was that I was to pick him up at the station, go to the Ashcrofts' house and confront her.'

'Was Don alone?'

'No. When I arrived at the station, I could see someone with him. I didn't think anything of it and then he brought him to the car.'

'Could you describe this person?'

'No. He had a hoodie on. He kept his head down and had his back to me. I asked Don who he was, and he said it was someone who was on our side. He didn't give me a name. I then . . . I don't know panicked. It was all well and good talking about confronting her, but I'd started to see more things in the chat. Disturbing things.'

'Like what?'

Laurence stood up, walked to the corner of the room and pressed himself against the wall. Henley let him, knowing that the microphones would be able to capture his voice. 'It was a video of a woman. She was on the floor and screaming, never heard anything like it and she was covered with feathers.'

'Who posted the video.'

'I'm not sure, but I just thought about that video, and I couldn't do it. Whatever they wanted to do, I just couldn't do it.'

'So, what happened next?'

'I told Don no. That I'd changed my mind,' Laurence said, returning to his seat. 'But he told me it was too late. I told him I was going home but he . . . took out a knife and put it to my stomach. Told me again that it was too late.'

'At the last interview we showed you footage of your car on Lordship Lane shortly before the attack on the Ashcrofts.'

'That was my car, but I wasn't driving. Don told me to get out of the car. He had a knife, so I did. He told the other guy to get in which he did and then they drove off. I thought he was just trying to frighten me, not that I wasn't already scared as fuck, but I thought he was going to come back. But he didn't.'

'So, what did you do?'

'Nothing at first. Just stood there like a mug and then I went to the pub. The Dartmouth Arms. I had a couple of pints, tried to get my head together and then I got an Uber and went home. I'm sure they've got cameras, and you can check the Uber app on my phone.'

'We'll do all of those things,' Henley replied, suddenly feeling exhausted by the lengths to which Laurence had gone to get some kind of justice for his wife. 'How did you get the car back?'

'Not that night but in the morning, I got a text from a different number. Telling me to pick up the car.'

Henley turned over the pages of the phone report and ran her finger through the messages. '6.49 a.m.. "Thanks. Keys behind the wheel. Driver's side.". There's no location,' she said.

'I got a location notification after the text. He'd left the car in New Cross. I can't remember the road name, but the car was parked next to an allotment. I got the train there and found my car. Windscreen shattered. Bumper fucked up. I just got in and hoped that you lot didn't stop me.'

Henley gathered the pages of the report together as she watched Laurence grow smaller as he made his admissions.

'How much trouble am I in?' he asked.

'I'm not sure yet,' Henley admitted. 'Are you telling me that you were definitely not involved in the attacks on the Ashcrofts.'

'I promise you,' Laurence said vehemently. 'I didn't do anything. Not a thing.'

'You didn't see the blood on the back seat of your car?'

Laurence lowered his head. 'I didn't check the back of the car.'

'Did Don contact you again?'

'No, I think he knew that I was done, that I was out but I saw what had happened. There were photos in the group. I wish I'd never met him.'

'I'm going to terminate the interview at 11.46 a.m.,' Henley said, tapping the stop button on the touchscreen.

'I'll do what I can to convince the CPS to take no further action against you, but I can't guarantee it,' she said as Larry leaned forward on the table with his head in his hands and began to cry.

'I just wanted her to say sorry,' Laurence said his cries becoming louder and uncontrollable. 'That's all I wanted. For her to say sorry for killing my wife.'

41

'Thanks, boss,' Ezra said, rubbing his stomach. 'That was much needed.'

'I can't believe you convinced me to buy you an all-day breakfast,' said Pellacia, closing the door to the café.

'Excuse me, I was here at the crack of dawn. I was here so early that I met the cleaners for the first time and, to be honest, you looked like you needed it. Late night, was it?'

'You know what, I let you get away with too much cheek,' said Pellacia as he pulled his cigarettes out of his coat pocket.

'And you should really give that up. You're too pretty to die.'

Pellacia laughed as he looked at the packet in his hand and put it back in his pocket. 'Thanks. If anyone asks, I'm at the Yard. Should be back before the end of the day, but any problems, then—'

Ezra patted Pellacia's shoulder affectionately. 'I know, you're always available,' he said. 'Such a devoted boss.'

'You really are a joker,' Pellacia said, shaking his head as he walked off in the direction of Greenwich train station.

Ezra didn't wait for the lights to change to red and crossed quickly. The time he'd spent serving a sentence in Coldingley Prison had made him hyper aware. He noticed things that wouldn't be out of the ordinary to most people. No one would have thought twice about the man sitting on the bench that faced Greenwich police station, where the serial crimes unit was based, but Ezra did. To Ezra the man seemed as though he was in the middle of making a choice and was waiting for someone.

Ezra walked past but then something made him stop. He turned around as the man who was wearing a baseball cap raised his head.

'I know you,' Ezra said, curling his fingers around his staff ID card, unsure exactly how he would use it as a weapon if needed. 'You're the . . . Kaiden. Soteria.'

'Is there somewhere we can talk?' Kaiden asked. 'I really need to talk to you. I called the office, but I was told you were out for lunch.'

'You want to speak to me and not the Inspector?' Ezra asked, looking around as though checking to make sure that no one was playing a prank on him.

'No, you. I want to talk to you about the—'

'I am not a police officer. Ones and zeros, that's what I deal—'

'I'm the one who did it,' Kaiden hissed, his eyes wide with panic.

Ezra stared at Kaiden. 'You're Spectercipher393?'

Kaiden rubbed his face with distress.

'A couple more hours and I would have had you,' Ezra said. 'You need to come inside. One of the—'

'I'm not going inside. They'll arrest me and I . . . I need time. I just want to talk to you.'

'Bruv, I told you. That ain't my job and I don't want to get in trouble and talking to you, right now, is getting me in trouble.'

'I'm not an idiot. I already know I've activated the clock by even being here and that you'll tell them but . . . I don't know. I suppose I'm just asking for a bit of grace.'

Ezra screwed his face in concentration. He relented. 'Come on. We're not going inside, just around the back, it's a big building but there's only us in it.'

'Thank you,' Kaiden said as he followed Ezra across the road, and they entered the old custody yard.

'So, what is it?' Ezra asked, positioning himself so that if needed, he could run but Kaiden couldn't.

Kaiden took off his hat and wiped the sweat off his forehead. 'It was never meant to go this far,' he said. 'No one was ever meant to die.'

'You made it look like someone had hacked the monitoring system?'

'I thought I'd done a good job of covering my tracks but then I went back and saw what you'd downloaded. I realised then it was only a matter of time before I was fucked.'

'You really should be talking to Inspector Henley about this.'

'I know, I know, but I just wanted to . . . I don't know, maybe because you're not a cop, I feel that I can trust you.'

'How involved are you?' asked Ezra. 'Is it just downloading stuff or is it . . . everything?'

'Everything.'

Ezra stepped back and looked at the rear door that led to the custody suite, trying to calculate how quickly he could get into the building.

'You don't have to be scared of me.'

'Mate, I spend half my time trying to avoid the murder board upstairs and you're telling me not to be scared of you. I've seen what you've done.'

'I've got a wife. Two boys and I'm about to lose it all. I want to hand myself in, but I just want to give myself a bit of time to get things sorted.'

Kaiden jumped as the sound of a police siren rang out, the volume increasing as it got closer.

Ezra held up his hands. 'It's just passing, nothing to do with us.'

Kaiden relaxed slightly as the siren reached its peak and then became quieter. 'I need to stop this, but I need to get things sorted at home first. Tell my wife. Say goodbye to my kids,' he said. 'You must get it. Wanting a chance to say goodbye.'

'I get that,' Ezra nodded. 'But I still don't know what exactly you want me to do.'

'An email address,' said Kaiden. 'I need to send you everything I've got. Everything that implicates me and the rest of them.'

'Mate, I'm not sure. Why don't you just come in and wait for the—'

'No. I want to do it this way even though I know you'll call Inspector Henley as soon as my back is turned.'

'Of course I will,' said Ezra.

'I promise you I'll be the one to hand myself in. First thing tomorrow morning. I'll come straight back here. You have my word.'

Ezra sighed. 'Ok, give me your phone.'

Kaiden pulled out his phone, unlocked it and handed it to Ezra.

'My email and direct line,' said Ezra.

42

An enlarged photograph taken from Kaiden Longley's driving licence was on the smartboard next to a composite of the man who had chased Ben and answered to the name Josh. The composite of 'Josh' had arrived on Henley's phone at the exact moment she was talking to Ezra. She and Ezra were sure. Kaiden Longley and Josh were the same person.

'I can't believe he was here,' said Copeland, stepping back from the smartboard. 'Why didn't Ezra call someone?'

'Ezra did call someone. He called me,' Henley said defensively. She popped two paracetamols out of the packet and swallowed them down with water.

'And this Kaiden guy was long gone by the time Eastie and I got downstairs,' said Stanford, shooting Copeland a look.

'What exactly did he say to Ezra?' asked Ramouter.

'That things have gone too far. That he didn't expect people to die. Which is all well and good, but the fact is that four people are dead,' said Henley. 'So, what exactly do we know about him?'

'Kaiden Longley. Aged forty-two. Born in Boston, Massachusetts,' said Ramouter, reading from his notes. 'His wife Rachel Longley is from London. They got married in the States eleven years ago and have two sons aged eight and five. They moved back to London four years ago and he started working for Soteria. No previous convictions in this country or the States and he has a clean driving licence.'

'Is there any indication, any social media that could tell us why he would get involved in a vigilante gang?' asked Eastwood. 'I mean on paper he seems decent.'

'None that I could find,' said Ramouter.

'I hate that he's just disappeared into the wind,' said Henley. 'Officers from Stoke Newington police station went to his home address but there was no one there.'

'What about the wife?' asked Stanford.

'City of London Police attended her office in Fenchurch Street. She said she last saw her husband when she assumed he'd left for work at 7.30 this morning,' said Henley. 'She hasn't heard from him since and all calls to his phone are going straight to voicemail.'

'So, what are we supposed to do?' asked Copeland. 'Just sit and wait for him to turn up tomorrow morning with a cup of tea and a bacon butty?'

'Right now, we don't really have much choice,' Henley said, fighting to keep the anger out of her voice. 'If what Ben Trezeguet told you and Ramouter is correct then this man is running scared.'

'The question is scared of what?' said Stanford, leaning forward and placing his elbows on his knees. 'This man is not scared of the police, that much is obvious, because he came to our front door, which must mean he's afraid of Iron Shadow.'

Henley picked up the control for the smartboard and brought up the sketch artist composite of the man that Laurence Durant had called Don. 'Kaiden was called Josh by the man who was at Nathan Hall's house, so I'm assuming that this guy has a fake name too. Laurence said he met him at the victim support group. I spoke to Jorge who confirmed that a man who he knew as Don attended three group sessions last year, but he has no other information. No last name and no idea why he was actually there.'

'Do you think this Don wasn't a victim?' asked Eastwood as Pellacia entered the room his face flushed as though he'd run up four flights of stairs.

'When Mark spoke about the pack mentality of vigilantes the other day,' said Henley, 'he said that the leader may not necessarily have been a victim themselves, and I can't think of a better place to find people to save than a victim support group.'

'It's almost predatory,' said Ramouter.

'Not almost, it *is* predatory and manipulative,' said Pellacia. 'How sure is Ezra that this Kaiden Longley will come back, if he's not picked up?'

'He's pretty confident,' said Henley 'And before you ask, no he hasn't received anything yet, but he'll let us know as soon as something drops in his inbox. So, onto next steps. We're waiting for both Lewisham council and TFL to locate CCTV from Forest Hill and New Cross Stations and also Amersham Vale in New Cross. I'm hoping that we'll get actual footage of this Don character.'

'What about this composite image of him? Do we want this circulated now or would you prefer to wait until we can join it up with some actual footage?' asked Pellacia.

'I think that people's memories are more likely to be jogged with actual footage,' said Copeland. 'So it might be best to hold off.'

'I agree with Copeland,' said Henley begrudgingly. 'The sketch is good but not the best but let's put a time limit on it. If we're still at square one at 9 a.m. tomorrow, then we release it.'

'Sounds good to me,' said Pellacia, standing up and turning to Henley. 'Are you all right to have a quick word before I let you get on?' he asked.

'Of course,' Henley replied, grabbing her phone from the desk.

'Before you lot go,' said Stanford. 'Where are we with the prison? We're wasting time here.'

'You're good to go first thing tomorrow,' Pellacia replied over his shoulder as he held the door open for Henley. 'Jo's got the paperwork.'

'Look before you say anything, I need to apologise. About the handing in my notice thing,' said Henley. 'I lost my temper and—'

Pellacia held up his hand and shook his head. 'Don't. You don't need to apologise. I didn't handle things the right way with you. I should have done better and I'm sorry.'

Henley felt the muscles in her shoulders relax. She hated fighting with Pellacia. He had been on her side for so long both as a colleague and a friend that the thought of losing him filled her with an indescribable dread. 'So, is that it or is there something else?' she asked.

'Ezra,' Pellacia admitted, unbuttoning his top button and removing his tie. 'I would have been with him if it wasn't for this stupid meeting at the Yard, talking about fucking nothing. He shouldn't have dealt with that on his own.'

'If it helps, Ezra seems fine. He's not shaken.'

'It's not the point though, is it? I don't give a shit whether this Kaiden Longley has regrets or not. He came here and he came looking for Ezra.'

'I'm not going to pretend that I'm pleased about it either. We were both at Soteria's office, but Kaiden Longley chose Ezra specifically because he's not a police officer.'

'That doesn't make me feel better. I've got a long history with Ezra – I was the one who arrested him, for God's sake – and I was the one who brought him into the SCU. I'm responsible for him.'

Henley sat down next to Pellacia. 'Come on,' she said gently. 'He's not in danger.'

'Even so, I'll drive him home tonight and I'll pick him up tomorrow morning.'

'His own personal chauffeur service. You'll never hear the end of it,' Henley said as she squeezed Pellacia's arm. 'Look, I was thinking, we haven't had a proper welcome drink for Copeland yet—'

Pellacia looked up at Henley with surprise. 'You've changed your tune,' he said.

'I'm trying to do the mature thing and, also, I think this lot need it but not tonight, I've got to—' she paused not wanting in that moment to let Pellacia into her date night plans with her husband. 'How about tomorrow night?'

Pellacia reached up as though to touch Henley's face but then pulled away. 'Tomorrow will be fine,' he replied.

43

Kaiden stepped out onto the balcony of his flat on the tenth floor of Primrose House in Little Portugal. This enviable view of London, with the neon pink lights that decorated the London Eye, the bright lights of the Shard, the cluster of geometrically shaped buildings that made up the finance sector of the city and every towering residential block that reached the black skies. It seemed as though everything was possible, but all Kaiden could feel was despair. That, like the disintegrating plaster on the balcony, his entire life was crumbling. Kaiden grunted with disgust as he pulled out the cheap bottle opener and prised the cap off the beer that had been sweating in his hand. All of his lies were unravelling. His wife was going to discover that he'd been using their flat for his illicit activities and had not put it on the market after the last tenants had left. He'd sneaked into his house earlier through the back door, taking the chance that the police weren't staking out his home. He'd kissed his boys goodbye and had told his wife that he loved her. He couldn't bring himself to tell his wife that, just like he had in Boston, he'd gone too far – but this time was worse. He'd barely raised the bottle to his lips when the intercom buzzed insistently. He checked his watch. 8.46 p.m.. They were early. Too early.

Kaiden put his eye to the spy hole and breathed a sigh of relief when he saw Mika's face and that she was alone. He pulled the chain off the hook and opened the door.

'I know, I'm early,' Mika said apologetically. She entered the hallway and walked through the flat as though she'd been there before. 'I'm sorry. It's just . . . you know what, never mind.'

'No that's—' Kaiden gasped as his attempt to close the door was blocked by a black, mud-encrusted trainer. He looked up to see a gloved hand grip the door and push it back. Kaiden stepped back into the narrow hallway as Don, his face barely visible under a black hoodie, closed the door.

'Sorry, I should have told you Don was coming,' Mika said. She stopped at the open door that led to the balcony. 'You're extremely lucky to have a view like this. Stunning.'

'Yeah, it is pretty spectacular,' said Kaiden, joining Mika on the balcony, keen to get away from Don whose hot breath he could feel on his neck when he'd followed him into the living room. He picked up the bottle which he'd left on the patio table and drank quickly in an effort to settle his nerves.

Mika turned and faced Kaiden. 'Ever since you called me this afternoon, I've been trying to work out why you want to see me,' she said. 'I thought maybe you'd changed your mind about leaving us, which would have been fine, but then I got a message from Don.'

Kaiden watched as Mika took her phone out of her jacket pocket. She tapped the screen a couple of times.

'Take a look,' she said, holding out her phone.

Kaiden cleared his throat, put down his beer and took the phone from Mika's outstretched hand. The fermented liquid travelled back up his throat, making him gag when he saw the photograph. It was him, sitting on the bench opposite Greenwich police station, where the Serial Crimes Unit was based. He swiped right. A photograph of him walking towards the building with Ezra. He scrolled down and saw screenshots of his pinned location on Google Maps. The first taken at 13.02 on Wednesday afternoon after he'd left his office near Cannon Street station and taken the train to Greenwich and walked to the police station where the SCU was based. His finger had hovered on the bell for a few seconds before he'd chickened out and returned to work. The second pinned location was taken an hour before he met Ezra.

Kaiden shook his head vehemently. 'It's not what it looks like,' he insisted.

Mika snatched her phone back. 'Are you telling me that it doesn't look like you went to the police twice?' she asked with genuine curiosity. 'Don saw you walk off with the black boy. What did you tell him?'

'Nothing. I didn't tell him anything.'

'So, you gave him something?' Mika asked, her words tripping over each other as she spoke more quickly and furiously. 'Information about Iron Shadow. About our cause?'

'No, the detective. She asked me to come in for a voluntary interview about the hacking of Soteria's system. I thought it would be a good thing, I could see where they—'

'Why on earth would they ask you?' Don spat. 'You told us that—'

Mika raised her head and tutted. 'I am an idiot. They were always talking to you. You're the boss at Soteria.'

Kaiden nodded.

'I was honest with you. Let you in. I feel betrayed. Don't you feel betrayed Don?'

'He's grassed us up,' said Don.

'No, I didn't . . . I wouldn't,' said Kaiden.

'What did you say to that boy?' asked Mika.

'Nothing. I didn't . . . you can trust me.'

'He's talking fucking bollocks,' said Don.

'Obviously, 'Mika said with a smile. She left the balcony.

'Mika, please. Let me—'

Kaiden stumbled back as Don's fist connected with his face, his nose breaking instantly. He screamed out as Don grabbed him by his shoulders, spun him around and punched him in the face again. Kaiden fell heavily against the bookcase and slid down to the floor. He felt warm blood drip down his face. Through his blurry vision he saw Mika pick up his mobile phone from the dining table.

'No,' Kaiden groaned as Don grabbed him by his feet and dragged him out towards the balcony. He twisted his body and grabbed the door frame. He screamed out, praying that his voice would be heard above the sound of drum and bass escaping from his neighbour's window. He cried out for a second time as Mika kicked his hands repeatedly until he let go. Don released Kaiden's legs and there was a crash as he kicked out. Kaiden's foot connected with a large monstera plant, toppling it. He tried to get up, but Don pushed him down and punched him for a third time. Kaiden's head spun as waves of concussion seeped into his brain. Don grabbed him by the waist but Kaiden was too weak to fight his way out of the macabre embrace. Don groaned and lifted him onto the balcony wall. There was a fleeting moment when Kaiden's eyes caught a plane crossing the night sky as the crescent of the new moon rose in the east and fire engine sirens played a dying symphony on their way to an emergency. He stretched out his hand, his fingertips brushing against the balcony wall as Don pushed him over. Kaiden screamed. The air whipped around his face as he thrashed him arms, willing himself to fly. He didn't hit the ground straight away. His neck connected first with the edge of the large communal wastebin and broke instantly. Kaiden was dead before he hit the cracked concrete.

44

'Did you know that they used to hold executions here?' Stanford asked, pointing at the entrance of HMP Manchester which, despite the name change more than thirty years ago was still referred to as Strangeways. 'Had its own execution chamber and everything.'

'I'll try to remember that if I'm ever a contestant on *Who Wants to Be a Millionaire*,' Eastwood replied. She raised her arms and stretched. 'You can drive back. My back is fucked.'

'Gladly. The sooner we get this job done and get back to London the better. Did I ever tell you that Gene wanted us to move up here a few years ago? He went to Manchester University and, according to him, those were the best years of his life.'

'Aww, bless him. He's got all of those lovely memories and now he has to wake up to your ugly mug every morning.'

'Do you know what, Eastie, you're very lucky that I don't have self-esteem problems.'

'No, you just have "I'm a snooty Southerner who doesn't like to go north of the M25" problems,' Eastwood said, opening her bag and pulling out the letter from the governor of HMP Manchester authorising their prison visits to see Gareth Humphreys and Karim Messenger.

'I hope this doesn't end up being a wild-goose chase,' said Stanford. 'This case is already doing a number on my head.'

'It's the scalping, isn't it?' Eastwood said, lowering her voice. 'It takes this case to a completely different level and the people doing it. They're beyond wicked.'

'Excuse me, Detective Sergeants Stanford and Eastwood here. Met Police,' Stanford called through the speech panel on the reception desk.

A few seconds later a man appeared at the desk. Eastwood pushed their warrant cards and authorisation letter through the service hatch.

The receptionist wordlessly turned his back and walked to his desk at the end of the room.

'Bloody hell, you wouldn't think we had a murderer to catch, would you?' Stanford huffed.

'What's wrong with you? I know we had to leave at the crack of dawn.'

'We left before that.'

'Whatever. As Henley would say, you spent most of the drive-up with a screwed face.'

Stanford leaned his head back and sighed. 'We got a call from the social workers yesterday.'

'Has the adoption fallen through?' said Eastwood, reaching for Stanford's hand.

Stanford shook his head and laughed. 'No, it turns out that our . . . well our, yeah, our son, has a sister. She's three. She's been in foster care but with another borough and they only found out about her a couple of days ago.'

'Oh, wow. Oh shit.'

'Exactly. It's . . . I'm trying to get my head around it. We were getting the house ready for one kid and now . . . fucking hell, Eastie.'

'How's Gene dealing with it?'

'Oh, he's not. He got pissed last night and passed out on the sofa. He was still there when I left this morning. We've got—'

A loud rapping on the security glass interrupted Stanford.

'Right, you've got a problem,' the receptionist said loudly as Stanford and Eastwood approached and he roughly pushed their warrant cards and authorisation letter back through the service hatch. 'Karim Messenger is refusing to come out of his cell. He doesn't want to see you and unless you're planning to arrest him for something, I don't think there's much you can do about it.'

'Thank you for the legal advice,' said Eastwood. 'What about Humphreys?'

'He's still good to go but he's currently appearing via video link at Manchester Crown Court.'

'He's back at court?' Stanford asked as the receptionist pressed a button under the desk and a staff door opened. 'What for?'

'Threw a kettle filled with boiling water and sugar at his cellmate when they were rioting,' the receptionist replied as he ushered them into the prison.

Gareth Humphreys adjusted the blue, torn bib over his protruding stomach as the prison guard slammed the door shut. 'The weird thing is that I've been sitting in Strangeways for what, six months, and no one has visited me. And today, I'm Mr Popular,' he said.

Gareth smiled revealing a gap where his left incisor and canine tooth should have been. His face showed all the signs that he'd been in a fight. A bruise covered his left cheek and lower jaw with a row of black stitches across the bridge of his nose. He ran a hand through his thick brown hair revealing another cut on his forehead. 'Even my own mam and kids haven't visited me,' he said.

'They've probably had enough of you,' Eastwood said. 'Hurry up and sit down before the guards start getting concerned.'

'Dutifully noted,' Gareth replied. The table edge pressed into his stomach as he settled himself into the seat. 'So, who exactly are you?' he asked. 'All they told me was that the police wanted to see me, but you're from London and according to my social diary, the last time I was down in London was to watch City in a Champions League game about six years ago.'

'I'm DS Eastwood and this is DS Stanford. We're from the Serial Crimes Unit.'

Gareth paled as his eyes darted from Eastwood to Stanford and then the door. His Adam's apple bulged as he swallowed, his hand reaching for a cup of water that didn't exist. 'Why would . . . why do you want to talk to me? Don't you lot deal with serial killers? I wouldn't know anything about that.'

'We think you do know something,' said Eastwood. 'We want to talk to you about the group you were a part of, Iron Shadow.'

'Why?' asked Gareth. 'I'm not involved in any of that stuff anymore.'

'That's only because you're stuck in here,' said Stanford.

'No, no,' Gareth said, shaking his head. 'It was all over with them after I did that first stint inside for assaulting that fucking paedo.'

'You mean Mantell. Your brother-in-law.'

'Who else would I be talking about? I still can't believe my sister stood by him. Defended him in court. The sick fuck.'

'But that's not true, is it, that you weren't involved in that stuff anymore?' said Eastwood. 'You were released on licence in October 2019 and was suspected of being involved in another assault a month later.'

Gareth's eyes grew smaller, his stomach rising and falling as he inhaled sharply. 'Are you planning to arrest me for that again?'

'No. We just want information. We're investigating the murder of three people and the attempted murder of two others.'

'Down in London?'

'Bloody hell, you're quick,' said Stanford, rolling his eyes. 'Yes, down in London. Look, you and Messenger both did time for harassing and assaulting Mantell and even though you were still serving your sentence when Gong Bo Hyoo was attacked, we suspect you know who was involved and told them how to really painfully punish someone.'

Gareth sniffed as though he'd suddenly developed a cold, his face reddening and developing an oily sheen as sweat pushed through his large pores.

'Someone attempted to tar and feather Gong Bo Hyoo by using sulphuric acid,' said Eastwood. 'Which kind of fits with your MO. Weren't you in court half an hour ago to enter a plea to a charge of causing grievous bodily harm with intent? Poured boiling sugar over an inmate.'

Gareth licked his dry, cracked lips and swallowed again. 'That was self-defence, and I pleaded not guilty. I'm allowed to defend myself. The law says so.'

'We're not here to debate what the law says,' said Eastwood. 'Tell us about Iron Shadow. How you met. Who the members were or are.'

'You should really talk to Karim,' Gareth said. 'He's the one who got me involved.'

'We're not talking to Karim. We're talking to you.'

'What do I get for it? Co-operating with you lot I mean,' Gareth said as the corners of his mouth turned upwards in a smile. 'I'm not a grass, but for the right price.'

Stanford straightened up and leaned forward on the table, the space between him and Gareth growing tight and claustrophobic. 'I'm tired, fed up and hungry. I didn't spend nearly five hours on the motorway to play games with the likes of you. Do you understand?'

'Understood.'

'Good. Now tell us about the group,' Eastwood said, clicking her pen.

'It started with Karim,' Gareth said quickly. 'His little sister was abused by her teacher. He got away with it and Karim didn't take it well. One night, we were in the pub talking about it and in he walked, that dirty paedo who abused Karim's sister. He was in the pub with his missus, acting like . . . I don't know, he was God's gift. His missus left and he stayed until closing and we followed him. That's all I'm going to say about that. You can fill in the gaps. Anyway, I don't know, it like triggered something and it . . . it was a rush.'

'Are you saying you started the group?' asked Eastwood.

Gareth shook his head. 'No, Karim found them, or they found him on Facebook, I think. The next thing I know, he's dragging me along to a meeting.'

'Who was in this meeting?'

'I wouldn't even call it a meeting. I was expecting a massive thing, but there was only one person at first. Called herself Mika. She said that her and her partner wanted to expand beyond chasing perverts with a phone through the park.'

'What did she mean by that?'

'I had no idea to start with,' said Gareth, the chair creaking under his weight as he leaned back. 'And then she explained how the courts were getting it wrong. How people like that teacher were getting away with murder because the jury weren't always equipped to make the right decision. And she had a point, right? Look what happened with my niece.'

Eastwood and Stanford both remained quiet. Their gaze fixed on Gareth.

'Anyway, after that first meeting. Karim started getting information on targets. And it was good information. Full name, home address, bail address, information about their cases, emails and, sometimes, phone numbers.'

'And what would you do with that information?' asked Eastwood.

'Use your imagination,' said Gareth. 'Think about what you would want to do if someone hurt – and I mean really hurt – your wife, boyfriend, your kid, your dad. Bloody hell, even your dog. Whatever you're thinking about, it was probably done.'

'All this information you got about the . . . victims,' Stanford said carefully. 'Where did it come from?'

'I'd always wondered the same thing, because the info Karim and I got, it was like a little dossier. Sometimes we got copies of witness statements so we could get a real feel for what our victims went through.'

'You mentioned that this Mika had a partner. Did you ever meet him or her?'

'No, but I know his name. Elliot. Karim met him. I got the impression that neither of them liked to get their hands dirty. She never came out with us. Just gave us our orders.'

'But you met this Mika?'

'A couple of times. She wasn't what I expected at all. She looked like she should be decorating the church on a Sunday, do you know what I mean?'

'If we got a sketch artist—'

'I got an A-level in art and I'm a graphic designer by trade. I could draw her myself,' Gareth said proudly. 'Give me your pen and a sheet of paper and I'll draw her for you now.'

'You've just appeared in court for violently assaulting a prisoner and you want me to give you a pen that you could use as a weapon?' Eastwood was incredulous.

'You have my word that I will not shank you,' Gareth said, making the sign of the cross.

Eastwood looked across at Stanford who gave a slight shrug.

'Fine,' she said as she ripped out a sheet from her notebook, took another pen from her pocket and slid both across the table.

'I always liked doing portraits. People's eyes tell you everything,' said Gareth as he started to sketch.

'So, what happened to her, what happened to the group?'

'They must have got new members because my perverted brother-in-law ended up in the bottom of the canal when Karim and I were inside.'

'But you got in back in touch with Mika when you were out?'

'The best way I can describe it, is that it's like an addiction. You're always looking for that rush of making people pay. So, we got back involved but it wasn't just us. There were more people in the group and not just from Manchester. There was a couple of people from your end because I remember seeing screenshots in the WhatsApp group of a guy that someone had doxxed in East Ham – I think it was – and there was also an online chatroom thing.'

'Was murder ever discussed in the group?'

'I mean people said things like "I wish so and so was dead" but I didn't take any of that seriously and you've got to remember that I didn't know my pervert brother-in-law was dead until after I was released from prison. It's not as if my stupid sister was visiting me and giving me updates. Also my kids and mam weren't talking to me. Nothing new there.'

'How did you find out?'

Gareth shook his head with a look of disbelief on his face as though he was reliving the moment. 'I met Karim for drinks in the pub and when I got there, he wasn't alone. There was guy with him, tall, stocky, think he had a beard, and he had a London accent. I can't really describe his face because I was already a bit pissed. We went outside to have a cigarette and to do a couple of lines. Anyway, we're out there and this guy brings up that pervert Douglas and then he asked me to put my hand out which I remember thinking was weird, but I was buzzing and then—'

Gareth put the pen down and his face paled, making his bruises almost glow under the harsh fluorescent light. 'This thing fell into my hand. Have you ever seen a chicken that's been plucked? Imagine that but with thick, greying black hair on it. That's what it looked like, a slice of chicken skin. I remember it feeling dry.'

'What did you think it was?' asked Eastwood.

'At the time, I wasn't sure. I just dropped it and then I left.

It was only afterward that Karim told me that it was Douglas's scalp.'

'Had scalping been discussed in the group before?'

'Not when I first joined but it was mentioned when I was released and got involved again.'

'And how did you feel about it?'

'Listen, when you're dealing with crazy, well you've got to go crazy too,' said Gareth. 'But in all honesty, it wasn't for me.'

'You were given an additional two years because you assaulted another cellmate and nearly scalped him and you're now saying that it wasn't for you?' said Stanford.

Gareth looked up at him. 'I think the doctors were exaggerating,' he said, calmly resuming his sketch. 'Do you know how much work it would take to scalp someone without a proper knife. Did I shank him in his head? Yes, but the idiot then fell back against the bed frame and sort of ripped his head open. I was not expecting that. Don't get me wrong, it was nasty, but I didn't scalp him.'

'OK. You said that Mika and her partner were the ones who got the information and basically handed it out?'

'That's right. Mika sent the information.'

'Including the information on Gong Bo Hyoo?'

Gareth twisted his mouth. 'Most likely, but remember I was still in here, in Strangeways.'

'But you know who was involved in the Gong Bo Hyoo tar and feather assault and her murder?'

'Now, why would I admit to knowing that? But what I will tell you is that in November 2019 the WhatsApp group was deleted. Just like that,' Gareth said, snapping his fingers. 'No warning.'

'Did you ask Karim about the group being deleted After all, he was the one who introduced you.'

Gareth nodded. 'He said that Mika's partner had got a new job and that they were moving down south, but they said they would be able to carry on with their duties or "our cause" as Mika liked to call it.'

'Do you know what either of them did for work?' asked Eastwood.

'I had my theories; I thought that maybe one of them worked for the CPS or the police, but you really need to ask Karim. I think he saw or bumped into her somewhere and speaking of her—' Gareth smiled as he slid both the pen and sketch towards Eastwood. 'Told you I was good,' he said.

45

Ramouter enlarged the image on Henley's phone. 'Who's that?' he asked. 'She reminds me of Ethan's teaching assistant.'

'Apparently that is the woman who was leading the vigilante group in Manchester and has now moved down here,' said Henley. 'According to Eastwood and Stanford she and her partner were the ones who picked the victims.'

'Do we have names for them?' Ramouter asked.

'Mika and Elliot. Even though the sketch is good I'm not too keen on stamping it with a Crimestoppers logo and releasing it to the public until I've got something a little bit more solid in terms of identification.'

'Maybe Kaiden Longley will be able to enlighten us.'

'It's gone past eleven and he hasn't shown up yet. Copeland called and confirmed that he's not at home,' said Henley as Ramouter pushed open the door to Ezra's room. 'His wife is in a panic and convinced for some inexplicable reason that we're responsible for his disappearance.'

'Ez, have you heard from Kaiden?' asked Ramouter.

'Nope,' Ezra replied as Henley passed him a brown bag containing his breakfast. 'First the big boss insists on dropping me home and picking me up and now you're bringing me sustenance. I should get approached by criminals more often.'

'Don't even joke about it,' said Henley, handing out coffees. 'So, what did Kaiden send you?'

'I'll tell you one thing; this guy is paranoid. He encrypted everything he sent me last night which I had to spend most of the morning, well, decrypting,' said Ezra, carefully unwrapping his bagel.

'So did you get in?' Henley asked.

'Of course I did,' Ezra said his mouth full.

'Ezra, we ain't got all day,' Henley said.

'Look up at the big screen, it will be easier than you watching over my shoulder.' Ezra typed and brought up a list of files. 'This first batch are case files. I checked and they're all London court cases.'

Ramouter and Henley approached the screen.

'Our victims are on here,' said Ramouter. 'Nathan Hall, Sian Fox-Carnell, Tabitha Ashcroft.'

'Ezra, open the Nathan Hall file,' Henley ordered.

'Bloody hell, everything is here,' said Ramouter. 'Section 51 letter from the CPS to Hall's solicitors, full case papers. Ezra, open the file named CC, please.'

'These are downloads from the Crown Court digital case system,' said Henley. 'Certificate of trial readiness, witness list for the prosecution and defence. Hall's bail application, trial forms completed by the judge.'

'How the hell did Kaiden Longley get hold of this?' asked Ramouter. 'The court wouldn't send Soteria copies of witness statements or a completed plea and trial preparation form. All they would need is the defendant's personal details and bail address.'

'Ezra, is there any way of finding out where these documents originated from? They don't look like scans,' said Henley.

'They're not. They were downloaded straight from the system,' Ezra answered.

'We need to check how many of these cases are active,' said Ramouter. 'The case files of our four victims are here. There are . . . how many are there, Ezra?'

'In that batch fifteen, but I still haven't gone through everything,' Ezra said as Henley's phone rang.

'It's Stanford,' Henley said, stepping out into the corridor. 'Hey, you. What's going on?'

'What isn't going on?' said Stanford. 'Eastie worked her magic and convinced Karim Messenger to see us.'

'What did he tell you?'

'That he thinks the man who he knew as Elliot worked for the court. He just can't tell us which one. He met him once with Mika in a park and he said that he could see a purple lanyard around his neck. He could only see the top of it, but he said that he could see the letters HMC before this Elliot pulled up his collar.'

'Just missing the letters T and S at the end. Her Majesty's Court and Tribunal Service,' said Henley.

'We were thinking of attempting to talk to the court staff but we're looking at a minimum of four courts if we include the magistrates, Manchester Crown Court and Manchester Minshull Street Court. I'm not sure how far we'll get without getting permission from the resident judge to talk to the court staff.'

'No, leave it,' said Henley. 'Whoever this Elliot is he must have transferred to a London court. I'll ask Pellacia to speak to whoever is responsible for the court staff at the Ministry of Justice.'

'We've got a viable list,' said Copeland, turning away from her screen. 'Ezra found nineteen defendant cases in the material that Kaiden Longley sent him. Fox-Carnell, Ashcroft and Hall were on that list. Nine cases have been adjourned to next year for trial and three have changed their plea to guilty and have been remanded in custody pending sentence. Three of the remaining four are currently in the middle of trials. Bartholomew Gardner, Mason and Paige Jones and Catlin Ferguson. The fourth, Primrose Welch, her trial is due to start on Monday.'

'Bartholomew Gardner,' said Pellacia. 'I've heard of him. Owns a chain of discount sport shops.'

'On trial for human trafficking at Southwark,' said Ramouter. 'I've just come off the phone with the list office. The time estimate for the trial is nine weeks and they're only on week four.'

'And the others?' asked Henley.

'The jury are out deliberating on Ferguson's case at Wood Green Crown Court. She's on trial for a Section 18 on her sister. Acid attack.'

'She's looking at a possible fifteen-year stretch if convicted,' said Copeland. 'That leaves the Jones trial at Woolwich. The jury is out deliberating.'

'Mason and Paige Jones have been in the news,' said Ramouter. 'Husband and wife own a wellness company in Shoreditch. A couple of women allege they were drugged and sexually assaulted on their manifesting yoga retreats.'

'Any one of those are targets for our vigilantes,' said Copeland.

'But it all depends on the verdict,' said Pellacia. 'We can't just sit here waiting for them to make a decision before we act.'

Henley stood up and paced the room. She felt as though she was a beginner in a chess match against a grandmaster. Every move she wanted to make had already been anticipated by her opponent.

'Henley,' Pellacia called. 'What do you want to do?'

Henley turned around and faced the remainder of her team. 'Let's get the public involved,' she said. 'British Transport Police, City of London and our people are already on the lookout for Kaiden Longley but let's release his image and the composite image of the man known as Don.'

'What about the sketch that Gareth Humphreys drew?' asked Copeland. 'I don't mean to be funny, it's good, but that woman could be anybody. A fantasy of his imagination.'

'It could be, but Eastwood showed it to Karim Messenger, and he said that the woman was Mika,' said Henley. 'I know it's not an official composite sketch but right now, with multiple potential victims at risk we can't be wasting any more time.'

'I'll get onto the press office and also chase up the MOJ with the court staff transfer request. Where are Stanford and Eastwood now?' asked Pellacia.

'They were at Cambridge services an hour ago,' said Henley. 'They should be here by four, give or take.'

'Hopefully we'll have some answers by then.'

46

'I've had a chat with a couple of the boys in CID about our new recruit,' Stanford said. He handed Henley her vodka and tonic. They both turned to their left where Copeland was talking animatedly to Ramouter and Ezra on the other end of the table. The early arrival of Stanford and Eastwood, from Manchester, had also meant the promise of welcome drinks at their local being granted.

'Have you been gossiping again?' Henley jested back to Stanford.

'You may call it gossiping, but I call it reasonable enquiries.'

'What are we talking about?' Eastwood asked as she ripped open a packet of crisps.

'The woman who you're not a fan of,' said Stanford.

Eastwood tutted. 'She grates me.'

'You're not the only one,' Stanford whispered. 'Apparently, her guvnor has been looking for a way to get rid of her months. She's undermined him more than once and was reprimanded in court for her overzealousness when arresting a suspect.'

'I should be surprised, but I'm not,' said Henley as Copeland broke out into laughter at whatever Ezra had just told her.

'The guy I spoke to—'

'You weren't speaking to my ex, Terry, by any chance?' asked Eastwood. 'You know what he's like. He has a very strange relationship with the truth.'

Despite the seriousness of the conversation, Henley couldn't stop herself from laughing. 'That's an understatement. So, was it Terry?' she asked.

'No, it wasn't. It was his partner, Phil,' said Stanford.

Eastwood rolled her eyes. 'Tweedle Dee and Tweedle Dum,' she said.

'The point is, according to him, Copeland isn't averse to throwing her colleagues under the bus to get what she wants,' said Stanford as Pellacia returned to his own seat next to Eastwood and picked up his pint. 'Whether that's a result or to be lead on a case.'

'Why do I get the feeling you three are conspiring,' said Pellacia.

'Us three. Conspire? Never, guv,' said Stanford.

Henley tuned out as Stanford, Eastwood and Pellacia talked about a new piece of gossip that had made it to his ears. She couldn't help but feel unsettled as she watched how Copeland was interacting with not just Ramouter, but with Ezra. There was a smugness about her that Henley didn't like.

'Copeland,' Henley called out as she nudged Stanford to get out of her way. 'Do you mind stepping out for a bit?' she said with a smile.

Copeland looked up with clear suspicion in her eyes. 'Of course, guv,' she finally said.

'What are you doing, Anj?' Pellacia hissed.

'It's fine,' said Henley, picking up her drink. 'I'll bring her back in one piece.'

'Is everything all right, guv?' Copeland asked. She pulled the sleeves of her jumper over her hands, protecting herself against the chill.

'I know that joining the SCU can be a bit of a baptism of fire,' Henley said, making it clear that she was not going to answer Copeland's question.

'I can't say I'm not surprised with how intense it's been, but that's not to say I can't handle it.'

'No one is saying that you can't handle it, but it's the way you've handled it.'

'Is this about the Ben Trezeguet interview?' Copeland asked in a manner that suggested she'd been preparing for the conversation. 'Did Ramouter say something?'

'No, DC Ramouter hasn't said a word,' Henley lied, feeling an overwhelming wave of protectiveness towards her partner. 'I'm the SIO so I'm going to be reviewing everything, which includes watching the interviews conducted by my team.'

'I don't think I did anything wrong. I asked the right questions,' Copeland said defensively.

'Anyone reading the transcript will probably agree but it's different when you see it. You went in too hard and you revealed sensitive information about the scalping to a man who makes his living by trespassing on crime scenes and talking about it on YouTube. You risked undermining not only yourself but also DC Ramouter. You don't get a prize for being the loudest one in the room or for breaking down a witness.'

'Ben Trezeguet was a suspect not a—'

'Copeland, two things. Learn how to adapt to changes and second, learn to take advice. Understood?'

Copeland nodded reluctantly.

'Good,' said Henley as she finished her drink. 'It's my round. Red wine for you?'

'Yes,' Copeland replied flatly as she followed Henley back into the pub.

Ramouter searched his jacket pockets and came up empty. 'Bollocks,' he said. His phone was definitely not there. The last time he could remember using his phone was when he'd shown Stanford his fantasy football stats in the pub. He felt lost. There was no way of calling Michelle to check if she and Ethan's train had arrived at Euston Station.

'Oh, shut up,' Ramouter said to the chirping budgie on his way back to the kitchen. He was cutting cucumbers when there was a loud knocking on the flat door.

He left the kitchen, knife still in hand, and opened the front door.

'Wow, I've never seen someone look so surprised in my life,' Copeland said with a laugh. She pulled out her hair from under the collar of her parka. 'Also, word of advice from one copper to another. Maybe you shouldn't answer the door with a huge knife in your hands.'

Ramouter looked down at his hand. 'Sorry. I wasn't . . . what are you—'

Copeland held up her hands mockingly and laughed. 'Don't panic. I'm not stalking you. I convinced Eastwood to give me your address, not that she made it easy for me and the main door was already open.'

'Right,' Ramouter said, still confused as to why Copeland was at his flat.

'Your phone,' Copeland said. She reached into her pocket and removed Ramouter's phone. 'I found it under the table in the pub.'

'Thank you so much. I didn't even realise,' Ramouter said, taking his phone.

'It's been ringing a lot,' Copeland said as Ramouter swiped the screen. Missed calls from Michelle, messages from the WhatsApp group that he was in with his brothers and cousins. He rang Michelle back but was immediately answered with her voicemail greeting. He pondered why his wife's phone was off when Copeland coughed.

'Oh, I'm sorry,' said Ramouter. 'Come in and thanks for doing this, especially as it's so out of your way.'

'Not a problem. I'm never in that much of a hurry to get back to Kentish Town,' she said as she followed Ramouter back into the kitchen. 'What are you making?'

'Lasagne,' Ramouter replied 'It's the one thing I can cook that makes Michelle think she married a gourmet chef even though we both know the sauce came from a jar.'

'Lucky woman,' said Copeland as she leaned against the counter. 'My ex could burn water and the last time I tried to make a lasagne, well, it's best not to talk about that disaster.'

Ramouter smiled politely as he took the garlic bread out of the fridge. He could hear Henley's words repeating in his head, warning him to be careful with Copeland. He still wasn't sure if Henley was just being overprotective of him or simply didn't like the fact that Copeland hadn't been afraid to challenge her in front of the team. He didn't say anything as he caught Copeland taking off her coat as though she intended on staying for dinner.

'I know we had a nice time in the pub earlier but, I'm not sure how to bring this up,' Copeland said. She picked up a jar of mixed herbs and turned it over in her hands before placing it back on the counter.

'Bring what up?' Ramouter asked.

'I was just wondering if Henley was being nice to me because I spoke to the guvnor about how she was treating me.'

Ramouter's eyes widened with the realisation that Stanford's guess that Copeland had complained about Henley was true. 'Why would you do that?' he asked.

'Would you have let someone talk to you the way she did?' Copeland asked. 'It was embarrassing. She couldn't make it any clearer that she didn't want me in the team.'

'I don't think that's true at all. Henley's always grateful when we get any kind of extra support.'

'She has a funny way of showing it. She said some things to me outside that made me think she was the reason my previous applications to join the SCU were refused. You know what the force is like, always spreading stupid rumours.'

'I haven't heard anything about you,' Ramouter said quickly as his ears picked up the sound of activity at his front door.

Copeland moved and blocked Ramouter's way. 'You don't have to spare my feelings,' she said. 'I know what people have said about me. A couple of appearances before the misconduct panel and your name becomes mud. People are allowed to make mistakes, but people seem very reluctant to move on. Why do you think I've been stuck at Detective Constable level for so long.'

'You think you've been blocked from promotion because of what—'

'I know I have,' Copeland said urgently. 'The only person who hasn't prejudged me is the guvnor and you, but Henley—'

'Look, I didn't know about the misconduct panel and I'm sure that whatever happened, well, you've learned from it.'

'You're very kind,' Copeland said, taking hold of Ramouter's arm. 'It's a good thing I met you when I did.'

Ramouter could feel Michelle staring at him before he even heard her.

'Daddy,' Ethan shouted. He dropped his rucksack onto the floor and ran towards Ramouter.

'Have you grown in a week?' Ramouter said. He picked up Ethan who squealed with laughter and kissed him. 'How is my boy?'

'Good. Who are you?' Ethan asked with all the innocence and audacity of a five-year-old as he looked down at Copeland.

'I'm Xania,' said Copeland. 'I work with your dad.'

'My daddy goes to work with Auntie Anjelica,' said Ethan stubbornly. Ramouter lowered Ethan to the ground, and he ran off to retrieve the remote control from the sofa.

'Auntie Anjelica?' Copeland said. She adjusted her coat in her arms. 'I didn't realise you were so close.'

'Aye, Ethan loves hanging out with his Auntie Anjelica,'

Michelle said, joining Ramouter's side. 'Is something burning?' she said to Ramouter as she kissed him on the lips.

'Oh crap,' Ramouter said. 'The lasagne.'

'Good. I'm starving,' Michelle said. 'So, you work with my husband?' she asked Copeland.

'Yes, I joined this week. It's nice to meet you, Michelle,' said Copeland. She extended her hand but withdrew it when she saw that it was not being received.

'Salim never mentioned that there was a new member of the SCU.'

'Oh well, things move quite quickly. An opportunity came up, and I took it,' Copeland said.

'She popped over to give me my phone,' Ramouter said loudly, and Ethan looked at him strangely. 'I dropped it in the pub.'

'So that explains why you didn't pick up when I called,' said Michelle.

'We got in a big taxi,' Ethan said.

'I couldn't handle jumping on the tube after that train journey. It's been a long day,' Michelle said pointedly to Copeland.

'Yes, I should be going. Got to get on the tube myself. No way to avoid the hell of the Northern line on a Friday night,' said Copeland. 'I'll see you Monday, Ramouter.'

'I'll show you out,' Michelle said with a smile, ushering Copeland towards the door.

'Bloody hell,' Ramouter muttered as the door slammed shut.

'I didn't have "strange woman who you've never mentioned standing in my kitchen" on my bingo card,' Michelle said as she entered the kitchen, opened the fridge door and pulled out a bottle of Chablis.

'I have mentioned her,' Ramouter protested weakly. He pulled Michelle towards him and kissed her.

'You definitely did not,' Michelle said.

'I missed you.'

'Did you really? How could you when you've got, what's her name, Xena warrior princess?'

Michelle picked up the roll of kitchen foil and initiated sword fighting.

'Miche,' Ramouter said, defending himself with a teatowel. 'She was just dropping off my phone.'

'She probably hid your phone in the first place. Needed a reason to come over and check out your space, to see how gone away with the fairies your wife really is?'

'Why would you say that? Copeland is just a colleague from work and she's—'

'Trying to seduce you.'

'Seriously. Is that how you're carrying on?' Ramouter said as Michelle started laughing. 'The scary thing is that I don't know if you're just joking or if you're deadly serious under that smile.'

'Oh, I'm serious. There's something there. I've got good instincts, Salim.'

'Yeah, you do,' he said quietly.

'I'm going to take a shower and then we can sit down and talk about my plans over dinner,' Michelle said, pouring herself a large glass of wine.

'What plans?'

'Work. I've been talking to my consultant, and he agrees that it wouldn't be a bad idea for me to go back to work.'

'What are you talking about?' Ramouter asked, clearly shocked.

'I'll explain once I've had a shower.'

'How can you go back to work?'

'Salim, you're looking at me as though I've grown two heads. Shower. Eat and talk.' Michelle kissed him. 'I promise you it will all make sense.'

*

'You can watch TV for another thirty minutes and then you're off to bed,' Ramouter said as he watched his son carefully carry his plate and place it in the sink.

'Can I watch *X-Men*?' Ethan asked as he spun around in the kitchen in his version of a superhero landing.

'One episode and then bed.'

'He's got far too much energy,' said Michelle. 'It was exhausting watching him run around with his cousins.'

'It's good for him though,' said Ramouter, tearing a slice of garlic bread in half. 'To be around family.'

Michelle leaned back in her chair. 'You sound as though you want to go back to Bradford.'

'What? No, I'm happy here. We're happy here and the last thing I want to do is to uproot us again. We all need stability, which is why—'

Ramouter paused as he reached for his glass of wine.

'Go on say it,' Michelle said, staring him dead in his eyes. 'Go on,' she repeated.

'I don't understand how your consultant can suggest that you go back to work,' he said. 'Isn't that a bit irresponsible?'

Michelle rolled her eyes. 'You sound just like my mam.'

'You discussed it with her first and not me.'

'It wasn't like that. She was eavesdropping on my call. You know what she's been like ever since she found out that I went walkabout before I moved down here. Hovering over me at every opportunity to make sure I don't lose my way.'

'You didn't just go walkabout, Miche,' Ramouter said, working hard to keep his voice gentle. 'You went missing and broke into our old house.'

'It was hardly a break in. I had a key,' she replied with a short laugh.

'It's not funny. Early onset dementia is not funny.'

'And no one knows that better than me.'

Michelle took a breath, reached for a glass of water, changed her mind, picked up her glass of wine and took a sip. 'I had all these plans for my life, Salim. Not just my life but ours and none of them included not having any memory of you or our son and even that annoying budgie by the time I'm fifty.'

Ramouter reached across the table and took hold of Michelle's hand. 'I know that it's hard for—'

'No, sweetheart. You don't know how hard it is.'

Ramouter straightened up and shifted his chair closer to Michelle. 'Tell me what the consultant said.'

'I'm doing well. A lot better since he changed my medication. My symptoms have reduced, so I'm a lot less agitated and the memory recall is improving. I'm more confident than when I first got here, and he's suggested that I try cognitive simulation therapy.'

'What is that?'

'Sitting with a bunch of strange men in the park playing chess.'

'I really don't know if you're serious or not.'

'Half serious. It's focusing on activities that help improve my memory and thinking skills. Forty-five minutes every week. I can handle that, which is why Mr McNamara suggested working part time. Obviously not as an accountant but I was talking to one of the mams at Ethan's school. I've told you about her, she has the bookshop on Honor Oak Road.'

'You want to work in a bookshop?'

'Why not? It's better than sitting at home watching repeats of *Death in Paradise* all day. It will just be for a couple of mornings during the week. My life isn't over yet, Salim.'

Ramouter buried his face into Michelle's neck, breathing in her hair and hiding the fact that tears had filled his eyes.

'It will be ok,' Michelle said, pulling away as Ramouter's phone began to ring. 'That's probably your girlfriend Princess Xena wondering if you can—'

'Stop it,' Ramouter replied. He picked up his phone from the sideboard and held it up to Michelle.

'Oh, she's fine,' Michelle laughed when she saw Henley's name on the screen and left to join Ethan.

'Everything all right, boss?' said Ramouter.

'I'm really sorry to do this to you,' said Henley. 'But a body has been found.'

'Who is it?'

'Kaiden Longley,' Henley sighed.

'I'll be with you in thirty minutes.'

47

Kaiden Longley's spilled blood had been washed away by the morning rain. Ramouter crouched down next to his body. Rat bites and small, ravaged cuts left behind by foxes searching for food were visible on his arms and calves. His twisted and broken body resembled an action figure that a child had taken apart limb by limb and put back together back to front.

'How long has he been here?' Ramouter asked Dr Linh Choi who was standing nearby writing notes.

'His rectal temperature was 26.167°C and he's in full rigor mortis,' said Linh. 'Best estimate, he's been dead for at least twenty-four to twenty-six hours.'

'It's—' Henley checked her watch. '10.28 p.m. now so that would place time of death at around this time last night. A whole bloody day.'

'Give or take. I'll get a better estimate when I take the liver temperature.'

'Who found him?' Ramouter asked.

Henley turned around and pointed to a low wall about fifty metres away which separated the car park from the recycling and rubbish area. A young couple were with a uniformed officer, the woman occasionally pacing and shaking her head as though trying to get rid of the images inside her head.

'According to the officer they're with, they were bringing down rubbish to the bins,' Henley said. 'The woman, Juniper, said she saw the body and thought it was a crackhead who had fallen asleep. She said it wasn't the first time, but then she got closer and realised he was dead.'

'Who called the police?' Ramouter asked.

'Her brother. I just can't believe he's been lying here all night and all day. I mean look around you. Look how busy this estate is,' Henley said, shaking her head.

The presence of not just the police but a forensic service van had garnered a lot of attention. Heads could be seen poking out of the windows above while groups of people stood on the large grassy mound that faced the rubbish area.

'The people around here either really didn't notice a dead man on the ground or they ignored it,' she said.

'Wouldn't be the first time,' Linh said. 'Especially if it's the norm to find passed out drug users next to the bins.'

'That doesn't excuse it,' Henley said bitterly.

'No, it doesn't,' Linh said.

'Can you say if it was the fall that killed him?' asked Ramouter.

'For now, all of his visible injuries, the positioning of his limbs are consistent with a fall, a great fall,' Linh said, looking up towards the upper floors of the block of flats. But you know the rules, youngling.'

Ramouter rolled his eyes. 'Nothing conclusive until you open them up,' he said.

'Exactly. You're learning,' Linh said.

'Do we know that it's definitely him, Kaiden Longley? His face is a mess,' Ramouter asked Henley.

Henley held out the small plastic evidence bag, containing a blue Barclays debit card and the familiar pink colours of a UK driving licence. She turned the bag around and showed Ramouter the side of the licence that contained the photograph and personal details of the man who was dead on the floor.

'I've got a couple of officers stationed outside his flat,' said Henley. 'Tenth floor and word of warning, the lift is broken.'

'Why are the lifts always out? I used to be the fastest 1,500 metre runner in my school. Ran for the county and now look at me,' Ramouter said. He placed his hands on his thighs and tried to catch his breath.

'The better question is why are the council estates always in a state of disrepair?' Henley replied. She leaned against the wall, her view of London slightly obscured by the green anti-bird netting that stretched from the balcony wall to the ceiling. A policewoman stood outside flat 85, shifting from foot to foot as she spoke to a CSI officer, adjusting his camera.

'It's quite a view,' said Ramouter as his breathing steadied. 'London keeps on surprising me.'

'And it won't stop,' said Henley. 'Right now, unless there's an eyewitness or there's evidence inside to tell us otherwise, we're working on the premise that he's a victim.'

'Thrown and didn't fall,' Ramouter said with a nod as they walked towards the flat. 'I noticed that the communal door lock is broken.'

'There's no cameras around the communal area, on any of the floors and I didn't notice any at the rear of the building where the body was found,' said Henley as the officer recorded both of their names in the logbook.

'It's a maisonette,' Ramouter observed as he pointed at the narrow staircase.

'Must be two bedrooms minimum,' said Henley as she turned back and checked the front door. 'No signs of damage to the lock.'

'It hardly looks lived in. It reminds me of my place before I moved in,' said Ramouter as he entered the living room which was minimally furnished with a single armchair and a small circular dining table.

Henley's eyes tracked the clumps of damp soil and moss to a giant monstera plant that was on its side, roots exposed. A spattering of broken plaster and a screw still attached to a red wall plug was next to the empty bottle of beer near Henley's feet. She looked up above the door that led to the balcony. The first hook on the curtain rail had pulled away from the wall causing the curtains that framed the door to unevenly drag on the floor. The room told a story of struggle.

Ramouter pointed at the carpet close to his feet. 'He resisted,' he said. Soil had been ground into two heel shaped marks slightly wider than hip distance apart which merged into two thick drag marks leading to the balcony.

'We've got blood on the back of the armchair and on the door frame,' said Anthony who was standing on the opposite side of the room writing a note on his chart. 'It's not a lot of blood but it's enough.'

'So, he's attacked in here and dragged out to the balcony,' said Henley. She turned and faced the open door that led into the hallway. 'But there's no damage to the front door, so he must have let them in,' she mused.

'My wife used to leave the door on the latch for me all the time back in the day,' said Anthony. 'But I only do it when I'm putting the bins out.'

'We're assuming that it was our victim who left the door on the latch?' Ramouter said as he stepped out onto the balcony followed by Henley. The balcony was chaos. Soil and broken pieces of ceramic plant pot were scattered on the ground. A second beer bottle was in pieces next to an upended teal coloured bistro table and chairs.

'All of the struggle takes place right here,' said Henley as she looked over the balcony, the view of Kaiden's body now obstructed by a white forensic tent. The crowd below had thinned out. Henley straightened up. She had the feeling that she was being watched. To her left, the occupants of number 83 were on their balcony straining to see their neighbour's flat.

'This time last night, Kaiden was dragged kicking and screaming and thrown to his death,' said Henley. 'I'm finding it difficult to believe that no one heard a thing.'

Ramouter blew out his cheeks. 'Maybe they did and just ignored it. Just another day on the block.'

'Any signs of a disturbance upstairs?' Henley asked Anthony.

'No,' Anthony said. 'But there's more stuff up there than there is down here.'

The first bedroom showed signs of living with an opened duffle bag filled with clothes, and a blue towel on top of the unmade bed.

Henley opened the door of the second bedroom. 'Oh wow,' she said.

'Bloody hell,' said Ramouter, following Henley into the room. 'Ezra would pass out if he saw this.'

The bedroom had been converted into a computer room. Two large monitors sat on a desk. A black PC base unit, with a violent neon light glowing through a transparent side panel was on the side. An opened laptop also sat on the desk next to an expensive digital camera. However, the computer equipment wasn't what held Henley's attention. On the third wall was a noticeboard covered with a map and photographs of the victims on the SCU's murder board, but it was the photograph on the top of the board that had caused a tightness in Henley's chest. The image was crystal clear, picking up every leaf on the trees that the council had neglected to prune. In the distance was a little girl, her back turned, as she faced the woman in front of her. Even if Henley hadn't been sure of the identity of the second woman in the photo, wearing a trench coat and a baseball cap, she was 100 per cent sure of two things: that was her street and the little girl in the photo was her daughter.

'Boss, is everything all right?' asked Ramouter.

'This photograph was taken outside my house. The day that Sian Fox-Carnell turned up,' said Henley.

'Are you sure?'

'That's my street and that's Emma,' she said, pointing at the photo as she shook with anger. She did everything she could to protect her family, but it never seemed to be enough. There was always an unseen danger at her doorstep. She wanted to tear the photograph in two, to remove the shame and fear, but she couldn't. The photograph was evidence.

'But she wasn't watching you. He was clearly following Fox-Carnell.'

'Doesn't make it any better though.'

'No, I wouldn't think that it would,' said Ramouter as he rubbed his right ear. 'But look at her. Look at your daughter. She knows that she's safe with you and don't forget that I've got your back. I'm your eyes and ears too. It's my job to see the stuff that you can't.'

Henley fought back the tears. Ramouter's dedication to not only her but her family was a testament to how far they'd come since first meeting. She looked at Emma in the photograph and was immediately taken back to the moment when she'd asked Stanford to be her godfather. The tears burned again. She trusted Stanford to take care of her daughter if anything happened to her but yet she hadn't entrusted him with her discovery that Rhimes had been murdered. Henley turned her back to the noticeboard, wiped her eyes and took a breath, grounding herself and mentally locking her emotions away. She looked around the room, her eyes stopping on the tight purple buds of the orchid plant on the windowsill; flowers that Kaiden Longley would never see bloom.

'Why kill him?' Henley asked as she and Ramouter walked back towards her car. 'Someone he knew killed him but why?'

'There's only one answer,' said Ramouter. 'Iron Shadow, well what's left of them, discovered he was talking to us. If they were able to track Fox-Carnell it's more than possible they were keeping an eye on him.'

'But Kaiden Longley didn't talk to us. He talked to Ezra. If the remaining members of Iron Shadow were following Kaiden and saw the two of them together, they'll be asking themselves: what did Kaiden tell Ezra. How much does Ezra know?'

'Do you think we need to ask the guvnor to do more than just pick Ezra up in the morning?'

'Most definitely,' said Henley. 'It's clear that these people have an agenda. They wanted to frame Kaiden Longley,' said Henley as she got into her car and started the engine. 'You saw that flat. They left everything upstairs, all the photographs. Implicating Kaiden Longley and only him.'

'That doesn't mean they're going to stop though,' said Ramouter as the black body bag containing Kaiden Longley was wheeled towards the open doors of the private ambulance. 'These are people who didn't even stop when half of their crazy group was put in prison and for whatever reason they moved to a different city.'

'No, you're right,' said Henley as she did a U-turn and drove through the estate. 'Whether they find someone new to take Kaiden's place or they just stick with who they've got. They're not going to stop.'

48

'Are you sure that pushing this Rhimes conspiracy theory is a good idea? Because if you ask me—'

'It's not a conspiracy theory and I wasn't exactly asking you, Rob,' said Henley. It should have been a normal Saturday afternoon, preparing for a children's Halloween party, but she'd woken up to a message from Chris Snyder. She'd thought the mundane activity of sorting out the laundry would settle her nerves, but she'd become more anxious with each passing minute. She'd picked up her phone twice to cancel her meeting with Chris but that would have meant breaking her promise to Eloise. Henley had never been a woman known for breaking her word and she had no intention of starting now.

'Because if you ask me,' Rob continued as he slammed the dishwasher door shut. 'It's not. If what you told me is right, if what Linh has told you is right, you're placing yourself in danger.'

'I've been placing myself in danger for over ten years. The first time I went out on independent patrol I was attacked by a seventy-eight-year-old woman in Sainsbury's who'd stolen six bottles of Johnnie Walker.'

'You being hit with an umbrella by Supergran is not the same thing as you chasing after people who may have killed not just your boss, Anj, but your friend. I've lost count of the times I've watched you asleep in bed and told myself it's a miracle you're still here, especially after—'

'Don't say his name. I don't need to be reminded of what I've been through, what I've endured. I see my scars every single day.'

Rob leaned his head back and exhaled loudly as the sound of Emma screeching in the living room with her cousins and Ramouter's son, Ethan, filtered through the house.

'I see your scars too,' he said.

Henley looked down at her hands and saw that she'd been twisting the tea towel in her hands so tightly that it resembled a line of rope.

'I can't not do this,' she said. 'I spent a lot of time trying not to feel anything when I got the call that Rhimes was gone. If I didn't feel it, then I could convince myself that it hadn't happened but then that switched to anger. As weird as this sounds, I was angrier about Rhimes than I was with my mum.'

Henley paused as she felt her eyes burn with tears. She'd resisted everyone's – Rob, her brother, dad and her therapist – efforts to drag her out of the dark abyss of grief. The only person who'd found a way to reach her was Pellacia.

'Mum was sick. I didn't want to admit that, but I knew she was going to die but Rhimes wasn't sick,' Henley said.

'There's nothing I can say that will change your mind is there?' asked Rob as he pulled Henley towards him. She could feel the muscles in his chest flex and contract as he slowed his breathing. An attempt to lower the temperature of his frustrations.

'I love you' he said. 'And I hate that I can't protect you.'

'Rob. I don't—'

'You may not need me to protect you but that's how I feel and I also know that I'll lose you if I try to control you. So, all I can do is remind you that I love you and will never stop worrying about you.'

Henley squeezed her eyes shut but the photograph of Fox-Carnell watching her and Emma burned brighter in her mind. She pulled away from Rob as her phone beeped with a message.

She picked up her phone. 'It's Chris. He's running ten minutes late.'

'I really do wish you would reconsider,' Rob said. He cocked his head in the direction of the living room.

'They're too quiet,' Henley said, reading Rob's thoughts.

'Which means they've broken something or are plotting something. Let me see what they're up to but, Anj,' said Rob, taking hold of Henley's hand and intertwining her fingers with his. 'I know I've asked you to step away from the job before.'

Henley raised her eyebrows.

'All right, I've been an arse about it,' said Rob. 'But this is different. I don't care what Chris tells you, I'm asking – no – I'm telling you to step away.'

'One day I would like you to just call me and ask me how I'm doing and if I fancy a drink,' said Chris, handing a coffee cup to Henley.

'We are out for a drink,' Henley replied, welcoming the warmth of the cup in her palms.

'When you first called me, I thought it was a wind up,' Chris said as they walked towards Hilly Fields. 'It's a good thing you're wearing your trainers because I'm thinking you should run.'

Henley stopped and looked up at Chris, searching his face for any traces of the humour that had been present a few moments earlier but there was nothing. His lips were so pressed together, they'd nearly disappeared and a frown line had deepened between his eyebrows.

'Chris, I just need some answers,' Henley pleaded.

'The account number isn't one that technically belongs to the NCA,' Chris said, dropping the volume of his voice as they continued to walk. 'It's kind of a floating bank account that's used by the NCA to pay their informants and I don't mean the informants grassing up the local drug dealer.' He paused. 'He wasn't a grass, Henley, and he wasn't involved in things that would land him in prison. The account that transferred money to him is also used to protect whistleblowers. It could be that Rhimes discovered something, like corruption, and the NCA wanted more.'

Coffee swirled and escaped from the mouth of her cup and ran down Henley's hand. She looked down, for a brief moment finding the trembling of her fingers hypnotic.

'Are you ok?' Chris asked, concern etched on his face.

'No, not really,' Henley replied, stepping away and dropping her cup into a bin. 'How can I be when you're standing here telling me that someone wanted Rhimes out of the way to stop him from revealing, what exactly?'

'That I do not know. And you've got to realise, I'm not necessarily talking about corruption in the Met – not that there isn't any. The NCA were the ones paying Rhimes, but just because we're London based . . .'

'Doesn't mean he was necessarily investigating the Met,' said Henley. 'There are forty-three police forces in the UK.'

'And I don't know which one.'

'Informants have handlers,' Henley said assuredly. 'They're not out there on their own. Rhimes would have had to report to someone.'

'Yeah, he would have.'

Henley knew this was the moment when she should walk away and return back to her family.

'This is the last thing I'm going to ask you to do for me,' she said.

Chris groaned as he rubbed the back of his neck. 'Shit,' he said. 'You have no idea the hornets' nest you're kicking.'

'I know I don't. All I'm asking you to do is to find his handler. A name. That's all I want.'

'Fine,' he said. 'I'll let you know when I have a name.'

Henley tried to remember the last thing Rhimes had said to her. It had been something innocuous about booking flights to see his brother in Florida. Rhimes was a man who had plans and many reasons to live and that was why she couldn't walk away and leave his secrets buried with him.

'What are you thinking?' Chris asked.

'That I should have paid closer attention to the things that weren't being said. I worked with Rhimes every day for years and I couldn't see that there was something deeper going on with him.'

'There is another way of looking at this,' said Chris. 'They say that people who whistleblow have a stronger sense of integrity. It's not about them. Rhimes took his ability to put others before himself to another level.'

'I can't believe I'm learning more about the sort of man Rhimes was in death than I ever did in life.'

'That ain't a bad thing, Anj. In a strange way, Rhimes is teaching you something important.'

'And what's that?' Henley asked.

'To never walk away and that this job isn't just about clearance rates,' said Chris. 'It's about protecting those who are unseen.'

49

'Catlin you have to prepare for the fact that things may not go our way on Monday,' said Hugh. He stood at a place of safety behind the large and ornate kitchen island. 'There's no point being in denial about this. Your solicitor has told you; your barrister has told you that—'

'Will you just stop? I don't want to hear it,' Catlin shouted, slamming the soapy mug hard onto the granite worktop. She looked down and saw the handle had broken into two, and a shard of porcelain had embedded itself into her soft flesh. Blood oozed across her palm, turning the white suds pink as she removed the shard.

'You're hurt,' Hugh said, grabbing sheets of kitchen towel. 'Let me—'

'Don't touch me,' Catlin spat viciously as she forcefully pulled her wounded hand away. 'All of this is because of you.'

Hugh watched Catlin open a drawer, and search for a box of plasters. 'You and that woman.'

'I didn't betray you. Our marriage has been over for a long time and it's not because of anything I've done,' said Hugh, slowly backing away from Catlin. 'You hurt your own sister, scarred her for life and you broke your family. If it wasn't for our son, and the fact that I know you're looking at a prison sentence, I would have kicked you out.'

Catlin silently watched Hugh.

'Twelve to sixteen years,' Hugh said boldly, surprised by the confidence that had swelled in him. 'The judge will take into account that you've never been in trouble before, that you're a respected member of the community, charitable,' Hugh said, repeating the barrister's advice that he'd committed to memory.

'I'm not going anywhere,' said Catlin. 'I'm innocent.'

'You threw acid in your sister's face,' said Hugh.

'I was defending myself.'

Hugh stared at his wife with disbelief. He'd sat in Wood Green Crown Court for two weeks watching the jury intently and listening – not always to the evidence, but – to them. He'd worked as a sound engineer for twenty-seven years and his ears were finely attuned to the sounds people weren't aware they made; the tuts, the snorts of disbelief, a cough to conceal a snigger, the shuffling of discomfort, heavy short breaths to conceal disbelief and disgust. He'd heard it all from the jury and he'd deciphered the sounds as twelve people deciding that his wife was guilty.

Hugh picked up his tumbler of whisky and walked past Catlin. 'I'm going upstairs,' he said.

Catlin grabbed Hugh's upper arm, her nails digging into his skin. 'Why?' she demanded.

'Your barrister said to pack a bag,' said Hugh, shrugging her off. 'One of us needs to be prepared.'

The wind did the job of slamming the front door shut for Catlin. The leaves and tree branches danced chaotically, the yellow streetlamp casting demonic shadows on the pavement as she walked away from her house.

'Bastard,' Catlin muttered under her breath as she walked. She squinted as the full beam of a car headlights turning on Artesian Road hit her square in the face, the engine revving as it gathered speed. She stopped momentarily and put a hand to her chest. The palpitations had returned, pounding on the door of her increasing anxiety. She'd been telling herself that women like her don't go to prison but she was struggling to believe it. She felt her heartbeat slow down as the car passed. She could see the light of the corner shop in the distance and quickened her pace as the wind whipped grit into her eyes.

'Hey, Ca—'

The increasing wind coupled with the sounds of a group talking loudly as they left The Draftsman pub on the corner drowned out the person who was calling.

'Hey, Catlin, I thought that was you.'

Catlin turned around as a figure moved out of the sealed church doorway.

'Yes, it's definitely you. Recognise you anywhere.'

The headlight of a motorbike approaching in the opposite direction placed a temporary spotlight on the person standing on the street, giving Catlin a moment to search the person's face.

'Sorry, I don't—' Catlin paused when she saw the large bottle in the woman's left hand. For a millisecond, Catlin thought the woman had thrown water into her face, but then her skin started to burn as though she'd been doused in petrol and set alight. Catlin's screams travelled down the road. The burning intensified as the acid penetrated her retinas, stripped through her skin, melted the hair on her head and fell in rivers down her face. The material on her chest and the gold chain around her neck dissolved and welded to her skin. She ran blindly, screaming and pleading for help. A heavy blow in her back propelled her to the floor, her legs contorting, her torso twisting as she withered in pain. In the tortured mist she felt cold steel pierce her back, tearing through her thoracic aorta. She weakly stretched her arm along the ground, her cries reaching out to the sound of voices who would be too late to save her.

50

'I can confirm that following a horrific incident that took place on Artesian Road in Notting Hill a forty-eight-year-old woman has died as a result of the injuries sustained after she was attacked with a corrosive substance believed to be sulphuric acid.'

'Superintendent, can you confirm the status of the other people who were injured?'

'As I stated last night, the two police officers and three members of the public who attended the scene all sustained minor injuries due to chemical burns caused by the acid. All five received medical treatment at Hammersmith Hospital and were discharged in the early hours of this morning.'

Pellacia paused the television. 'The woman who was murdered has been identified as Catlin Ferguson,' he said.

'Oh, for fuck's sake,' said Stanford, throwing his jacket onto the desk. 'When did this happen?'

'Saturday night but she died in the early hours of yesterday morning.'

'Why are we only hearing about this now?'

'Because she wasn't formally identified until last night. Acid burns made her unrecognisable and, for reasons unknown to me, her husband didn't report her missing until yesterday morning,' Pellacia explained.

'This doesn't make any sense,' said Henley. 'If the vigilantes are responsible for this, why would they kill her before there's even been a verdict? When Ramouter checked on Friday, the jury had only just retired.'

'That's right,' said Ramouter. 'According to the list office, they'd gone out just after 11 a.m. and then the judge sent them home early at 3.30 p.m.. Killing someone before a verdict goes completely against their MO.'

'They're escalating,' said Pellacia. 'They're not even waiting for a court to reach a verdict that they don't like.'

'Was she scalped?' asked Eastwood.

'No. Her attackers would have ended up in hospital if they'd touched her,' said Pellacia. 'But this entire attack was different. It was in public for starters,' said Pellacia as he walked over to Henley and handed her a single sheet of paper. 'OIC details for the Ferguson case.'

'If our vigilantes are responsible,' said Ramouter as he remained standing. 'It means that they're even more dangerous now.'

'How so?' Copeland asked.

'They're becoming unpredictable,' Henley answered. 'We had a narrow area in which to cast our net when our hypothesis was that they were targeting defendants who they believed had taken advantage of the system and had been wrongly acquitted. But with Ferguson, they're not even waiting for the court process to conclude. Iron Shadow are now the jury.'

'That means that the Joneses, Bartholomew Gardner, and Welch are all in immediate danger,' said Copeland.

'Where are we with Kaiden Longley?' asked Pellacia.

'Anthony should get forensic results to us by the end of the day, but the post-mortem was completed yesterday,' answered Henley. 'A broken neck as a result of the fall is the cause of death. No eyewitnesses either to the fall or to anyone entering his flat. We've recovered personal items but not his phone which shouldn't be too much of a problem because the cell site report from the phone company landed in my inbox half an hour ago.'

'Keep me updated,' said Pellacia. 'I'm going to see the borough commander and see what we can do about the defendants who are at risk but first I'm going downstairs to speak to Ezra. He's feeling bad about Longley.'

'He's got absolutely no reason to feel guilty,' said Stanford. 'Longley made his choices and, unfortunately, he's paid for them.'

'Right, this is what we're going to do,' Henley continued. 'Copeland, I want you to go to Wood Green Crown Court and speak to the prosecutor for the Ferguson trial.'

'This is crazy,' Copeland said as she picked up her covert harness and police radio from her desk.

'Stanford and Eastwood, I need you to go through all of the property that was recovered from Longley's flat and also the Crimestoppers call logs. Most of the people calling up since we released the composites have been cranks but there has to be something there. And I'll speak to the OIC dealing with the Ferguson acid attack,' said Henley. 'We need to find these people before anyone else ends up dead.'

51

Copeland grimaced as she left the security desk of Wood Green Crown Court and took the stairs to Court six. There was an atmosphere in the air that was unique to court buildings. A palpable sense of anticipation mixed with the unmistakable scent of denial that permeated from the pores of defendants who had yet to understand the gravity of their situation. Copeland found a barrister sitting outside Courtroom Four with a bemused look on his face. Copeland took out her phone and double checked the screenshot that she'd taken off the barristers' directory 9 Kemble Hill Chambers.

'Barnaby Spada?' Copeland asked the barrister.

'Who's asking?'

'DC Copeland. I'm attached to the Met's Serial Crime Unit,' she said, flashing her warrant card. 'I understand that you're prosecuting Catlin Ferguson.'

'Are you here to tell me that you found her? The judge issued a bench warrant about an hour ago.'

'Found her . . . no,' said Copeland. 'Is there somewhere private we can talk?'

'Private? What exactly is going on?'

Copeland stepped forward, lowering her voice. 'Catlin Ferguson is dead.'

Barnaby's eyes widened. 'What do you mean. How?'

'An acid attack on Saturday night which is why I need to—'

'Hold on,' Barnaby said, stepping away from Copeland. His

voice travelled and echoed around the tiled hallway as he shouted urgently. 'Kerry, Will.'

A female barrister turned around and looked at Barnaby quizzically.

'My room,' Barnaby said, picking up his laptop and papers.

'Who are you?' Kerry asked, removing her wig as Barnaby closed the door of the CPS office.

'DC Copeland, this is Kerry Murphy, defence counsel for Ms Ferguson,' said Barnaby 'And this is Will Summers, Ms Ferguson's solicitor.'

'Have you found her?' Will asked.

Copeland glanced at the clock on the wall. Ferguson had been dead for nearly thirty-six hours. She couldn't understand why she, a police officer from a unit on the other side of the river, was delivering the death message.

'On Saturday night a woman was attacked with acid in Notting Hill and died yesterday morning,' said Copeland. 'That woman was identified as Catlin Ferguson.'

'Excuse me, what?' Will exclaimed as his briefcase fell out of his hand. 'She can't . . . are you sure?'

'Her identity was confirmed and her family have been informed.'

'Why are *we* only being informed now?' asked Kerry as she looked across at Barnaby and then back at Copeland.

'I don't know why you or the court haven't been informed by the investigating officers,' said Copeland softening her voice, aware that she was getting defensive.

'Aren't you the investigating officer?' Will asked suspiciously.

'No, I'm attached to the Serial Crimes Unit,' said Copeland. 'It's early doors and we're just making all the necessary enquiries now to determine if Ferguson's murder is a part of a series of vigilante attacks.'

'Christ,' Will said. 'How can the verdict stand if the defendant is dead?'

'The verdict has to be set aside. Excuse me.' Kerry grabbed her belongings, pushed past Copeland and left the room.

'Verdict?' Copeland asked as Barnaby also picked up his belongings. 'The trial isn't listed until 11 a.m..'

'The wrong time was published online,' Barnaby explained. 'The case was called on at 9.45 a.m. and the judge sent the jury out almost immediately. He then called us back in at 10.25 a.m. and issued a bench warrant because we thought Catlin had failed to surrender. I think the jury had already made up their mind because, forty minutes later, there was a verdict.'

'Guilty,' said Will. 'Unanimous. Not that I was surprised. She should have bloody pleaded. She would have been serving a prison sentence but at least she would have been alive.'

'I was hoping that the OIC would be around. I wanted to ask him if Catlin had reported incidents of harassment,' said Copeland as she moved and blocked the door. 'Was there anything that happened recently, any incidents at court? I'm not asking you to break legal privilege, Mr Summers, but did—'

'She thought she was being followed,' said Will. 'I assumed she was being paranoid and overdramatic as per usual.'

'Was there anything else other than being followed?' Copeland asked.

Will blew out his lips as he rubbed the top of his bald head. 'I'm assuming you already know about the slashed tyres and shit through her door?'

'No, I didn't,' said Copeland. 'Did she report it?'

'I advised her to but—' Will stopped as his phone rang. 'Sorry, it's the office. I need to take this.'

'There was also the incident last Friday with her sister, Siobhan,' said Barnaby as Will left the room and the sound of the tannoy crackled.

'*All parties in the case of Ferguson to Court Six immediately.*'

'That's us, but you might be in luck. Siobhan has been here

for every single day of the trial. Check with witness services. I'm sorry, I really have to go but also don't leave the building, just in case the judge wants to hear from you.'

'Siobhan Perez,' Copeland shouted as she ran across the small car park towards the woman who had her hand on the door of a blue Mini. The woman jumped back, her car keys firmly between her fingers.

Copeland did her best not to gasp. The foundation couldn't conceal the red, scarred and fragile skin on the left side of Siobhan's face. The twisted skin of her left eyelid looked heavy as it concealed her weeping eye.

Copeland held out her warrant card. 'I didn't mean to startle you,' she said. 'My name is DC Copeland. I'm with the Serial Crime Unit.'

'Am I supposed to know what that is?'

'We're a specialist unit based in Greenwich. We're making enquiries into—' Copeland paused and turned her face buying herself more time. For the second time in less than an hour she was going to deliver the death message. 'Your sister.'

'I'm not really interested in hearing about my bitch of a sister, unless you're here to tell me you've found her and she's on her way to prison,' Siobhan said furiously.

'I'm afraid I have some bad news,' said Copeland. 'Your sister was attacked on—'

'Good. Hopefully she's dead,' Siobhan said, lowering herself into the car seat.

Copeland grabbed the top of the car door to stop Siobhan from slamming it shut. 'Your sister was attacked with acid on Saturday night. She died in the early hours of Sunday morning,' she said.

Copeland waited for any expression to cross Siobhan's face. Shock, bewilderment, denial or even acceptance but they never came. She remained impassive. Copeland suspected that Siobhan would have shown more emotion if she'd been listening to an electricity meter reading.

Siobhan stared back. 'What are you expecting of me? For me to be sorry?'

Copeland bit the inside of her cheek, fighting the temptation to answer in the affirmative. 'Look, I understand that your relationship with your sister was tumultuous but—'

'Tumultuous?' Siobhan scoffed, pointing at her face. 'Look at me.'

'I'm sorry for what happened to you. I just need to ask you a few questions and then I'll let you get on. I understand your sister had breached her bail conditions by visiting you?'

'She's a psychopath and a narcissist,' said Siobhan. 'I'm a psychiatrist and you would have thought I'd have been able to see the signs in my own flesh and blood. The day before the trial, she turned up in my house.'

'What do you mean, "in your house"?' asked Copeland.

'I gave a spare key to my nephew which she obviously took. I came home from work, and she was sitting there in my kitchen, drinking a glass of wine as though we were—'

Siobhan turned her face, her voice cracking for the first time.

'What did she want?'

'For me not to give evidence. To either not turn up at all or to stand in that courtroom and lie. Tell them it was someone else who threw acid in my face.'

'What did she do when you told her no?'

'Offered me money. A lot of money. Which was just like her. If she couldn't manipulate you then she would throw money at the problem. I told her to get out. Threatened to call the police.'

'And did she?'

Siobhan nodded. 'I came to court every day, but there are all these rules, which meant I had to wait in the witness room until they were ready for me. I didn't see her again until the day I gave evidence. She sat in the dock, looking at me as though I was a piece of shit and then she sat up there in the witness box, all fucking sanctimonious and acted as though she was the victim.'

'Did you attack her outside the court last Friday?'

'It was hardly an attack. It was just . . . she looked at me as though she was so sure she was going to get away with it and I just—' Siobhan lifted up the central console, pulled out a bunch of tissues and wiped her weeping eye. 'Thank God Mika was there to stop me.'

'Mika?' Copeland asked, her grip on the car door growing tighter. 'Who's Mika?'

'She's works in witness services. Victim support,' Siobhan replied cautiously. 'To be honest, I don't know what I would have done without her. She's been a godsend these past two weeks.'

'And this Mika works here at the court?' Copeland asked as she released the door, took her phone out of her pocket and went to her emails. 'Come on,' she said as she tapped repeatedly on the jpeg icon attached to Stanford's email, desperate for it to open.

'You won't have much luck out here. The reception is awful. You're better off inside.'

'This Mika. Do you know her surname?'

'No, I don't.'

'And have you seen her today? Was she with you when the verdict was delivered?'

'No, she wasn't. I doubt very much that I was the only victim on her list.' Siobhan pressed the ignition button and the car engine purred. 'Can I go now? This has all been a lot and I really want to go home.'

'Of course,' Copeland replied as she stepped back from the car door. 'Oh, but before you go, can you describe Mika?'

'Has she done something?' Siobhan asked suspiciously.

'It's just routine in an investigation like this.'

'Ok. She's about five foot five, slim build. Shoulder length blonde hair, dyed. She has a small mole under her right eye. Late forties, early fifties, I think. Sorry, I'm not the best with guessing ages. That's it. Just ordinary really.'

Copeland stepped into the large court admin office. There were only three people in there as the court morning session hadn't yet concluded. A short, middle-aged Asian man with his glasses hanging around his neck on a chain, stood by the photocopier, while a younger woman was on the phone.

'I'm DC Copeland attached to the Serial Crime Unit. I'm looking for a woman called Mika,' she said exasperatedly as her phone finally connected to the court Wi-Fi. 'She was looking after a witness in the Catlin Ferguson trial. Court Three. She's blonde, about five foot five. Has a mole. Late forties.'

The third woman, whose name badge identified her as Pearl, approached Copeland who showed her the photograph of the sketch that Stanford had emailed to the team.

'Can't say that I recognise her. Hold on. Terri,' she said, turning to look behind her. 'You're covering Court Three, aren't you?'

'Yes, not that there's much to cover at the moment. The defendant was apparently murdered over the weekend. Acid attack,' said Terri. She put down the phone and approached Copeland. 'Is this what you're here about?'

'Yes,' Copeland replied as the man who'd been by the photocopier picked up a coat from the back of a chair and walked out. 'Do you know this woman?'

Terri wrinkled her face as Copeland held out her phone. 'That looks like Mikaela. She's the new witness services manager. She lets the witnesses call her Mika.'

'Where is she?' Copeland asked.

'What has she done?'

'Where is she?' Copeland repeated urgently.

'I don't know, but you can ask Elliot. She's his wife. He was just standing by . . . Pearl, wasn't Elliot just here?' Terri asked.

'He just left. Must be grabbing a cigarette break,' said Pearl.

'The man who was standing by the photocopier?' Copeland asked.

'Elliot Fonseka. He's Judge Tarlov's—'

'And this woman is his wife?'

'Yeah, he introduced her to me.'

'Find the police liaison officer and tell them I need backup, now! I've got a suspect on the run,' Copeland shouted. She ran out of the office, into the empty hallway and stopped at the lift. Copeland ran down the stairs. She wished she'd paid closer attention to the man standing innocently next to the photocopier. She reached the ground floor and turned to the lift. The doors were closed, and the lift was on its way to the second floor.

'Did an Asian man just leave? He works here. A clerk. Elliot,' Copeland shouted at the surprised security guard.

'Yes, a few seconds ago,' the guard replied.

Copeland pushed through the glass door and stood momentarily at the top of the steps.

'Police!' she shouted as the man who'd been walking quickly through the car park turned left and ran across the wet grass of the Court grounds. Copeland grabbed and extended her baton as she sprinted after Elliot.

'Stop! Police!' she shouted again. It didn't take long for Copeland to catch up with Elliot and grab him by his coattails. Elliot screamed out; his arms wild. He punched Copeland in the face.

Copeland gasped as she landed heavily on her back. She turned over and scrambled to her feet, picked up her baton and gave chase again, her trainers slipping on the wet grass.

'You little shit,' Copeland muttered, striking her baton hard against Elliot's arm and pushing him to the ground. She dropped to her knees and turned a wittering Elliot around as the police liaison officer ran towards her.

Copeland straddled Elliot and grabbed hold of his left arm. 'Elliot Fonseka, I'm arresting you for murder,' she said.

'Ow, you're hurting me,' screamed Elliot, his Manchester accent broad.

'Shut up,' Copeland ordered, grabbing his right arm and placing the handcuffs on his wrists as she cautioned him.

'Tell her to let me go. She's made a mistake,' Elliot shouted as Copeland pulled him to his feet and handed him over to the police liaison officer.

'I told you to shut up,' Copeland repeated. She winced as she bent down and picked up her phone which had fallen out of her pocket and dialled Henley.

52

Elliot Viran Fonseka's custody photo filled the smartboard. His thin-rimmed, black glasses were sitting unevenly on a face that looked resigned to its fate. Broken blades of grass were in his wavy salt and pepper hair.

Henley stepped back and took in all the contours and heavy jowls of Elliot's face. She'd learnt a long time ago not to make assumptions about what a person would look like based on the crimes alleged against them, but Elliot surprised her. There was nothing striking about his appearance. He was someone who'd been born to walk through the world unnoticed.

'He reminds me of Penfold from *Dangermouse*,' said Stanford, who was perched on the edge of his desk with tea in hand.

'He does a bit,' Eastwood agreed.

Copeland walked into the room. A raw graze was visible on her left cheek and her eye was bruised and swelling.

'How are you feeling?' Henley asked.

Copeland removed the cold compress from her face. 'I wasn't expecting him to come out swinging like that,' she said. 'I shouldn't have been surprised. He did make a run for it. So where are we with him?'

'Right now, Fonseka is sitting in the cells at Lewisham. He's been booked and samples have been taken,' said Henley. 'His fingerprints haven't been matched with any of the prints that were retrieved from the crime scenes.'

'DNA?' Eastwood asked.

'We've asked for the lab to deal with it urgently but you know how it is. We can ask but we may not necessarily get,' Henley replied, turning towards Copeland. 'So, about Elliot Fonseka.'

'He's fifty-four years old and has been working for the Crown Court Service for twenty-six years.' Copeland winced as she sat down. 'We're still waiting for a breakdown of his full employment history from HMCTS but according to colleagues he started working at Wood Green Crown Court nearly two years ago. He has no criminal record.'

'Working for the court, that wouldn't be a surprise,' said Ramouter.

'No, it wouldn't, and it wouldn't have been a surprise to see him accessing confidential information on the court's database because that is literally his job,' said Copeland. 'He didn't make any comments on arrest or during the drive from Wood Green to Lewisham. Spent the entire time sniffling in the back and staring out of the window.'

'What about the wife?' asked Eastwood.

'Mikaela Elizabeth Fonseka. Maiden name Colbert,' Henley replied, turning back to the smartboard, she brought up a driving licence and zoomed in on the photograph. 'forty-nine years old, no previous and little is known about her employment history, other than that she's a volunteer for the witness support service.'

'Where is she now?' asked Ramouter.

'No idea,' said Copeland. 'The witness service manager gave us her phone number but she didn't pick up. I have a feeling that her husband may have contacted her just before I arrested him. She was scheduled to work this afternoon but there's been no sign of her.'

'Her description has been circulated to all units and we're going to release her image to the public this afternoon. We have to find her,' said Henley.

'List of possible targets is down to three,' said Ramouter. 'The list officer at Harrow Crown Court called and confirmed that Primrose Welch's case was adjourned because there was no jury available. The judge amended her bail conditions and she's booked on a flight to Dubai, leaving tonight. She won't be rushing back anytime soon. Her trial has been moved to June.'

'June,' Stanford exclaimed. 'I don't know why I'm surprised. The criminal justice system is completely broken.'

'We can discuss the broken criminal justice system at a later date. Our priority is the Fonsekas,' Henley said firmly. 'Ezra has been given remote access to Elliot Fonseka's work computer and his login for CCDCS. A Section 18 search has been carried out on his desk at Wood Green Crown Court.'

'What about his home?' asked Eastwood.

'The Fonsekas live in Tulse Hill. Brixton CPU have spared a couple of officers to search the property, I'm just waiting for confirmation that they're ready. Copeland are you good to assist on the search?' Henley asked.

'Of course,' Copeland replied.

'Thank you,' said Henley. 'Stanford and Eastwood, I want you on Mikaela Fonseka and the CCTV footage from the Ferguson acid attack has come through. I need you looking for anything that can help us identify the third person in Iron Shadow. Ramouter and I will be interviewing Fonseka but I don't want him on record until we've got something concrete to put to him. At the moment all we've got is that he's left the court building and didn't stop when Copeland ordered him to.'

'Don't forget the assault on a PC,' Copeland said, removing the cold compress and pointing at her swollen eye.

'Don't worry, I'll be asking him about that too. Right, everyone get to it, and Copeland can I have a quick word?' Henley said, gathering her things.

'Yeah, of course, guv.' Copeland followed Henley outside. 'Is everything ok?' she asked.

'Everything is fine,' Henley said. 'I didn't want to talk in there with everyone pretending they're working and not eavesdropping.'

'They're not exactly subtle.'

'No, they're not. I wanted to say well done, for today. You did good work.'

'It was just luck really. We would still be at square one if I hadn't caught Siobhan Perez in the car park.'

'Don't diminish what you did. You followed through and you got a result that has moved this case forward. You're a good addition to the team.'

'Oh, thank you,' Copeland said, visibly surprised.

Henley's phone vibrated in her hand; she replied to the text message. 'That's Brixton CPU,' she explained. 'They're ready to go. I'm forwarding the address and the officers' details to you now.'

'I'll keep you updated,' Copeland said.

Henley waited until the door slammed shut behind Copeland, before turning around and pressing her forehead against the cold wall. She was grateful that the text message had arrived and stopped her from going that one step further and apologising to Copeland. Despite her protestations and a gnawing feeling that she shouldn't trust Copeland she couldn't deny that she was a good detective.

Elliot Fonseka was both shaking and sweating. Large sweat patches were visible in the underarms of his blue shirt and his top lip glistened as the hands holding on to the plastic cup of water shook. His solicitor, a man named Arthur Crooks who had been knocking around the criminal courts longer than Henley had been alive, sat next to Elliot. The room reeked both of body odour and desperation.

'Elliot, DC Ramouter has reminded you of the caution which you've confirmed you fully understand. I'm going to question you about the allegations made against you,' Henley said. She spotted a box of tissues on the ground, pulled out one and handed it to Elliot.

'Before you do that,' said Arthur, tearing a page from his notebook, 'I have a prepared statement from Elliot Fonseka which I'm going to read out.'

Henley leaned back as Ramouter sat with his pen poised. Prepared statements weren't unusual in a police interview. Most people thought they had only two options when being interviewed by the police, to answer questions or answer no comment but there was a third option: to give a statement prepared by your lawyer which either denied the offence or admitted it but also laid out a defence.

Arthur cleared his throat and read: '"I, Elliot Fonseka, will say as follows: I deny having any involvement in the murders of Catlin Ferguson, Nathan Hall, Sian Fox-Carnell, Douglas Mantell, Gong Bo Hyoo, Kaiden Longley and the attempted murder of Tabitha and Graham Ashcroft. I have no knowledge of a conspiracy to commit murder. I deny running away and attempting to avoid arrest when I saw DC Copeland at Wood Green Crown Court. I was leaving the court for a cigarette break. I was not aware that DC Copeland was a police officer and was acting in self-defence when I punched her. I believed that I was being attacked. My actions were reasonable and not excessive." The statement has been signed and dated by Mr Fonseka. I have a scanned copy so you can keep the original.'

Henley, took the statement from Arthur. 'Just because you've given a prepared statement doesn't mean that the interview is over,' she said. 'But you would know that, being a court clerk.'

'And he's been advised to answer no comment to all questions following on from his statement,' said Arthur.

'Elliot, you've been working for the court system for a long time. Twenty-six years,' said Henley. 'We've got a copy of your employment history. You started as a legal advisor in the old Bow Street Magistrates' Court and were there until it closed in 2006. You then transferred to Blackfriars Crown Court where you were a clerk for eleven years and then you moved to Manchester Crown Court. Why?'

'My dad was ill, and I moved to be closer to him. He died four years ago.'

'I'm going to remind you of the advice I gave you in consultation,' said Arthur without looking up. 'To answer no comment to all questions put to you.'

Elliot picked up his water, sipped and replied, 'No comment.'

'How did your dad die?' Ramouter asked.

'He was mugged when he was leaving the betting shop. He was pushed and banged his head. He died before the ambulance arrived,' said Elliot as Arthur gave an audible sigh, signalling that he'd given up.

'Did they catch the person who mugged him?'

'He was charged with manslaughter and was given a two-year sentence. Can you imagine that? He killed a defenceless old man, and he got a shorter sentence than someone convicted of being in possession of a fake passport,' Elliot said angrily. 'That wasn't justice.'

'Two years. That's not long at all is it, Inspector Henley?' asked Ramouter. 'Especially when two years doesn't even mean two years.'

'The man who killed your dad would have been out of prison after serving half his time,' said Henley.

'It's wrong,' said Elliot.

'Did your wife, Mikaela, or Mika, feel the same way?'

'No comment.'

'You answered questions about your dad, but you don't want to answer questions about your wife?'

'No. I won't talk about her, and you can't force me,' Elliot said petulantly.

'You're right, we can't force you, so let's talk about your time at Manchester Crown Court and Douglas Mantell. This is a copy of the first page of the trial transcript. You will see that it states who was present at court before the prosecution opened their case,' said Henley, handing a copy to Elliot. 'You're listed as the court clerk assisting His Honour Judge Keir.'

'That's right,' Elliot confirmed.

'And it's correct that your wife, Mika, had started working for witness services at the same court six months earlier?'

'Yes she—' Elliot pressed his lips closed, prematurely ending his answer.

'It takes a certain type of person to sit there day in, day out listening to the prosecution tell the jury how a man sexually abused his daughter and allowed others to do the same. Twenty-six years is a long time. It must take its toll,' said Henley.

'It's my job and I do my job. I'm not paid to have an opinion. My job is to assist the judge, diary management, liaise with counsel. I don't take the job home.'

'That's not true,' said Henley, producing a short stack of prints from a folder. 'This is a log of all of the cases you accessed on the Crown Court digital case system since you transferred from Manchester to Wood Green Crown Court. Now that's a lot of cases.'

'But what is most interesting about these cases is that you accessed cases that weren't taking place in Wood Green,' added Ramouter, tapping his pen against a name highlighted in yellow. 'For example. R v Christopher Hayes. Isleworth Crown Court and we go down a bit. R v Bolade Yesufu. Snaresbrook Crown Court and there's more. Pick any Crown Court in London and we'll find a defendant's case that you tried to access.'

'That's not against the law. I have the right to access the system,' said Elliot unconvincingly.

'But do you have the right to download case papers and upload those papers to your personal Google drive?'

'I didn't do that.'

'It's not a good idea for you to lie to us especially when the evidence is right in front of you. Highlighted.'

'I accessed papers, but I didn't download them.'

'Can you explain why you downloaded not only the case papers but the court file and the DART recordings from trials.'

'DART? I don't know what you're talking about.'

'Stop playing games, Elliot,' Henley snapped. 'The digital audio and recording transcription and storage system that every court uses. The system that records every single word uttered in a court hearing. You downloaded the recordings for Tabitha Ashcroft's trial at Croydon Crown Court. Nathan Hall's trial at Southwark, Sian Fox-Carnell didn't have a trial, but you downloaded the court file which contained her bail address. What did you do with them?'

'I was doing my job.'

'It wasn't your job to take this information home. Whose idea was it to take actions into your own hands?'

'No comment.'

'Was it your wife's idea?'

'No comment.

'Was it Don's?'

Henley watched the recognition spread across Elliot's face as she put the composite image in front of him. 'What's his full name?' she asked.

'I don't know.'

'How did you meet him?'

'I never met him. I don't know who you're talking about it.'

'We've found fingerprints and DNA at the crime scenes. We know it doesn't belong to you. You're not the one who injected fentanyl into Sian Fox-Carnell's blood stream or broke Nathan Hall's legs with a sledgehammer.'

Elliot's cup fell from his shaking hands and water spilled onto the table. 'What?' he exclaimed. 'What do you mean?'

'In your job you shouldn't really be surprised that a pre-meditated murder is usually the worse kind,' Henley said soothingly as she blotted away the spilled water with a tissue. 'The planning that goes into that type of murder. The decision to not only murder but to desecrate a body by, DC Ramouter, why don't you enlighten, Mr Fonseka?'

'Oh, you mean the scalping?' said Ramouter. He opened a blue, spiral-bound A5-sized photo album and placed it in front of Elliot. Nathan Hall's broken body – the Y incision visible on his chest was the first photograph. Ramouter turned the pages before stopping at the photograph of the back of Nathan's Hall's head.

'Thankfully Hall was already dead when Don – or maybe it was Kaiden Longley – cut away a piece of his scalp.'

Elliot put a hand to his throat as he audibly heaved. 'I didn't . . . didn't. Oh my God.'

'What was that? You didn't know?'

Elliot shook his head vigorously and pushed the photo album away.

'You're involved in the murder of five people. You're the one in the middle of all of this. None of this is possible without you. Did your wife introduce Don to you?' asked Ramouter.

'I told you that I'm not talking about her,' Elliot said shakily.

'Are you scared of her?'

'Of course not but I've told you I'm not talking about her. She's not involved.'

'I don't think that's true. Do you know Gareth Humphreys and Karim Messenger? They're both serving sentences in Strangeways but they've both given descriptions of you and—'

'Stop. Stop. I need to talk to my lawyer. I'm allowed to stop the interview to have a consultation with him. You said it,' Elliot said, standing up and pointing at Ramouter. 'You said I could.'

'Aye, I did say it. Calm yourself and sit down,' said Ramouter as Arthur grabbed Elliot's arm, forcing him to sit. 'I'm suspending the interview at 4.24 p.m..'

'How long do we keep on pushing him?' Ramouter asked as Henley walked away from the closed door of interview room four.

'We've only been in there for twenty minutes and look at the state of him. He's ignored his lawyer's advice and he's talking,' said Henley.

'Except when it comes to his wife. He refuses to talk about her.'

'Because he doesn't want to incriminate her, but I reckon that if we keep pushing with the questions about Don he'll crack. Are you happy to take the lead with the rest of the interview?' Henley asked as the interview door opened and Arthur stepped out.

'Inspector Henley, can I have a word?' Arthur asked.

'Feel free,' Henley said.

'Mr Fonseka wants to make a deal,' Arthur said unenthusiastically.

'A deal,' Henley repeated. 'He's in no position to make a deal.'

'Well, Mr Fonseka thinks that he is. Section 72 of the Serious Organised Crime and Police Act allows for the prosecution to give an undertaking that any information a person gives will not be used against them.'

'He wants us not to take further action against him if he grasses? Is that what you're telling me? That he wants immunity from prosecution?'

'Something along those lines. If you agree he would become a co-operating witness and not a suspect.'

'Wow. He's delusional,' Ramouter said.

'Your words not mine,' said Arthur as he pulled out a packet of Nicorette gum from his pocket and popped a piece into his mouth.

'He's a court clerk. He must know that only a prosecutor can make that decision and not me?' said Henley. 'And to be honest, he's in this up to his neck. There's no way—'

'Those are my instructions,' Arthur said, holding his hands up in defence.

'Tell him that the best I can do is put the offer to the prosecutor once he's charged.'

'I will pass on the message, but I will be repeating my advice to him to answer no comment to any questions that you put to him.'

'We'll see how long that lasts,' Ramouter muttered as Arthur went back into the interview room. 'I can't believe he's asking for immunity.'

'That's because he knows there's no way out for him,' said Henley as Arthur poked his head out of the door and waved at them to return.

'You push him,' Henley said. 'And make sure Elliot Fonseka breaks.'

53

'Ez, are you sure you don't want a lift, cuz?'

Ezra adjusted his rucksack on his back. 'Bruv, you make absolutely no sense,' he said. 'We both live ten minutes away and you're driving.'

'Don't start on me,' said Zyon. 'Acting all sanctimonious about my little car's carbon footprint.'

'The last time I checked, a Land Rover Evoque wasn't a little car,' said Ezra, playfully shoving his cousin.

'It's electric.'

'What do you want, a medal?'

'Nah, a gold star would do,' Zyon laughed, stepping aside to allow a couple to enter the gym. 'All right, suit yourself. Message me when you get home.'

'Great,' Ezra said to himself as the first raindrops splashed against his forehead and Zyon drove away. He pushed his AirPods into his ears, turned the volume up high and walked quickly down New Cross Road. Ezra's plan for the evening was simple: go home, jump in the shower, eat whatever experimental dish his sister had cooked, and then go to bed. He was three houses away from his front door when the first blow connected with his head, the force ejecting his AirPods out of his ears like a projectile.

A second blow landed in Ezra's stomach, and he fell back into a trio of wheelie bins. His chest muscles seized as he struggled to breathe. He opened his eyes to see the orange glow of the streetlamp bouncing off the dull steel of the standpipe that was being held aloft. Ezra willed himself to turn over, his hands reaching for the low crumbling wall in front of him. The sounds of speeding traffic and trains pulling into New Cross Gate station drowned out Ezra's screams as the third blow landed on his back, swiftly followed by a kick to his head.

Ezra cried out as the force of a kick to his back propelled him along the pavement. He rolled over twice and ended up with his face flat against the wet pavement. The smell of mouldering leaves and a blocked drain filled Ezra's nose. He yelled again as he was roughly turned over onto his back. There was a tight pressure on his chest as his attacker straddled him. Somewhere in Ezra's head, he heard an instruction, and he scratched weakly at his attacker's hands.

'You little fuck,' his attacker said as he punched Ezra in the face and smashed his arm against the ground. Ezra tried to open his eyes, but he was blinded by the glow of the streetlight and then another blow to his head. Ezra wanted the high-pitched ringing in his ears to stop. He wanted the pain to stop. A final blow to his head gave him his wish.

The sharp sound of Henley's phone pulled her forcefully out of sleep. She pushed Rob's arm off her chest and turned over, scrambling in the dark for her phone on the bedside table.

Henley reeled the charging cable in like a fishing line and pulled the phone onto her chest. She squinted at Pellacia's name on the screen and then the time, silencing the phone as she did so. It was 2.13 a.m.. She scrambled out of bed and pressed accept.

'Anj,' said Pellacia. The pain in his voice was clear. 'Anj. Are you there?'

'I'm here,' Henley said. She closed her bedroom door and sat down on the top step of the stairs. 'What's going on?'

'It's Ezra.'

'What's happened?'

'This is all my—'

'Stephen! Where is he?'

Henley got up and opened the door to the spare room, grabbed a hoodie and a pair of leggings from the pile of clean clothes on the bed. She put the phone on speaker. She could hear Pellacia taking a breath, steadying himself.

'Lewisham hospital,' he said. 'He's been attacked.'

The harsh overhead lighting struck the tense muscles in Pellacia's jaw as he stood in front of the window staring out into a night sky. He turned around as though autotuned to Henley's presence.

'This is my fault,' Pellacia said, his voice low and pained.

'Stop it,' Henley said, making her way to his side. She silently counted to three, hardening herself, sealing off her emotions and her attachment to Ezra before she asked, 'What happened?'

Pellacia opened his mouth just as the lift pinged and Ramouter stepped out, his face fixed in a combination of anger and determination.

'What the hell happened?' Ramouter demanded in a tone that made it clear that in that moment he had no respect for rank.

'His cousin Zyon said they left the gym on New Cross Road at about 9.15 p.m.,' said Pellacia, his voice hardening with each syllable. 'He offered Ezra a lift home, but he refused, because it was only a ten-minute walk. Zyon said he was expecting a call or text from Ezra by 9.30 p.m. to let him know he was home, but he didn't get one. He called but got no answer. He called Natalie, Ezra's sister and she said he wasn't home. Zyon decided to go to Ezra's house but when he got to Jerningham Road, well the place was lit up. Paramedics and police. Ez—'

Henley remained where she was as Pellacia's voice broke, and he turned his back. She looked at Ramouter and for the first time since getting to know him she couldn't read his expression.

'Who called 999?' Henley asked.

Pellacia turned around. His eyes wet. 'A couple who were walking home saw a man hit Ezra multiple times with a standpipe.'

Ramouter placed his hands on his head and turned his back. Henley closed her eyes.

'This man then ran off when the couple shouted at him. A cab driver was completing a drop off at the same time and he also called 999.'

'Were they able to give a description?' Ramouter asked as Stanford and Eastwood arrived.

'I haven't seen their statements yet or spoken to the officers from Peckham who were there,' Pellacia answered. 'But CSI did retrieve the standpipe, and they've got Ezra's clothing.'

'So, what was it? Is this to do—'

'Ramouter stop,' Henley said to no avail when she saw the intense anger in his eyes.

'Say it,' Pellacia said through gritted teeth. 'I can hear it in your voice. You blame me.'

'Of course I fucking blame you,' said Ramouter, his voice cold but amplified in the hallway. 'It's this case. We've got two lunatics out there and they both know that Kaiden Longley was talking to Ezra. You left Ezra out there exposed even though you—'

'Do you know what, you can stop talking right now,' said Pellacia his face reddening as he stepped up to Ramouter.

'Hey, hey,' Stanford said, moving swiftly in front of Ramouter and pushing Pellacia back. 'What are you playing at? This ain't the—'

'He's just a kid. I know that he gives it the big I am, but Ezra is a kid,' said Ramouter. 'You're the one who brought him into the SCU and—'

Pellacia inhaled sharply. 'Don't even—'

'You told me to say it, so I'm saying it,' Ramouter challenged.

'All right, stop,' Henley said firmly as she and Eastwood both grabbed Ramouter and pulled him back. 'We're not doing this here. In fact, we're not doing this at all. Do you understand me?'

Ramouter turned his head away as the dull tone of an arriving lift rang and a doctor stepped out.

'Ramouter, did you hear me?'

'Yes, boss,' Ramouter said quietly.

'We're taking a walk,' Stanford said to Pellacia in a tone that made it clear he was not messing about.

'Get off me,' Pellacia said his voice low.

'You either walk or I fucking carry you,' said Stanford.

'Stephen, please,' Henley said. 'Go.'

'For fuck's sake,' Stanford said as Pellacia shoved past him.

'Come on,' Henley said, taking Ramouter's arm leading him towards the ICU entrance. She pressed the intercom button and identified herself to the disembodied voice.

The door to the ICU opened and Henley put her hand on Ramouter's back to push him through, but he turned and called after Pellacia, his face twisted in fury and pain.

'It's all on you if Ezra doesn't make it.'

54

Stanford handed Henley a large cup of coffee. 'Any updates?' he asked.

'Not good. Ezra's not good at all,' Henley replied. 'Fractured skull, swelling on the brain. Broken collarbone, cracked ribs and a broken wrist. He's in critical condition but stable. We just have to pray that he comes around when they pull him out of the medically-induced coma.'

'Shit,' Stanford replied, his voice thick with tears. He placed his mug on the window ledge and pressed his forehead against the glass. 'He doesn't deserve this. He's just a fucking kid.'

'Paul,' Henley said, fighting back her own tears as she joined him at the window and put her arms around him. 'He's going to be OK.'

'You don't know that.'

'I have to believe it.'

'He should be walking in here with his disgusting green juice and moaning about the murder board,' said Stanford. He pulled away from the window and wiped his face. 'I can't believe that fucking group of vigilantes decided that a kid was a threat to them.'

Henley shook her head. 'It was one man according to the witnesses and he would have killed Ezra if he hadn't been interrupted.'

'Who's dealing with it?' Stanford asked.

'Peckham CID. Ezra's case is nothing to do with us, but the

OIC has promised to keep us updated,' Henley said. She put her mug down and rubbed her puffy eyes.

'What time did you finish last night?' Stanford asked with concern. 'You look knackered.'

Henley groaned as she checked the time. It was almost 8 a.m.. 'We finished interviewing Fonseka at around 9 p.m. but I didn't get home until midnight. I'd just fallen asleep when Pellacia called. I haven't even been home to change,' she said, looking down at the hoodie she was wearing that belonged to Rob.

'You should sleep. Take a nap downstairs.'

'I'm too wired to sleep,' Henley said as Pellacia walked in, making his way to his office without acknowledging either of them.

'He looks even worse than you do,' Stanford said. 'Can't say that I'm sorry.'

'Are you going to talk to him?'

'Nope. I said everything I had to say to him earlier. Ezra should never have been put in harm's way. He took his eyes off the ball.'

'Did you tell him that when you led him away?' Henley asked.

'Something like that,' Stanford admitted. 'Not my finest hour but he was behaving like a twat. What about you?'

'Me? Absolutely not,' said Henley as she watched Pellacia's closed door. 'I know him well enough to know that he wouldn't even hear me right now and the last thing we need is for him to think we're bitching about him. Best to leave him, but more importantly we need to keep Ramouter out of his way.'

'I've never seen that side of Ramouter before,' Stanford said with surprise.

'I don't know what he would have done if you weren't there.'

'Don't even think about it. Eastwood said she was taking him to the café. Trying to get him in a good place before he comes back to work.'

'It will take more than a full English to put Ramouter in a stable mood,' Henley said as the phone on her desk rang and Southwark CSI appeared on the display screen.

'Let me know when you're ready to get started,' said Stanford, turning his chair and waking up his computer.

Henley nodded as she picked up the phone.

'Inspector Henley, SCU.'

'It's Anthony. I've got news for you. It's up to you whether you take it as good or bad.'

'What is it?' Henley asked, catching the exhaustion in Anthony's voice.

'Members of my team were allocated to Ezra's case. I made it a priority and there's no way I wasn't going to keep you in the loop.'

'Thank you,' Henley said, sipping the coffee that Stanford had made extra strong. 'So, what have you got for me?'

'We were able to recover fingerprints from the standpipe that was used to assault Ezra and DNA from the broken strap of Ezra's rucksack. Unfortunately, we didn't get a hit with the fingerprints but Ezra being a clever little bugger had a lot of skin under his fingernails.'

'He must have been scratching away, defending himself,' said Henley.

'Getting evidence for us,' said Anthony. 'The labs are chocked full with a backlog so I can't say when we'll get a DNA result back.'

'Shit,' Henley said as an image of Ezra lying in the hospital bed, his face swollen and bruised and his head heavily bandaged as the monitor recorded his vitals flashed in her mind and hot coffee spilled on to her fingers.

'You all right?'

'Not really,' Henley paused as the door opened and the borough commander, Geraldine Barker, walked in. 'Anthony, I've got to leave you, but thank you.'

'So, let me see if I've understood this correctly,' said Barker as she stood in front of the SCU team. 'Fonseka will only reveal the name of the man we know as Don if he's granted immunity from prosecution?'

'That's the long and short of it, ma'am,' said Henley.

'How much time do you have left on Fonseka's custody clock?'

Henley checked the clock on the wall. 'Four hours and thirty-four minutes,' she said. 'As far as I'm concerned, I've had enough of Fonseka wasting our time with this immunity nonsense.'

'I agree. You've got more than enough to charge him with conspiracy to murder and misconduct in a public office,' said Barker. 'It's between him and his legal team to propose a deal to the prosecution. I want him charged and out of my cells before lunchtime.'

'We can do that,' said Pellacia who had been sitting quietly next to Henley.

'Are we any closer to identifying this Don?'

'Not yet but we've circulated enhanced CCTV images of the vehicles seen at the scene of the acid attack. We've also got the description that Laurence Durant gave us. The composite image is on the Crimestoppers website and has been shown on the local news. We're also arranging for the witnesses at the acid attack scene to give their full statements,' said Pellacia.

'And what about Mikaela Fonseka?'

'No idea,' said Henley. 'The last sighting of her was about an hour after Elliot Fonseka was arrested. A neighbour saw her entering her home and leaving forty-five minutes later.'

'And what about the Section 18 search?'

'We retrieved copies of court documents from the garden office, and we seized the computer equipment but there were signs that someone had left in a hurry, ma'am,' said Copeland. 'The wardrobe in the main bedroom was in a state of disarray and what appeared to be a document folder had been emptied on the bed. We recovered Elliot Fonseka's passport, birth certificate and insurance papers but nothing for his wife.'

'She's clearly on the run but I don't think that the remaining defendants on their list are safe,' said Pellacia. 'Bartholomew Gardner, Mason and Paige Jones.'

'Which is one of the reasons why I'm here this morning,' said Barker. 'UK protected persons services are refusing to offer protection on the grounds that there isn't a real and imminent threat to their lives.'

'The fact that we've got eight people on our board, six of them dead, isn't evidence of a real and imminent threat?' said Stanford.

Barker raised her eyebrow at Stanford.

'Sorry, ma'am,' he added.

'Look, I understand the frustration, but that is the reality. My hands are completely tied and, before you even suggest it, I do not have the bodies spare to sit on Gardner and the Joneses until they're either convicted and remanded immediately in custody, or your outstanding suspects are caught.'

'There's no reason why I couldn't do it,' said Stanford. 'I did a stint in parliamentary and diplomatic protection.'

'I know that the SCU can often behave as though they're a law unto themselves but that is not happening,' Barker said sternly. 'One of your team is already in the hospital. That should be warning enough.'

'So, what's the plan, Henley?' Ramouter asked as Pellacia led Barker into his office and closed the door. 'We just can't sit here waiting for another defendant to end up dead.'

'I'm very aware of that,' Henley said, fighting against the waves of exhaustion. The lack of sleep and the energy it took to be strong and not be overwhelmed by not only her emotions and attachment to Ezra but also the rest of the SCU, was taking its toll. She'd had to lock up her emotions when Joanna had broken down in tears when she'd heard the news about Ezra.

'Stanford, you're covering the charge of Elliot Fonseka,' said Henley. 'I sent over the file to the CPS last night, which means that they've got everything they need for a charging decision.'

'Just to be clear, we're opposing bail, right?' asked Stanford. 'Perverting the course of justice, commission of further offences.'

'Add fail to surrender. Remember he ran from Copeland. Tell the CPS the clock is ticking, and we want Fonseka in front of a judge this afternoon. Eastwood, you're happy to stick with the CCTV?'

'That's fine. I've also just received an email from the OIC who was dealing with the Ferguson acid attack. He's sent me CCTV footage retrieved from the pub's external cameras. I've got enough to keep me busy.'

'That just leaves us with Gardner and the Joneses,' said Henley as she faced Copeland and Ramouter. 'Copeland, you're on Gardner. We may not be able to provide him with protection, but we can bloody warn him and also find out if there's any instances of harassment. Basically, anything that would make him believe his life is at risk.'

'I'm off to Southwark Crown Court then?' asked Copeland.

'Yeah, and you're also on Mika Fonseka. We asked the bank and her credit card company to alert us if there's any activity on her cards but—'

'I'll chase them,' said Copeland, gathering her things.

'So, I take it that we're dealing with the Joneses,' asked Ramouter, his eyes fixed on Pellacia's closed door.

'We are. The last thing this unit needs is anyone complaining that we sat on our hands and did nothing when we knew people's lives were at risk but first, you and I need a chat,' said Henley.

'Boss, I don't think that—'

'I don't need you to think. Meet me in the old canteen in fifteen minutes.'

Henley joined Ramouter on the old sofa and handed him a cup.

'More coffee,' said Ramouter.

'I doubt that any of us had much sleep,' said Henley. 'How are you feeling?'

'Do you want the truth or a lie?'

'The truth.'

'And can you not be my boss in this moment?' Ramouter asked.

Henley sighed with exhaustion and resignation. 'You get a wild card,' she said. 'I'm not going to sit here and pretend I'm not upset and that it didn't scare me to death to see Ezra in that hospital bed. I've been asking myself if there was more I could have done to protect Ezra.'

'It's not your fault. You didn't—'

'Ezra's my responsibility too and I didn't do my job. I was the one who took him to the Soteria offices. He wouldn't have met Kaiden Longley if it wasn't for me,' Henley insisted as Ramouter put his head in his hands.

'He's just a kid,' Ramouter said, choking back tears. 'And he's a good kid.'

Henley swallowed back her own tears as she gently placed her hand on Ramouter's back. They sat there silently for a few minutes.

'Ezra will pull through,' said Henley.

Ramouter sat up and picked up his coffee. 'We don't know that,' he said angrily.

Henley groaned. 'Ramouter you need to—'

'I'm fucking angry. Ezra is in a hospital bed because of Pellacia.'

'That's not fair, Ramouter. You can't blame—'

'Of course I can. He had an obligation to protect him, but he exposed him to people like Kaiden Longley and whoever this fucking Don is. Pellacia should have done better to protect Ezra. He knew that Ezra was in danger, and he did nothing.'

'Are you done?'

Ramouter leaned forward and took a sip of coffee. 'Aye.'

'Now I'm talking to you as your boss,' said Henley. 'Pull yourself together. I've told you more than once that this team doesn't work if we're not supporting each other. I need you to focus and not let Ezra's hard work be in vain. Don't let your anger with Pellacia get in the way. You're better than that. He's hurting and you're hurting.'

'Are you telling me to apologise?' Ramouter asked.

Henley stood up. 'No. You'll know when it's the right time to do that.'

'Is that it?'

'We've got a case to deal with and I need a partner who's got his head screwed on. So, are we good?'

'Aye, boss,' said Ramouter. 'We're good.'

55

'I've got you,' Eastwood said triumphantly. She paused the CCTV footage and picked up her can of Coke. Her eyes were burning, and she was convinced that she'd developed repetitive strain injury after spending hours moving the mouse to rewind, pause, zoom in and peer at frozen images. But her diligence had paid off as she stared at the van that a cab driver had said had driven away at speed shortly after Catlin Ferguson was attacked. She zoomed in and then leaned forward as she attempted to decipher the blurry images that made up the van's number plate. She jumped as she felt a tapping on her shoulders.

'Bloody hell,' she said, removing her headphones. 'You nearly gave me a heart attack.'

'What do you want, an apology?' said Joanna.

'I'm going to let that go because we're all having a shitty day and praying for Ezra. So, what is it?'

'Crimestoppers have transferred a call over to us. Line seven.'

'Ok, but before you go. Look at this,' Eastwood said as she pointed at the van's number plate. 'Can you make that out.'

'It's a bit blurry but it looks like GN20. Sorry I can't see the rest.'

'Jo, you did a better job than me,' Eastwood said. She picked up line seven. 'Serial Crimes Unit, DS Eastwood speaking.'

'Oh hello, my name is Jennifer McMahon.'

'I'm sorry but I can barely you hear you,' said Eastwood. She increased the volume on the phone but to no avail.

'I don't want to speak too loudly. I'm in my office. The man you're looking for . . . I think he's in my house repairing my conservatory. I saw his picture, the sketch on the news this morning and then I went on the Crimestoppers website and I'm sure that it's him, the one who was wanted for the attack on that couple in Dulwich.'

'And this man is in your house?'

'He's been working here for the past few weeks on my garden and the conservatory. He's such a nice man but—'

'Shit,' Eastwood said as the composite image of the man who Laurence Durant called Don appeared on the screen. She stood up and walked away from her desk, towards Pellacia's open door, until the cord was taut.

'Jennifer, what is this man's name?' Eastwood asked as she waved frantically at Pellacia.

'Donovan Hernandez,' she whispered. 'I found him on one of those find a tradesperson sites.'

'Ok, I need you to give me your address and we're coming to you now.'

'What shall I do?'

'Nothing. I want you to do nothing but stay in your office,' said Eastwood as Pellacia walked over. Copeland pointed at the screen and mouthed. *We've got him.*

'I know you're my boss and that it's not my place to question your orders or to tell you what to do, but with all due respect, guv, I really don't think you should be here,' said Eastwood as she watched Pellacia secure his stab vest.

'You're right, I am your boss, and you follow my orders. It's not the other way round,' said Pellacia.

'Guv, I know how close you are to Ezra, and I just don't think—'

'I'm well within my rights as your boss to tell you to stand down and go back to Greenwich. Do you want to go back?'

Eastwood took a breath and looked away. 'No, guv, but—'

'I've told you that I want to be there when they place the cuffs on him and that's what's going to happen.'

Eastwood sighed with the realisation that she'd lost the battle. She followed Pellacia to the corner of Buckingham Mews in Gypsy Hill where three police officers were waiting.

'Sir, we've got officers at the rear of the property,' said PS Lyons as he lowered the volume on the police radio.

'Has there been any movement from the property?' asked Pellacia.

'A man matching the suspect's description left the property to retrieve items from his van and went back inside but nothing since then.'

'What about the homeowner?' Pellacia asked Eastwood.

'I texted her and she's aware we're here. She said the door is open, and she's locked herself in her office upstairs,' said Eastwood. 'That was less than five minutes ago.'

'Right, let's go,' said Pellacia, marching ahead.

'Is your guvnor all right?' PS Lyons asked Eastwood as they followed. 'He looks pissed.'

'No, he's not,' Eastwood replied. 'Make sure you get your hands on Hernandez before he does.'

'I get it,' PS Lyons said, jogging ahead.

The mews was set away from the main road and was quiet due to the wet weather keeping people off the streets. Eastwood paused as she stepped into the driveway and saw the van. She felt a swell of anger in her stomach as she caught sight of the first part of the van's number plate: GN20. She looked up to see a young woman's face in the window.

'Ready,' Pellacia said as he pressed his hand against the door, pushed it open and stepped in. The conservatory was accessible from both the kitchen and the living room. The smell of wet plaster hung heavy in the air. They followed the sound of Heart FM as they made their way through the house.

Donovan was crouched, with his back turned, scooping plaster with a trowel onto the plastering hawk. The conservatory door leading out to the garden was open.

'Donovan Hernandez,' Pellacia barked as he stepped hurriedly into the room.

Donovan stood up quickly and turned around. Confusion, and then realisation, spread across his face as he dropped the plastering hawk onto the floor.

'Donovan Hernandez, you're under arrest for the—'

Pellacia didn't have the opportunity to finish as Donovan threw the trowel in his direction. Pellacia stumbled back as the sharp edge of the trowel pierced his cheek.

'You fucking little shit,' Pellacia shouted as Donovan bolted through the conservatory and ran into the garden.

'He's heading towards the back,' Eastwood shouted into her radio as Donovan sprinted across the wet garden, opened the gate and slammed it shut. Pellacia pursued Donovan. Eastwood slipped on the grass but scrambled to her feet as Lyons ran past her and through the now-open gate. She could hear voices shouting as she reached the gate and stepped into the alley. She stopped in shock when she saw Pellacia grab Donovan, punch him and throw him to the ground.

'Stephen. Stop!' Eastwood shouted as Pellacia kicked Donovan in the side.

Lyons grabbed Pellacia and pushed him against the fence as two more officers entered the alleyway. 'Calm the fuck down,' he shouted as Pellacia pushed back. 'I said stop,' Lyons repeated as another officer helped to restrain Donovan.

'He attacked me,' Donovan screeched. He held onto his side and rolled onto his back. Blood streamed from his nose and his face was grazed.

'If I was you, I'd stop whining,' Eastwood said. Another officer turned Donovan over, handcuffed him and brought him to his feet. 'Donovan Hernandez, I'm arresting you for murder, attempted murder and assaulting a police officer in the execution of their duty. You do not have to say anything. But it may harm your defence if you do not mention when questioned something which you later rely on in court. Anything you do say may be given in evidence. Do you understand?'

'Fuck you,' Donovan said as he spat bloody saliva at Eastwood's feet.

'You need stitches,' Eastwood said as the tissue Pellacia was holding to his face turned red.

'I'm fine,' Pellacia replied, his gaze fixed on the police van transporting Donovan Hernandez to Croydon police station.

'You're not bloody fine. You're bleeding all over the place and,' she dropped her voice, 'you nearly beat the shit out of Hernandez.'

Pellacia stared at Eastwood stony-faced. 'Did you really expect me to go easy on him?' he asked.

Eastwood raised her head to the overcast sky and took a breath. 'I've called Stanford and told him to meet me at the station. There's no way you're sitting in that interview room with Hernandez.'

'Are you forgetting who's in charge of this unit? It's not your—'

'I have not forgotten and if you want to stay in charge of this unit *and* keep your job, you'll stay away from Croydon police station.'

56

Pellacia groaned in pain as he exited the police car that had escorted him from King's College Hospital to the SCU. No one trusted him not to go to Don Hernandez's cell at Croydon police station and finish what he started. He groaned for a second time when he saw Ramouter cross the car park on his way to the SCU entrance.

'Ramouter,' Pellacia called.

Ramouter ignored him and kept walking.

'For fuck's sake,' Pellacia muttered. He jogged and stopped in front of Ramouter. 'Did you not hear me?' he asked.

'What can I do for you, guv?' Ramouter asked with clear disdain.

'I just . . . last night or this morning. Neither of us were ourselves,' said Pellacia, fighting to keep his tone conciliatory. 'We both said things that we—'

'No,' Ramouter said firmly. 'I meant everything I said.'

Pellacia tutted. 'I didn't realise you were so hardheaded.'

'You're a fine one to talk,' said Ramouter, inching closer to Pellacia. 'If your priorities were in order Ezra wouldn't—'

Ramouter paused as the door creaked open behind him.

Pellacia turned around to see Henley staring intently at the pair of them.

'Ramouter, you're needed upstairs,' Henley commanded. 'Now,' she said more forcefully as Ramouter showed no signs of moving.

'Yes, boss,' Ramouter said bitterly.

Pellacia silently watched as Ramouter made his way into the building.

'Was it your plan to end up in a hospital bed next to Ezra?' Henley asked Pellacia. 'And then have to explain yourself in a misconduct hearing?'

'Please don't start,' said Pellacia, placing an arm on the safety railing. 'I've already had an earful from Eastwood.'

'An earful wasn't enough,' Henley replied as she stepped down. 'I saw the body worn camera.'

Pellacia's face fell. 'Whose?' he asked.

'Does it matter?'

'I'm going to lose everything,' Pellacia said. He sat down on the step. 'I can't even say that I saw red. I saw Hernandez and then Ezra and that . . . It's like I blacked out.'

'You're going to need to come up with something better than that,' said Henley, joining him on the step. 'Hernandez was screaming about police brutality all the way to the station.'

'The man is facing life in prison for multiple murders, and he nearly killed Ezra.'

'We've got no evidence that Donovan Hernandez was involved in the assault on Ezra,' Henley said regretfully.

'Of course, he's fucking involved and me kicking the shit out of him is the least of his problems,' Pellacia said as he gingerly pressed his fingers against his red and swollen cheek.

'How many stitches?' she asked.

'Three. I need a drink. This fucking day, Anj.'

'I know, but I'm going to tell you the same thing that I told Ramouter. We need to focus; this isn't about us.'

'Try telling Ramouter that. He blames me. You saw the look on his face.'

'He's angry and you know what it's like when we're hurt. It's easier to take it out on each other, but we have to move on.'

'You make it sound so easy.'

'That's because I know you're one of the good ones,' said Henley. She put her arm around Pellacia, and he buried his head into her neck.

'I'm not feeling that right now,' he said.

Henley felt her neck become damp with Pellacia's tears as she held him a little bit tighter. She could feel it in her own body the overwhelming feeling of exhaustion, hopelessness and anger. Henley heard the sound of squeaking door hinges. She turned around to see Copeland standing in the doorway with a quizzical expression on her face.

'What is it, Copeland?' Henley asked as Pellacia quickly moved away from her, picked up his stab vest, which had been at his feet, and stood up.

'We've got a bank alert on Mika Fonseka,' said Copeland.

'It's four alerts actually,' said Copeland, back upstairs 'She made a cash withdrawal from a Post Office in Bruce Grove. A purchase at a chemist in Lower Clapton and another purchase in Marks and Spencer in London Bridge.'

'Does anyone else get the impression that she's heading south?' asked Ramouter.

'It certainly looks that way,' said Henley. 'What was the fourth purchase?'

'She hired a car,' said Copeland. 'But not with a physical business. They're called Whiz Cars. You go online, enter your postcode, find an available car closest to you, pick it up and go.'

'How can you just go? What about the keys?'

'You open the car with an app and the key is usually in the glove box,' Copeland explained. 'The problem we have right now though, is that even though we know she's hired a car we've got no other information. We don't know what type of car she's hired or even where she picked it up.'

'We need to get hold of someone at Whiz Cars,' said Pellacia.

'I don't know how easy that's going to be with a purely online business.'

'Ezra would have found a way,' Ramouter said mournfully as he turned his back to Pellacia.

'Have there been any updates?' Copeland asked.

'His sister, Natalie, called a little while ago. He's no longer critical but they're keeping him in a medically-induced coma for the next twenty-four hours to help reduce the swelling on his brain,' said Henley.

'Poor kid,' said Copeland.

'He'll get through it,' Henley said resolutely, trying to lift the air of dejection that emanated from Pellacia. 'I also got an update from Eastwood. Hernandez is refusing to talk. He's lawyered up and has gone no comment to everything. Eastwood said he wouldn't even confirm his name. They've taken a break, but they don't expect him to deviate from no comment once they resume the interview.'

'I'm about to head down to Southwark to do a viper ID with Laurance Durant,' said Ramouter. 'A positive identification from Durant and the fact that we've got a fingerprint match for Hernandez will be enough for the CPS to authorise a charge.'

'Before you go, what happened with Gardner and the Joneses?' asked Pellacia.

'Gardner turned into a quivering wreck when I told him he was a target,' said Copeland. 'He's been staying at the Hilton hotel next to the court and has his own security. I can't see Mika trying to make a move somewhere so public.'

'And the Joneses, Ramouter?' Pellacia asked pointedly, forcing Ramouter to look at him.

'Mason Jones was found guilty and remanded into custody awaiting sentence,' Ramouter replied flatly. He picked up his coat and case file. 'Paige Jones was acquitted. The boss tried to convince her that she should request protection, but she wasn't having it.'

'I'm going to have another word with her,' said Henley. 'She doesn't live far. I'm going to pass by her house on my way home. If Mika is nearby and she's watching, then maybe the sight of police presence will scare her off. I'll also get on the radio and see if any cars in the area can do a drive-by.'

'You're going home?' Copeland asked with surprise.

'Only for a shower and a change of clothes. But make sure you call me the minute you get confirmation of Mika; do you understand?'

'Of course,' Copeland replied.

57

Copeland stood at the window eating a slice of pizza. The rain had finally stopped, and a few stars had managed to break through the cloudy night sky. Her mind kept going back to the moment when she saw Henley and Pellacia sitting on the stairs. There was something in their body language that suggested to her that this was more than just one colleague comforting another. Her phone interrupted her thoughts.

She rubbed her hands on the front of her jeans and jogged over to her desk.

'DC Copeland speaking.'

'Hi, this is Jed from Whiz Cars. I'm sorry that it's taken a while to get back to you. We had to speak to the compliance team, legal and then our systems went down.'

'That's fine,' said Copeland as she dropped into her chair and reached for her pen. 'What can you tell me?'

'Mika Fonseka hired a Volkswagen Golf, the electric one, at 2.48 p.m.. She entered her location address as SE1 9RT, which came up as Guy's Hospital and she picked up a car on Pocock Street at 3.07 p.m.,' said Jed.

'This is a stupid question but are you able to continuously track your hire cars?'

'All of our cars have a tracker and anti-theft technology but an hour ago Mika Fonseka ended the hire of the car.'

'Shit. Where?'

'She left the car in Kellerton Road in SE13.'

Well, thanks for—'

'No, that's not all,' said Jed, 'She then hired another car, using the same card, on Dorville Road in SE12.'

'What car was that?'

'A Hyundai Ioniq. Black. And we last picked it up in Waveney Avenue at 8.22 p.m..'

'Excuse me,' Copeland said as she turned over the pages of the Paige Jones custody record and found her home address. 'Did you say Waveney Avenue?'

'That was twenty minutes ago, but I can't tell you where the car is now because our system just crashed.'

Copeland checked the clock. Henley had told her that it would be a quick trip home, but she had not yet returned to the SCU. Copeland knew she should call Henley and tell her that Mika Fonseka was on the move and that she had Paige Jones in her sight. Copeland looked around the empty office. She was finally part of the SCU and she wanted to stay. Being the one to arrest Mika would make her temporary position permanent. She picked up the key to the pool car, and left the building. Adrenaline pumped through Copeland's body as she got into the car and started the engine. She drove out of the car park but hit the brakes before she turned onto Greenwich High Road. She should tell Henley she was on her way to possibly apprehend Mika Fonseka, but Copeland knew that if she did, she was at risk of being told to stand down. So, instead, she called Ramouter.

Henley had made the mistake of lying on her bed after she'd showered and dressed. Warped images of Ezra, Sian Fox-Carnell and Pellacia had flooded her mind as she'd napped. The sharp ringing of her phone had woken her. She sat up and picked up her phone. It was Ramouter.

'Are you back at the SCU?' Ramouter asked.

'What? No. I fell asleep, I'm going to make my way there now.'

'We've got a problem. I just got a call from Copeland. She's possibly in pursuit of Mika Fonseka.'

'What the hell do you mean that she's in pursuit?'

'She got a location notification from Whiz Cars. The first was at Paige Jones's home address. Copeland went there but there was no sign of Fonseka or Paige.'

'Have you been in touch with Paige?' Henley asked as she left the bedroom, ran down the stairs and searched the hallway for her trainers.

'Her phone's going straight to voicemail, but Copeland spoke to Paige's sister, who's staying at the house. She told her Paige had gone to her studio in Bermondsey.'

'Ok, where are you now?'

'I was eating a Big Mac in Greenwich when Copeland called, I'm still here, just outside.'

'Let me think,' Henley said as she put on her trainers, grabbed her car keys and raced out of the house, the door slamming shut behind her. 'Get on the DLR and I'll pick you up on Elverson Road,' she said. 'I shouldn't be more than ten minutes.'

58

Mika turned off the car engine and sank back into her seat. She'd kept a safe distance from Paige Jones as she followed her but had also checked her rear mirror regularly for any signs of the police officer who'd turned up at Paige's home. When she'd seen Paige's Instagram story, a plan had formed. She invited her followers to join her for a live Q&A and a manifestation session. The high iron fencing surrounded a small industrial estate where a clothes factory had been converted into three buildings that housed recording studios, a boutique gym and office space. Mika got out of the car, opened the boot and reached for the large duffle bag that she'd hurriedly packed. She winced as rough canvas brushed against the acid burns – the skin raw and peeling – on her hand. She removed the knife that had been used to scalp all of her victims and cable ties. She closed the boot and ran across the road and into the estate, making sure to keep to the spots where the streetlamps couldn't reach as she made her way to Paige's recording studio.

The sound of screeching brakes pierced through the silence as Copeland stopped the car in the middle of the estate. She'd been forced to listen to Henley chastising her over the loudspeakers of the car, accusing her of entitlement and recklessness as she'd driven at speed towards Bermondsey. She stepped out into the estate and looked around as she adjusted her stab vest. The lights were on in the gym, but the windows were frosted – it was impossible to see in or out. She turned to her left and saw the building that had made a regular appearance on the Joneses' website and social media pages. To the outside world the building which housed the Joneses' office and recording studios was a sign of a commitment to manifestation and their wealth, but it was only the people who'd sat in Courtroom Two who'd known the true horrors of what had taken place on the top floor. Copeland wasn't convinced that Paige Jones could ever rebuild her tarnished reputation. She stopped momentarily at the main door as Henley's voice emerged from her police radio.

'Copeland where are you?' Henley demanded.

'I've just arrived,' Copeland replied. She pulled fruitlessly at the main door and then pressed the buzzer for 'Floe Studios'.

'We're seven minutes away. Do not go into that building until we and back up arrive.'

'Little chance of that,' Copeland said. She turned left and walked towards the side of the building, stopping at the external staircase. 'The main door is locked. I'm just checking the fire escape.'

'Is there any sign of Mika?'

'The rental car is parked nearby but there's no sign of her,' said Copeland. She walked up the staircase and pulled at the fire door. She heard a click, pulled it open and stepped into the dark hallway. 'I'm in the—'

Copeland gasped as someone pushed her hard from behind. She fell forward, the rough carpet tiles grazing her bruised face. She rolled over on to her back as the fire door slammed shut. The dimmed lights illuminated Mika's face which was contorted with rage.

'Shit,' Copeland breathed when she saw that Mika was holding a small fire extinguisher. She scrambled to her feet, but she wasn't quick enough to defend herself and Mika swung the fire extinguisher hard against her arm, breaking the bone. Copeland screamed in pain. Mika kicked Copeland in her side as she dropped the fire extinguisher. Copeland cried out as Mika fell to her knees, grabbed her head and banged it hard against the floor. Her head rocked. She blinked twice and inhaled sharply in an effort to force herself to focus through the intense pain ricocheting through her body.

Copeland gingerly raised her head and then her upper body. She saw Mika moving determinedly down the corridor. Copeland shoved herself backwards until she was against the wall, her left arm limp, tears streaming down her face. She used her good arm to grab her police radio but when she patted the top left-hand side of her stab vest it was empty. She shakily pulled herself to her feet and looked along the ground, her gaze stopping when she saw the white glow of the display screen on the radio near the fire escape door. She cried out, the turbulence in her head making her nauseous. She limped towards the radio, convinced that her ribs – as well as her arm – were broken. Copeland froze as Mika stopped at the end of the corridor and turned around. Copeland fought through the pain to snatch her police radio and press the red emergency call button. She pushed the radio into her pocket and grabbed the fire escape door handle when she saw Mika running towards her. The cold night air hit Copeland, momentarily sobering her up as the door swung open, and she stepped out onto the steel landing. She could hear a cacophony of sirens, but the building concussion in her head made her unsure if they belonged to police, ambulance, fire department, or all three. She had one foot on the first step when she heard the screech of car tyres and saw the flashing blue lights. Copeland stumbled as she took the second step. She tried to steady herself when she felt hot breath in her ear. She turned around and faced Mika.

'You're in my fucking way,' Mika said as she pushed Copeland hard in the chest.

Copeland tried to grab hold on to the railings, but she was too weak and unable to stop herself from being pushed over the edge.

*

Paige cried out, the rope tight around her wrists. She'd been adjusting her microphone when her studio door burst open. She screamed when she found herself staring at a woman who closely resembled the woman in the photo that Detective Inspector Henley had shown her. The soundproofed room had trapped her screams as the woman grabbed and pushed her. Paige fell heavily against the desk and the computer monitor, and mixer console had landed on her. She fought to disentangle herself from the cables when she felt a pair of hands around her ankles, and she was dragged across the floor.

Warm spittle had fallen on Paige's face as the woman had stood over her and screamed, 'You should not be here,' and slapped her face hard.

Paige had begged and screamed that she'd done nothing wrong when the woman grabbed a fistful of her hair. She'd kicked out and knocked over the trio of scented candles as she was dragged to the corner of the room. It was only when the woman pulled a syringe out of her pocket that Paige realised what the woman was going to do. The accusation against her was that she and her husband had drugged the guests on the retreat and one of the women had woken up to find herself tied to a bed. Paige felt the sharp scratch of the needle, and the first waves of disorientation hit her. She had no idea how long she'd been out for when she felt the heat of the flames against her face.

'Which building is it?' Henley asked. She pulled out her phone and dialled Paige Jones's number again, as the sound of police sirens grew louder.

'The one on the left. Steele House. Paige's car is here and so is the rental but there's no sign of Copeland,' said Ramouter as they walked briskly towards the building. 'She said she was on the fire escape before she pressed the alarm.'

Henley looked up at the building as her call to Paige went unanswered. 'I can smell smoke,' she said.

'Are you—'

Ramouter didn't finish as he took off at speed towards the fire escape.

'Where are you . . . oh my God,' Henley exclaimed when she saw the light from the side of the building shining on the crumpled body on the floor. She gave chase after Ramouter.

Copeland was on her back, her left leg clearly broken and her right arm across her chest. Blood trickled from her nose and glistened on the arm of her sweatshirt.

'Is she alive?' she asked as Ramouter fell to his knees and pressed his fingers against Copeland's neck.

'There's a pulse,' he said as Henley activated her radio and requested an ambulance, fire services and confirmed that an officer was down.

Henley looked up at the open door of the fire escape as a police car drove into the car park. 'Stay with Copeland until the ambulance gets here. I'm going in,' she said, taking the steps two at a time.

Henley entered the corridor, looked left and saw nothing but a blank wall. She tripped over a fire extinguisher on the floor as she walked forward, the smell of smoke growing stronger. As she reached to pick up the extinguisher, she heard a blood curdling scream. She removed her baton and sprinted along the corridor.

'I'm on the first floor. Suspect at large,' Henley shouted into her radio as she turned the corner. She stopped momentarily when she saw the glow of flames but another scream from Paige propelled her to run faster.

'Police! Get the hell away from her,' Henley screamed when she ran into the studio and saw Mika kneeling behind Paige with a large knife at her scalp. She could feel the heat of the flames as they licked the walls and ate away at the carpet. There was a toxic scent of burnt rubber from the melting cables in the air. Henley raised her baton and swung it at Mika's hand. Mika cried out as the knife flew out of her hand and clattered against the wall. Henley gasped as Mika lunged and fell against her. Henley held onto Mika, and they fell into a heap into the floor as Paige swivelled herself around the column, trying to avoid the flames inching towards her. Henley could hear Ramouter's voice over the radio as she pushed Mika off her.

Mika jumped up and screamed, 'You're ruining everything.'

Henley grabbed the side of the table and pulled herself up as Mika ran out of the room.

'Help me,' Paige shouted, trying in vain to loosen the ropes around her wrist.

'Ramouter, she's on the run,' Henley screamed into her radio as the flames suddenly hit the ceiling, a panel crashed onto the floor and a window exploded.

Ramouter stepped away from Copeland who was being attended to by paramedics. The car park was aglow with the flashing lights of the emergency services as police officers ushered away the people who'd left the gym to observe the chaotic activity. Ramouter looked up as the fire door flung open and Mika stepped out. She looked wild eyed at the scene below and ran back in.

'Stop,' Ramouter shouted as he ran around the paramedics and up the stairs into the smoke-filled hallway. He gave chase after Mika, who was surprisingly quick. She turned right and ran down the stairs. He thought that she would try to escape through the front door but instead she ran ahead. At the end of the corridor, Ramouter could see a green, fluorescent fire escape sign on the wall. He heard Mika scream out as she pushed the bar down and opened the door. Ramouter was a few feet behind and grabbed the door to stop it from slamming shut in his face.

'Mika Fonseka. Stop. Police!' Ramouter shouted as Mika turned left and found her route blocked by a wall. 'You have nowhere else to go,' Ramouter said, reaching for his CS gas canister. 'The only way you're leaving here is with me, in handcuffs. Now, let's do this calmly.'

'Get out of my way,' Mika said, moving to the side and looking beyond Ramouter at her exit. She looked down, picked up a beer bottle and threw it at him.

'Stop,' Ramouter said, moving swiftly to his right as the bottle smashed against the door, far too close to his head. Mika screamed at him like a wild animal, ran to the corner and picked up a broken brick that had fallen from the crumbling wall behind her.

'For fuck's sake,' Ramouter said as Mika threw the brick and he ducked out of the way. 'Stay exactly where you are or I will be forced to use the CS spray and believe me you do not want that,' he said.

Mika picked up another brick. 'Move,' she screamed.

Ramouter removed the CS spray and held it at arm's length. 'Put the brick down, Mika. I'm counting to three. I'm giving you a chance . . . shit,' Ramouter said as Mika screamed wildly, threw the brick and ran towards him. He pressed the button and Mika screamed again as the full canister of CS gas hit her face. She fell blindly against the wall, her eyes streaming as the skin on her face flushed scarlet.

'I can't breathe,' Mika spluttered before collapsing onto the ground.

'I don't really care. You're under arrest,' Ramouter said, the CS gas burning his throat as he turned Mika onto her front, grabbed her arms and cuffed her.

Henley removed the oxygen mask and jumped out of the ambulance when she saw Ramouter and a second police officer escorting Mika to a waiting police van.

'You're OK,' Ramouter said with relief once the doors were slammed shut on Mika.

Henley coughed deeply and worryingly. 'A bit of smoke inhalation, but I'm fine,' she said. 'How are you doing?'

Ramouter splashed the remainder of the water that the paramedics had given him onto his face to relieve the burning sensation of the CS gas. 'I forgot how irritating that stuff is, but I'll live. How's Paige?' he asked.

'The shock has got her. She hasn't said a word since the firefighters rescued us. Physically, she's got cuts and bruises but she's lucky. If we'd been just five minutes later, Mika would have killed her.'

'What about Copeland? I left her with the paramedics. She was breathing but . . . fuck, Henley. Why didn't she listen? Why didn't she wait?'

'Don't,' Henley said, gently taking hold of Ramouter's arm. 'We can't focus on that right now. The most important thing is that she's alive. They're taking her to Guy's and she's going to be in the best hands.'

'When are we going to deal with her?' Ramouter said as the van containing Mika Fonseka headed towards the exit.

'First thing in the morning,' said Henley as a cough rattled her chest.

'Mika's in that van screaming her bloody innocence, saying she's been framed. That I attacked her.'

'She's desperate, Ramouter,' said Henley. 'Donovan and Elliot. We've got them and Mika knows there's no way out. So let her scream.'

59

Mika Fonseka sat on the opposite side of the table in a grey police station issued tracksuit with her arms crossed. She'd declined to have a solicitor, or anyone informed of her arrest and had objected to every part of the booking in process including having her samples taken.

'I want it on the record that I do not recognise the authority of the Metropolitan Police, and the justice system is a farce,' said Mika.

Ramouter rolled his eyes.

Henley coughed and took a sip of a water. 'Doesn't really matter whether you recognise it or not. The fact is that you're sitting here because you've been arrested for the murder of six people,' she said.

'How is it six?' Mika asked.

'Douglas Mantell, Gong Bo Hyoo, Sian Fox-Carnell, Nathan Hall, Kaiden Longley and Catlin Ferguson.'

'I didn't kill any of those people. I wasn't even there. That was all down to Donovan Hernandez and my husband.'

'Oh wow. Straight in there with the cutthroat,' said Ramouter.

'You've also been arrested for conspiracy to murder Tabitha and Graham Ashcroft and Paige Jones, the attempted murder of DC Xania Copeland and assault on DC Ramouter and me,' said Henley.

'You forgot arson with intent to endanger life and kidnapping,' said Ramouter.

'I did not attempt to kill that policewoman. I had no idea who she was, and I was defending myself, and as for you,' Mika said, pointing at Henley.

'Let's not do this. I identified myself,' said Henley. 'What I want to know is why?'

'Why did my husband and Donovan decide to kill those people? I have no idea,' Mika shrugged. 'You know when they say that you don't really know people. Well guess what? That's true. I had no idea my husband was a monster.'

'You're saying you had nothing to do with this? That this wasn't all your idea? That you didn't manipulate your husband to provide you with the full case details for the victims you were supporting? Is that what you're telling us?'

'Yes,' Mika smirked. 'I wouldn't be the first wife to be blindsided by her husband. Manipulated. Gaslighted.'

'The burns on your arms and face,' said Ramouter as he pressed play on the laptop and turned it towards Mika. 'The HCP – that's the health care practitioner – who assessed you when you were booked in, said that your injuries were consistent with acid burns. This is footage from last Saturday when Catlin Ferguson was attacked. As you can see, we've enhanced the footage.'

Mika remained silent as the footage played. Catlin turning around and facing a heavy-set white man. A woman running into view with a bottle in her hand. Mika shuffled in her seat and looked away when she saw her own face.

'We searched the car you hired,' Henley said. She picked up an unsealed plastic exhibit bag that contained four small, sealed exhibit bags and placed them in front of Mika. Human hair was attached to pieces of dried skin. 'Samples have already been retrieved and are currently with the forensic services but I'm pretty confident they'll confirm they're a DNA match for Mantell, Bo Hyoo, Fox-Carnell and Hall.'

'They were obviously planted in my belongings. Must have been Elliot,' said Mika.

'Elliot. Your husband who was remanded two days ago to Brixton Prison, somehow managed to plant evidence in your bag. A bag that contained your clothes and passport. Is that what you're telling us?' asked Ramouter.

'That's exactly what I'm telling you. You seem to think I'm the bad person here. That I've done something wrong. That woman on the footage isn't me. I didn't kill anyone or try to kill anyone. You won't find my fingerprints or DNA anywhere.'

'What about Paige Jones? You waited outside her home, followed her to her studio,' said Henley.

'I found her there. In fact, I was trying to save her.'

'Save her? You wanted to kill her. You injected her with Rohypnol, tied her up and had a knife to her head when I stopped you. Tell me, which part of that was saving her?'

Mika tapped her leg against the table, watching Henley defiantly, as she ran her finger across the bandage on her right hand.

'Why, Mika? Six people dead. They were tortured, made to suffer. Punished because you persuaded your husband, Donovan Hernandez and Kaiden Longley to kill for you.'

'I didn't ask anyone to do anything for me,' said Mika. 'But can you imagine how it would feel to spend sixteen years sitting with victims. You sit with those victims, hold their hands and tell them that the court will hear them, really hear them and do the right thing. You hold their hands, give them tissues when they cry, escort them to the court room and watch as they give evidence. You see the jury sit there transfixed, nodding away, believing them. You hear how strong the prosecution case is, and you think to yourself that yes, this poor woman, man, child will get justice. You promise them that this tiresome, cruel court process will be worth it and then you get the call that the jury's ready. You're convinced that their abuser, murderer, rapist will be convicted and punished but then for some inexplicable reason they walk away. No justice. How is that fair?'

'So, you took it upon yourself to deliver justice?' asked Henley.

'I never said it was me. I just posed a question.'

'What about Catlin Ferguson? You killed her before the jury delivered their verdict,' said Ramouter.

'I didn't kill her,' said Mika. 'That was clearly Donovan on the street. I don't know who that other woman is.'

'The jury delivered a guilty verdict. Unanimous.'

'You're lying,' Mika said as she pulled herself up. 'She was going to walk. I could see it on their faces. Elliot could see it too.'

Ramouter took a printout and handed it to Mika. 'This is a copy of the trial record. As you can see, on Monday at 11.26 a.m. a verdict was returned. Guilty. Unanimous. You interfered with justice.'

'No,' Mika said, her eyes scanning rapidly across the page. 'You made this up. This is fake. You're a fucking liar.' She ripped the page in two, screwed up the pieces and threw them at Ramouter.

'Why don't you help yourself and admit that you were involved, and that this entire thing was your idea?' said Henley.

'I've told you. I had nothing to do with any of this. It was my husband and Donovan.'

'Here's the thing. Both your husband and Donovan Hernandez have become quite talkative in the past twenty-four hours,' said Henley. 'When they were first interviewed, they were, I suppose loyal is the word, but the realisation that they were going to spend the rest of their lives in a prison cell sobered them up.'

For the first time, there was fear in Mika's eyes as she looked at Henley and Ramouter. 'What do you mean?' Mika asked, her voice low.

'Before Donovan Hernandez was produced at court this morning he gave a statement to our colleague.'

'What did he say?'

'That you were the ringleader. That he was following your

orders including an order to throw Kaiden Longley from the balcony of his flat.'

'That's not true,' Mika said softly, her fingernails scraping against the burned skin on her face.

'And then there's your husband. I don't know whether the prison air does something to your senses, but he also had a lot to say,' said Ramouter. 'In fact, I've got a copy of my colleague's notes right here. "I, Elliot Fonseka make the following admissions. I obtained confidential court information on the request of my wife Mikaela Fonseka. I obtained these documents under duress. I—"'

'No, no, no,' Mika screamed. 'How could he? The liar.'

Mika stood up, banged her hands repeatedly on the table and swept all the exhibit bags and folders to the floor.

Ramouter raised his eyebrows, and pressed the alarm strip that ran around the perimeter of the interview room.

'Suspend it?' he asked Henley as the door flew open and the custody sergeant appeared with a plain clothes officer.

'Yes,' Henley said. She picked up the exhibit bags containing the scalps of Mika's victims from the floor.

'Interview suspended at 11.36 a.m..'

Henley stood outside the gates of Lewisham police station and breathed in deeply. She could still taste smoke in the back of her throat and the headache was taking an age to shift.

'Can I say that I think she's crazy,' said Ramouter, zipping up his coat.

'Mika Fonseka is not crazy,' said Henley. 'That woman knew exactly what she was doing. She's manipulative and evil but the irony is that she's going to be asking the jury to believe that she's the innocent one in her husband's sick games.'

'They won't fall for it,' said Ramouter as they walked towards Henley's car. 'They're all going to sit in the dock, blaming each other and they're all going to go down.'

'I bloody hope so,' Henley said as her and Ramouter's phones both rang at the same time.

Ramouter paled as his thumb hovered above the green accept button. 'It's Eastwood,' he said.

'Pellacia,' Henley replied. She pressed accept, closed her eyes and silently prayed as she listened to Pellacia. He was short. To the point. Emotional. She ended the call and wiped her eyes.

'Ezra's awake,' Ramouter said quickly with a broad smile on his face. 'Awake and talking.'

'Thank God,' Henley said, exhaling with relief.

'I want to see him,' Ramouter said as the 199 bus which stopped at Lewisham hospital approached.

'I need to see Copeland at Guy's first. She shouldn't be alone. You go and I'll catch up later.'

Henley's phone rang as she watched Ramouter board the bus. She felt the pressure push at the base of her skull when she checked the screen. It was Chris Snyder from the NCA. Her thumb hovered over the green accept button for a few seconds and then she silenced the call. Whatever information Chris had for her about Rhimes's handler could wait. Her priority now was the living.

'Well look at you,' Henley said as she stood at the door of Ezra's room. He'd been barely recognisable the last time she'd seen him with an oxygen tube down his throat. The swelling on his face had reduced slightly, his head was still heavily bandaged, and his left arm was in a cast, but he looked more like himself.

'Hi, boss. Look who's here,' Ezra said, his voice hoarse, raised his right arm and pointed to Linh who was sitting by his side trying to turn on the TV.

'Honestly, the price they're charging for this one to watch another episode of *Squid Game*,' Linh said. 'Can you believe he had the cheek to ask me for a bed bath.'

Henley laughed and wiped away the tears that were flowing

mainly with relief, but also part anger that someone she cared about had been treated with such violence.

'It wasn't like that,' said Ezra, placing his head back against the pillow.

Henley sat down next to Ezra and tenderly touched his brow. 'Are you in a lot of pain?' she asked.

'My head is banging, and my chest hurts but I'm pretty much high as a kite,' said Ezra. He picked up his morphine pump and held it aloft.

'I'm so glad you're awake. The doctors said you're going to make a full recovery.'

'That's because he's got a hard head,' said Linh, laughing.

'Linh, honestly,' said Henley.

'It's better to make jokes instead of standing over him bawling my eyes out like Stanford.'

'Grandad got emotional,' Ezra said, but his laughter was brief as he groaned in pain. Henley grimaced in sympathy and took hold of Ezra's hand. She gently massaged his palm. She remembered how effective the small action had been, when Pellacia had taken her hand when she'd been in her own hospital bed after being stabbed. Henley smiled at Linh as Ezra visibly relaxed.

'Right, I've sorted out your TV. I'm off,' said Linh, kissing him gently on his swollen cheek. 'I'll check up on you tomorrow and bring you some decent food. Anj, I'll call you.'

'I'm sorry,' Ezra said once Linh had left the room.

'Ez, you have absolutely nothing to be sorry for,' said Henley. She took a tissue and wiped the tears from his eyes. 'I don't ever want to hear you apologise for this. Do you understand?'

Ezra nodded.

'Can you remember what happened?' she asked as a police officer arrived at the door and nodded at Henley.

'Just random bits,' said Ezra, pointing at the glass of water on the table.

'This officer is here to talk to you,' said Henley as she held the straw to Ezra's mouth and he drank greedily. 'Don't put any pressure on yourself to remember. You're healing. They can come back.'

'Oh,' Ezra said as Henley kissed him and left his side. 'Did they find my laptop?'

Henley turned to the police officer who shook her head.

'It's got a tracker,' said Ezra.

'That's good to know,' said Henley, turning to the police officer. 'Go easy with him. He's very important to me.'

Henley felt the headache and nausea, a side effect of the smoke inhalation, finally subside as she stepped out into the cold air and headed to the car park. She made a silent prayer that her next case wouldn't involve ghosts from her past.

'What is that?' Henley asked as she noticed an envelope stuck behind the wipers on her windscreen. She looked around at the other cars, thinking that it was the usual adverts for a car wash service, but their windscreens were empty. She removed the envelope and opened it. Inside was a single sheet of paper. She unfolded it and immediately felt sick. There were four words written in red ink across a picture of Harry Rhimes's grave:

LET THE DEAD SLEEP.

Henley placed the photograph back into the envelope and pushed it into her pocket. She looked up at the hospital where Ezra was recovering from his injuries. Donovan Hernandez had repeatedly and vehemently denied attacking Ezra and insisted that he had an alibi. The alibi couldn't be corroborated and the SCU believed it was only a matter of time before Peckham CID charged Donovan Hernandez with the attempted murder of Ezra.

'We've got it wrong,' Henley whispered to herself before

throwing up onto the grass verge. Her frantic pulse pushed hard against her temples and the muscles in her chest spasmed. She took out the bottle of water from her bag and focused on rinsing her mouth as she willed herself to calm down. A minute later, she took out her phone and called the number she knew by heart.

'Hey,' Pellacia answered, his voice heavy and dejected.

Henley got into her car, locked the door and started the engine. 'Where are you?' she asked.

'Home. The borough commander *suggested* I take the day off. To get my head together.'

'Are you alone?'

'Yeah, I . . . what's going on?' Pellacia asked as dejection changed to concern.

'I'm coming over. Now,' Henley said. She drove out of Lewisham Hospital car park, turned left in the direction of Hither Green and towards Pellacia.

Acknowledgements

Acknowledgements are a strange thing. After you've spent many months of writing and then editing your book, you have to write your acknowledgements and for a moment you say to yourself, I acknowledge me. I thank me. I'm the one who sat there alone, making bad diet choices while I wrote this book. I'm the one who had to deal with finishing this book while dealing with the trauma of being in the middle of a category 4 hurricane (*yes, that did happen to me*). However, once you have a word with yourself and kick your ego to the kerb, you remember that there are many friends and family to acknowledge because the funny thing is, you did not do this alone. So here we go.

Thank you to every single person, friends, family, and all of my WhatsApp groups (and yes, I know I have quite a few). Whether you indulged me as I ran storylines by you, asked you random questions, checked in just to see how I was doing, or gave me that much-needed nudge to keep going, you all played a role.

To all the readers, bloggers, and content creators, thank you. Whether you've read one book or followed Inspector Henley from the very beginning, I'm deeply grateful. Thank you for your reviews, your posts, your YouTube breakdowns and TikToks. I know how much time and thought that takes, and I appreciate every single one of you for staying on this journey with Henley, the SCU and me.

A special thank you to the TV series *Lawmen: Bass Reeves*.

I'm always trying to push my books a little further, to take a risk, to twist something just a bit differently. While working on this book in Grenada, I knew there was something missing, that the villains needed something more. A unique hook. And then I watched *Lawmen: Bass Reeves* and had one of those rare lightbulb moments. A specific scene gave me an 'A-Ha' moment and was the inspiration behind my villains' unique calling card.

As I've always said, you don't do this alone. Thank you to my agent, Oli Munson, my editor Manpreet and my publishing teams at HQ and Hanover Square.

And as always, love and thanks to my mum and dad, my brothers Gavin and Jason, and my best friend, Gaynor. I love you all. Thank you for being my constants.

Gripped by *The Shadow Carver*?
Don't miss the spine-tingling and chilling debut!

There's a serial killer on the loose.
When bodies start washing up along the banks of the River Thames, DI Henley fears it is the work of Peter Olivier, the notorious Jigsaw Killer. But it can't be him; Olivier is already behind bars, and Henley was the one who put him there.

The race is on before more bodies are found.
She'd hoped she'd never have to see his face again, but Henley knows Olivier might be the best chance they have at stopping the copycat killer. But when Olivier learns of the new murders, helping Henley is the last thing on his mind . . .

Will it take a killer to catch the killer?
Now all bets are off, and the race is on to catch the killer before the body count rises. But who will get there first – Henley, or the Jigsaw Killer?

Don't miss another suspenseful and thrilling read!

In this room, no one can hear you scream . . .

The Serial Crimes Unit are called in to investigate when a local pastor is found stabbed to death. As DI Henley assesses the crime scene, she discovers a hidden door that conceals a room set up for torture – and bound to the bed in the middle of the room is the body of a man.

When another body is found, also tied down, Henley realises there's someone out there torturing innocent people and leaving them for dead. But why?

There's nothing that connects the victims. They didn't know each other. Their paths never crossed. But someone has targeted them, and it's up to Henley and the SCU to stop them before they find another binding room . . .

Make sure you've read this shocking and jaw-dropping serial killer thriller!

He will come for them, one by one . . .

Five shocking murders

Twenty-five years ago, DCI Harry Rhimes arrested Andrew Streeter for the brutal murders of five young people. Streeter's 'kill list' was found in his home, leading to his conviction.

A legacy under threat

Now, Streeter's convictions are being overturned as new evidence suggests corruption in the original investigation. DI Henley is shocked; this case is personal, as Rhimes was her old boss and can't defend himself. When the killings resume, Henley must confront the possibility that Rhimes got it wrong.

A hunt for a killer

Henley and her team reopen the original cases, setting aside feelings, as the real killer works through a new kill list . . .

ONE PLACE. MANY STORIES

Bold, innovative and empowering publishing.

FOLLOW US ON:

@HQStories